C000005707

THE TIME OF OUR LIVES

THE TIME OF OUR LIVES

Abby Williams

First published in the United Kingdom in 2019 by Aria, an imprint of
Head of Zeus Ltd

ISBN 9781789540703

Aria
c/o Head of Zeus
First Floor East
5–8 Hardwick Street
London EC1R 4RG
www.ariafiction.com

For the real Craig Evry – a million times more
magnificent than the fictional version

One

Erin

I never thought I'd be one of *those* brides. You know, one that reads all those magazines with pictures of puffy white dresses and articles on how to achieve the wedding of your dreams on a shoestring budget. I mean I don't want to sound like a stuck-up cow, but I had an architectural engineering degree, I spoke fluent French and if I'm honest I'd always imagined myself wearing a pair of jeans when I got married, with just my groom and a couple of strangers we'd dragged in off the street to witness the momentous occasion. I just wanted it to be about me and him, that was all that mattered. Yet something strange had happened since I got engaged six months ago to the love of my life, Brad Masters. I had started to linger longingly outside bridal shops, admiring white meringues, and deep down I had a feeling I wanted to wear something other than denim on the biggest day of our lives.

'Don't tell me,' my best friend Cara giggled now down the other end of the phone. 'You're at work, sitting at your desk pretending to do some work when actually you're admiring your engagement ring for the umpteenth time this morning and flicking through *Brides* magazine when you think the boss isn't looking.'

Immediately I stopped twirling my one-carat diamond engagement ring around my finger and shoved the magazine hurriedly to the edge of my desk. That's the trouble with best friends: they know you too well.

'Luckily for me,' I chuckled, 'I'm on very good terms with my manager.'

'Nothing like getting engaged to the boss to ensure you're happy at home *and* work,' Cara replied, a hint of steel to her voice.

I felt a pang of guilt. Cara had been dumped a year ago by her own fiancé, Ian. He decided that he was too young at twenty-seven to get married. Why he hadn't worked that out before he asked her was a mystery to me and everyone else. However, I'd held my tongue and offered her a shoulder to cry on instead.

I changed the subject. 'So are you ready for tonight?'

'Erm, about that, I really don't think speed dating's my thing,' Cara whined.

I sighed and ran a hand through my long red hair. 'Cara, it's been a year. You've got to move on. Ian's in Australia living on a surfboard, dating some bikini-clad surf-type girl, creating a new life for himself; you've got to do the same.'

'I just don't fancy sitting in a room full of strangers making polite chit chat, looking at the door ready to make my escape.'

'It won't be like that. It'll be fun. We'll go for an Indian after and you can give me all the goss. What do you say?' I put on my best begging tone that never failed to win Cara round. 'My treat.'

Cara paused for a moment as if thinking about my offer. 'Will you throw in the lagers as well?'

'Lagers and poppadoms,' I chuckled. 'Though don't go getting any ideas about pudding! Brad might be my boss but he still pays me a pittance.'

I heard laughter down the other end of the phone. 'I think it's time you got creative and asked for a raise!'

I giggled. 'I'm going now. I'll meet you outside the King's Arms at nine and don't even think about getting out of it!'

Putting the phone down, my thoughts turned to my history with Cara. We had been best friends since we were babies. Born a couple of days apart in the tiny cottage hospital just outside Bath, our mums bonded over our birth twenty-six years ago and it was only natural we did the same. Growing up, we went to the same nursery, primary and secondary school. We were more like sisters than friends, despite the fact we looked nothing alike. Cara was petite and dainty with long dark hair, hazel eyes and olive skin. As for me, I was tall and towered over her, my red hair, green eyes and freckled complexion only making me stand out all the more. We told each other our deepest fears and darkest secrets. I had never forgotten the time Cara, at the age of eight, wept on my shoulder after her parents divorced, or the time she asked me to drive to Birmingham in the middle of the night after she dropped out of university. When I passed my driving test (on the fifth go), Cara was the one I told first, just as she was when visiting lecturer, Brad Masters, owner and CEO of Brad Masters Architects asked me out while I was in my last year at Bath university.

He had been giving a talk on the role of responsible urban development, only I hadn't heard a word. For the first time since enrolling on the degree programme, I hadn't been fixated on studying. Instead I couldn't tear my eyes away from Brad. Cara told me to go for it when I asked her if it was appropriate for me to date him, and when he offered me a job as his PA, which would allow me to gain the work experience I needed to become a proper architect, she gave me her seal of approval again – the only caveat being I clear it with human resources first. 'You find love in the strangest of places,' she'd concluded.

Brad and I had been together for three years, and now I was a fully qualified architect but still also worked as his PA. Watching him now as he walked along the open plan office towards me I felt my heart bang against my chest. Tall, with chocolate eyes and thick, black hair, Brad still gave me butterflies.

'Erin, have you got my itinerary for the conference tomorrow?' he asked, standing in front of my desk.

'Of course,' I replied, pulling out a glossy brochure from my in-tray and handing it to Brad. 'I booked you into your usual hotel for two nights and I've arranged for the hotel business centre to set up your presentation material so you don't need to worry.'

Brad smiled. 'Thank you, that was very thoughtful.'

'All part of the job,' I replied sweetly.

As Brad ran his finger down the itinerary, he frowned. 'Actually, could you book me an extra night? I've just noticed my old boss is giving the closing address, it might be nice to try and catch up with him over a few beers rather than rush straight back.'

'Of course,' I said, making a note on my iPad. 'And before I forget, you have a new business meeting with a firm in London on Thursday morning.'

'Gowerings are interested? Why didn't you tell me?' he asked excitedly. 'We've been chasing them for months!'

I smiled, his enthusiasm infectious. 'I stayed on at the architectural business awards dinner last week after you had to rush off. I got chatting to Gowering and of course sang your praises. He called to ask if you would be free to talk when you're in London this week and I found a space in your diary that worked for you both.'

'Erin, I don't know what to say.' Brad stood there looking at me, open-mouthed.

I chuckled. 'You can make it up to me later, out of office hours. Now is there anything else?'

Brad looked thoughtful for a moment. 'I need you to open the office tomorrow morning as I'm off to London first thing on the early train. That all right?'

I groaned inwardly. I had hoped that he might ask his junior partner Andy to do it instead. Opening the office was one of my least favourite jobs. Not only did it involve being here at just after seven in the morning, but it also meant I missed out on my morning chat with Phil, my favourite coffee guy, who ran a lovely café near the park I had been going to for years.

Naturally I said nothing, understanding only too well the boundaries between work and home and set a reminder on my phone, as Brad perched on my desk causing my carefully hidden copy of *Brides* to fall to the floor.

Embarrassed, I leapt to my feet to pick it up, but wasn't quick enough, and Brad got there first.

'What's all this?' He frowned.

'Just getting some ideas.' I tried to take the magazine from Brad's hands. Just because I was engaged to the boss didn't mean I wanted to be caught taking the proverbial on company time.

'So I see,' he smiled, turning back to the magazine.

'I just thought that we've been engaged for a little while now, maybe we ought to think about setting a date soon? Plus, I'm so tall, it'll take me ages to find a dress,' I babbled.

'A hundred and one ways with favours,' he read, ignoring what I'd said. 'Find the dress of your dreams, and oh look, how to keep your family on side when they hate the groom.'

'It doesn't say that,' I said, snatching the copy away from him and shoving it in my drawer.

'No, but maybe there should be an article on what to do when your future in-laws hate you,' he said gloomily.

Hurriedly, I glanced around at my fellow co-workers. Even though I was in a private office next to Brad's, I always felt as though people liked nothing more than watching us together. Some days it felt like we were the office entertainment.

'They don't hate you,' I said.

'Yes, they do!' Brad exclaimed. 'You don't talk to your parents because of me.'

'And you should appreciate my loyalty.' I said, shuffling awkwardly on the spot.

Brad got to his feet and looked at me pleadingly. 'And I do. But we can't get married with you still not talking to your parents. Perhaps it's time to put things right.'

'There will never be a time to put things right,' I said, folding my arms firmly across my chest. 'It's better this way.'

'So you honestly want to get married without your parents there?' Brad asked, his tone incredulous.

I nodded. 'I've made my choice. I'm not happy about it, but it's not as though I haven't tried over the years to sort things out with them. Look what happened when we drove over there last summer to announce our engagement.'

We both looked away at that point. Nobody wanted to remember the way my dad had told Brad to get out of the restaurant we had booked, after he thought he saw Brad checking out one of the waitresses. I mean, as if he would have done that when we were announcing our engagement. Mum and Dad had been too hard on Brad and to say it irked me was an understatement.

Brad looked uncomfortable as he interrupted my thoughts. 'Look, I just think that we ought to start married life in the right way. And that means you having a relationship with your family.'

'It's not as simple as that—' I began, only for Brad to cut me off.

'Why? Because they hate the fact I'm twenty years older than you? Because I'm divorced?' Brad paused for a moment squeezing my hands gently again. 'Why don't we invite Cara round later and we can see what she thinks?'

'I can't,' I muttered. 'She's going speed dating later, but I said I'd meet her for a curry after.'

'Speed dating?' Brad raised an eyebrow. 'I didn't think that would be Cara's sort of thing.'

I shook my head. 'I don't think it is really. But she needs to start dating again.'

Brad chuckled. 'Fair enough. Just as long as she doesn't think she's going to meet Mr Right at one of these things.'

I returned the grin. 'No, but she might meet Mr Right Now!'

Brad shrugged his shoulders in mock despair as he stood up. 'Just be careful Erin,' he warned. 'I would hate to see her heart broken all over again.'

With that, he walked away. As I watched him go I felt a warm glow of happiness burn inside. I may not have a family, but I had a fiancé I was very much in love with and maybe after tonight Cara might find as much love and happiness as I had.

Two

Lydia

Up until this moment, I had always loved this room. Right at the top of the house you could see across the rooftops with the entire beautiful Georgian city spread out before you. If I craned my neck, on a good day I could see the splendour of Bath Abbey and next to it the beautiful Pump Rooms, made famous by Jane Austen but still just as splendid today as a place for residents and tourists to mingle. And if that wasn't enough, the majestic stone buildings of the city were framed with lush countryside, the sight of which couldn't help but make your heart soar. Well, usually, but today as I sat in the room that had once been Harry's study, I felt nothing but gloom-laden. In this particular moment I hated this room. I felt as though it wasn't the picture-perfect paradise I always believed it to be, but instead a huge vault, a prison for secrets if you will. As my eyes darted wildly about the room I felt like crying. Harry, my husband of fifty-six years, had suddenly died of a heart attack three weeks ago, but that wasn't the only reason I was so upset. I wanted to sob my heart out because he had left his affairs in such a flaming mess. There was paperwork strewn across the desk, folders were missing, corrupt files had been found on his desktop and terrifying letters from the tax office, seemingly hidden from me for years, were stuffed in a drawer. For the umpteenth time that morning I wondered why I had been stupid enough to let Harry take charge of everything. I didn't have a clue about any of this stuff and, at seventy-eight, felt I was a bit long in the tooth to start getting a grasp of it all now.

I threw the sheaf of papers across the room in anger. 'Why did your father keep such bloody complicated accounts?'

My son, Luke, jumped in surprise. 'They're not that complicated, Mum. It's just a simple in and out accounting system. Though I'll confess, Dad's paperwork is a bit lax.'

'Lax!' I exclaimed. 'He told me he was on top of everything, yet there are years' worth of missing accounts, not to mention letters from the tax office demanding back-payments. I still haven't found the details of half of our investments. I don't know if I'm coming or going.'

I pinched the bridge of my nose to stem the tears. It had niggled away at the back of my mind for years that I had nothing to do with any of our finances; I didn't even know how much the gas and electric bills were. Deep down I had known it was stupid just to let Harry deal with everything. Recently I had suggested I got to grips with our affairs in case something happened to either one of us, but my darling husband had waved my concerns away. Two months later, we were in our favourite café enjoying a coffee with our old friend Phil when Harry had complained of chest pains – an hour later he was dead.

'Mum, are you all right?'

I felt my only child's hand rest gently on my shoulder. Just the weight of it there gave me comfort. Lifting my head, I met Luke's gaze and felt a rush of love for him. He was being so patient with me in the wake of his own grief. The least I could do was try and keep a lid on my emotions.

'Yes, I'm sorry, love. A bit tired, I think.' I got to my feet and surveyed the room. At times like this there was only one thing to do and that was to gulp down a glass of wine. Sadly, I knew the fridge was bare, and so the second-best thing would have to do. 'Tea?'

As Luke nodded, I planted a kiss on top of his head and walked back down the three flights of stairs to the kitchen. Flicking on the kettle, I suddenly felt very weary and old. Sinking into one of the dining room chairs, I gazed out across the garden. It needed work, I realised with a sigh. The lawn needed mowing, the path re-laying, the shrubs tending and the shed a patch repair on its roof. Harry and I were always so busy with the antiques business we had run together, we didn't have much time to worry about maintenance. Then when Luke had left home, Harry had wondered if this house was too big for us.

'We've got five bedrooms and it's a listed building,' he had protested. 'I know we run an antiques business, but we don't have to live in an antique as well for the rest of our lives. That's the trouble with living in a World Heritage site! Most of these other properties around us have all been carved up and turned into flats. Why don't we do the same and live in one of them? We could make a tidy sum on the investment as well, Lyds.'

The idea had horrified me just as much then as it did now. 'We bought this house before Luke was born, we can't convert it into flats.'

'It's too big. We don't need all this space,' Harry had tried again. 'We don't have to leave Bath, but perhaps we could find somewhere smaller? Move out of the centre perhaps?'

'But we've always lived here!' I had screeched. 'People come to our house for parties, I may dislike them but we're famous for it.

'People will still come even if we live on the other side of town in a two-up, two-down.' Harry had countered.

'Over my dead body!' I had said.

I'd meant it too. It had been me that had found this house a month after we married. Harry and I had been living in a studio flat on the busy main road out of town. The place was riddled with damp and our closest neighbours were a family of rats. To describe it as a dump would be more than generous.

I had been on my way to the auctioneers in town one morning where I worked as a secretary and had seen the house up for sale. I always walked through the Circus, it was a bit out of my way, but I loved to pretend I was living in a Jane Austen novel for a few minutes.

Taking my usual route, I found myself peering up at the houses as I always did, picturing who had lived here over the years. Steeped with history, these Georgian houses could tell a story. Then, about halfway down, I saw what I thought had to be a mirage. There, right in front of me, was a man attaching a 'for sale' sign to the iron railings outside. I mentally pinched myself. Houses around here never came up on the market!

A quick call to the estate agent when I arrived at work told me it wasn't a joke, but the place did need renovating which was why the monthly mortgage payments wouldn't be much more than the rent we paid on the studio flat. I wasn't put off and made Harry come with me to see it later that day. As we walked through the hallway, I had already moved in. The place was beautiful, filled with original features such as the foot scraper outside to wipe the muck off your shoes. While Harry roamed from room to room moaning about the cost of rewiring, re-plastering, rebuilding and the difficulties associated with listed buildings, I cut across my husband and put an offer in to the estate agent there and then.

It didn't matter to me that women couldn't get mortgages on their own without the approval of their husbands; I knew this house was the right one for us and I was determined to make our dreams come true.

The kettle boiling jolted me back to reality and I poured the water into the teapot, enjoying the motion of stirring the leaves before I put the lid on. I knew some people thought tea leaves were old fashioned, but my father had always taught me that if something was worth doing, it was worth doing right. I very much counted a cup of tea as something worth doing right.

'Mum, have you got a minute?' Luke asked, bursting into the kitchen.

I turned around and saw his face was a picture of worry. 'Are you all right?'

Luke leaned against the architrave and said nothing. I watched him curiously. He seemed to be struggling with what to say. He might have just turned forty-eight in December, but to me he would always be my little boy. Pouring the tea, I kept quiet. Luke was never very good when he was rushed, just like his father. I would have to simply wait until he was ready to tell me whatever it was that was wrong and judging by the desperate look in his eyes I didn't think it would be very long.

'It's…' he began.

'Go on,' I coaxed.

'There's a bit of a problem with Dad's affairs.'

I stood against the worktop and took a sip of tea. 'Well, I know that. How we'll pay off that tax bill I don't know. I suppose I'll have to dip into our savings.'

'The thing is, Mum… there aren't any savings,' Luke said nervously.

'Of course there are!' I said, laughing. 'Your father may not have been a very good administrator, but he knew a sound investment. That's why we've still got an attic full of stock for the online business. Your father was very savvy, I'm sure whatever he chose to invest our money in will be worth a small fortune.'

Luke shot me a plaintive glance. 'I don't quite know how to say this, Mum, but I think savvy is the last thing Dad was. The online business hasn't traded in years. There are no investments or savings. They're gone.'

I stared at him. He must have got it wrong. But the sparkling blue eyes that he got from me, along with my blonde hair and sloping Roman nose, told me there had been no mistake. If anyone was savvy, it had always been Luke. He made his living from banking.

Taking the chair opposite him, I took a deep breath and steeled myself. 'I'm sorry, Luke, but I don't quite understand what you're telling me. Before your father died, he and I had a frank chat about money and he told me that if anything should happen to either one of us we were more than adequately provided for.'

'I think Dad might have been telling fibs, Mum,' Luke replied, sitting down and pushing a file towards me.

'What's this?' I asked, flipping through the contents of the A4 buff folder. Luke said nothing as I pulled out statements of accounts all with a closing balance of zero, along with letters from insurance companies confirming the cancellation of our life insurance.

'I don't understand,' I said shutting the folder and passing it back across to Luke. 'What does all this mean?'

Luke closed his eyes and breathed heavily. 'It means that Dad cashed everything in. From what I've been able to look through so far I think he was using your investments and savings to fund your lifestyles.'

I felt as if I were on a rollercoaster – and I definitely wanted to get off. I couldn't think straight, this couldn't be happening. How could Harry have done something so stupid without talking to me?

'So you're telling me everything's gone?' I asked with finality.

Luke nodded. 'He cashed everything in over the past few years.'

I shook my head in disbelief. There had to be an alternative. 'But what about the online business? Why do you say it hasn't traded in years? Harry always told me how well that was doing.'

Luke grimaced. 'It seems Dad shut that down two years ago. It was costing more to run than it made.'

I gasped. Only last month we'd had a conversation about going back to the souks in Marrakech to source more stock just as we had when we had run the shop near the park.

'Why did he lie to me?' I whispered in horror.

Luke reached out and laid his hand on top of mine. 'I think he wanted to protect you, Mum.'

'But he must have known this ridiculous plan couldn't last,' I wailed. 'He should have talked to me.'

Luke shrugged. 'Downsizing would have been your best option. Dad knew you didn't want to do that. He knew how much this house meant to you.'

Guilt gnawed away at me. Luke was right. Harry was well aware of how much I adored this house. He must have been worrying himself sick if he had been juggling so much and keeping so many secrets. Even so, I was his wife; we had built a life together.

'There is some good news. There's enough to pay the tax bill,' Luke said gently.

'Oh, let's throw a party to celebrate,' I said sarcastically.

'And there are other things you could do.' Luke said, ignoring my caustic tone.

I felt a flash of hope. 'Like?'

'You could sell up and come and live with me and Hannah in New York.'

I let out an involuntary shudder. I didn't like Luke and his wife Hannah living in such a big city. I adored travelling but never liked the bustling concrete jungles where it was noisy twenty-four hours a day. They had been living there for four years, moving when Hannah got a new job as a fashion buyer for some very impressive company and of course Luke went with her. He had no problem getting a job, not with his qualifications, and they now lived a wonderful life on the Upper East Side, which Harry always insisted meant they were doing very well for themselves.

Harry and I had visited regularly at first but over the past few years Luke and Hannah had come to us several times a year as I was beginning to find air travel tiresome. All those security checks and then of course there was the jet lag. The last time we had gone over to visit I had felt dreadful and they could tell the journey had taken its toll on me. Naturally, I missed Luke and I adored Hannah, but whenever we visited I always looked forward to getting back to my home in Bath. New York wasn't me, and even allowing for the air travel and the jet lag which I knew I would eventually get over, I felt far too old to make a move like that.

'Okay.' Luke grinned, seeing my reaction. 'You could downsize on your own then.'

'After the lengths your father went to to ensure I could keep this house, you must be joking,' I said stubbornly.

'All right, you could start up the antiques business online yourself,' Luke suggested.

I barked with laughter. 'Oh, sweetheart, I can barely send an email! Don't you remember how I accidentally copied all your colleagues into a message I sent Hannah with photos of you as a baby?'

Now it was Luke's turn to shudder. 'Okay, how about a lodger?'

I opened my mouth ready to protest, but Luke held up a hand to silence me. 'Just hear me out, okay?'

Nodding, I closed my mouth, already disliking the direction of this conversation.

'This house is huge, you could rent out one of the rooms and never see anyone for days,' he began.

'But I don't want strangers around me. You remember those parties I always hosted for your father's sake? To be honest, I could never wait to see the back of everyone!'

Luke laughed before his face turned sombre. 'I also think it might be a good idea for you to have someone with you. Think about it, Mum. Dad did everything around here, you don't even drive! And you're only short, you'll never reach the high shelves in the kitchen without me or Dad around. Surely you don't want to live alone?'

With a start, I realised I hadn't given the idea of living on my own much thought. It was true I was five-foot-nothing, and had always been a passenger rather than driver. But I thought I'd coped rather well. Yet the moment Harry passed away, Luke had stepped on a plane and had been by my side ever since. I knew it was stupid but I had sort of assumed Luke would never go home.

'I've got to get back to Hannah and the bump at some point,' Luke reminded me gently. 'I can't leave them, and you won't come with me.'

Tears felt dangerously close as I took in my new reality. How in the space of a month had I lost my husband, my future, my lifestyle and now my sense of self? I took another glance around the kitchen, the memories of the last fifty years flooding back.

When we'd moved into this house, I had been fearless, believing there was nothing I couldn't do. But slowly, over time, that girl had gone, replaced by a woman who let her husband take care of everything. I got to my feet. What lay ahead was terrifying but if I was going to survive, I needed to see if I could find that girl again.

Three

Erin

The smell of coffee wafting through the air jerked me awake. Blinking my eyes open, I saw Brad wearing a smug grin as he stood over me with a plate of toast in one hand and a coffee in the other.

'For me?' I rasped gratefully, forcing myself to sit up.

'I don't know anyone else that might need an extra strong Americano and carbs this morning,' he chuckled, handing me the cup and setting the toast down beside me. 'Good night last night?'

I took a gulp of the strong liquid as Brad perched on the bed next to me and desperately tried to recall the events of last night. I remembered meeting Cara in the pub after speed dating as planned. It had not gone well and I'd needed to get a gin and tonic into her immediately as she told me story after story of hopeless, chauvinistic, desperate and even old men, clearly past the age restriction. I felt so guilty I'd made her give speed dating a try, I ended up pouring as much gin down my throat as Cara's, so it was no surprise that the curry had been forgotten in place of a liquid dinner instead.

'Not bad.' I smiled, my head banging like a drum. Turning to look at Brad, I felt a stab of regret as I realised that he was off for three nights. I had wanted to spend some quality time with him last night after a couple of hours with Cara. Shaking my long red hair behind my shoulders I looked at Brad and gave him what I thought was my sexiest come-to-bed look.

'Do you have something in your eye?' he asked frowning.

'No!' I exclaimed, before trying to be seductive again. 'I just thought we could say goodbye properly.'

Brad looked at me warily. 'Sorry sweetheart, it's just gone half six and you need to be in the office in half an hour to open up. I've got a train to catch.'

With an evil glint in his eye, Brad ripped the duvet from over me.

'Hey!' I shrieked. 'There was no need for that.'

'There was every need for that.' Brad smirked. 'Come on! I'll go and make another coffee.'

As Brad stalked off to the kitchen, I stood up and groaned.

Stepping into the large rain shower, the hot water that sprang enthusiastically from the state-of-the-art jets Brad had installed was like a balm to my poor, aching body. Like everything else in our flat – well, technically Brad's flat – the shower was beautifully designed, expensive and top of the range.

The two-bed he owned, just outside the city centre, had been fully renovated and designed by Brad. As well as the modern bathroom with twin basins and under-floor heating, our bedroom boasted a walk-in closet for each of us, while the kitchen looked like something that belonged in an episode of *Star Trek*. As for the electrics, I always felt you needed a degree in computer science just to turn the lights on, as everything was controlled by iPad. Much as I appreciated the gadgetry of it all, my parents' home in nearby Bristol was much simpler, with light switches and TV remote controls you operated yourself rather than with some computer that could seemingly read your mind.

As the hot water cascaded over my body I couldn't help thinking about my parents. Usually it was too painful, and so I always pushed them out of my mind, but since my discussion with Brad yesterday I hadn't been able to forget about them so easily.

We had always been such a close family. With there just being the three of us, Mum, Dad and I had formed a tight little unit over the years. I knew I was spoilt rotten – nothing was ever too much trouble for my parents when it came to me – but I always appreciated the love and devotion they showed me.

I always told them everything, along with Cara, never feeling the need to keep secrets from my parents like some of my friends. My mum and dad knew when I'd tried cigarettes and alcohol for the first time and when I'd skived off school because I hated maths. They didn't bat an eyelid at any of it and, instead of having a go at me, would always talk to me about any problems I was having.

Everyone at school thought they were amazing and wished they were their parents. I had to admit they were cool. Dad had been a hippy growing up in San Francisco, with his mum and dad taking him to Woodstock when he was a baby. Mum was an activist at Greenham Common.

Although they both became solicitors, running a practice together in Bristol, that hippy spirit never left them. As a kid, I had fond memories of them taking me to marches against the Poll Tax or the Iraq War in London and so I learned early on what it meant to be responsible not just for yourself but other people too. That's why it was such a shock when Mum and Dad took against Brad so quickly. They had always taught me to be tolerant of everyone, and naturally I assumed that they would take Brad in to their hearts just like I had.

Yet, if I was honest with myself, I think I did suspect there was every chance Mum and Dad might not completely accept Brad into the fold. Mum's sister Sandra had been a bit of a wild child and had married a divorcee twenty-five years her senior when she was only twenty-one. Despite Sandra telling everyone Jerry was the one, Jerry clearly had other ideas. After developing a worrying gambling habit, not to mention an eye for the ladies – something Sandra refused to believe – Jerry finally did what we all expected and four years later he took up with a younger model named Tina. Not only did he set up home with Tina straight away, but he left Sandra with a load of his gambling debts to pay off. To add insult to injury, he sold the house from under Sandra, meaning Mum and Dad had to bail her out. I'd lost count of the times Mum told me to be careful with my assets and to be careful who I trusted, but I still thought that she would take the time to get to know Brad before deciding they wanted nothing to do with him. Yet the moment I introduced them, Dad went puce and Mum shook her head in disbelief. Pulling me aside in the kitchen she asked me if I'd learned nothing from Sandra's situation, insisting that

Brad would do just the same to me as Jerry had done to Sandra. I couldn't believe what I was hearing. Brad was a world away from Jerry. For a start he didn't gamble – well only occasionally in the casinos and that was for business – and he had never so much as looked at another woman.

But Mum and Dad weren't convinced. Mum said that the fact Brad had given up on one marriage was a worry, never mind the fact he was closer to their age than mine. She was sorry but she couldn't go through an emotional mess like this one again. It had been hard enough being there for Sandra, she said, when Jerry constantly broke her heart and she reckoned it would kill her to see her own daughter go through the same thing. There had been a pause then as she and Dad looked at each other before Mum said, in a rather shaky voice, that I had to choose: Brad or them. In that moment I felt a rage like no other. I stared at them, anger pulsing through me that they were putting me in this position. I had never given them a reason to doubt my decision-making in the past – they ought to support me now. Furiously I refused to choose and said that if that meant they cut me out of their lives, that was up to them, but I wasn't being held hostage like this. They said they couldn't support my decision to be with him and although they would always be there for me if I needed anything, it would be best if we didn't speak while Brad was in my life.

I had left the house that day in tears, unable to believe what had happened. Brad had been a huge comfort, insisting that they would come around eventually. I hoped he was right, but the one thing I never told him was how much I missed Mum and Dad. They weren't just parents, they were friends. I missed talking to them about my day or the silly things that made up the rich fabric of our family life: like the way Dad would do a bad Tommy Cooper impression round the dinner table or the way Mum began nearly every sentence with, 'In the *Guardian* this morning…'

Most of all I just missed having them on my team and as much as I told myself I was fine with their decision, I knew Brad was right. I didn't want to get married without them there, and would do anything to fix it.

Turning the water off, I swaddled myself in a large fluffy towel as Brad shouted through the door.

'Hurry up, babe, you'll never make it at this rate.'

'All right, all right,' I grumbled, snatching the door open and stalking past him in my towel. 'I don't know why you need me to open up so early anyway. It's not like anybody ever starts at that time.'

'*I* start at that time,' Brad said firmly. 'And I, as your boss, have asked you, so that's the end of it.'

I rolled my eyes as he sat on the bed and watched me get dressed in the navy-blue suit he had laid out for me. Quickly running a brush through my hair, I spritzed on some perfume and reached for my bag.

'See, I'm ten minutes early,' I said gleefully, shoving my watch under his nose.

Brad gave me a wry smile. 'Makes a change!'

'Cheek!' I chuckled, swatting him playfully with a pillow, before kissing him softly on the lips. 'What time will I see you on Friday?'

'I don't know, sweetheart,' he replied, kissing my nose. 'I'll text you. Now go!'

'Okay, I'm gone!' I stepped out into the hallway. 'Have a good time.'

There was no reply as I slammed the front door shut and walked out into the cool air. Pulling my wool coat tightly around me, I began my walk down the hill noticing the mid-March grey skies. It looked like it was about to throw it down at any minute and I quickened my pace, eager to get to work before I got drenched.

Thankfully, we lived just close enough to the centre that you could walk, and this morning I had a feeling I could use the fresh air. Taking a deep breath to try and fight off the feelings of nausea, I wondered if Cara felt as badly as I did this morning. She was a cabin crew manager and I knew she had a long flight to Florida to prepare for. Reaching into my bag for my phone to text her, I frantically scrambled through my belongings, pulling out tampons, hand cream, nail varnish, tissues, keys and my purse – but no phone. A creeping sense of dread surged through me as I realised that in my hurry to get to work on time I'd left my phone on my bedside table charging.

I let out a frustrated squeal, resisting the urge to unleash a full-on toddler tantrum before turning to walk back home. By the time I reached the flat twenty minutes later, I was out of puff and looked like a drowned cat with my bedraggled hair plastered to my head. There was nothing for it, I thought, fishing the keys out of my bag and quickly unlocking the door, I'd have to get a cab to drop me off at work.

Standing in the hallway, I quickly shucked off my rain sodden coat and wandered through to the living room. Hearing the sound of Brad's gravelly laugh, my heart sank when I realised he hadn't left for London yet. I had hoped I might miss him and save myself the embarrassment of him knowing I'd be late after all.

'Sweetheart, are you here?' I called, wandering from room to room.

But there was no reply. I frowned. Perhaps the hangover was worse than I thought if I was imagining noises.

'Brad?' I called again but there was nothing.

Instead I carried on walking towards the bedroom. As I rested my hand on the door handle, something made me hesitate.

I couldn't put my finger on what it was, whether it was a smell or a feeling, but something told me that beyond that door lay danger.

Cocking my head, I listened for a sound to confirm my instincts, but there was none. I rolled my eyes, frustrated with myself. I was too old to be this hungover on a work day, and if I was imagining things then clearly the weekday drinking had to stop.

I pushed open the door and immediately felt like I was falling. I realised with sudden clarity my instincts had been right. There in my bed, the bed I had been sleeping in less than an hour ago, was Brad with another woman.

A wave of sickness crashed over me as I stood rooted to the spot. Then, from nowhere, I felt a rage burn through me. I opened my mouth cleared my throat causing the two of them to spring apart as if they had been burned. Turning to see me in the doorway, Brad's face drained and his eyes widened in shock. It was clear he had been so carried away by the moment he hadn't heard my dulcet tones.

'Erin, I'm sorry,' Brad said, his voice barely a whisper.

But my gaze swept past him, towards the woman now sitting upright in the place where I usually slept. Sheets clasped to her chest and her mouth opening and closing like a goldfish, she was clearly stunned as she desperately tried to think of something to say.

'It seems I didn't have to worry about your hangover after all,' I remarked in an oddly calm voice. 'You look like you're doing just fine to me, Cara.'

My former best friend went as red as my hair, while Brad said nothing, merely glancing from me and then back to Cara in alarm.

I wanted to flee but it was as though my legs had other ideas. No matter how much I willed them, they refused to budge. The scene was like a train wreck and I was unable to tear my eyes away from the devastation. I opened my own mouth again, prepared to shout and scream at the betrayal of the two people who up until five minutes ago had been my world. But the moment I did, I caught the smell of sex hanging heavily in the air, and suddenly the only thing I wanted to do was throw up. So I did, all over Brad's expensive beige wool carpet that we had picked out together. For a brief second I stared at the floor, filled with disgust at what I had done. Then with what dignity I could muster, I squared my shoulders and stalked out of the bedroom, my mind whirring.

Forgetting my phone, or the change of clothes I had promised myself, I bolted back down the hallway, unsure what to do or say, but just knowing I had to get the hell out of there immediately. Reaching the front door, I shoved my feet into a pair of trainers and picked up my rain-sodden coat from the floor. I had just managed to get one arm in when Brad appeared. I looked up and was mildly grateful he at least had had the good grace to put on boxer shorts.

'Erin I'm sorry,' he began, only for me to hold my hand up to stop him.

'Don't,' I said, with a boldness I didn't feel.

He took a step towards me and reached for my hand. Immediately I shrank back as if I had been scorched. 'No! You do not get to speak to me, you do not get to touch me.'

Angrily I shoved my other arm into my coat. I was so tense I felt as though my arms and legs could break in two. I had to get out of here, I had to breathe but before I did I had to know the truth.

'Has it been going on long?' I whispered, hating myself for asking the question.

A mixture of remorse, guilt and anxiety crossed his features. 'A month.'

My hands flew to my mouth as I realised this wasn't some one-off. This was a relationship.

'Do you love her?' My voice sounded small and scared.

A flicker of regret passed across his face as he gave a brief nod. 'I'm sorry.'

His words hit me like a punch to the stomach. I felt floored, so brutal was the truth. Somehow I found the strength to open the door, and without looking back I fled from the flat. I ran and ran and didn't stop until I reached the bottom of the hill, where I ducked behind a tree and threw up again.

When I was finished, I sank onto a nearby bench and took a deep breath. I wanted to wallow, I wanted to cry, I wanted to beat my fists against a wall and scream *why me?* But I refused to do any of that. In that moment I made a silent promise to myself. That although my heart was broken, I would not let the fact my best friend and my fiancé had fallen in love define me.

Four

Lydia

There was only one flaw in our beautiful house that I had never been able to solve and that was the boring but vital issue of parking. Now, as I looked out of the window at the street below, the early morning rain soaking passers-by, my eyes came to rest on Harry's bright red E-Type Jaguar. Even though I could barely tell one end of a car from the other, I knew it was undoubtedly a classic. Harry had always loved the attention it brought and would chat to admirers night and day about it, given the opportunity. He had bought it after we sold the shop and treated himself to something he had always wanted, ditching the old Honda we'd had for years.

To say it was his pride and joy was something of an understatement. Dating back to the sixties, it was an antique in its own right, and in the same way I adored this house, Harry had adored that car. He would spend every Sunday morning cleaning it, buffing it and tinkering with it, before taking it out for a drive. Looking at it now, parked just where he had left it three weeks ago after his final Sunday jaunt, I felt a pang of sadness. It couldn't stay parked there forever. Denise, the chairwoman of our residents' association, was frankly a battle-axe and always looking for ways to exert her power over us poor residents. It was clear I was going to have to do something with the car, but what?

'You could always sell it,' Luke suggested, standing alongside me in his fluffy blue dressing gown.

I turned to him and smiled. 'You always were good at reading my mind.'

'It's an option, Mum.' Luke shrugged. 'It's worth a lot of money. I'm afraid that once we've cashed in what little of the investments Dad didn't touch there's not going to be a lot left after those back taxes are paid.'

'I know that, Luke,' I hissed. 'But I'm not parting with your father's car! It was as precious to him as this house.'

Luke let out a loud groan. 'But you don't even drive. You'll have to go to the DVLA and get a SORN.'

'Who? What?' I said, a bit too snippily.

'See, Mum! How on earth are you going to take care of yourself in this big old house when you don't even know what the DVLA is!' Luke replied in frustration. 'When are you going to see sense?'

'When I'm six feet under,' I snapped, turning away from the car and sinking into my favourite armchair. 'And if you carry on nagging me like this then I don't think I'll be far behind your father.'

Luke sighed as he sat opposite me. 'I'm not trying to give you a hard time, Mum, I'm just trying to get you to see reason. You cannot carry on living as you have been.'

I resisted the urge to put him over my knee and instead took a deep breath. That was something else nobody ever told you about getting older – how irritating it is when your children think they know better than you. I realised Luke was only acting out of concern, but frankly there were fleeting moments when I wished he would go back to Hannah. I wanted to get on with the business of grieving for my husband in private, without the constant threat of my future hanging over my head. I just wanted to wallow over the loss of more than fifty years of marriage and friendship, and the fact there was no more Harry and Lydia. Was that really so wrong?

Luke's blue eyes met my own. 'I'm sorry, Mum. I don't mean to go on. I know this is hard for you. It's all been a surprise to me too. I keep thinking how I was only speaking to Dad three weeks ago. He seemed fine, couldn't wait to get back on the golf course and was talking about coming to the States to see me, Hannah and the baby when he or she was born... Now he's gone and he'll never meet his grandchild and I'll never see him again.'

There was a sudden sob and I realised my precious boy had completely broken down. Immediately I got up and wrapped my arms around him, letting him bury his face in my neck, not caring that he was drenching my shoulder. I clung to him as though he were a lifeboat and I a desperate swimmer cast adrift, as he wept for the only father he had ever known and loved.

I thought back to the day I had lost my own father. I had been a little older than Luke at fifty-five but it had still hurt like hell, even though he was ninety-one and we all knew it was coming. I had always been close to my father, an engineer with a heart of gold, and when he went I felt so lost. In the first few months without him, I had felt like a little girl again as I wept myself to sleep, crying for my daddy.

My mother had died before I was born, so Dad was both mother and father to me and my sister, Stella. In those days, of course, many children without mothers were shipped off to boarding school but Dad refused. He had been quite the maverick and instead did his best to muddle through the difficulties of raising two girls alone.

The experience taught me you could get through anything if you tried and as Luke's tears began to subside, it occurred to me that my son wouldn't be pushing me into action if he didn't think it necessary.

'Okay then,' I whispered. 'I'll make some changes.'

Luke lifted his head and smiled, his eyes shining with tears. 'You'll consider getting a lodger?'

I gave a curt nod of my head. 'If you really think that there's no other way.'

Luke nodded, this time wiping his tears away with the back of his hand. 'It will be good for you to have company and if you choose carefully you can make sure whoever it is will be perfect for you.'

I sniffed at that. 'Luke, you know I have never made friends easily. Phil is the closest friend I have and even he was someone I shared with your father. I rather doubt there's someone out there that's perfect for me.'

'You might love this house Mum, but it's too big for you to manage on your own. If you offer a reduced rent, then you can invite someone to help you look after it and even drive you about.'

I stopped for a moment and caught my breath. Who did I know that would be home during the week? Then it hit me – my old uni mate Rachel. She was home on maternity leave from her job as a junior architect with her six-month-old daughter, Matilda.

At the thought of a coffee with my friend and a cuddle with her baby, my heart soared. Settled on my mission, I rounded the corner before reaching Rachel's place, not far from the further education college.

Rachel and her wife Lily had bought a derelict flat when they left uni. At the time I had been amazed they had become so responsible so quickly, but now as I pressed the bell on the old Georgian townhouse, I had never felt so grateful for a responsible friend.

Seconds later I heard the sound of a sash window being pulled up. I looked up and saw Rachel's beaming face quickly turn to concern as she took in my red-rimmed eyes and bedraggled appearance.

'What the hell's happened to you?'

'Brad's cheated on me with Cara,' I shouted up at her.

Her jaw dropped open but then, to her credit, she quickly composed herself and threw the keys down for me to let myself in.

'I'll get the coffee on. Come straight up.'

Relief flooded through me as I made my way up to their apartment. It always made me feel safe, and right now that was all I wanted.

Rachel opened the front door and led me to the sofa, where I sank down and leaned my head against her. She didn't rush me or make me talk. Instead she wrapped her arm around my shoulders and kissed my head, telling me how sorry she was.

When I felt better, I wiped my tears away. 'I caught them in our bed. There's no mistake. He says he loves her. She wants me to come round, that she's sorry but she and Brad are meant to be.'

As I said this last part, my voice broke, the effort of saying the words out loud too much to bear as the truth of the situation hit home.

'That pair of bastards,' Rachel growled. 'I know she's your oldest friend, but I have never liked Cara. She's always looked down her nose at Lily.'

Privately I knew that wasn't true. Lily was a make-up artist and had taught Cara all the tricks of the trade over the years. However, I appreciated Rachel's support and wasn't about to start defending Cara now when everything about her was indefensible.

'What do you want to do?' Lily asked softly, having just arrived home for lunch to hear the tail end of my story.

I shrugged my shoulders. I was so tired all of a sudden. 'I want to sleep and then I want to get my stuff from Brad's place. Just my clothes and things. Nothing Cara would have touched. I ought to go to work too. Do things properly at least.' I sank my head into my hands. It all seemed so much to deal with. 'Brad's out of town on a conference, or that's what he told me, so at least I don't have to face him. If one of you don't mind giving me a lift, I can go up and get my stuff later when I'm sure he's gone.'

Lily smiled kindly and looked at her wife. 'We can manage a bit more than that can't we?'

'Tell you what,' Rachel reached behind her for a rug. 'Why don't you stay with us for a couple of days until you get sorted? In the meantime, have a nap, then you can nip into the office for a chat with HR? While you're doing that, I'll get your things from Brad's.'

'I can't ask you to do that,' I exclaimed.

'You didn't. I, or rather we, offered,' Rachel replied firmly. 'Besides, you can't want to run the risk of seeing him again, especially now. It's fine, give me your keys and I'll throw everything together.'

'You really don't mind?'

'Not at all, as long as you don't mind looking after Matilda.' She grinned, gesturing towards the sleeping baby.

'It would be my pleasure,' I said, meaning it.

Rachel got to her feet and I handed her my house keys out of my bag. 'And it would be my pleasure to cut off Brad's balls if I see him.'

After two days with Rachel, Lily and Matilda, I felt a lot stronger. The first night had been horrible. I kept waking up on their sofa-bed wondering where the hell I was and feeling sick and angry at all that had happened. But the following night I slept like the dead, my mind finally catching up with my body, seemingly in need of rest. I think the fact I had a mountain of paperwork, as well as all my stuff to sort through, thanks to Rachel, had helped. In all honesty, I had been dreading going into work and talking to HR, but they had been brilliant when I explained, without going into too many details, what had happened and why I felt it best if I left immediately.

As I was owed some holiday there was no problem and they even sorted out my final salary payment. It wasn't huge but would be enough to tide me over until I found something else. Then there was just some exit interview stuff to go through, which they assured me could be done over the phone.

'Do you feel like going for a walk to the park?' Rachel asked me as I finished getting ready after my morning shower.

'That sounds nice,' I said as Matilda let out a healthy burp in her mum's arms. 'Maybe we could even call in at Phil's afterwards?'

Rachel's face lit up at the suggestion. 'Brilliant! After this one kept me up all night, I need several espressos to get me through the day.'

In the end we abandoned the idea of a walk, as Rachel said she was just too tired. Instead we went straight to Phil's and ordered our usual from Ginger, the world's grumpiest but most efficient barista.

'My favourite ladies,' Phil cried, ushering us towards my usual table by the window. 'And how are the three of you this morning?'

'Fine.' Rachel smiled. 'Tired, but I'm hoping one of your legendary coffees is going to sort me out.'

Phil smiled, his brown eyes crinkling with understanding. 'It's hard being a parent, yes?'

'It is,' Rachel sighed. 'And please don't judge me, but there's a small part of me that can't wait to get back to work! There's only so many times I can listen to "Baby Shark" without wanting to stab myself in the eye!'

As Phil and I roared with laughter at the mix of amusement and guilt spread across Rachel's caramel features, Ginger appeared with our order.

Taking a grateful slug of coffee, I felt Phil's eyes turn to me. 'And what's wrong with you Erin? You don't seem yourself.'

'I'm fine,' I lied.

Rachel rolled her eyes. 'If fine means you're all right after your fiancé sleeps with your best friend, then yes, Phil, Erin is totally fine.'

'Not Cara!' Phil gasped.

'The very same,' Rachel confirmed.

Phil's jaw dropped open. 'How could this have happened? I knew that Brad was trouble from the moment he came in here, but as for Cara, I'm disgusted.'

As Rachel nodded her agreement, I let their chatter pass over my head. Phil adored his regular customers and said he thought of us all as family. Even though he had been born and bred in Bath, his parents were Spanish and had brought him up to believe in the very Spanish tradition of family coming first. Named Philippe but far more comfortable with Phil, I felt his kindness once more as he pushed another croissant, that had somehow magically appeared, towards me.

'Erin, what will you do now?' Phil asked gently, bringing me back to the present.

I shook my head. 'Don't know. Rachel's letting me sleep on her sofa but they haven't really got the room.'

'We have,' Rachel insisted, draining her cup dry. 'You're welcome to stay as long as you like.'

'That's sweet but you and Lily are new parents and you only got married a couple of weeks ago! I can't cramp your style.'

At that Rachel made no protest, and I smiled gratefully at my friend as Phil tried again. 'What about your family? Have you any other friends you can stay with?'

'No,' I said quietly. 'My family and I haven't spoken in three years, I can hardly turn up now.'

Phil raised his eyes to the ceiling for a moment, his lined face clearly deep in thought. 'I have it!' He suddenly shrieked with delight, banging the table for emphasis. 'For you, Erin, I have the perfect solution.'

'You do?' I asked doubtfully.

'Yes, yes,' Phil said excitably. 'But first, Erin, can you drive?'

I nodded, feeling bewildered. 'What's that got to do with anything? Oh, Phil, do you want me to work here and be your delivery driver? That's so kind but—'

'No sweetie,' Phil replied, somewhat sadly. 'I have no money or need for your services. But I have another suggestion. Wait here just a moment,' he said, scuttling across to the community noticeboard.

'What's this?' I asked as he set a white lined index card down in front of me.

'It's your new home.' He grinned, looking decidedly pleased with himself. 'I know this lady. She is lovely and, like you, has just lost someone close to her. She needs someone like you and you need someone like her.'

Glancing down, I began to read.

Houseshare available with an elegant and mature lady. Room to rent, reasonable rates, in exchange for help around the home and driving duties. Car provided. Enquire within.

I looked up at Phil feeling confused, only for him to smile and pull out his phone. 'She brought this down only the other day. I'm sure the room will still be available, I'll give her a call.'

Six

Lydia

I had only just got back from the bank when I saw Luke put the phone down, a bright smile plastered across his face.

'That was Phil,' he said, 'you know from the café.'

'Oh, yes?' I asked expectantly as I hung my coat on the rack under the stairs.

'He said he's got someone for the room!'

'So soon?' I gasped. 'I only dropped the card in a couple of days ago.'

Luke clapped his hands together in excitement. 'I know! Isn't it great? He's sending her up now and she can move in straightaway.'

I walked into the sitting room and tried to steady my nerves. This was all happening far too quickly. When I had left the advert with Phil, he had assured me that he wouldn't let just anyone enquire about the room. Instead he would guard it with his life, ensuring that only the right person was sent my way.

I believed him. When Harry keeled over in Phil's coffee shop, I had been too shocked to help, so it had been Phil that had sprung into action, calling the ambulance and keeping customers well away.

After the unthinkable happened, Phil had been so kind, popping up to the house with flowers and a card. Then he insisted on making all the food for the funeral and giving me a very welcome discount which at the time I had no idea I needed.

Harry and I had come to know Phil very well. He had set up shop forty years ago, just as we were starting our own antiques business two doors along. Phil wasn't just an excellent barista, but a good friend and I trusted his advice. If he thought he had the right person for me, then no matter how quickly I thought this was all moving, I had to believe him.

'Is the room even ready?' I asked suddenly. 'We were going to clear it out and give it all a quick vacuum before showing anyone round.'

'I gave it a going over last night when you went to bed.' Luke smiled, sitting down beside me. 'Mum, please relax. I'm here to help you vet whomever it is Phil's sending up. If we don't like her then she doesn't move in. It really is that simple, I promise. You don't have to do anything you don't want to.'

I said nothing and patted Luke's knee affectionately. How could I tell him that over the last few weeks my life had been filled with things I didn't want to do? From burying the love of my life to selling my husband's things and now living with a complete stranger. None of these were things I had particularly wanted to do.

But I said nothing and instead when the doorbell rang, I got to my feet sharply and hurried towards the front door. I briefly checked my appearance in the hallway mirror, patting my greying blonde locks into place and then, ignoring the butterflies in my stomach, opened the door.

Although I hadn't really given much thought to my ideal tenant, the girl on my doorstep was definitely not it. She was only in her mid-twenties and I had envisaged someone a lot older. Not only that but she looked desperately pale and thin. I felt my maternal instinct kick in as I wondered if she was ill.

'Mrs Harper?' she said in a gentle tone, as I stood there gawping.

'Yes, but it's just Lydia. Please do come in,' I said, holding the door open as I remembered my manners. 'I'm so sorry, I didn't speak to Phil and so I don't know your name.'

'Erin Matthews,' she replied politely.

'Can I take your coat?' I asked, echoing her well-mannered tone.

Erin smiled her thanks and handed it to me as I led her downstairs and through to the kitchen.

'Shall we have a cup of tea? Then I can show you the house.'

She followed me inside where Luke had already boiled the kettle and was pouring fresh water into the pot. Pleased to see he was using leaves rather than bags, I gestured for Erin to take a seat and tried not gasp in horror as she made a beeline for Harry's chair.

'So, Erin,' Luke began, laying a hand on me warningly as he set the pot down. 'Tell us a bit about yourself.'

'Yes, go on dear.' I smiled, knowing it was important to be friendly. 'Are you from the area?'

48

The girl nodded as Luke poured the tea. 'I'm originally from Bristol, but I went to uni here in Bath. After that I never left. What about you? Have you always lived here?'

'More or less – like you I was born in Bristol, but have lived in Bath all my married life. My son Luke' – I nodded at him – 'was born and bred here though.'

'Although I live in America now. I'm just back visiting Mum,' Luke put in.

Erin nodded again, taking in this new bit of information. 'I wondered. I was sure the advert said you lived on your own.'

'Yes, I might as well tell you: Harry, my husband, died very suddenly three weeks ago. He was seventy-nine and still full of life' I said, baldly. 'It's taken us by surprise somewhat. Luke, number one son that he is, flew back at the drop of a hat to be with me, but of course he can't stay forever. He has a wife that needs him and he thinks it would be good for me to find someone to help around the house, keep me company, drive me around, that sort of thing.'

'And what do you think?' Erin asked.

I found myself chuckling at the girl's directness. Full marks for saying what she meant.

'I think I would rather live by myself and try to get over Harry's death in private,' I replied honestly. 'But I agree with Luke that it's not the best option financially and if I can find someone who will tolerate me then I can make the best of a bad situation.'

My son smacked his hand against his forehead and groaned. 'Why did you have to say that, Mum? You'll put Erin off if she hasn't been put off already.'

'It's fine.' Erin's eyes crinkled with mirth. 'After the few days I've had, I appreciate a bit of honesty.'

I raised my eyebrows. There was a story here. 'Oh?'

The girl bit her lip, clearly wondering if she had said too much. But if I was going to share my home with someone, then I wanted to know everything about them, warts and all.

'The truth is that up until a few days ago I was living a very happy life in a swish flat on the other side of town. I had a best friend, a fiancé and a brilliant job as an architect,' she said.

'So what happened?' I asked, keen to get to the nub of the matter.

Erin lifted her chin in defiance. 'And then I caught my fiancé sleeping with my best friend in our bed. As I also worked for him and lived in his flat, I'm now homeless and jobless.'

Luke reached over and squeezed the girl's arm. 'I'm so sorry, that's a horrible thing to discover.'

'Thanks,' Erin said, squaring her shoulders. 'But you don't need to be sorry, you didn't do it. The only ones that should be sorry are my fiancé and best friend, but they won't be, they're "in love",' she said sarcastically.

I took another sip of my tea and offered Erin a genuine smile. I admired her for putting a brave face on for the world, even if she did fall apart in private. She was, of course, young enough to find someone else, but also to not know that men like this fiancé of hers, not to mention the best friend, were fickle. I wanted to tell Erin she would be far better off without the pair of them. But I said none of that. I might have been old and a bit forgetful, but I wasn't stupid. It was too early for Erin to hear that, in the same way as it was too early for me to hear from strangers at my husband's wake that there was still time to remarry.

'What are you going to do with that ring?' I asked catching sight of the sizeable diamond on her finger.

Erin looked at it in surprise as if she had forgotten it was there at all. 'Give it back, I imagine. I want nothing from him.'

I couldn't hold back any longer. 'Don't be a fool. There's a deposit for a flat or car on your finger. You always keep the jewellery, dear. Especially if they can't keep it in their trousers.'

Erin and Luke looked at me in shock. I took another sip of tea and tried to think of a less controversial topic. The young were so easily upset.

'And how do you know Phil?' As I mentioned his name, Erin smiled, her whole face lighting up as she did so.

'I used to revise in his café when I was at uni and he would bring me incredibly strong lattes to help me concentrate, often for free. He's always been so kind to me.'

'Phil is a wonderful man,' I agreed.

'He is,' Erin gushed. 'But I don't want you to think I took advantage. When Ginger was ill in hospital last year, I took some holiday from my job and helped him out without payment. He always does so much for other people, I wanted to do something for him.'

I had to confess that was a kind and thoughtful gesture. Perhaps Phil had known a little of what he was doing after all.

'Shall we have a look upstairs at the room?' I suggested, draining my cup. 'Then you can see if you think you might like it.'

'I'd like that,' Erin replied, following Luke and me upstairs to the second floor.

As I pushed open the door, I was delighted to find Luke had done a bit more than cleaned and vacuumed. He had cleared the room out, put fresh sheets on the bed and even set up a little television. The result was quite homely and I shot my son a grateful smile.

'So what do you think?' he asked Erin, who was peering out of the window at the grass beyond. I had always thought it a lovely room overlooking the Circus itself and this morning the room was bathed in a warm glow, now the clouds had given way to bright sunshine. From nowhere, I found myself hoping that Erin loved it up here as much as I did.

'I really like it,' she said shyly. 'It's far nicer than I could have hoped for.'

'I'm so pleased,' I beamed.

'So does that mean you want to move in then?' Luke asked excitedly.

I rolled my eyes at my boy. It was a good job he never played poker.

'There's no hurry to decide,' I offered.

Erin took a step towards me, her lovely smile lighting up her whole face. 'If you're happy to have me, I'd love to move in.'

'Then let's give it a try,' I suggested, holding out my hand for her to shake. As she gripped it firmly, I felt a fleeting glimpse of happiness. It seemed no accident Erin had found her way to me. Perhaps together, she and I would help each other find ourselves again.

Seven

Erin

I sank onto the double bed, my belongings strewn all around me. When Rachel had collected my stuff from Brad's flat, I was sure I didn't have that much. Yet between Rachel, Luke and I, it had taken two trips to get everything into my new home.

Home. I shivered at the sound of the word. But as I looked around this bright, sun-filled room, I realised that's exactly what these four walls were. I bit my lip. It wasn't where I had expected to find myself but when I stood up and peered out of the large sash window that overlooked the Circus, I felt a shiver of delight at the decadence of living in such a posh house.

When Phil had told us the location of Lydia's house, neither Rachel or I could believe it. Even Matilda had let out a cheery wail, which we all assumed meant she was as delighted as we were. After all, the Circus was one of those very famous, very prestigious addresses where you couldn't quite believe real people lived, as it seemed to be too perfect.

As I watched two children play a game of French cricket on the circular lawn outside, I hugged myself. Although I would never in a million years have chosen this particular fresh start, I had realised as soon as I knocked on Lydia's front door that fate was finally smiling on me and I didn't want to mess it up.

If I'm honest, I thought Lydia was a bit prickly at first and I was glad she became a bit friendlier after a cup of tea. Though frankly, after all she had been through I thought it was a miracle she was still standing. When she explained her situation to me, I could understand why she felt a bit reluctant to welcome me inside with open arms. Like me, she was having a change forced upon her. I could only hope that she would make the best of it, just as I was trying to do.

It seemed we had a lot to learn from each other. Because although I found it incredible that in the twenty-first century Lydia had known nothing about the finances she shared with her husband, she was still pretty savvy. That crack about keeping the ring told me that beneath the navy Marks & Sparks twinset, there was a firecracker waiting for her chance to shine.

I stared down at the sparkler that still sat on my ring finger. I had been so excited when Brad had whisked me off to Las Vegas and proposed on a gondola ride at the Venetian. When he had somehow got down on one knee and placed it on my finger in the narrow boat, I'd felt so happy. It had cost a fortune and I'd loved wearing it, but now it felt gaudy and cheap. Just the existence of it was weighing me down and without further thought I slipped it over my knuckle and off my finger. Holding it up to the light, I admired the way it sparkled for one last time and then slipped it into my jewellery box for safe keeping – I would know what to do with it when the time was right. Maybe Lydia was onto something: maybe I should sell the thing. After all it wasn't as if I wanted to keep the reminder of how my best friend and fiancé had betrayed me.

As my thoughts turned to Cara, I wondered what she would make of Lydia and the fact I was now living in such a posh house. And then I realised with a sudden jolt that Cara wouldn't be able to give me her opinion because Cara wouldn't know, just as she would never know anything about my life ever again. It hit me then in a way it hadn't hit me before: Cara really was gone, and I wanted to wail, the agony of losing her felt so raw. My mum had always drummed it into me that the power of female friendship was far more important than a romance with any man. Sandra had been living proof of that. I think that was one of the reasons I had never really bothered about boys before Brad came along. I hadn't needed their approval or validation in a way that many girls my age did. I had Cara, and she had me, only now I didn't. I had lost a relationship that had been formed before I was born and it felt too terrifying for words. I was just about to fling myself onto my bed and scream into my pillow when there was a knock at the door and Lydia's smiling face appeared. 'How are you getting on, dear?'

I did my best to plaster on a smile, waving at her to come inside. 'Fine, I think. Just working out where to put everything. Is there anything you'd like me to do or not do?'

Lydia frowned for a moment. 'I don't think so. You're probably a bit old to start Blu-tacking posters to the wall, aren't you?'

'Yes, my Backstreet Boys days are over you'll be glad to know.'

'Backstreet what?' Lydia's face clouded over with confusion before she shrugged and changed the subject. 'I just came to ask if you would like to join me and Luke for supper?'

I smiled gratefully. With all the moving, hefting and lifting I had done today I was starving but hadn't thought to get myself any food. 'That's very kind, but only if it's no trouble.'

Lydia's face lit up. 'We would love to have you. It'll be ready in about ten minutes.'

Checking my watch, it was my turn to frown in confusion. Surely there was some mistake. On busy days at work I had eaten lunch at around this time. 'It's only five o'clock.' I pointed out.

'Exactly, supper time. It's just chicken Kiev and salad.' She smiled, before her expression changed to one of panic. 'Oh lord, you're not one of those vegetarians, are you?'

I couldn't help laughing at the look of horror on her face and swallowed any feelings of annoyance I had at eating so early. It was sweet of her to try and make me feel welcome even though I didn't usually eat dinner at this time. I had to make a success of this odd house share and didn't want to fall at the first hurdle – after all, wasn't life all about compromise? 'No, and that sounds lovely,' I said. 'Thank you.'

As she turned to walk back down the stairs, I followed her into the kitchen and pushed all thoughts of Cara firmly from my mind. Instead I decided to see if there was anything I could do to assist. The ad had said help was required and I wanted to get off on the right foot.

After Lydia and Luke waved my offers of assistance away, I took a seat at the large kitchen table and admired the garden view. It was such a lovely room and, despite the darkening skies outside, was surprisingly light. Pine cabinets lined two of the walls, while gleaming white worktops reflected the light, making the whole place feel warm and inviting.

I turned to watch Luke mash a huge saucepan of potatoes. To my horror I saw he wasn't going easy on the butter and cream. I was a keen runner, but that amount of fat was going to cost me a few extra miles this week.

'Only one way to eat mash,' he said with a grin, licking the spoon before sticking it in the dishwasher. 'Hannah never lets me eat like this and as it's my last day, I'm going to make the most of Mum's cooking – or rather my cooking.'

I chuckled. 'I didn't realise you were going so soon.'

'Yes, unfortunately, work have been ringing wanting to know when I'm coming back.' He sighed, dividing the mash across three plates. 'That, and Hannah's worried the baby's going to come any day even though she's not due for another five months.'

Lydia smiled at her son. 'Time to go back, love. Life carries on.'

I couldn't fail to notice the fleeting look of sadness that passed between their matching blue eyes and I realised they had lost something far more important than I had. Lydia had lost the love of her life, her best friend of fifty years. Luke, his father, a relationship that could never be replaced.

What had I lost? A fickle man and equally fickle best friend. The love I thought ebbed and flowed between us was non-existent, unlike the love Luke and Lydia so obviously shared.

'So Erin, have you given any thought to job hunting?' Luke asked as he doled out the plates and sat down.

Lydia flashed him a look of warning. 'Luke, Erin has only just arrived. She's paid a deposit and her first month's rent in advance – I think we can save the lectures, don't you?'

Luke had the good grace to flush with colour. 'Sorry, Erin. I didn't mean to sound as though I was hassling you. I was just making conversation. It was stupid of me, sorry.'

I waved his concerns away. 'It's fine. You were right to ask. If some strange woman was living with my mum then I'd want to make sure they weren't some freeloader as well.'

'Really, dear, there's no pressure at all.' Lydia said, her voice rich with concern. 'You've had a traumatic time. You need to take care of yourself. Don't rush from the frying pan into the fire.'

'Thank you,' I said gratefully. 'The truth is I don't know about work at the minute, everything has happened so suddenly. Rachel says that there might be a job going at her firm, but she's still on maternity leave. Otherwise I thought I might start looking over in Bristol. I could easily commute on the train.'

'Just don't feel you have to rush into anything,' Lydia said comfortingly. 'I see too many young people running around complaining of stress these days. You need to take stock a bit, find something you love.'

I smiled as I took another mouthful of mash and groaned in delight. I had to admit that it did taste incredible.

'So were antiques something you and Harry loved then, Lydia?' I asked.

The moment I mentioned antiques it was as though a light had been switched on and I had a feeling I had discovered another of Lydia's passions besides this house.

'Yes, I think they were. I had worked in an auction house and loved the antiques we handled from day one. I was always fascinated with the history behind every piece. Harry had learned the trade up in London after his father told him he either had to get a job or go in the Army! He chose the former after hating his time doing National Service and a friend of a friend got him a job shifting boxes for an antique dealer. His love grew from there.'

I chuckled. My own father was American and although he came to the UK to study law at 18, always feared he would be drafted into the US military, so I could understand Harry's reluctance to do anything but join-up.

'And were there any antiques you and Harry specialised in when you had your shop?'

'We used to go all over the world,' Lydia said, a faraway look in her eyes as she recalled happier times. 'I liked early twentieth-century Burmese – or Myanmar you would call it now, wouldn't you? Well, anyway, I always enjoyed collecting Oriental pottery. Harry was more of a furniture and wood man.'

'Remember that Chippendale sofa he bought that was a knock-off.' Luke grinned, his eyes lighting up at the memory.

Lydia shook her head, eyes twinkling with laughter. 'He knew it was a knock-off as well. But he was determined.'

'Why?' I asked. 'Surely as an antiques collector a fake is the last thing you want to buy?'

'Harry thought it had once belonged to Simon of Simon and Garfunkel fame.' Lydia smiled. 'I expect you're too young to remember, but they were huge at one point and Harry and I adored them.'

'You even started that club, do you remember, Mum? What was it called?' Luke gestured excitedly.

Lydia grinned. 'The Simon and Garfunkel Appreciation Society. We had twelve members at one point – all antiques dealers. We used to go all over Europe and have impromptu meetings after we'd spent the day selling our hearts and lungs out at fairs. Our AGM was after the famous Paris fair in September. We'd spend the night at a little restaurant in the eleventh arrondissement armed with Simon and Garfunkel records where the waiters would play them for us all evening long.'

I clapped my hands together in delight. 'How lovely.'

A dreamy look passed across Lydia's face as she strolled down memory lane. 'It was after a Simon and Garfunkel concert I told Harry I was pregnant with Luke.'

Luke raised his eyes. 'Did you? You never told me that before.'

'I'm sure I did.' Lydia frowned. 'Well, anyway, we had gone to see them in 1970 at the Olympia. It was wonderful. And afterwards as we walked out into the cool Parisian night air, I broke it to Harry that he was going to become a father. We summoned all twelve members of the Society afterwards to celebrate and drink pastis well into the night.'

'Mum!' Luke hissed. 'You can't drink when you're pregnant.'

Lydia rolled her eyes. 'It was a different time, Luke. Besides, you're all right, aren't you?'

I could sense Luke was about to say something else so I cut across him before the evening could sour. 'Well, if I had been around then you would have had thirteen members.'

Putting her fork down in surprise, Lydia gazed at me open-mouthed. 'You're too young to know who Simon and Garfunkel are!'

'Not at all! I was brought up on them,' I told her triumphantly. 'My dad always used to make me listen to "The Sound of Silence" when I was a baby apparently.' I rolled my eyes. 'It was his attempt at irony I think, when I was busy screaming my lungs out preventing him and Mum getting some sleep. Anyway, something must have stuck because I loved them growing up and still love them today.'

'I can't believe it.' Lydia gasped.

'Neither can I,' said Luke drily.

'Well, Erin, I still have a stack of records should you ever want to join me and listen to them one day. I usually stick them on when I'm doing the dusting.' Lydia shook her head in wonder.

'Or drinking a glass of wine, which is nearly every night.' Luke laughed gently as he finished his last forkful of mash and cleared the plates.

Lydia swatted him with her tea towel. 'When you get to my age, dear boy, you too will have earned the right to a glass of wine each evening while listening to your favourite band. And speaking of wine, I think it's time you pour Erin and I one.'

Luke did as he was told and poured us each a glass of delicious Malbec. Then, standing with the tea towel folded over his arm, looking for all the world like a sommelier, he addressed us both in a mock posh voice. 'Anything else, ladies?'

Lydia roared with laughter. 'Not tonight, Jeeves. As you were.'

Tugging his forelock, Luke gave a small bow. 'Very good, ma'am. In that case I shall leave you to it and get on with my packing. I want to have a lie-in tomorrow as I won't get a wink of sleep on the flight.'

With that, Luke dashed off upstairs. I took a sip of wine and found myself thinking about my mum and dad. They had been on my mind a lot the last few days. I couldn't help wondering what they would think about Brad, Cara and the fact I had now moved in with Lydia.

Mum and Dad would like Lydia. No nonsense, a sense of humour and direct, she was just their cup of tea. As for Brad, I knew that if they heard about our break-up, they would open the champagne. I wasn't sure what they would say about Cara. She was an unofficial part of the family and so I was pretty sure they would feel horrified and betrayed.

'Penny for them.' Lydia said, interrupting my train of thought.

I smiled. 'Just thinking about my mum and dad.'

'You should invite them over.' Lydia's face lit up at the idea. 'I was never fond of socialising, but I did always used to throw good dinner parties. I would love to meet them, and I'm sure they would want to know a bit more about the old bird you're sharing a house with.'

'That's very kind,' I said. 'But I haven't spoken to my parents in three years. Well, apart from once when I got them to come to a restaurant on false pretences because

I wanted them to hear about my engagement, but other than that never. They cut me out of their lives when I got together with Brad. There, that's my secret out of the way.'

As Lydia stared at me in shock, I mentally kicked myself. I hadn't meant to tell her so soon about how they disapproved of Brad, and of course how right they had been. Still, she had been honest with me, so I took a deep breath and told Lydia everything. I left nothing out, including how Brad was two decades older than me, had been married before, how Brad had bought me a latte when he found me at Phil's after the lecture he had given. We had got chatting and when he asked me if he could take me out for dinner that night I had instantly said yes. As Lydia nodded her head encouragingly, I told her how I had tried, on more than one occasion, to make things right between me, Brad and my parents.

'The funny thing is, that's why Brad said we couldn't get married yet, because of Mum and Dad's disapproval,' I said sadly, once I'd told Lydia the whole sorry story. 'He said that it wouldn't be fair to get married without them there. Now of course, I know he was just using that as an excuse because he was sleeping with my best friend.'

I made a face and Lydia reached over and clasped my hand. The gesture took me by surprise. I hadn't realised just how much I needed to feel some affection. Silently, I looked up at her and felt a warm glow as she gave me a lopsided grin that reached her sparkling blue eyes.

'Don't you think you might like to try and reconcile with your parents now?' she suggested gently. 'I'm sure they would be devastated to know what's happened. As a parent I know only too well how frustrating children can be, but we love them so much, all we want is for them to be happy.'

I sighed. 'I've thought about it. But at the moment I can't face it. I just want to adjust to my new life and settle down for a bit. I don't think I could take it if they rejected me all over again.'

At the thought of my parents turning their back on me once more, my eyes brimmed with tears. Before I could stop myself I found them streaming down my cheeks. Quick as a flash, Lydia was on her feet and had pulled me up into her arms for a hug. Resting my head on her shoulder, I allowed myself to give into tears, feeling the release of all the stress the last few days had brought.

When I was finished, I pulled away, wiped my eyes and gave Lydia a watery smile. 'Sorry.'

'Nothing to be sorry for,' she said kindly. 'You've had what can only be described as a right bugger of a time.'

I laughed at her unexpected turn of phrase. Usually she sounded so posh. She smiled at me again as she returned to her own seat and topped up our wine.

'It's hard in life when you don't have your mum and dad to turn to,' she said thoughtfully. 'As children we take them for granted, and as parents we know that we will love our children far more than they will love us, that's the way it is. My own mother died just after my sister was born, leaving our father to raise us'

'Oh, I'm so sorry,' I gasped as Lydia waved my sympathy away.

'It was a long time ago now, but I used to dream about what it would be like if my mother hadn't died and just run off somewhere. Even though I knew it was pure fantasy I never gave up dreaming about her coming back for me. I think I wanted that happy ending, I wanted to be like all the other children.'

'What does your sister say?' I asked.

Lydia smiled sadly. 'Stella died two years ago. Cancer, it was so cruel.'

'Lydia, how awful,' I said softly.

'It was for the best. She had suffered a long time and when she went she wasn't in pain any more. But I think she reached a place of acceptance over our mother. She always said we had a perfect dad who was worth two parents – that was good enough for Stella.'

I nodded. 'Sounds like she was very sensible, your sister.'

'She was. But Stella taught me that you have to make the most of what you have, even if you don't think it's enough.'

Wise advice, I thought as Lydia got to her feet and smiled at me.

'Which is why you've got to make the most of the relationships you do have, and you still have your parents in your life so it might be worth trying to contact them again,' she suggested. 'Now, can I show you the sofa that may or may not have graced Simon or Garfunkel's bottom?'

I laughed at the skilful way she changed conversation and realised that in that moment there was nothing I wanted more.

Eight

Lydia

The sight of Luke's overfilled black suitcase by the front door hit me squarely in the pit of my stomach. Although I knew it was time for my son to return to his own family, I couldn't bear the idea of us being apart. He had been home for almost a month and looking at him now, hoisting his rucksack – stuffed full of the Cadbury chocolate he adored – onto his shoulders, I felt a sob catch in my throat. The action reminded me of when he was a little boy starting his first day at school. In that moment all I wanted to do was pull him in my arms and never let him go.

I felt as though I had been suddenly cast adrift with everyone leaving me so suddenly. How would I cope without him or Harry by my side? Suddenly the pain inside me felt as raw as it did the day doctors told me Harry had died.

Luke must have sensed I was doing my best not to cry as he looked up then and gave me a smile. 'Come on, Mum. I'll be back soon, and next time I'll be bringing your grandchild to see you.'

'It's the only reason I'm letting you go,' I joked as I opened my arms, and he rushed towards me. I breathed in his familiar musky scent, savouring the smell of him for later when he had gone. Luke had been a tower of strength these last few weeks and I would miss him. However, even though it was hard, I knew it was time for him to go back to his own life.

As we broke away, I became aware of Erin standing awkwardly in the hallway. I turned to her, saw that lovely smile of hers light up her face and immediately felt myself relax. There was something about Erin I found strangely reassuring.

'Please don't worry, Luke,' she said, stepping forward to give him a hug. 'I'll take really good care of your mum.'

'I know you will. I think that's the only reason I feel ready to go back, knowing you're here, Erin,' Luke replied into her shoulder.

I shook my head irritably. I knew they meant well, but last time I checked I was still a grown woman with all her faculties. After all, Erin was my lodger, not my carer.

However, that's not to say I didn't appreciate all the hard work Erin put in after dinner last night. Not only did she stack the dishwasher, but she cleaned the kitchen from top to bottom, even digging out my old slow cooker and promising a delicious beef stew one night for supper.

I had been delighted and had gone to bed feeling better about the decision to let a lodger move in. Not only that, but it had been a revelation to discover she adored Simon and Garfunkel as much as Harry and I had. Watching them now as they broke apart, I felt a wave of maternal instinct wash over me. Erin wasn't much more than a kid herself and she had been treated appallingly by the two people she had trusted most in the world. I could see from the couple of days she had spent with us so far that she was surprisingly capable, but I knew inside her heart must be breaking. I wanted to help her move forwards with her life, as I strived to do the same with my own.

'Right then,' I said brightly. 'Are you sure you don't want me to come to the airport with you? It doesn't seem right waving you off like this at the front door.'

Luke shot me a wry smile as he shook his head. 'Don't be silly, Mum. It's six at night, you wouldn't get home until God knows what time. Besides, where's the sense in you taking a train to Heathrow and wasting all that money?'

He was right. Until I had a light-bulb moment. 'Erin could drive you in the E-Type.'

I turned to Erin and saw she had gone as red as the classic car that was parked on the street outside.

'I can't drive that!' she hissed. 'I'm used to small cars, not a great bit Jag – and especially not in the dark! I'm not even insured, Lydia.'

'Exactly,' Luke agreed. 'Though, Erin, you are insured. I fixed it up last night, but you're right, I don't think your first drive in Dad's pride and joy ought to be a hundred miles down the motorway to the airport in the pitch black. Better to take a drive around town and get used to it first.'

A flush of relief passed across Erin's features and I couldn't help laughing. 'Okay, Luke's right. London is a bit too far, but perhaps you could have a drive another time?'

Erin nodded. 'All right. Maybe I could go to the supermarket or something later in the week? Get the ingredients for that beef stew I promised.'

'Well, it looks to me as though you ladies don't need me any more,' Luke said as he picked up his rucksack and opened the front door. Bending forward to kiss my cheek, he gazed at me with his sparkling blue eyes. 'I'll ring you the moment I land. I love you, Mum.'

'I love you too,' I whispered.

Watching him walk down the street, his suitcase rolling noisily along behind him, I felt the tears I had worked so hard to keep at bay run down my face. I was going to miss my boy so much.

Just then I felt the weight of Erin's hand on my shoulder. She didn't say anything, she just squeezed it, and somehow the feel of her touch gave me strength. I could get through this.

'I'm all right, dear,' I whispered.

'I know,' she whispered back just as her phone rang. Pulling her iPhone out of her pocket, I saw her frown at the number before silencing the ringer.

'Anyone important?' I asked, knowing full well I was being a nosey old bat, but I wanted to think about something other than Luke's departure.

'Just one of the temp agencies I registered with the other day,' she admitted. 'They said they could get me some data entry work, but Rachel has said she'll help me find something. I won't be under your feet all day for long, I promise.'

'There's no rush,' I said firmly. 'Take a few days to adjust, you've had a shock. You've moved house, broken off your engagement and discovered your best friend isn't who you thought she was. You need to take some time – you've been through a lot.'

'Thank you, Lydia.' Erin smiled gratefully. 'But I need to keep busy. I'm not very good if I'm not doing something. My mind starts going to places where I really don't want it to go.'

I said nothing, I knew only too well how that felt. Since Harry's death, I had been kept fairly busy going through all his papers and things. With Luke's help, we had managed to get a lot of it sorted out. We had worked out a repayment plan with the tax office and Luke had streamlined my finances as well, whatever that meant. Yet there was still so much to do. I was well aware that as part of Luke's careful financial planning for my future, I had to go through the attic and sell some of the goods that had never made it to the online business, but I hadn't been up there for years. It had always been Harry's job to sort out the attic, but after seeing the state of his study, I had a horrible feeling about what I might find up there.

Luke had suggested I sell the goods online for a quick profit, but I had refused. I didn't know anything about online selling but I did know an awful lot about antique fairs. It was how Harry and I had supplemented the business and a little part of me was excited at going back to my roots.

I glanced at Erin. I wondered if I could persuade her to help me sort out enough stuff for a fair soon. I knew the rent was reduced but I didn't want to overwhelm the poor girl when she had just moved in.

'If you want to keep busy, would you mind helping me sort through the attic? I thought I'd take what's suitable to a nearby antiques fair and set up a stall,' I said, deciding to chance my arm.

Erin's face lit up. 'I'd love to. Me and Mum always used to do car boots when I was little and I loved haggling with the customers.'

'It sounds like you're a natural for the antiques business,' I chuckled. 'How does now suit?'

'I can't think of anything I'd rather do.'

Standing in the attic, my heart beating wildly, I was sure I was on the verge of a panic attack at the sight of so much junk.

I hadn't seen a lot of this stuff for years. In fact, I had thought we had sold most of it through the online business years ago. Now, as it stared me in the face, I felt a surge of anger – it was yet another reminder of Harry's lies.

Suddenly, I became aware of Erin standing next to me, whipping her head around like a spinning top as she took in the scene before us. Looking at the chaos I felt a pang of guilt at asking her to help. I knew it would be bad, but never this bad. In fact, I'd brought a bottle of wine and two glasses up with me, thinking we could listen to Simon and Garfunkel on the little stereo we kept up here and get to know each other a little better while we worked.

Despair coursed through me as I picked my way through picture frames, carved wooden walking sticks, marble chess pieces, Tiffany lamps and even a couple of teak sideboards.

'I'm sorry, Erin,' I groaned. 'I don't expect you to help me clear all this lot. I'll call in some home removal people, they can just take the lot away.'

'Lydia, no!' Erin exclaimed as she rushed towards me. 'Owwww!'

'Sorry,' I grimaced as I watched her hop around in bare feet, clearly in pain.

'What is that?' she asked.

'Lego, I think.'

She looked at me in disbelief. 'You have antique Lego?'

'Don't be silly. It's Luke's!' I giggled. 'Listen, I'll open the wine, you find the stereo and we'll make a start.'

Twenty minutes later and we had done just that. We agreed to start systematically, beginning at one corner and working our way across the room to the other side. The fact the Sancerre I had brought was chilled to perfection helped too, and as the alcohol took effect I relaxed and began enjoying myself. Not only was I getting to revisit memory lane, but it was nice spending time with Erin. I had to confess that since she moved in, even though I liked her enormously, I had experienced brief pangs of doubt that our situation would work.

After all, not only were we generations apart, but worlds apart too. We might both have a shared love of Simon and Garfunkel but I wasn't sure that a relationship could be based solely on that. Erin liked trashy dating shows and fast food. I liked early suppers and good detective dramas. But I began to realise that although Erin might be a lot younger than me, there was a possibility this might work out. There was something about Erin I admired. She wasn't afraid of hard work, she had a no-nonsense attitude and most of all I thought her incredibly brave. The issue with her parents was dreadful, but I could see it from both sides; clearly, this was a situation that had got badly out of hand. Her parents obviously adored their daughter and had perhaps hoped that by refusing to have anything to do with her while she was with Brad, they might shock her into ending the relationship. It was a gamble that had backfired massively, but I had thought of little else since Luke had left and wondered if there was any way I could help reconcile them.

'So what was your first date with Harry like?' she asked, interrupting my thoughts.

I smiled, delighted at the chance to talk about older and happier times. 'He took me to a dance hall in Bath in 1961. I had said no at first because I was still in love with my old boyfriend, Jack, but there was something about Harry that drew me to him.'

Erin cocked her head to one side. 'What happened to Jack?'

I paused, it still hurt after all these years to talk about Jack. 'He went into the Army and we had promised to wait for each other. But he was killed shortly after he was posted overseas.'

'Oh, Lydia, I'm sorry,' Erin said sympathetically, as she reached for the bottle of Sancerre and topped up my glass.

I took a sip and gave Erin a watery smile. Even after all these years it hurt when I thought about Jack Harrison, the boy I thought I would grow old with. 'In 1957 I was living in London with my father and sister. Dad had got a job there when I was ten so we moved to Islington and it was there I met Jack when I was only sixteen and he was seventeen. We were neighbours.'

'Aww, childhood sweethearts.' Erin grinned.

'Something like that,' I replied, returning her grin. 'We were together for a year before Jack turned eighteen and of course back then boys had to do their National Service. When Jack was conscripted, we promised to wait for each other.'

'So, what happened?' Erin urged.

'Well, Jack did his basic training in Leicester, which lasted six weeks then he was posted up to Sunderland for a while. His mother, Anna, and I were relieved he wasn't sent abroad as we knew that after the war a lot of people had been sent to Malaysia and Kenya to protect British interests, which seemed dreadfully far away. But then towards the end of 1959, Jack had been away over a year and he wrote to us to say he was being sent to Palestine.'

Erin raised an eyebrow. 'Was it as dangerous there then as it is now?'

I nodded. 'Worse, possibly. Jack was in the Signals and his job was to repair telephone cables when they were sabotaged. All very well, but the place was full of snipers, bumping off the British army – certain people didn't want the phone lines repaired you see.'

'It sounds terrifying.'

'It was for all of us,' I said quietly. 'Jack had been gone a month when Anna received a telegram from the Army explaining that Jack had been killed by the snipers we were all so worried about.'

'Then what happened?'

'It was just before Christmas and I fell apart. I couldn't stand the idea of a life without Jack. As far as I was concerned, I no longer had a life. Anna encouraged me to move on, told me that Jack would hate me to stop living because of him, but I couldn't, I loved him.'

I paused and took a sip of my wine. I hadn't thought about this part of my life for a long time, it had been too painful, but sharing it with Erin, felt natural somehow.

'Lydia, my gosh, you must have been devastated,' Erin whispered, her eyes brimming with tears.

'I was. But I learned very quickly that just because you want life to stop for a bit, life won't stop for you. The following year, my father's firm transferred him to Bristol, so we all moved back this way. I was broken-hearted. I felt that by moving away, I was leaving Jack behind. All I could do was give Anna our new address, and beg her to keep in touch. It felt as though she was my last link to Jack, you see, and I didn't want to let go.'

'But you never heard from her again?' Erin quizzed gently.

I shook my head. When I thought of how Jack had been killed, the pain felt as raw now as it did the day I discovered he had died.

'I never forgot about Jack, but I tried to follow Anna's advice and get on with life. I knew Jack wouldn't want me to mope around, he was always full of fun, mischief and honour. He was the boy that would think nothing of diving into the Thames to rescue a couple of kids who weren't strong swimmers one minute, then have a few too many in the pub afterwards to toast their health. He always told me to make the most of every minute of life, that the war had proven we never knew how long we had.'

'He sounds as though he was a lovely lad,' Erin replied gently.

'Jack really was, he was more than lovely,' I said. 'Everyone adored him, that was half the reason it was so hard to move on.'

'So, what made you finally agree to date Harry?'

It was a question I had often asked myself. Lord knew that when I left London I could never picture myself with anyone other than Jack.

'Harry had a quality I couldn't put my finger on. I felt drawn to it,' I said eventually. 'He was quieter than Jack, but he was kind, decent and principled. I know that probably doesn't sound terribly exciting to you young people, but something told me that Harry was my future and I didn't want to let him go when I finally gave in and went to the dance with him.'

'Did you tell him about Jack?' Erin asked.

I nodded. 'Yes, I think it was after we had been out a few times. It was important to me that we were honest with each other, and Harry understood immediately. He said that there was no rush, and that I must feel as though I had a foot in the past and the present, and that was it exactly. It was seeing how he understood me that made me realise he was the one.'

'And how long was it before you and Harry got married?' Erin asked.

I put down the box of records I had been sorting through and smiled at the memory. 'Two years later to the very day that we met, January 1963. We married in Cotham Church and had a do back at my father's old place nearby. It was lovely, my sister made the cake.'

'It sounds idyllic,' Erin smiled. 'Where was your honeymoon?'

'Italy,' I smiled. 'We went to the Cinque Terre in the summer, which was considered very exotic back then. I had some savings from my secretarial work, and Harry had earned some good money in London.'

Erin seemed impressed.

'Of course, that was all a long time ago now,' I sighed. 'We had our whole lives ahead of us and thought anything was possible.'

'But anything is still possible,' Erin exclaimed. 'What's stopping you? What have you always really wanted to do?'

I chuckled. That was the thing about young people – they were always so good at taking risks. They never thought about how difficult it became when you had so much more to lose. At my age it was harder to get about with all those aches and pains, and of course money played a large part. Unlike youngsters, I wouldn't get another chance to earn any money again. If I made a mistake there was nobody to bail me out – it paid to be cautious.

I tried to think, what was it I really wanted from life now? Looking around at the belongings strewn across the attic, realised that actually, after we bought this house, I had stopped being reckless and had instead become much more cautious. Just where had it got me? My husband had still lied to me and I was here now at the age of seventy-eight without two pennies to rub together, and forced to start living on my wits again. Hadn't I said just a few days ago that I wanted to find that girl again that used to be fearless? Perhaps it was time to start throwing caution to the wind.

Nine

Erin

The next morning, I woke up with a splitting headache. As I eased myself upright, I reached for the glass of water on my bedside table and gulped gratefully at the cool liquid. I hadn't been drinking much in the few days since Brad and I split up as I hadn't wanted to feel maudlin. I also hadn't wanted to risk drunk-dialling him, and calling him and Cara all the names under the sun.

Thankfully, I hadn't done that. In fact, as I pulled on the fluffy robe Rachel and Lily had bought me for Christmas, I realised I hadn't thought about Brad or Cara at all last night. I had been so focused on Lydia's stories about her love life, I had thought about nothing else – clearly Lydia was proving a very positive distraction.

'Morning!' Lydia said, beaming at me with a very welcome pot of coffee in her hand as I walked into the kitchen.

'You're very cheerful.' I smiled back at her as I pulled out a chair and sat down at the table. The April sunshine was out in full force this morning and I relaxed into the chair enjoying the feel of the warmth on my skin.

'I know.' Lydia set down a plate of toast, her eyes shining with delight. 'I'm in a good mood this morning. We got a lot done last night.'

I sipped my coffee. 'We definitely made some headway, but there's so much to go through. A lot more than I expected.'

'I know.' Lydia sighed. 'Harry was always full of surprises.'

'Do you still want to try a fair this weekend? Have we got enough stuff?' I asked, taking another sip of much needed coffee.

Lydia took a bite of her toast. 'I think if we could sort out a bit more this week we should have enough to get started.'

'Okay.' I yawned, stretching my arms above my head to try and wake myself up. 'I said I'd go over to Rachel's tonight, so maybe tomorrow?'

Lydia looked disappointed. 'Oh, I was hoping we could carry on tonight.'

'Sorry.' I smiled at her affectionately. 'I'm free tomorrow night though.'

'I suppose,' she said, her tone flat.

A mixture of guilt and frustration gnawed away at me. I wanted to get on with rebuilding my life, but then, a new part of my life was Lydia. My reduced rent meant I had to help her get back on her feet and drive her about.

'Why don't you invite Rachel over here?' Lydia asked suddenly. 'I could cook supper.'

I looked at her doubtfully. 'I don't think Rachel can get here for five and I don't think she's going to want to clear out the attic either.'

Lydia rolled her eyes. 'Of course she doesn't. But she's a good friend of yours and I would like to get to know her. As for eating at five, how about we eat at seven instead? What do you think?'

I hesitated. I had been looking forward to a night out with Rachel but instinct was telling me not to leave Lydia alone tonight.

'Let me text her,' I said, pulling my mobile out of my dressing gown pocket. Almost immediately after I pressed send, Rachel texted back with a thumb's up emoji.

'What on earth's that mean?' Lydia asked as I showed her the screen.

'It means she thinks it's a good idea.' I smiled, texting Rachel back and telling her when to arrive.

'Well, then why doesn't she just say that?' Lydia frowned. 'Why is she using pictures instead of words.'

'They're not pictures, they're emojis.'

'Emo-what?' Lydia asked, getting to her feet. 'No forget it, I won't understand and to be quite honest I don't want to,' she said, peering in the fridge. 'Hmmm, does Rachel like roast chicken? I've all the ingredients here for a roast.'

'That sounds perfect.' I got to my feet. 'I'll give you a hand a bit later on. I thought that I would look at hiring a van for the weekend if you think we've got enough stuff.'

Lydia pulled her head out of the fridge and looked at me in alarm. 'Will we need a van?'

'We won't fit a sideboard in the E-Type,' I said.

'But can you drive a van?' Lydia looked concerned. 'They're rather large.'

I rolled my eyes. 'Yes, Lydia I can drive a van! I can do anything, and so can you!'

With that, I took a final sip of my coffee and ran back upstairs. Even though Lydia had been in a grump, I felt a bit worried about her. With Luke gone, the responsibility to look out for Lydia now fell on my shoulders and I wasn't sure I was capable – after all, I hardly knew the woman. All right, I knew a little about what she was going through but my experiences were very different. The love of my life hadn't died suddenly, he had just cheated on me. It was sweet of Lydia to say I had every right to grieve, but I didn't feel as though I had the right to be as sad as Lydia – angry perhaps, but not grief-stricken.

I reached for my laptop and opened up a webpage, intending to start looking at van hire companies. Instead I found myself on Facebook hoping that one of Rachel's daily pictures of Matilda doing something cute would ease my hangover. Although Rachel and Lily were young to become parents, they were adamant that a baby was what they wanted. Lily hadn't been able to have children but Rachel had, and determined to make sure they had a baby that was the perfect mix of them both, they had asked Lily's brother Jake to step in and become a sperm donor which he had happily agreed to do.

Since Rachel's pregnancy, she and Lily frequently posted updates about Matilda and I loved seeing them.

Only, as I opened up Facebook, the first thing I saw wasn't a sweet picture of my friend's baby girl but an image of Cara and Brad. She was draped all over him at a party, while holding the camera in one hand. He was grinning and kissing her neck. The photo was simply captioned 'true love', and even though it had only been posted twenty minutes ago by Cara it had already got fifteen likes.

I felt sick. Of course I was angry with Brad for what he had done, but Cara's betrayal hurt far more. This new post might not have been deliberate but it was thoughtless and selfish and it was then it hit me – that was what Cara had always been. Her parents might not have offered her much love but that didn't give her the licence she thought it did to behave as she liked. In the past I had always forgiven her everything, simply because I felt sorry for her that her childhood had been fraught with so much pain, but not any more. People couldn't just go around hurting whomever they liked. With a start I remembered how Cara had been dumped by a guy in sixth form who had slept with someone else behind her back. She had been in so much pain, that when she went out with a guy who already had a girlfriend, she said she couldn't care less – the girlfriend wasn't her problem. I had been shocked at her cavalier attitude, but forgiven her, because well, I always did. But not any more. This time I was all out of forgiveness.

Just then there was a knock at the door and before I had chance to shout, 'come in', Lydia poked her head around the door.

'I've been thinking,' she began hesitantly.

'Sounds ominous,' I said. 'And please come in, you look like a weird floating head.'

'Sorry,' Lydia said walking into the room. 'I was just thinking if you're not doing anything now, we could always have another look in the attic.'

'Now!' My head was still banging and I felt so fired up with fury and upset I wasn't sure I was capable of making polite conversation with anyone. But when I turned to look at Lydia, I couldn't miss the flicker of excitement in her eyes. This was something she needed.

'Let me throw on some jeans, and I'll be right with you.'

'Thank you.' Lydia smiled gratefully. 'I've got some chocolates, I'll make all your hard work worth your while.'

I smiled politely, unable to say that actually it wasn't chocolate I needed, it was a machete, to bury in my ex best friend's head. Instead, I got to my feet, pulled on some clothes and slammed the lid of my laptop shut. It was time to forget all about Cara.

Ten

Lydia

It wasn't that we needed more items for the antiques fair this weekend. With my practised eye I could easily pull out a handful of things from the attic that would fly from our stall and besides, my reputation and knowledge alone would see seasoned buyers come flocking. No, it was more that the state of the attic troubled me. The amount of paraphernalia up there was shocking, especially as most of it was stuff I thought had been sold or thrown out a long time ago. When I woke up this morning, I wanted to get back up there and sort through as much as possible. It felt like unfinished business, a loose end that I hadn't known needed resolving.

And now I did, it weighed heavily on my mind. I needed to sift, pack, sell and sort in order to move on. I knew it was silly, and I knew it was a lot to ask Erin to help me again so soon but I hadn't been able to think about anything else. There was only one cure to ease my madness and it was keeping busy.

As I busied myself making a pot of tea for us to take up to the attic while we worked, I thought back over the events of the night before. What was it we had been talking about? I knew Jack had come up, and Harry too, but hadn't Erin asked me something important about my life? I had a feeling that she had but I couldn't remember what.

I put down the pot and felt a creeping sense of unease. I had been having trouble remembering things lately. But surely, I would have remembered saying something as daft as that? I rubbed my hands over my face as if trying to stir some memory. The trouble was everything felt so fuzzy these days – doctors said it was just the grief of losing Harry but it was so frustrating. Things I always used to remember were becoming more difficult. Of course, there were the usual things like going into rooms and forgetting what on earth I had gone in there for, but there was other stuff too. I could blindly forget entire conversations with people, yet still remember what my Secondary Modern teacher wore the first day I started school.

'Lydia, are you ready?'

Erin's voice jolted me swiftly back to the present and I looked up to see her standing in the kitchen doorway with a notepad and pencil stuffed under her arm as she clutched several crates.

'What are all those for?' I asked.

'I thought it would make it easier to organise if we could label stuff properly, then stack it in crates that are clearly marked,' she explained. 'The notepad will help us make a list of inventory.'

'My goodness,' I marvelled. 'You're a wonder.'

She smiled happily at the compliment and I felt my troubles ease. 'Once a PA, always a PA.'

'Well, Brad's loss is my gain,' I beamed, placing the teapot and cups onto a tray. 'Come on then, sooner we start the sooner we can open the champagne I've got tucked away for Rachel's arrival later.'

The attic looked even worse in the cold light of day than I remembered. Although we had clearly made a good start last night, there was also evidence of the fun we had shared as we got to know one another better. What looked like two empty bottles of wine stood on one of the teak sideboards while an unopened third bottle rested on the floor. Meanwhile two Kettle Chips crisp packets had been stuffed into an antique umbrella stand, next to an array of Simon and Garfunkel records that I definitely remembered singing along to.

'Looks like we had quite a party last night,' Erin chuckled.

I set the tray down and poured us each a cup. 'Judging by the mess I think we would have given the Simon and Garfunkel Appreciation Society a run for its money in its heyday, but this morning we've got to get down to business.'

'Yes, boss.' Erin gave me a mock salute and I laughed. Even though I didn't understand her emo-whatsits, Erin was a tonic. She made me feel revved up and enthusiastic about the new life ahead of me, helping me believe anything was possible.

'So I thought that rather than have a tidy-up we could sort through the things we want to sell first,' Erin suggested. 'We want to start strong if we're going to sell everything here. That way people will know our name and keep coming back.'

I smiled at her enthusiasm. 'You've got a good head for business, did anyone ever tell you that?'

She shoved a pencil behind her ear and shrugged. 'It's common sense. Besides, have you seen *The Apprentice*? An episode of that would tell you exactly what not to do in business.'

I said nothing. I had no idea what *The Apprentice* was. That was the downside of living with someone who was a couple of generations younger. Sometimes it felt as though they were speaking an entirely different language.

'We're also going to need a name for the business,' she called over a pile of boxes she was beginning to sort through. 'Any thoughts? What did you and Harry call your business?'

'H and L Antiques,' I replied. 'Not exactly ground-breaking but it worked for us.'

Erin pulled out the pencil from behind her ear and tapped it against her teeth. 'Not ground-breaking no, but it obviously served a purpose. Do you want to call the stall that now?'

I shook my head. 'No. I want a fresh start. H and L feels like we're going back to the past and this is about the future. What about L and E Antiques? You are helping me with this after all.'

'No!' Erin laughed. 'I mean, that's sweet, but I think we need something a bit more memorable.'

We both fell silent then in deep concentration. My eyes fell to the stack of records strewn across the floor and I had a surge of inspiration.

'The Simon and Garfunkel Antiques Brigade!'

Erin thought for a moment. 'I like it,' she said slowly. 'It doesn't do what it says on the tin, but it's a name people will remember, and that's the most important thing in business.'

I couldn't help myself and punched the air with delight. 'Yes!'

'What was that?' Erin laughed.

I felt my cheeks flame with colour. 'Not sure. I think I saw it on the television recently and it felt like a natural response.'

'It's a brilliant response! We can ask Rachel later to mock up some signs for us, she's brilliantly creative.'

'Wonderful.' I smiled, feeling pleased at the progress we were making so quickly. With Erin's boundless enthusiasm and organisational skills, I had a feeling it wouldn't take us long at all to get this attic into some sort of order and our new business venture on the road. I could already see how we could theme our stalls each weekend. Rather than just piling up stuff and hoping for the best, which is what I knew a lot of dealers did, we could run an Asian-inspired stall and then another week we could do a Renaissance event. One week we could specialise in pictures and another week we could concentrate on woodwork, I thought, silently cursing Harry's weakness for carved walking sticks.

'What do you want to do with personal things?' Erin asked, breaking my train of thought.

'Like Luke's Lego?' I asked. 'Much as it pains me to suggest it, I think we'd better toss it. I had thought it would be nice to pass on to my grandchild, but I'm not wasting valuable luggage space shipping Lego to New York! Not when I know there's a perfectly wonderful FAO Schwarz just around the corner from Luke's home.'

'No, not Lego. Personal things like this,' Erin replied, waving an envelope in her hand.

I looked up from the walking sticks I had been sorting through and peered at the red, white and blue striped envelope in Erin's hand. Squinting, I looked a little more closely and saw it appeared to be an opened white envelope.

'Whose is that?' I asked puzzled.

'It's addressed to you,' Erin said, smiling. 'Oooh, is it a love letter from Harry?'

I frowned. The only letter Harry had ever left me was a note asking me to buy bread. This letter didn't look familiar to me at all.

'Can I see?' I asked holding out my hand.

As Erin passed it to me, I felt as though I might faint. The handwriting was as familiar to me as my own. Even though I hadn't seen it in more than fifty years, it took me right back to my teens, when I had lived for notes like this landing on the doormat.

I took in the address and saw it was addressed to me at the grotty old flat Harry and I had lived in before we moved to the Circus.

'Who's it from?' Erin urged again.

I sank back against the teak sideboard and fanned my face with the envelope. 'It's from Jack – my first boyfriend.'

'Your first love!' Erin gasped. 'You must want to hang onto that.'

'I think I'd better. Especially as this is the first time I've ever seen it.'

Eleven

Erin

Shock. That was the only word to describe the look on Lydia's face when she saw the letter. Complete and utter shock. In fact, she looked like she'd seen a ghost as she stood there staring at the handwriting, hardly moving.

I thought quickly. Lydia needed a tonic, something to snap her out of it. I didn't want to slap her, that seemed far too disrespectful and frankly plain rude. My eyes strayed to the wine bottles that stood on the sideboard and I saw that, though I had thought them to be empty, one was still about a third full. I quickly made a grab for it, pouring us both a measure into last night's dirty glass – any port in a storm and all that.

'Here!' I said, thrusting a glass into her trembling hands. 'It'll make you feel better.'

Lydia needed no encouragement and drank it down in one gulp, before holding her glass aloft for a refill.

'Make that one last,' I warned. 'Neither one of us wants to be leathered before lunchtime.'

'Not usually no,' she replied.

'So,' I tried again, my tone gentler now. 'Are you sure you've never seen this letter before?' I said, thinking back to how she'd forgotten about her plans to start running. 'Maybe you read it before and just forgot?'

'I didn't forget,' she said stiffly. 'This letter was opened by someone else. I've never seen it before.'

'It wasn't sent before Jack died?' I asked, confused by the whole situation.

'No,' Lydia said with a quick shake of her head, as she looked at the envelope again. 'This is postmarked December 1962. Jack was killed three years earlier. In December 1962 I was engaged to Harry and about to get married the following month.'

'Did you never hear from Anna at all?' I said, clutching at straws. 'Did she not mention that Jack was alive?'

Lydia gave me a taut smile. 'I think I would have remembered if Anna, or anyone else come to that, had told me Jack was still alive.'

'So you never heard from Anna again when you left London?'

'No, not a word.' Lydia sighed. 'Of course I thought about writing to her many times. But Dad always said that he knew what it was like when you were trying to move on with your life after something painful. He said that he was sure she wished me well, but that for both of us to heal after Jack's death I was better off leaving her be. So, I did as he suggested, but when Harry and I got engaged, I wanted to let her know. I just couldn't stand the idea of starting a new life without tying up all the loose ends. I wrote to Anna and told her I had met a lovely man named Harry and we were getting married. I said that I would always love Jack and I would never forget him. I also told her that I didn't want to upset her, but that in order to move forwards, I had to look to my past and that I hoped she understood.'

'Makes sense,' I said, nodding.

'In my letter, I gave her the address of Harry's flat in Bath and explained it would be best to reach me there if she ever wanted to, as that would be where I would live when we got married. Besides, by then I was there more often than I was at my own house in Bristol,' Lydia continued. 'I said, that if she ever wanted to talk to me or write then I would always love to hear from her, whether it was now or in the future.'

'What did she say?' I asked, as desperate for answers as Lydia now was.

'That's the thing. I never heard from her again, so I assumed that either it was too painful for her to write to me, or that she thought I had forgotten her son and was too furious to put pen to paper.'

'Maybe your letter or her reply to you got lost in the post?' I mused.

'Perhaps.' Lydia shrugged. 'But the wedding was drawing nearer and I suppose a part of me couldn't stand the heartache of worrying over whether Anna hated me for getting married. I realise that must sound incredibly selfish now.'

'Not at all,' I insisted.

'But Jack was alive and I never knew,' Lydia said desperately. 'Because here's the proof, this letter shows Jack was very much still with us in 1962 after all. I gave up too easily.'

'Lydia, why don't you read this letter and see what it says?' I suggested.

'I'm scared,' she replied in a small voice. 'What if he resents me for getting married?'

'There's only one way to find out,' I said gently, giving her shoulder a comforting squeeze. 'And after almost sixty years, I think it's time to face the truth about whatever happened.'

Wordlessly, Lydia tore into the envelope's contents. I saw tears pool in her eyes as she began to read aloud.

10 December 1962

My darling,

It was so good to get your letter to Mother. I hope you don't mind but I opened it instead as Mother passed away three years ago and I am now living in her home. I heard from neighbours you had moved away to Bristol, but nobody knew your address and with no way to contact you all I could do was hope, Lyddie, that one day you would find me. I tore the house apart looking for a forwarding address, then I found your last letter to Mother so I am writing to you here, praying this will reach you.

I imagine you must be surprised to hear from me after all this time, so please let me explain what happened. The truth is, as I'm sure you can tell from reading this letter, that I wasn't killed. I was shot during my time in Palestine, and taken to hospital where I spent six months convalescing. The Army assured me they had written to my family and explained what had happened, but in fact there had been a horrible mix-up. A James Harrison from another platoon was also posted out to Palestine at the same time, and it was he who was killed, not me. When the mistake was discovered, I wrote to you both to tell you I was safe and well, but you had already moved and Mother had died.

When I discovered what had happened to you both in my absence, I was beside myself and tried to track you down. I couldn't believe my mother had gone to her grave thinking I was dead and you were gone. I was heartbroken, Lyddie. No man should go through so much loss at the same time. When I was then posted to the Signals in Cyprus, it was thoughts of you that kept me going. I told myself that you would write to Mother, thinking she was still alive at some point, and then somehow, we would find a way to be together, but as time wore on, I gave up hope. When I left the Army in 1961 and returned home, I tried to look for you again, but it was like searching for a needle in a haystack. All I could do was hope and pray that you were safe and well somewhere. Reading your letter to Mother, I am so happy to see that you are. I have only ever wanted you to be happy, you know that, don't you? A brush with death teaches you things, Lyddie, and I have come to realise that your life and your happiness are more precious to me than my own. Truly, my love, I would die for you if it meant your happiness was secured. You are the only woman in my life I have loved and ever will love, but I understand why you fell in love with someone else. However, I have to ask you now, before it's too late, won't you please give us another chance?

I am sorry if this sounds selfish, to do this to you now with your wedding just weeks away, but after so long wondering where you were Lyddie, forgive me for taking this chance now. I can give you a life Lyds, the life you deserve. We could be so happy together, if you would only give us another chance. The thought of never wrapping my arms around you again, hearing your beautiful laugh, or simply holding your hand, our fingers entwined, is tearing me in two. I cannot imagine a life without you darling Lyds, you're my world, always have been and always will be. I won't rest if I don't tell you the truth and beg you for another chance.

But Lydia, I am not the man to keep you from true happiness. If your heart now belongs with another then I will never stop you, that is not who I am, and I do not think that would be the man you would want to be with.

Just know this, my darling, I cannot make you love me, but you cannot stop me from loving you. You, my precious Lydia, will have a place forever in my heart. I will hope more than ever to hear from you now, but if you don't write back I shall know that is your answer and I shan't trouble you again. Just know, my love, that I shall never forget you.

I worship you, always and forever,

Your Jack

When Lydia finished reading the letter we both had tears streaming down our cheeks. The letter was so emotional, so raw, it had left me feeling heartbroken, so I couldn't begin to imagine how Lydia must be feeling.

'Are you all right?' I whispered.

Lydia nodded as she smiled through her tears. 'All this time lost thinking Jack was dead and yet he was right here in England, safe and well!'

'I can't believe it, Lydia,' I said, smiling through my own tears of joy, so swept up was I in her story. 'And to think, his letter was above your head for decades.'

As I laid out this bald statement of facts, the happiness on Lydia's face disappeared, giving way to a fresh round of tears.

'Oh, Erin, you're right. If only I had explored this attic a bit more often, I might have found this letter sooner. I could have known Jack was still alive instead of imagining his death, worrying if he had suffered. Now, I don't know what to think.' She wept, pulling out a hankie from the sleeve of her cardigan and dabbing at her eyes.

'It's okay,' I soothed. 'You don't have to think anything.'

'But none of it makes sense. Why have I never seen this before? Did Harry keep it from me?'

'Not necessarily...' I said, carefully, determined not to make Lydia feel even worse. 'Maybe someone else opened it, you said you lived in a flat...'

Lydia reached for her wine glass. 'That's true. There was another flat in the building. Perhaps they took it and opened it by mistake, then gave it to Harry and he forgot to give it to me...'

'Anything is possible.' I said, not wanting to admit the idea sounded unlikely.

'But maybe it was Harry,' she said, sadly. 'That's the most logical explanation, isn't it, Erin? That my husband took my letter and hid it from me?'

'I'm sure it wasn't like that,' I said, desperate to console her. 'And even if it was, he only did it out of love for you. He was probably scared you'd run off with Jack or something. I mean, you did say you thought Jack might have been the love of your life.'

'But it should have been my choice to make,' she said tearfully. 'I should have been given all the information to make a decision, and I wasn't. I adored Harry, Erin. He was so different to Jack, but he was never cruel and yet, hiding this letter from me, whether he opened it or not, seems like an incredibly callous thing to have done.'

Neither of us said anything as we pondered the significance of Lydia's outburst. I couldn't imagine what she must be going through, and catching the sadness in her eyes was nothing short of heart-breaking.

'I'm sure that whatever he did, if in fact he did anything, would have been because he loved you,' I said, eager to offer some crumb of comfort.

'I know,' Lydia began. 'Harry and I worshipped each other, but it doesn't change the fact Jack must have gone through life thinking I didn't care, that I didn't love him any more.'

'You don't know that, Lydia,' I said desperately. 'It was all such a long time ago.'

'But what if he hated me?' she said stubbornly.

'I'm sure he didn't. Anyway, he's probably still alive, with a family of his own now and forgotten about all this,' I said, knowing that was unlikely to be true.

'I just wish I could talk to Jack, and explain what happened,' Lydia continued as if I hadn't spoken. 'I feel as though I need to make this right somehow.'

'Well, then, why don't you?' I suggested.

'Whatever do you mean?' Lydia frowned as she finished off her wine.

'I mean that although you can't talk to Harry, you could talk to Jack. Why don't we find out if he's still alive? If he is, you can tell him the truth,' I said.

Lydia's hands flew to her mouth. 'I couldn't do that!'

'Why not?' I smiled. 'You said yourself in your letter to Anna all those years ago that you couldn't move forwards with your future until you had sorted out your past. Maybe now is the time to go back to the past and set things in order.'

Twelve

Lydia

Since finding the letter from Jack, I hadn't let the precious piece of paper out of my sight. I had held onto it for the rest of the day, then all the way through our dinner with Rachel and even gone to bed with it that night, clasped in my hand as if it were some sort of talisman. Naturally, I hadn't slept a wink. Instead I had read and reread the letter, committing each word to memory, savouring the image of Jack sitting down to write the note, pouring his heart out onto the paper.

Two days later I still couldn't stop thinking about what Jack must have thought when I didn't reply to him. Not for the first time since my discovery, I felt a rush of guilt as I thought about how I had callously tossed Jack aside when I met Harry, marrying him at the drop of a hat. Sitting at the kitchen table, my robe wrapped around me as I watched the sun rise, I took a sip of tea and thought back to the very first day I had met Harry. It had been a cold wet day in January 1961. I had been on my way home from the library in Bristol, when all of a sudden someone on a bicycle had ridden right through a puddle, splashing my clothes and soaking me through. As I stood in the street shaking my fist at the rotter who clearly had no consideration for anyone but themselves, I felt a warm hand tap me on my shoulder. Turning around in astonishment I saw a young man a good foot taller than me with thick brown hair and twinkling brown eyes offer me a clean handkerchief and his trench coat.

'Oh no, thank you.' I smiled, so touched at the gesture my anger melted away in a heartbeat. 'I couldn't possibly, you'll need those yourself.'

The man had lifted his hat but refused to put down the trench coat or hankie. 'Your need is far greater than mine. Now please, I insist.'

Sensing he wasn't going to take no for an answer I took the items gratefully. 'Can I buy you a cup of tea as a thank you?' I asked, jerking my head toward the café that stood behind us. 'It's the least I can do.'

At the suggestion, the man looked at me and offered me a big toothy grin that lit up his entire face. 'What a lovely idea, but I insist on paying, it wouldn't be gentlemanly otherwise.'

'All right,' I said, returning the smile, 'but only if you let me pay for the next cup.'

The man looked at me in surprise. 'You mean there's going to be a next time?'

'I'm going to have to get this trench coat back to you sometime,' I replied.

There was a pause then as the man smiled again. 'Well, if we're going to see each other again, you'd better know my name. Harry Harper.'

'Lydia Day,' I said quietly.

From then on, a great love affair began. A love affair I hadn't known I wanted or was looking for. Harry had come to my rescue that day, just as he had every day in his life. I ran my fingers across the envelope once more, my thoughts a jumble of my husband and my first love.

I knew there was no point thinking like this, that what was done was done, but it was as though I couldn't switch my mind off. All night I had pictured different versions of my life, some with Jack, some without and some even on my own. The thing that troubled me most was that people had been hurt by whoever's decision it had been to hide the note from me.

Standing up, I walked across the kitchen to make myself another cup of tea. I had given up on sleep a few hours ago and with a new day ahead of me I knew I would need caffeine in one form or another to power me through.

Just then I heard a creak on the floorboards outside the kitchen and saw Erin's head appear around the door. I gave her a weak smile, as I glanced at her pale face. She looked as if she had got about as much sleep as I had and I felt a flash of concern. She had been a tower of strength since finding the letter, and I knew she had her own wounds to lick. It wasn't fair she was missing out on her sleep because of me.

'Tea?' I asked gently, holding a mug aloft.

Nodding, Erin smiled as she scuttled into the kitchen, and sat in the chair I had now come to think of as hers rather than Harry's. I reached for the tea as always and then with a flash of irritation opened the cupboard and helped myself to teabags rather than leaves, for once not caring about the right way of doing things. All my life I had tried to do things properly and look where it had got me. As I poured in the water and watched the bags rise to the surface, I felt something inside me stir. It felt surprisingly satisfying to do something different.

'What are you doing up so early?' I asked, setting the steaming mug down in front of Erin.

Erin smiled ruefully. 'Much the same as you, I imagine. I couldn't stop thinking about your mystery letter. I've been online most of the night trying to find him.'

I looked at her warily over the top of my cup, aware that my pulse was racing. 'And?' I asked as casually as I could.

Erin's face fell. 'Sorry Lydia but there are about a million Jack Harrisons. I've tried to narrow it down but in London alone I managed to find the best part of a thousand.'

My own jaw dropped as I glanced at Erin aghast. 'How on earth are we going to find him out of that lot?'

'Well, it would really help if you could tell me a bit more about him,' Erin said, pushing her laptop towards me. 'Do you remember if he had any brothers and sisters? Any idea of what he might be doing now?'

I suddenly felt overwhelmed at Erin's questions. I hadn't seen Jack for over fifty years, how on earth should I know where he was now? 'Could we write to his mum's old address? Someone there might know something?' I asked, feeling a flash of inspiration.

Erin raised an eyebrow. 'We can certainly try but I think we should probably explore other options too.'

'Like?' I sighed.

'Like any family members. Brothers are good as they don't change their name like women.'

I made a face. 'Jack only had a sister, Eileen. She was ten years older than him so it's possible she may not be alive.'

'Okay, anything else. You said he worked in the Signals, could he have worked in communications when he got back?'

'It's possible.' I shrugged, feeling hopeless. 'I thought this internet made life easier. Isn't everyone on this Facespace now?'

'Facebook,' Erin laughed, pushing a lock of hair behind her ear. 'And not everyone is, I mean you're not, are you?'

I shuddered at the thought. Everyone in the world knowing my personal business, it wasn't natural. I took a sip of tea as I glanced over Erin's shoulder and looked at the Facebook page she had up. I had to admit it looked fascinating. She was right of course, there were about a million Jack Harrisons but they all had pictures, information and friends.

'Look at that one!' I exclaimed. 'He's got nearly 500 friends! Perhaps he knows where Jack is.'

Erin looked at me in amazement. 'It doesn't matter how many friends he's got, he would still need to be the right man.'

'Oh,' I said, feeling crestfallen.

'But I bet if your Jack was on Facebook he would have a lot of friends,' she said in a kindly tone. 'I mean, given everything you've told me, he sounds as though everyone would want to be friends with him.'

I shot her a genuine smile. 'You're right. Jack was very popular.' I took another sip of tea, still enjoying the feeling of using bags for once and thought for a moment. 'Does this Facespace mean I could make lots of friends too?'

Erin looked at me in surprise. 'Yes, of course. But would you want to be on Facebook?'

'I don't know,' I said carefully. 'It might be nice to connect with Hannah and Luke a bit more once the baby comes. I imagine lots of people talk to each other, don't they, over photos and things?'

'That's right,' Erin said eagerly. 'Actually, it could be a good idea. It would certainly be a lovely way for you to keep in touch with them.'

'But would everyone in the world know what I'd been doing?' I asked doubtfully.

Erin shook her head. 'No, you can make your settings private so only the people you want to see your posts will be able to.'

'Okay then.' I smiled, feeling revved up. 'I would like to be on Facespace.'

'Facebook,' Erin said through gritted teeth. 'Well, let's make you a profile then. I'll need your email address and have you got a photo handy?'

I scribbled down my email address then stood up and reached for the photo Harry had taken of me shortly before he died. I had gone to the races with some acquaintances from my art class and Harry insisted on capturing the occasion, telling me I looked as pretty as I had when I was a girl. Something, I noticed with a flush of pride, Erin commented on as well, as she took a photo of my portrait with her phone.

'Beautiful Lydia,' she said, tapping a few buttons.

Swivelling the computer around to face me I could barely believe the image staring back at me. There was my picture, my name and according to the profile I already had a friend. It was nothing short of incredible.

'Who am I friends with?' I asked in astonishment.

'Me,' Erin chuckled. 'But don't worry, I've already asked Phil, Hannah and Luke to friend you too.'

'Really? Phil is on here?' My jaw dropped as I tried to take it all in. 'I had no idea he was so modern.'

'If it makes you feel any better, he wasn't until I set it up for him last year. Now he's always on it talking to family and friends in Madrid, not to mention posting pictures of all the yummy cakes Ginger has made.'

I nodded approvingly. I could see I had a lot to learn. 'So what do I do now?'

'Tell people what you're up to. Post pictures, ask questions. Let people know you're here.' Erin explained, holding the laptop towards me again. 'It could be really good for the antiques business as well. We could post photos of what we've got to sell, tell people where we're going to be selling.'

'What does your profile look like?' I asked, determined now to find out as much as I could.

With a few clicks, Erin brought up her own profile page. I could see she had posted a lovely photo of herself that showed her smiling as she sat down with a glass of wine with the sun beating down somewhere.

'You look gorgeous,' I said admiringly. 'Where was that taken?

'Los Cabos in Mexico,' Erin replied wistfully. 'Brad took it, that was the last holiday we went on.'

I wrapped an arm around her shoulders, able to tell that the memory was too much for her. 'Stupid bloody man. It's his loss. Now, why don't you show me what else you've got on this page so I know what I'm supposed to be doing.'

Quickly, she scrolled down the page and I saw photo after photo flash up, along with sentences and lots of those emo things that Erin had told me about the other day. As my eyes fell on a picture of a couple wrapped around each other, captioned 'true love', I watched Erin freeze.

'I take it that's Brad and Cara, is it?' I asked gently.

Erin gave a brief nod of her head. I said nothing, I could tell the image was nothing short of torture for her and I felt a despair that the men of today had no idea how to behave. Social media was all very well, but in my day the last thing you wanted was to see what an old flame was up to. Then again, I thought, sadly, perhaps if social media had been around when I was Erin's age I wouldn't have believed the man I thought was the love of my life had been dead for over fifty years.

'Come on,' I said, getting to my feet, and taking Erin's cup to the sink to rinse along with my own. 'Time we got on with the day. There's an antiques fair in Bridgwater I think we could have a go at this weekend and I want us to get the stock ready.'

'Fair enough,' Erin sighed, getting to her feet. 'I'll get in the shower.'

'Good,' I said, sitting back down and helping myself to Erin's laptop. 'Because I want to familiarise myself with this Faceache a minute.'

'Facebook!' Erin shouted as she walked up the stairs.

With a chuckle I glanced at the screen. It was hard to believe that I, Lydia Harper, was on social media. As my eyes roamed the screen, I realised there were so many things to explore. I could search antique stores and even find things to buy. Then out of nowhere I felt a flash of inspiration and let my fingers hover briefly over the keyboard. Erin had told me the names of her parents – Rosemary and Tom, and so before I could change my mind, I typed in *Rosemary Matthews* and pressed return. Erin wasn't the only one that could bring people together.

Thirteen

Erin

I knew I could get Lydia interested in Facebook, it would just require a bit of gentle persuasion. Although we had only been living together a short time I had quickly realised that telling Lydia what to do was the least effective way of getting her to do something.

The idea of getting her involved in social media hadn't come to me immediately, but as I began my search for Jack Harrison, I realised just how many older people were online now and how much good it might do Lydia to start reconnecting with old friends.

There was of course also the chance that one of them might know of Jack's whereabouts too. It was incredible just how many Jack Harrisons there were.

Now, as I pulled on my favourite jeans, I turned my attention to the fair this weekend. We had managed to get quite a bit done over the past couple of days despite Lydia's sudden drama and I was hopeful that getting back into antiques would be just what she needed.

Peering out of my bedroom window onto the Circus below, I shook my head in wonder. Not for the first time I wondered what the hell Harry had been thinking hiding that letter from Lydia like that. I mean it was obviously him, from everything Lydia had said there was nobody else it could possibly have been, but I wasn't about to sully her dead husband's good name.

In a way I could understand it. If the love of my life suddenly got a letter from a presumed dead old flame, I would probably have got rid of the evidence too. I wondered why Harry didn't do just that? He kept the letter, which made me think he wasn't all bad. Perhaps he intended to show Lydia at some point, or perhaps he just forgot.

I turned away from the window and sank onto my bed. It was all too much to think about, but at the very least it was taking my mind off Cara and Brad. I still hadn't been sleeping well most nights, and the very action of sleeping alone still felt weird. But then again, as Rachel had pointed out at dinner last night, it was far better to be alone than curled up beside a two-timing rat-bag.

The sound of the vacuum cleaner outside my door dragged me from my misery. I knew Lydia well enough by now to know that she only did that when she wanted something. For some reason she seemed to think this was a better option than simply knocking on the door.

'Everything okay?' I asked, pulling the door open to find Lydia vacuuming one spot relentlessly.

'Ah, there you are.' She smiled brightly, switching the vacuum cleaner off. 'I need a bit of help. I need you to come into town with me. I've got a little bit of money left over from your first rent cheque and I want to go shopping.'

'What for?' I eyed her suspiciously.

'I'm sick of all these old lady clothes,' she said, tugging at her navy twinset. 'I want something a bit more modern. I want to feel fresh; I want…' she paused with a sudden gleam in her eye. 'I want to wear jeans.'

My jaw dropped open in shock. Lydia was someone that took pride in the fact she had never worn jeans in her life. Where was all this coming from?

Two hours later and we were in Southgate ready to work our way back to town to some of the shops Lydia liked the look of. So far, our journey had been a roaring success. Lydia had not only purchased two pairs of jeans but she had also bought a very flattering understated leather jacket from All Saints, which I had to confess really suited her. Now she was after something other than a cardigan to keep her warm when we stood outside on our stall all day, but she had been unable to find something that was really suitable so instead we had taken a coffee break in Marks and Spencer. I'd tried to drag her into one of the trendier barista style coffee shops in Kingsmead Square but Lydia wasn't having it, claiming she needed a slab of fruit cake and a coffee before she could buy anything else and she didn't want to start being asked to give her name at the till when she ordered her drink, thank you very much. Given the magnitude of what we were taking on I didn't have the heart to refuse so I jostled my way to the front of the queue and watched in amazement as she devoured the cake in two mouthfuls.

Afterwards, we walked up and down Stall Street and Union Street, then made our way back to Abbey Churchyard for a rest on one of the benches. As hordes of tourists swarmed around us, I noticed Lydia watching them intently.

'What are they doing?' she asked, her tone incredulous as she watched a couple of Americans take a picture outside the baths with a selfie stick, the warm spring sunshine perfectly highlighting their faces.

'They're taking a photo.' I shrugged, following her gaze.

Lydia shook her head in amazement. 'But they look bloody ridiculous! Surely they can see that? Why on earth are they swishing their hair around like a couple of show ponies? And why is that one on the left making her lips look like they belong on a duck?'

A giggle escaped my lips. Lydia had never made a secret of the fact that not only did she dislike all the tourists that poured through the city, but she also hated anyone that posed for a selfie.

'They're young,' I said. 'They just want to look cool for their Instagram feed.'

'Well, they'd look a damn sight better if they stared into the camera normally rather than doing their best bird impression.'

With that she turned to me and stuck her lips out like one of the teenagers behind us, swishing her imaginary long hair back and forwards across her shoulders. I couldn't help howling with laughter as she preened into a pretend camera lens.

All too soon the teenagers realised what Lydia was doing and scowled. 'Is she okay?' one of them asked in an accent that was pure New York.

'Yeah, you know that to mock other people is, like, so rude,' the other one said.

I glanced at Lydia who was still preening into the pretend camera and swallowed another giggle. I was about to open my mouth and say something when instead Lydia surprised me by getting to her feet and turning on the tourists. 'It's not me that's rude, it's you lot! When I was your age, I wanted to experience life not look at it through a damned camera! You're being rude, you're turning your back on life itself, as if you're too afraid to experience the real thing. If you want my opinion the best thing you can do is throw that bloody thing in the baths over there!'

I hurriedly intervened. 'So sorry,' I babbled. 'Care in the community, you know, be grateful you don't have the NHS in America – this is the result. Come on Lydia, time to go.'

As I stood up, I began to half coax, half drag Lydia back along the street with me, fully expecting resistance but instead she accompanied me quite happily while the Americans shot daggers at us as we walked back towards the shops.

'What was all that?' I asked in astonishment when we'd rounded the corner back into the safety of the High Street.

'What was what?' Lydia asked innocently.

I rolled my eyes. 'All that back there. You were lucky they didn't call the police.'

Lydia let out a snort of disgust. 'The police! No doubt they would congratulate me for getting a pair of tourists to stop staring at their bloody phones for a minute.'

No longer able to help myself I threw my head back and roared with laughter. Lydia did have a point. I too hated the way people took selfies so seriously and it used to wind me up no end when Cara would preen and perfect her pout before taking the photo. I glanced across at Lydia and caught the satisfied smile on her face. The events of moments earlier seemed to have done her the world of good. So what if a couple of passing tourists got it both barrels in the process? Still, I thought, Lydia did need to be careful. This devil may care attitude may be funny now but it could end up getting her in serious trouble.

I was about to say as much when she stopped suddenly in the street. 'What are we doing now?'

'Going in there,' she said, pointing to a mobile phone shop. 'It's high time I got myself one of those phones.'

I stared at her aghast. Lydia could barely work the DVD player, what on earth was she going to do with a mobile? 'Why? You always say you think mobile phones are the scourge of all evil. That you take pride in the fact you don't want to be contacted at all times.'

Lydia's eyes flashed with excitement. 'That's true, but Erin I want to join the twenty-first century. I don't want to miss anything else.'

With that she stepped inside the store and pounced on the new display of smartphones. As I trailed in after her, I felt a mix of admiration and wonder – what on earth had happened to my housemate and landlady?

Fourteen

Lydia

I'd had my new mobile phone for three days now and, along with the letter from Jack I couldn't bear to part with, it was something else I had to have nearby at all times. It was such a wonderful invention I couldn't understand why I hadn't got one before. Not only did it mean I could keep in touch with Luke more easily by text message, but I could check my emails on the go and I was becoming rather obsessed with Facebook. I had to confess that when Erin fixed me up with an account I wasn't sure how much I would use it but I had become friends with so many old antique collectors that Harry and I had met over the years, it had been lovely reconnecting with old colleagues.

Sitting in Phil's café, mobile still in hand, I scrolled down the screen using my forefinger looking for the camera app, as Erin told me it was called. This morning I had walked out of the house in my new leather jacket and jeans, feeling a million dollars. I left Erin in charge of collecting the van for our trip to the fair in Bridgwater the following morning.

Spring was firmly in the air and I wanted to take a picture to send to Luke. He had always adored Parade Gardens as a child and as I glanced out of the café window into the walled gardens opposite, it was wonderful to see the flowers starting to bloom. The park in the heart of the city was always such a riot of colour that Luke and I had loved to visit when we could, even enjoying the concerts in the summer when a band would take to the stand. We'd watch the ducks in the pond and hire a deckchair, surrounded by the sounds of the babbling River Avon and the elegant Bath stone buildings providing an elegant backdrop. This tradition was something we had done right up until he left for New York. Looking at the gardeners toil away getting ready for the upcoming season, a pang of longing flooded through me as it hit me just how far away Luke was. But then I realised that the contraption in my hand was a way of keeping us close. So far, Luke and I were emailing every day and he was also trying to get me to do something called FaceTime which I didn't understand but Erin promised I'd love once I'd got used to the phone.

At the thought of Erin, I felt a surge of warmth. This added closeness with my son was her doing. She was a very welcome breath of fresh air at a time when I hadn't known I would need it. Now, I wanted to pay her back for all she was doing for me, which was why I had sought out Phil earlier. He was a wise old thing. I'd watched him snaking his way through the tables, an eager smile for all his customers as he carried a tray laden with coffee and cake.

'To what do I owe this wonderful pleasure?' Phil grinned as he passed me my flat white with extra foam, made just how he knew I liked it.

I took a sip, enjoying the first rush of caffeine slipping into my blood stream before I spoke. 'That's one of the many things I love about you Phil, you don't waste time beating about the bush.'

He shrugged and took a sip of his own latte. 'I don't see the point. We have been friends for many years now, Lydia. When you get to our time of life there isn't much time to waste beating a bush. How are things going with Erin?'

I gave him a wry smile. 'Very well thank you. I've become very fond of her since she moved in, but then I think you knew that I might.'

'I had a feeling the two of you might be well suited,' he chuckled before looking down at the mobile in my hand. 'Is she responsible for that too?'

'Partly,' I admitted. 'Since Harry's death I've wondered if I'm too set in my ways. As you say, life is short.'

There was a pause then as we reflected on all that had brought us here. Phil had lost his own wife, Rosa, five years ago and like me he had had a hard time adjusting to life without her. Unlike me he hadn't needed a lodger, but with no children of their own, he had been lonely and so he had taken in a rescue cat from the nearby shelter. Pico, a boisterous moggy had given him the lifeline he needed and along with the lifetime of memories he treasured of his life with Rosa, Pico helped keep him warm at night.

'Is that what's prompted this change of image then?' he said, gesturing to my new outfit. 'You look very chic, very Helen Mirren.'

I couldn't help myself and roared with laughter. 'Never mind her looks, I wouldn't say no to her money.'

'Touché.' Phil laughed, clinking his cup against mine before he frowned. 'Though what's all this about you shouting at some tourists?'

I shifted uncomfortably in my seat. I had been trying to forget about that part of the day. 'A moment of madness.'

Phil raised an eyebrow. 'I think you had your new houseguest a little worried.'

I pinched the bridge of my nose. How could I explain? 'The thing is I just had this great wave of irritation sweep over me,' I began. 'I looked at their silly faces, preening, pouting and generally wasting time and I let them have it.'

'Pretty savagely by the sound of it,' Phil chuckled.

'I may have gone a bit far,' I admitted.

Phil smiled, his expression softening. 'That's not like you, Lydia. I mean I know you don't suffer fools, it's one of the many, many things I've admired about you over the years, but you don't tend to lose your temper so suddenly. Is everything all right?'

I took a bite of the delicious cake he had pushed my way. Phil always did like to treat me, perhaps he would be able to offer me a slice of much needed advice this morning too.

'I had a bit of a blast from the past this week. It's rather shaken me to be honest, got me wondering if I've been missing out on life, so I decided to embrace change. I don't want a life half-lived any more,' I explained, roughly outlining the letter Erin and I had recently discovered had been hidden from me.

When I finished, I passed the letter across the table for him to read and watched Phil's face become grave.

'The very first time you saw this was a few days ago?' he said, his face pale.

I nodded. 'And since Erin suggested tracking Jack down, I feel confused. I keep going over my relationship with Harry. Since he died, Phil, I feel as though I didn't know the man I spent over fifty years with – he kept so many secrets from me. Did he love me at all?'

Phil put the letter down, leaned across the table and clasped my hand. The feel of his rough calloused hand against my smooth one grounded me. 'I think he loved you very much, Lydia, and that was perhaps the problem. All he wanted was to take care of you and give you the very best life possible. The trouble is you were capable of so much more than he thought.'

'Or I thought,' I muttered. 'Since Harry died I've come to realise that I can do things on my own, which makes me wonder if I ought to look for Jack. What will I achieve? My dear old dad used to say there was no point pursing a relationship if it wasn't going to go anywhere. I keep wondering if I ought to leave it. I mean, even if I do find him, what's the point? Maybe the answer isn't Jack or Harry.'

Phil shook his head and rested it on his hand. 'I think your instincts were right, Lydia. Sometimes we have to look back before we can go forwards. I think you should search for Jack and talk to him.'

I smiled, his kindness striking a chord. 'Then of course there's Erin. Since she discovered this letter, she's had the bit between her teeth. I can't help feeling this search for Jack is doing her a bit of good too. You know it's giving her something else to focus on besides that rotten ex of hers.'

Phil frowned. 'That girl is a treasure. She deserves so much better. I always thought she was too good for Cara.

That girl took advantage of Erin but I think she's only starting to see it now.'

I stiffened, privately thinking the same thing but choosing not to dwell. 'I want to get her to move forwards.'

'Has she got a job yet?' Phil mused.

I shook my head. 'I don't want to rush her. Besides, I've kept her busy working on the antiques side of things and we've got our new fair tomorrow. There's plenty to keep her occupied.'

'Ginger wants to go part-time. Her mother isn't well and she wants to spend more time taking care of her,' Phil said. 'I wonder if Erin would like to work here for a bit? Might get her out of the house – when she's not doing antiques business of course.'

I clapped my hands together in delight. 'That's a wonderful idea!'

'As long as she doesn't think we're meddling.' Phil frowned. 'I am very fond of Erin; I don't want her to think I am involving myself in her affairs.'

'We're not meddling, we're looking out for her which is more than that bastard of an ex and her so called best friend ever did,' I exclaimed.

Phil smirked at my choice of language and said nothing. Before Harry died, the worst expletive I had ever uttered was 'bloody'. In the last few weeks my language was becoming as coarse as a fishwife's and I had to admit there was a part of me that was enjoying it. Draining my cup dry, I set it down on the wooden table and glanced across at the community noticeboard. As usual there were the weekly yoga classes, guitar lessons and childminding services offered, but right in the middle was a poster I hadn't seen before.

Eyes narrowing, I got out of my seat and scurried across the café to take a closer look. Snatching it from the board, I brought it back to Phil and laid it out in front of us.

'Is this all booked up?' I asked, stabbing the poster with my forefinger.

Phil raised an eyebrow and shook his head. 'Ginger knows the organiser – I think she said this morning there were a couple of seats spare.'

'Not any more there aren't – book me and Erin on.' I grinned.

Phil's jaw dropped to the floor. 'Lydia, are you sure? I mean this all seems very sudden. Perhaps if you want to go out and socialise more we could go out for a meal? And what about Erin? This may not be something she wants to do.'

I waved away his concerns. 'Leave Erin to me,' I declared with confidence.

'But Lydia,' Phil cried, his tone beseeching now. 'Do you honestly think either one of you is ready for speed dating?'

I folded my arms and fixed Phil with my best steely gaze. 'Not only do I think we are both ready for it, I think we need it. I'm done with missing out on opportunities Phil, and Erin needs to realise that the best thing she ever did was cutting Brad and Cara from her life. The question should actually be, is speed dating ready for us?'

Fifteen

Erin

Perched on a cardboard box, the early morning wind whipping around my head, I glowered angrily at Lydia over the top of my paper coffee cup.

I hadn't woken up feeling this furious. In fact, when the alarm went off at five this morning I had bounded out of bed like an excited child, ready to start our very first fair as the Simon and Garfunkel Antiques Brigade. Together, Lydia and I had loaded our van with stock, packed our cash register, portable debit card machine and bags full of change, along with packed lunches, snacks and water to keep us going throughout the day. As we drove along the A39 towards Bridgwater, the early morning April sunshine lighting the way, I had been as excited as Lydia and I sang along to the radio and chattered non-stop about the potential customers we might meet that day. Summer was just around the corner, and it was the happiest I had felt since splitting with Brad, but then Lydia ruined it by dropping one massive bloody bombshell.

'So, I saw Phil last night,' she said casually as we passed through Wells, the empty road stretching out before us. 'Said he might have a bit of part-time work for you, if you want it?'

I blinked at her in surprise. 'Really? When I spoke to him before I moved in with you, he said he was fully staffed.'

'Well, that was before Ginger's mother took a turn for the worse. The poor girl wants to help her out a bit more and work part-time. You don't have to do it forever, but I thought it might help you get your confidence back.'

'I would love to,' I said, braking as a motorcyclist came out of nowhere and dangerously overtook me. 'It would be great to help him out as well, he's been so kind.'

Lydia nodded. 'He has. And of course, he was full of support about our search for Jack.'

I flashed Lydia a sympathetic glance. I still hadn't got any further forwards and hoped she hadn't become too disheartened.

'He said he thought it was a good idea, that it would help lay a few ghosts to rest, you know,' she said, her voice suddenly becoming high-pitched.

I glanced at her out of the corner of my eye. Her face was flushed and she looked as if she was bubbling with excitement.

'Was that all he said?'

'Yes,' she replied in her strange tone. 'Oh, and that we could have the last two places on Ginger's mixed age speed dating night at The Cow and Calf next Friday evening.'

'What?' I gasped.

The last thing I felt like doing was seeing anyone else. For a second, I wondered if Lydia was joking but the delighted smile that lit up her entire face told me that this was no joke and she obviously thought it was a good idea. Suddenly a sharp beep brought me swiftly back to reality and I turned the steering wheel just in time to avoid hitting a cyclist.

'Why?' I croaked eventually.

'Because you and I need this,' she said firmly. 'Since we found that letter last week, I'm not sure who I am any more. I feel like I need to try new things, have new experiences to find out. As for you young lady—' I glanced across at her as she wagged her finger at me, her face suddenly stern '—you desperately need to get out of the house and start realising there are other men out there that won't treat you as badly as Brad did.'

'I don't think that,' I gasped. 'We just broke up.'

'You've wasted too much time on him already,' Lydia continued as if I hadn't spoken, 'You're not getting any younger and neither am I. If Harry's death has taught me one thing it's that you don't know how much time you've got left. Your life could be snuffed out when you least expect it and I don't know about you but I'm not living my life in the shadow of a man any more.'

With that she turned and fixed her gaze straight ahead and we stayed like that until we reached our destination. As we unloaded the van, Lydia kept trying to talk to me but I was too furious to reply. Instead I focused on nodding quiet hellos to fellow stallholders, ensuring all the banners and signs advertising the fact we were the Simon and Garfunkel Antiques Brigade were straight, and then set about getting us some coffees. Despite the fact spring had arrived, there was still a nip in the air and I hoped a coffee wouldn't just thaw out my hands but dampen the burning rage that was threatening to swallow me whole as well.

Now, as I watched Lydia welcome the first few customers that wandered over to our stall, I took a deep breath and did my best to calm down. I knew that she had been acting in my best interests and she genuinely believed she wasn't just helping herself but me too. The trouble was that not only did I resent having my affairs meddled with, I hated the idea of speed dating. It was the last thing I had encouraged Cara to take part in and look how that had turned out. As I simmered over the dregs of my coffee, I felt a flash of realisation. The person I was mad at wasn't Lydia, it was Cara. I couldn't forget how, after the last speed dating session she had been on, we had gone for drinks and pored over the events of what I thought was her exciting single life, while all the time she was sleeping with my fiancé.

Throwing the remains of my coffee on the grass, I got to my feet and stood beside Lydia. 'I forgive you,' I whispered as she shoved a ten-pound note into our cash box.

She turned to me and grinned, her blue eyes alight with a mixture of kindness and mischief. 'I'm sorry. I know I overstepped the mark. But well, I saw there were two places left and thought it was fate. I'm sorry Erin, I shouldn't have booked us into the event without discussing it with you.'

I wrapped an arm around Lydia's shoulders. 'Please don't do anything like that again. After Brad and Cara's betrayal I can't cope with any more surprises, even little ones. Promise me?'

'Of course, I won't do it again.' Lydia smiled, before hastily turning to another customer who was examining an old Wedgewood vase. For a split second I thought I saw a flash of fear across her features, but then shook my head. Clearly the cold air and early start was playing havoc with my ability to think straight. This was all best forgotten, and perhaps Lydia was right, there was every chance I might even have a good time or at the very least a good laugh afterwards.

Feeling better, I looked around the rest of the fair properly for the first time. It was quite big, I realised, with car boot sellers, catering vans and small businesses all bustling with activity. Lydia had been right. This was a good place to start. Not only was it relatively close to Bath but it seemed popular with customers too. I stifled a yawn as I smiled at a potential customer browsing through the walking sticks we had laid out in an umbrella stand, then I turned to the petty cash tin. We had already made over £300 and it wasn't even nine in the morning.

'Not interrupting anything, am I?' I said, sidling up to Lydia and flashing a smile at her and the younger man she was talking to.

'Not at all,' Lydia exclaimed. 'In fact, I was just talking about you to John. John, this is Erin my business partner and lodger. Erin, this is John, a fellow antiques dealer from Bristol.'

I leaned forward to shake the man's hand and smiled. Tall and a good few years younger than Lydia, with a lopsided grin and bright red hair, he had a friendly look about him. 'Pleased to meet you.'

'Likewise,' he said in a broad Bristol accent. 'I hear you've got Lydia back into antiques. I'm delighted to have you back, Lyddie love, we've missed you.'

A hint of wistfulness flashed across Lydia's eyes, 'I have missed being a part of the antiques scene. It's been wonderful selling our stock again and talking to enthusiasts about their interests.'

'How long have you two known each other?' I asked.

Lydia and John narrowed their eyes at each other as if trying to work it out. 'Would it be about twenty years?' John said finally.

'I think so!' Lydia exclaimed.

'You don't look old enough, John,' I chuckled.

Lydia swatted me playfully with her arm. 'Thank you very much!'

I held my hands up in mock defence. 'I didn't mean it like that. Just, you know, you have to admit Lydia, John does have something of a baby face.'

For a minute John looked embarrassed. 'I'm actually older than Lydia here, but I didn't always look like this. For ages I was a right fat so and so. Always eating those bacon rolls when I sold my stock at fairs like these. Then I got a personal trainer and he's taken years off me.'

I nodded approvingly. It had clearly paid off. 'What's a personal trainer?' Lydia asked.

'It's someone that tells you how to train at the gym,' I explained helpfully. 'They help make you fit and healthy by working out your current fitness level and setting you a goal.'

'I swear by mine,' John said. 'Been seeing Mike about five years now. I've lost six stone thanks to him, and even my wife Annabel's started seeing him.'

Lydia's mouth fell open. 'Annabel is going to the gym? But she always hated exercise.'

The easy laugh that fell from John's mouth reverberated across the stall. 'That's before she saw the results I got. Not only that, but she was at a bit of a low ebb after her sister died. Mike's helped her come to terms with that.'

'Through exercise?' Lydia asked incredulously.

'Exercise is well-known for staving off the blues,' I said.

'Well I never,' Lydia gasped, before turning to John. 'Do you have his number? I think I should like to give him a call.'

'Yes, hang on a minute.' John fished out his mobile from his pocket.

'Lydia! Hang on. Are you sure you want a personal trainer?'

'Why not?' she chuckled, a glint in her eye. 'Maybe this Mike can take twenty years off me like he has for John.'

I watched in astonishment as John texted the number to Lydia. I was all for Lydia making changes and improving her life, but since we'd discovered Jack's letter she seemed to be trying to reinvent herself – was it possible she was changing too much?

Sixteen

Lydia

It had taken almost a week for Erin to properly forgive me for booking us onto the speed dating evening. She rallied at the antiques fair to put on a show, and afterwards as we drove though the countryside in darkness with an almost empty van, I could tell she was doing her best to remain even-tempered.

Now the evening was looming, I had to admit I was having second thoughts. I wasn't sure what had possessed me, and if it hadn't been Ginger that had arranged it then I would have cancelled and happily paid the money involved as a forfeit.

However, I hated letting people down so there was no choice. Erin and I were going to have to go through it and live with whatever happened next. Hearing the sound of footsteps outside the kitchen door, I smiled brightly as Erin appeared. Dressed in jeans and a smart white blouse Luke would have described as a doily, I glanced at the clock in surprise.

'Why are you up and dressed so early?' I frowned. 'It's only just gone seven.'

'I start my new job with Phil today,' she replied, helping herself to a bowl of granola. 'I want to make a good impression.'

'Of course, that's today. I completely forgot, I am sorry.'

'No need.' Erin smiled, sitting opposite me at the table.

'There's every need,' I said, feeling guilty. 'I'm sorry Erin, I wanted to wish you good luck.'

'Really, it doesn't matter.' She tucked a loose strand of hair behind her ear. 'It's not like I haven't worked there before. Besides,' she added playfully, 'shouldn't it be me wishing you good luck today. Isn't Mike coming round later to put you through your paces?'

I nodded excitedly at the thought of my new personal trainer. 'Yes. He's coming at eight to start whipping me into shape.'

With that I stood up and flexed a non-existent bicep while Erin looked at me, clearly perplexed.

'You do know that it takes time to build muscle?' She frowned. 'It won't happen overnight. And also working out hurts.'

Privately I had wondered if I was losing my marbles. First speed dating and now exercise. I knew outsiders might think I was having a three-quarter-life crisis, but I was rather enjoying trying new things and finding out who I was. Besides Jane Fonda was older than me and she looked fabulous. But it wasn't just about looking good, I was actually hoping exercise might help my mental health. I was always reading in the newspapers that the best way to improve your memory was to get fit and I wanted to give it a try before it was too late. Besides I'd been a bit forgetful of late, this could only help things.

'I know that,' I said loftily, 'but I told you Erin, I want to try everything at least once and you should too. Stop being so afraid of new adventures.'

With that, she arched an eyebrow and fell silent. I thought desperately of something else to smooth the waters. 'There's another fair next weekend in Swindon this time. Do you want to go?'

Erin turned to me and smiled that lovely smile of hers that lit up her entire face. 'Absolutely. I still can't believe how well we did in Bridgwater.'

I rubbed my hands together in glee. 'It was wonderful. I knew we had some good quality items but the way people flocked to our stall was a great surprise.'

'It was all the social media promotion,' Erin said authoritatively as she finished her cereal. 'I asked every customer afterwards how they heard about us and 90 per cent of them said they saw us online.'

'Really?' I asked in surprise. 'I didn't think it would have that much effect. Most of the business Harry and I had was through word of mouth.'

'Social media is a very powerful tool.' Erin stood up and rinsed her bowl in the sink. 'I'll start setting up the next lot of promotional material if you let me have all the fair details'

'Yes of course. I'll go and get ready for my exercise session and then I'll get the details together.'

With that, I made my way up to my bedroom. I already had my workout outfit planned, having gone into town and got myself a very nice pair of leggings, trainers and

T-shirt that the sales girl assured me would keep me very comfortable.

And while I would, of course, send Erin all the details of the fair, there was something else I wanted to get on with before Mike arrived and that was checking my Facebook. Last night I had taken myself to Harry's old office, sat at his computer with a glass of wine and rebooted my search for Erin's parents. I was still keen to bring them back together, and this morning there were a couple of profiles I wanted to take a closer look at.

Shutting the door to Harry's office, I crept over to the old desktop and waited for the machine to fire up. When the familiar four-note melody sounded, I pressed the internet icon and loaded up Facebook. Going to the search bar, I entered the name Rosie Matthews and looked at the two profiles I thought might be her. Erin hadn't given me much more to go on than her parents' names and I had already looked through at least fifteen profiles and none of them had been right. I was getting so desperate I was tempted to ask Luke for help but I could only imagine what he would say. I could almost see the familiar eye roll and hear the pleading tone in his voice as he begged me to leave well alone.

I nearly had, but then last night I had found one Rosemary Matthews and another named Rosie that both lived in Bristol I wanted to look at them last night but Erin had made some big fuss about me watching a film with her, and there hadn't been time. So now, as I clicked on the first one, I scanned the first profile. Although she lived in Bristol, she was apparently single and judging by the moronic stare she was giving the camera lens, I highly doubted she was clever enough to have become a solicitor.

Returning to the search bar, I clicked the next name down, and the moment the profile loaded I felt a shiver of excitement. The woman in the profile picture was the spitting image of Erin. With a bright smile, greying red hair and a glass of wine in front of her as she smiled confidently at the camera, I could see immediately where Erin got her self-esteem. This Rosie Matthews' smile alone would have you believing you could do anything. Once again I felt a pang of sorrow that this magnificent-looking woman and her daughter were estranged. Quickly I scanned the rest of her profile. Although she didn't say outright that she had a daughter called Erin she no longer spoke to, this Rosie Matthews did run a solicitor's firm in Bristol, did advocacy work for a women's refuge and her likes included several left-wing groups along with the *Guardian*. Oh, and her husband was Tom, just like Erin's father.

My heart pounded. Should I message her? If so, what should I say? Decisively, I clicked on the send message icon and as I waited for a new page to load I thought about what to say. What was the best way of telling a woman, mother to mother, that their estranged daughter was living with them, had been through hell and back and wasn't it about time they kissed and made up?

I rubbed my chin. No, even I wouldn't be that insensitive. My fingers hovered over the keyboard, and then common sense prevailed. If Erin had been upset about me setting up a speed date, I wasn't quite sure how she would take me trying to reunite her with her family, no matter how honourable my intentions. She had made no secret of the fact that was the one thing she hated – surprises. I didn't want to keep this from her.

As the front door slammed shut, I logged out of my Facebook account, resolving to think about it all later.

'Oww,' I muttered under my breath as I hobbled up to one of the bar stools in Phil's café.

Erin gave me a sympathetic smile. 'Why don't you sit down at one of the tables? You'll be more comfortable.'

'Because I can't bend down,' I hissed crossly, 'That workout was agony, you should have warned me.'

'I did try,' she chuckled. 'A personal trainer is not for the faint-hearted. What did he get you to do?'

I shuddered at the memory. It was more a case of what didn't we do. From the moment Mike arrived, he promised he wouldn't work me too hard. I thought that might mean a long chat about what I wanted to achieve followed by possibly one or two gentle exercises to get me in the mood. Not on your life! He had me doing star jumps, lunges and these horrible little bends called squats. After an hour I was begging for mercy and wondering if all this pain was really worth it. Given every part of my body felt as if it had been tortured, I decided once was enough and so after I gave Mike his money, I gave him his marching orders too.

'Let's just say it was more than I anticipated and I won't be doing it again,' I admitted, nursing the coffee Erin had presented me with the moment I arrived. 'How are you getting on anyway?'

'Really well I think,' she replied. 'It's been nice to be busy.'

I glanced around the café and saw that aside from me and another man in the corner drinking a latte, it was quiet. I had hoped it would be busier than this when I caught the bus into town. I wanted a private word with Phil about Erin's mother.

'You didn't have to check on me, though I appreciate the fact you did,' she said, bending over the refrigerated counter and cutting off a large slice of what appeared to be a very jammy Bakewell tart. 'Here you go. On me, just to say thanks for the support, you know, it means ever such a lot.'

As she placed the tart on a plate and slid it towards me with a fork, I felt a flash of guilt. 'I can't take this.'

'Nonsense.' she said firmly. 'You've earned it! In more ways than one this morning.'

I slipped her a small smile and eyed the tart. It looked delicious and in all honesty, I had worked up quite an appetite. 'Is Phil around?' I asked, forking off a small piece and savouring the delicious almond scent. 'Don't tell me he's left you running the show all by yourself on your first day.'

'He's just nipped upstairs to sort out something to do with one of the suppliers,' she explained, flashing a smile as a customer walked in. 'Do you want me to get him?'

I shook my head and devoured a mouthful of tart. 'I think I've more than enough to keep me going until the boss arrives.'

Just then I saw a pair of feet and some rather stout legs appear on the stairs behind Erin.

'Ah, Phil.' I smiled as his head and body emerged. 'I was hoping for a word.'

Setting a pile of paperwork down on the counter, he exchanged a mock nervous glance with Erin. 'What have I done?' he deadpanned.

'Don't ask me,' Erin said, shrugging her shoulders. 'Are you all right if I take my break now?'

Phil looked around the café wryly. 'Well, I mean we are rushed off our feet...'

As he trailed off, Erin kissed his cheek and tore off her apron in one swift movement. I laughed at their easiness together. They were almost like father and daughter and it was lovely to see how affectionate they were with one another.

Saying goodbye to Erin, I indicated my plate to Phil and raised my eyebrows. 'I'm actually here to arrest you for crimes against waistlines,' I sighed. 'This Bakewell is delicious.'

'It's Ginger's.' Phil smiled ruefully. 'She's a wonder in the kitchen.'

'I must ask her for the recipe,' I groaned, patting my stomach.

'Is that why you're here, Lyddie? Only I heard you were trying to rebuild the body beautiful this morning,' he teased, slipping another coffee my way.

I smiled gratefully. 'I insist on paying for this. You'll be bankrupt if you carry on being this generous. But no, Ginger's recipe book is not why I'm here. I want your advice.'

'Again? I'll need to start charging,' he teased. 'What is it this time?'

'Do you have a laptop?' I asked. 'I need to show you something.'

Perplexed, Phil nodded and reached down under the counter for an ancient-looking computer that looked as though its predecessor had been an abacus. Walking around the counter to join me, he lifted the lid, pressed a few buttons and brought the social media site I wanted to show him to life.

'Have you found Jack?' he asked excitedly as I clicked onto my own profile. 'Is that what this is about?'

'Sadly, no. We seem to have hit a bit of a dead end. But what I did want to show you was this.'

Pushing the computer back towards Phil, he gasped in shock as he saw who I had found. 'This is Erin's mother. What are you doing with this?'

'I want to reunite them,' I said baldly. 'As I keep saying, Phil, life is just too short and this family should be talking to one another.'

'But, Lydia,' Phil said beseechingly, unable to take his eyes from the screen, 'you can't go messing about in Erin's affairs. Yes, I agree it's ridiculous. But Erin is our friend and it is merely our job to support her not interfere. She told me she didn't really want to go speed dating tomorrow night but you've made her.'

I rolled my eyes. 'Erin's over all that now. Phil, what I want to know is do you really think it's a terrible idea if I contact her?'

Phil said nothing and instead peered at the screen. Running his eyes across Rosie's image he suddenly sighed. 'Erin is the spitting image of her mother, isn't she?'

'Yes,' I said sadly. 'And frankly as a mother, if my child had been through everything Erin has then, estrangement or no estrangement, I would want to know. Look, I've written her this note, and wanted your opinion before I sent it to her through the messaging service.'

Delving into my handbook I pulled out a handwritten sheet I had laboured over and passed it to Phil. As he placed his glasses on his nose and read it through, I was astonished to see tears pool at his eyes.

'Well?' I demanded. 'Do you think I should send it.'

Phil clasped my hand. 'It's a beautiful letter Lydia. And I think that we both know that it doesn't matter what I say, you'll send that note. All I can say to you is be prepared for the consequences.'

Seventeen

Erin

Stretching my limbs overhead, I yawned lazily, desperately trying to find the motivation to get out of bed. Yesterday had been my first full day at the café and although I was no stranger to hard work, my arms were sore from carrying overladen tea trays and my thighs were shattered after walking up and down that flight of stairs all day.

As the high-pitched ring of my iPhone beeped and vibrated, insisting that I get out of bed, I hit stop and tried not to scream in pain when I stood up. Sinking my feet into my sheepskin slippers, I reminded myself that this was the worst I would feel all day, and there was no point putting off the inevitable any longer.

Padding down the stairs to the kitchen, I reached for a mug and switched on the kettle. Although I wasn't due at Phil's today I did have to catch an early morning train to London. I had told Lydia I would be out most of the day helping Rachel sort out something at work. However, the truth was I had a lead on Jack Harrison's whereabouts but didn't want to get Lydia's hopes up until I knew more.

Even though I had drawn numerous blanks when it came to Jack, last week I'd had the inspired idea of joining one of those community groups that's plastered across social media for the area Jack and Lydia had lived in Islington. The other day I had put up a post asking for information about Jack as I was an old family friend and last night my phone beeped enticingly with an alert letting me know someone had answered.

Immediately, I logged on and discovered the message was from a woman named Becki who said her grandmother still lived in the street, remembered Jack, and how he had mistakenly been reported dead. When she asked me over for a chat to talk further, we messaged each other and Becki suggested her grandma was a bit old school, and preferred to chat about things of a personal nature face-to-face rather than over the phone. Consequently, I hadn't hesitated to agree to pay them a visit at her grandmother's home.

Of course, I'd said nothing to Lydia, and had hoped to be out of the house before she woke so I could avoid awkward questions. However, hearing her nearing the kitchen door I knew I was going to have to start lying through my teeth.

'Morning,' I said brightly, reaching for another mug as Lydia slumped into a chair. 'Sleep well?'

'If you can call it that,' she groaned.

I glanced across and felt a pang of worry. Even though it was just after six in the morning, a time when nobody ever looked their best, Lydia looked pale and her greying locks seemed even greyer in the half light.

'Everything all right?' I asked softly, setting the cup down in front of her.

She blinked her eyes open and rewarded me with a kind smile. 'Fine, thank you dear. I'll be right as rain after this.'

'You're not ill, are you?' I asked, worried. She was always appeared to be as strong as an ox, but this morning she seemed fragile somehow.

Lydia smiled again, and patted my hand consolingly, 'I'm absolutely fine. Think I just overdid it with Mike yesterday, that's all. I'm aching in places I never knew it was possible to ache.'

I grimaced. I honestly thought it was great that Lydia was changing her life and even embarking on an exercise regime, but I didn't want her overdoing it. It took the body time to adapt to change and Lydia seemed as though she wanted to alter her entire life in a heartbeat. After I got back from my tea-break yesterday, Phil and I had chatted about this at length. He told me that he was as worried as me but assured me that to try and force Lydia to change her mind was the worst thing you could do.

'She is her own woman, Erin,' he said with a smile that looked surprisingly sad.

I mopped up the coffee spills on the counter and frowned. 'But so much change all at once? New clothes, new shoes, new phone, new attitude. It's all so much Phil. This can't be healthy?'

Phil smiled at me kindly then. 'Who are we to say what is healthy and what is not. What I do know is that we all deal with grief and loss very differently. Lydia will settle down, I promise. But to try and force her to do it before she is ready will be a mistake.'

I rinsed the cloth in the sink under the counter. 'You don't think I should have a word with Luke then?'

Phil's eyebrows waggled in concern. 'No, I don't. Trust me Erin, less interference is for the best.'

Reluctantly I'd agreed, but now as I assessed Lydia's tired appearance I began to wonder how long I should keep that promise. Lydia was the only parent Luke had left, and I had a feeling he was also the only person Lydia would really listen to. Then again, she had put up with an awful lot lately – who was I to start telling her what to do?

'You should take it easy,' I warned her now as I blew across the top of my tea to cool it. 'Too much is as bad as too little.'

Lydia rolled her eyes. 'Yes, Mum.'

'Stop that.' I helped myself to a cereal bar for the train. 'I'm only saying it because I care.'

'I know that, my darling.' Lydia smiled. 'I'm lucky to have you.' She sipped her tea then, and looked at me in surprise as if it had just occurred to her that I was up ridiculously early.

'Where are you off to?'

I felt my cheeks flame with colour. I hated lying. 'Rachel's,' I babbled. 'I said I'd get there early so we could make a start on all the stuff for the antiques business. Lots to get through and I want to make sure I'm back in time to get ready for our evening tonight.'

'Oh yes!' Lydia clapped her hands together in delight as I mentioned our speed dating evening. 'I've bought a lovely top from Zara, I thought it would go well with my new jeans. What do you think?'

'Sound lovely.' I smiled, bolting out of the door before I was forced to tell any more lies. 'See you later.'

An hour later and I was sat on the 6:46 to London Paddington, having made it out of the house and into the taxi in record time. Fortunately, I hadn't bumped into Lydia again so hadn't had to feed her any more fibs. Now, as the train thundered through the Box Tunnel I felt myself relax. Not only did I have a seat all to myself, something that was unheard of at this hour, I had also managed to bag myself a latte and croissant in the platform café before diving on board.

As we drew closer to London, I looked around at commuters and saw they were half asleep, desperately trying to make the most of this precious time before their insanely busy days at work in the capital began.

I pulled my phone out of my bag to flick onto silent when the sound of a loud beep startled me and the bloke trying to grab an extra forty winks sitting opposite me.

'So sorry,' I mouthed, while silencing the ringer and ignoring the death stare he was sending my way.

Satisfied I had silenced my phone, I glanced down at the screen to see who it was and felt a flash of horror – it was Cara. What the hell did she want? And at this time in the morning!

Cautiously I pressed my forefinger against the screen to unlock my phone and clicked onto the message.

Erin, we need to talk. I know you hate me and never want to see me again but call me. It's important. Cx

A surge of anger crept its way through my body. C with a kiss at the end. Who did she think she was? Next thing I knew, she'd be sending me messages filled with cute emojis. Furiously, I wondered what the icon was for cheating snake of a best friend. A girl with bright yellow hair and python coiled around her neck perhaps?

I took a deep breath and tried to calm myself down. I had a big enough day ahead of me as it was without getting upset about Cara. Instead I looked down at the screen again and let out a snort of disgust. She probably wanted to tell me how she and Brad had broken up and she now wanted a shoulder to cry on.

Well, C with an x, I thought spitefully as I deleted the message, you can get lost because there is literally nothing you could say to me that would be of any interest whatsoever.

I was about to put my phone down when I noticed another text message appear. This time from Lydia. Immediately I clicked onto the message, hoping against hope she hadn't injured herself trying out one of the exercises Mike had given her to do.

Do you know any driving instructors?

I shook my head in wonder. What on earth was she up to now? I was about to fire a message back, when another message from Lydia appeared almost instantly.

I've just organised my provisional licence and now I need an instructor.

My eyes widened in horror as I reread the last part of her message. Surely she wasn't serious about learning to drive?

Fingers fired up ready to write a reply, I was about to start typing when the train guard's tinny voice sounded across the tannoy.

'We have now arrived at London Paddington which is our final destination. Please gather all of your belongings and make sure you have all your items before you leave.'

Quickly, I slipped my phone back into my bag and reached overhead for my coat. Lydia might be busy trying to sort out her future, but I was about to spend my day delving into her past.

Eighteen

Lydia

I had always wanted to drive but everyone I knew said I wasn't cut out for it. I'd had lessons when I was young, but given I panicked every time another car came near me, both my father and Harry felt it was best if I left the driving to someone else. An arrangement I had been perfectly happy with until of course my darling husband had died, suddenly leaving me not only bereft but without my freedom as well.

That morning after Erin had left I had gone back upstairs, only for the bright red car to catch my eye. For a moment I stared at it, imagining what it would be like to take that car out for a drive.

April was now very nearly May, and with lighter mornings and longer days ahead, I could think of nothing lovelier than driving along the open road, the wind in my hair. It had been something Harry and I loved to do when we retired and with a start I wondered if it was something Jack would have liked to do too? I realised I had no idea, but what was worse was I had no idea if this was something

I liked doing. This was yet another example of how I had let other people have far too much say in my life. What if I was actually good at driving and just learned in a different way? Too easily, I had been written off by men who, though full of love and concern, thought they knew best. I felt a flash of irritation then that many possibilities in life that had been taken from me. Or rather, I thought sadly, I had allowed them to be snatched from me. Well, no more. I wanted to give driving another try and while I knew many might think it strange I wanted to suddenly start learning at my age, I knew I would regret it if I didn't.

Despite the ache in every one of my limbs from yesterday's training session I powered up the stairs with renewed enthusiasm. After a quick shower I washed and dressed, then made another cup of tea before settling myself at Harry's computer.

As the old machine rumbled into life, I brought up the search engine and resisted the urge to look at an email Luke had sent until later. Quickly I typed in 'DVLA', 'old people' and 'first driving licence'. I wasn't sure what I was looking for but I knew that at seventy-eight I was no spring chicken and there may be certain restrictions. I scanned the website and found to my delight that there were no upper age limits. Gleefully, I discovered that as long as I was of sound mind and body then there was no reason at all why I couldn't learn to drive. As someone over seventy, it was my responsibility to make sure my eyesight was fine, and every three years declare I was well enough to drive but apart from that there was no reason at all why I couldn't learn. I thought for a moment – my optician had said my eyesight was rapidly declining when I saw him for a check-up last month but it wasn't as though I was blind. I stared again at the screen and decided this statement must apply to the really old duffers that were stupid enough to try driving on the road when they could barely see a hand in front of their face.

I drummed my fingers against the desk. Was I really considering this? My eyes fell to a photo of Harry and I in a frame next to the monitor. Taken shortly after our wedding, we were leaning into each other in the way newly-wed couples do when they are so in love. I smiled at it fondly, remembering only too well the day it had been taken. We had been out for lunch with my father in Bristol and he had insisted on taking the snap on his old Box Brownie.

'Come on, shuffle up,' Dad had called as Harry and I posed on College Green, arm in arm.

'Yes, come on,' Harry had said, smiling down at me, as he pulled me in tighter. 'We want this photo to show our grandchildren that we were young once.'

I'd beamed happily up at him. 'And very much in love.'

'Very much,' Harry had whispered tenderly, bending down to kiss me lightly on the lips.

At the touch of his lips against mine, I had felt a flush of happiness like no other. I had felt safe, loved and wanted and knew I was the luckiest woman in the world to have married a man as wonderful as Harry Harper.

Only now, as I picked up the frame and peered into Harry's eyes I couldn't help wondering what he was hiding from me as he smiled into the camera lens. Did he know then he would lie to me throughout our marriage or did that come later? Placing the photo back on the desk, I came back to the same question that had been reverberating around my mind for days since discovering Jack's letter.

Just who would I have become if Harry hadn't seemingly hidden a myriad of secrets from me?

In that moment I felt a surge of determination – I was going to do this. With just a few clicks I had somehow managed to order my provisional driving licence. I sank back in my chair feeling rather pleased with myself, and wanted to share my good news with Erin.

Quickly, I typed a short text message to Erin asking if she could recommend any driving instructors but no reply came. I knew it was silly but I felt deflated until I remembered there was a message from Luke. Tapping into my email, I felt tears pool at my eyes as I read my boy's scant but loving message.

Hi Mum,

Just wanted to say hello and see how you and Erin are. How was the antiques fair? Things are all good here. Hannah is getting bigger by the second and we found out the other day we're going to have a little boy, Mum! Can you believe it? Baby boy Harper will be running about the place at the end of September – is the world ready? I'm not sure I am!

Speak to you soon Mum and take care – maybe lay off the exercise sessions, eh? I'm not sure we want you in hospital with a broken hip thanks to one too many enthusiastic burpees.

Lots of love,
Luke

I clapped my hands together in delight. A baby boy! At the thought of my first grandchild I felt a rush of emotion. I was about to tap out a quick reply when I saw a message flash up from Facebook. Frowning I clicked onto it and froze – Rosie Matthews had sent me a message.

My heart banged against my chest. This was now a reality, whatever it was Rosie Matthews had to tell me. I knew there was no going back. I couldn't pretend that I hadn't meddled in Erin's affairs, and whatever the outcome I would have to deal with the consequences as Phil had so wisely pointed out the other day.

Dear Lydia,

Many thanks for your message. I must admit your note came rather out of the blue and both Tom and I were rather shocked to hear from anyone connected with Erin's world and we needed a bit of time to think, I hope you understand.

First of all, let me thank you for letting me know about Erin's situation. I am sure she is devastated and as a mother yourself, I know you must understand what I mean when I say no parent wants to see their child in pain. When Tom and I told Erin we would have nothing to do with her while she was with that man, we truly believed we were acting in her best interests, and that by keeping our distance Erin would see what we saw the moment we met Brad. We were blessed that Erin was always so open and honest with us. She told us everything about Brad, how he grew up in Cheltenham, how he was twenty years older than her and how his first marriage to Cassandra had ended the night she cheated on him. I'm afraid the moment Erin told me about her new man, Tom and I became rather narrow-minded — well, me perhaps more than Tom. My own sister was treated in a very callous way by someone who had a similar history to Brad and I'm afraid all I could see was history repeating itself. I hoped that by shutting Erin out she would realise how devastating this relationship would be for her future. I am only sorry she had to find out the truth so brutally. If I'm honest, Lydia, I never liked Cara. I always thought she was a manipulative and rather selfish girl. She relied far too much on the excuse that she came from a broken home, and used it to get out of homework and detention, as well as to help herself to whatever she wanted from my daughter, whether it be toys, clothes and now boyfriends it seems.

Let me thank you, Lydia, from the very bottom of my heart, for giving my daughter a home and salvation when she needed it most. For that, I shall forever be indebted to you. Erin has always been a clever, intelligent and wise girl. It's why Tom and I were so stunned when she fell for Brad and seemed unable to see what he truly was. I never stopped caring and loving my daughter, Lydia, I do so hope you know that. In hindsight, we perhaps handled things badly and I regret that now. In truth it's something I have regretted for a long time and there's nothing I long for more than to pick up the phone and be with my daughter again, but I know that a lot of time has passed — we aren't the same people we were, but I would so like to reconcile. Do you think now this would be possible, and if so would you help us?

If you have the time I would like very much to meet you so we could perhaps discuss this further. I appreciate discretion is key and so I will await your reply eagerly whenever you have time.

However, before I sign off, allow me to thank you again, for being a friend to my daughter when I couldn't. That is a kindness I shall never forget.

Yours with gratitude,
Rosie Matthews

I read and reread the note three times more, scanning the it for any clues or any other piece of valuable information I may have missed but could find none.

My heart went out to Rosie. I wasn't sure what I had been expecting, but this was more than I could have hoped. Here was a very real possibility that I could reunite Erin with her parents – and I felt wonderful.

The only trouble was meeting Rosie. Obviously it would be easier and far more discreet to go to Bristol as I didn't want Erin to find us. She had been betrayed enough in her life already, and I could only imagine what she would say if she caught me in cahoots with her mother, no matter how honourable my intentions.

No, this would require some thinking about, and it wasn't a decision to be rushed into. With a sigh, I got to my feet, closed down the computer and drained the last of my tea. Right now, I had a driving instructor to find and a speed dating evening to prepare for.

Turning back to face the photo of Harry and I so in love, I ran my fingers over the glass and smiled. What on earth would my darling husband say if he could see me now?

Nineteen

Erin

The tree-lined street looked extremely inviting. With the classic London brick terrace and immaculate wrought iron fences, it reminded me of the houses in the *Mary Poppins* film, and as I walked past the yummy mummies clad in Lululemon activewear, I half expected to come face to face with Julie Andrews, who would probably have replaced her magical umbrella with a yoga mat.

I turned my face towards the sun to revel in the warmth and shucked off my denim jacket, tucking it over the top of my bag. The idea of Lydia living on this street now was something I struggled to picture. She hated anything too trendy, although, I thought with a rueful grin, that was before she suddenly decided to buy up half of All Saints in her quest to change her entire life. It was quite possible that this street and everyone that lived in it would now be her idea of bliss.

Peering over the top of my sunglasses I searched the houses for number 26. With their uniform black doors, it was quite hard to pick out any distinguishing features, but as I got about halfway down the road I saw the house Becki had told me was her grandmother's. Walking up the stone steps, I rapped the brass knocker firmly and braced myself for whoever answered the door. Thankfully I didn't have to wait for very long, as just a few seconds later a woman a few years older than me with a bright smile and blonde hair opened the door.'

'Becki?' I asked hopefully.

'Erin,' she replied warmly, welcoming me inside.

I stepped into the narrow hallway, framed with black and white prints of what I guessed were family members, and followed Becki down the corridor towards the back of the house.

'Thanks so much for talking to me today,' I babbled. 'I've been trying all sorts of things to find Jack and wondered if I ever would.'

'Oh, you're welcome,' Becki replied warmly 'It will be nice for Gran to relive old times. She'll be back soon; she's just gone out for her coffee morning at the club on the corner. In the meantime, I thought we could chat in the kitchen, it's cosier than the rest of the house.' She pushed open a large white door that exposed a bright white kitchen.

'Very trendy, your grandma, isn't she?' I said admiringly, taking in the gloss white kitchen cupboards, Corian worktop and large, American style fridge.

'To be honest, although this is my grandma's house, she very kindly gave it to me and my husband Nick when we got married,' Becki admitted a little sheepishly. 'She lives with us now and, I still think of it as her house.'

'Generous grandma,' I murmured.

'I know.' Becki fired the bean to cup coffee machine into life. 'But you didn't come all this way to talk about me and my gran's living arrangements.'

'No,' I replied, reaching into my bag for the photos of Jack and Lydia I had brought with me. 'I've brought some pictures that I thought might help jog your gran's memory.'

I pushed them across the table towards Becki as she placed a large cappuccino in front of me. Taking a grateful sip, I watched Becki's face break into an affectionate smile.

'These are wonderful,' she beamed. 'They'll definitely help. Actually, I meant to say to you when we spoke on the phone the other day, don't be surprised if Gran gets a bit confused.'

As Becki made a face, I chewed my lip trying to understand what she was getting at. 'How do you mean?'

'I mean, Gran has Alzheimer's. 'It's one of the reasons she gifted us this house and one of the reasons we moved in. We help take care of her, or at least I do.'

'Oh, I'm sorry,' I said quietly. 'Listen, I don't want to cause any problems for her.'

Becki smiled at what I imagined was my stricken face and shook her head. 'Not at all. If anything, it'll do Gran good to talk about the old times, it brings her back to life a bit, you know.'

I nodded, not really understanding, but wanting to. 'How long has she had it?'

'About three years.' Becki wrapped her hands around her own mug. 'At first we thought she was just getting forgetful but then there were other things too.'

I took a sip of my coffee. 'Like what?'

'Like she would suddenly fly off into rages or suddenly become very aggressive.' Becki sighed. 'When she started losing her eyesight, it was her optician that suggested she be assessed for dementia. After a series of tests, she was diagnosed with Alzheimer's.'

'I'm sorry,' I said, meaning it. I didn't know much about Alzheimer's but I knew it was a difficult condition for all those affected and I felt even more grateful to Becki and her grandmother for taking the time to help me with my search for Jack.

'Don't worry, though,' Becki said confidently as she took a sip of her coffee. 'Today's been a good day for Gran so you've come at just the right time.'

Just then, the sound of the front door opening echoed down the hallway closely followed by the sounds of footsteps coming towards us.

'Hi, Gran,' Becki called loudly, 'we're in here.'

'Well, I didn't think you'd gone to Timbuktu,' I heard a clear North London accent shout in reply before a head appeared around the door.

I got to my feet and smiled at the older lady. With a wide, welcoming face and brown eyes, she looked friendly and I was hoping she would be able to help. 'I'm Erin, Erin Matthews. Thank you so much for meeting me today, Mrs Elwood.'

'Sit back down, love.' The old woman smiled as she kissed Becki on the cheek and took a seat at the table opposite me. 'And it's Vera, not Mrs Elwood, that was my mother-in-law, God rest her. You getting me a cuppa or am I gonna die of thirst, darlin'?' Vera asked her granddaughter cheekily.

Rolling her eyes affectionately, Becki got to her feet and made her way to the kettle. 'Don't show me up when we've got company, Gran!'

Vera chuckled under her breath and winked at me. I giggled back. There was something incredibly warm about Becki's grandma, Alzheimer's or no Alzheimer's.

'So, what is it you want to talk to me about?' she asked. 'Are you here about them drains outside love? I called you lot up the council all last week, not one of you took a bleedin' bit of notice.'

I opened my mouth about to explain who I was when Becki jumped in, 'I told you yesterday, Gran. Erin's here to talk about Anna Harrison and her son Jack.'

'Oh yes, of course,' Vera replied, mollified. 'Now, what do you want to know about Anna and Jack? You know, of course, his mum went to her grave thinking her poor son had died.'

I nodded, all too aware of the sad story. 'That's sort of why I'm here. My friend was engaged to him but she too believed he died up until recently. She found a letter in her attic that he sent to her years ago begging her not to marry again. She only just found it and is understandably upset.'

Vera looked at me wide-eyed in surprise. 'Bloody hell! Sounds like something from *EastEnders*! This a cock 'n bull story?'

'Gran!' Becki admonished as I slid the photo of Lydia and Jack across the table to her. Picking it up, she examined the photo and smiled in recognition. 'Oh, it's little Lydia Day and Jack Harrison. . Those two were so in love it made you pig sick.'

'You remember her then?' I asked eagerly.

'Only too well.' Vera smiled, setting the photo down on the table. 'In fairness she was a lovely girl, Lydia, broken-hearted when she found out what had happened to Jack. I thought she'd never get over it, always had a face like a busted clock and eyes full of tears after she discovered he'd died. Tell you the truth I was relieved when she moved so I didn't have to look at her miserable face every day.'

'Gran! That's a horrible thing to say,' Becki said, setting her tea down on the table and turning to me. 'I'm sorry, Erin, please forgive Gran, she doesn't mean it.'

Vera's cheeks flushed with irritation. 'Don't speak for me, girl. I might be losing my marbles but I can still string a sentence together.' She turned to me then and looked apologetic. 'Sorry, love, I shouldn't have said that. I dunno what's up with me sometimes, my mouth opens before I've had a chance to think about what it is I'm going to say.'

I waved her concerns away, not wanting to break her concentration. 'Don't worry,' I said soothingly. 'But you do remember Jack then?'

'Course I do. I was about five years older than him when he came back. Torn apart he was, like those bags of broken biscuits they used to sell up Woolworths. Devastated to discover his mum had gone and Lydia too with no forwarding address. Up and down the houses he went trying to find out where she'd gone.'

I took another sip of my coffee. The irony that I was following in Jack's footsteps by asking the neighbours where *he* had gone was not lost on me.

'But you didn't have an address for her?' I quizzed.

Mrs Elwood shook her head, 'Lydia and me weren't that close really, being older than her we weren't exactly friends. I knew she'd gone back down to the West Country which is what I told Jack, but I didn't know anything else. He went off like a mad March hare, turned it into his own private mission he did, trying to track her down, but I don't think he ever did and I don't think he ever got over what happened neither. It was a relief when he met Liz Penway.'

'Jack got married?' I gasped.

'In the church on the corner,' Mrs Elwood confirmed. 'Must have been about seven years after Lydia left. I think he accepted he was never going to find her so he moved on. She was from Bromley way I think, so they moved over there, but he still kept in touch with my brother, God rest his soul.'

'Your brother?' I frowned.

'Yes, Jack and Freddie were great mates, right up until Freddie died last year. Jack came over for the funeral, he hasn't half aged. Still, I s'pose we all have,' Vera sniffed.

My heart was banging so loudly against my chest at this new piece of information, I was sure Becki and her grandmother could hear it.

'Jack's still alive then?'

'Very much so,' Mrs Elwood said. 'We had a letter last week off him, didn't we Becki?'

'Yes of course, I completely forgot!' Becki mock-smacked her head against her hand. 'Let me get it.'

'Do you hear from him a lot then?' I asked, unable to believe my luck that Jack Harrison wasn't only still alive, but that there was an address for him too.

'Not really,' Vera said. 'He sends the odd note, enquiring after my health, that sort of thing. But now Fred's gone, it's not the same and of course Jack's got his own crosses to bear now Liz is dead.'

'Oh, I'm sorry.'

'Ten years ago or so now,' Vera replied sadly. 'Breast cancer got her in the end. She was a lovely girl, Liz. Jack couldn't bear to be without her, so he ran off, nobody knew where he'd gone or why. Certainly not his family or our Fred who was worried sick. But then he turned up right as ninepence. France, would you believe?'

I leaned back in my chair and regarded Mrs Elwood cautiously. Was she sure she had the right end of the stick?

'Don't you look at me like that young lady,' Mrs Elwood snapped. 'You wait 'til you're my age. You think you're so smart now with all your bleedin' faculties, well, I was like you once. I had the pick of the fellas and looks to die for. Then one day I woke up and I saw an old crone staring back at me. You might look at me with pity in your eyes now, but you'll be me one day, and don't you forget it.'

I shrank back in my chair. 'I'm sorry,' I began. 'Truly, I didn't mean any harm.'

Just then Becki reappeared and looked at me in horror, 'Gran, come on, don't be mean to Erin.'

To my horror I saw tears pool at Vera's eyes. 'Sorry darlin', I dunno what came over me. I think I need a lie down now, Becki, I'm ever so tired. Sorry again, love.'

'I'll help you,' Becki said quietly, reaching a hand out to her grandmother to ease her out of the chair.

'Won't be a minute.' She smiled apologetically as she passed me. 'I'll just settle Gran down for a nap. In the meantime, I've scribbled down Jack's address.'

Gratefully I took the notepaper and I checked the address. Maison Retrait, Paris. I took a photo of the paper with my phone as a back-up, and then stuffed the address firmly in my purse. Finally, we were getting somewhere. Jack Harrison had been found and was very much alive.

Twenty

Lydia

In the end I chose a more classic ensemble for the speed dating night, picking out an old navy wrap dress that I knew Harry had loved. Teaming it with a pair of grey ankle boots for a more youthful appearance than heels, I surveyed myself in the mirror feeling oddly anxious. This evening was only supposed to be a bit of fun. I didn't expect to meet anyone and honestly speaking, didn't want to, but this was the first time I had put myself in a position where potential romance was in the air, and in a funny way it felt as though I was cheating on Harry. But then again, I thought, smoothing a crease from my dress, now I knew about Jack's letter I couldn't help feeling as though my marriage to Harry meant I had been cheating on Jack.

I shook my head and flung open the bedroom door. It was all such a muddle and tonight I wanted to forget the past and focus only on the future. Clattering down the stairs, I found Erin in the kitchen drinking what looked like a fishbowl of red wine.

'Dutch courage?' I asked, raising an eyebrow.

Erin shot me a weary smile. 'Something like that. It's been a long day.'

'Rachel work you hard?' I asked, helping myself to a glass from the cupboard and pouring a generous measure of Malbec straight into it.

'Mmm.' Erin gave a non-committal shrug, taking another slug of her drink.

Taking a deep gulp from my own glass I looked across at Erin. She was staring at something on her phone. I wanted to ask her what was so important but she looked as if she might bite my head off so I held my tongue.

'Looking forward to tonight?' I tried again, taking a seat opposite her at the table.

Erin put the phone down and rolled her eyes. 'I think "looking forward to" is a strong term Lydia, but I've made up my mind to make the best of it, if that's what you mean.'

'It's a start,' I chuckled, 'and I'm pleased to see you've made an effort. You look lovely.'

Self-consciously, she looked down at herself as if seeing her outfit for the first time. She was only wearing jeans and a blouse, but the blouse was a vivid emerald green that skimmed her curves and complemented her hair so beautifully, she looked utterly gorgeous.

'It was the first thing I found,' she said ruefully. 'I only got back twenty minutes ago.'

'Well, you've scrubbed up well,' I teased.

'Thank you,' she replied. 'You look lovely as well. I love that dress.'

I gave a mock swish of my hair. I'd had it cut into a bob earlier on and was still getting used to a cold neck. 'This old thing?' I said in a fake American accent. 'Hopefully I won't send all those suitors running for the hills.'

Erin narrowed her eyes and looked at me crossly. 'Don't say things like that. You're a fabulous looking woman and any man would quite frankly be lucky to have a date with you. Don't put yourself down like that, Lydia, there's plenty of life in you yet.'

I set my wine glass down in surprise. This was the most animated I had seen Erin in days. I was about to ask if she was all right when I saw her glance at the clock.

'Shall we go? It's gone half seven and I don't want to get on Ginger's bad side.'

'*Nobody* wants to get on Ginger's bad side,' I agreed, getting to my feet.

We made our way out into the cool evening air and began our walk into town. The pub that was the venue for tonight's speed dating event wasn't far away. In fact, nowhere was far away thanks to the Circus's closeness to the city centre, which was another reason I'd never bothered to learn to drive. I glanced across at Erin. She still looked deep in thought. I pursed my lips; whatever this was, it stopped right now.

'Right, that's it. Out with it,' I demanded stopping in the middle of the road.

Erin whirled around in surprise. 'What do you mean?'

'I mean you've got a face like a smacked arse, as my father candidly used to say. Whatever is wrong?'

'I had a message from Cara today,' she said in a quiet voice. 'She wants to talk to me, but I can't face the idea of talking to her.'

'Cheeky madam. Hasn't she caused enough damage?' I growled. 'And is that what's really on your mind?'

Erin's cheeks flushed red. 'Yes, why do you ask?'

'No reason.' I shrugged. 'I just wasn't expecting you to come out with it so easily.'

'Oh.'

'So I take it you've ignored her?'

'Yes, but I can't stop thinking about what she wants.'

'It doesn't matter what she wants,' I pointed out. 'She can tell you she's about to marry Prince Charles and become Queen of England, it has no bearing on your life because she isn't in it any more.'

There was a pause then as Erin seemed to think through what I'd said. 'And what about if she doesn't feel the same way? What if Cara keeps on at me? She can be relentless sometimes.'

'Well, it seems simple enough to me,' I said. 'Why don't you just block her number? And Brad's too for that matter. There's no reason you ever have to hear from them again if you don't want to. They don't know where you live or work now, and I'm fairly confident from what I know of Rachel that if they try to ask her for details she'll tell them where to go.'

'I can't do that!' Erin gasped, before the tiniest bit of doubt passed across her face. 'Can I?'

'Of course you can!' I said crossly. 'They have stolen enough of your life, Erin, do not let them take any more. Now is that it?'

Erin nodded, clearly thunderstruck at either my outburst or the fact I knew about blocking numbers on mobiles.

'So let's go then,' I said more gently this time as I linked my arm through hers. 'There's no reason for those terrible people to bother you any more.'

With that, Erin flashed me the first genuine smile of the evening and together we carried on down the hill towards the pub where destiny awaited.

An hour later, the wine was flowing and I sat at a table waiting to see what the evening held. The moment we arrived, we were handed a glass of lukewarm prosecco and told by the bar staff that were running the event we would have two minutes with each man before a bell rang, indicating they were to be sent on their way. Then we were handed a sheet of paper, told to make a note of anyone we liked and at the end if any of the men we liked had also ticked our box, so to speak, we would be paired up.

The room was divided into three tables: twenty to thirty, thirty to fifty and fifty and over. I was delighted to see that I wouldn't be faced with the indignity of having to chat up a child in their twenties and so took my place next to a woman in her fifties who looked frankly terrified.

I smiled at her, trying to put her at ease and then glanced across the room at Erin. She seemed to have calmed down since her revelation about Cara and was now happily chatting to another woman her own age at the twenty to thirty table. I tried to catch her eye but all too soon a large gong sounded and then what seemed like a horde of men appeared from a door behind Ginger.

It was hard not to stare and make judgements as they all filed into the room like cats flocking to an open tin of tuna.

Some were fat, some were thin, some clearly hadn't made an effort with ripped jeans and too much aftershave. And then there were the ones that looked as if they were about to be hanged, drawn and quartered. I watched as they all sat at their appropriate tables, and looked expectantly at a well-dressed man in his sixties who came to sit opposite me. Tall with a full head of hair and what appeared to be all his own teeth judging from the smile he flashed me as he sat down, I smiled in what I hoped was a welcoming fashion.

'Lydia,' I began, extending my hand out for him to shake.

'Marcus Reiss,' he said, ignoring my offer of a hand to shake and instead kissing the back of it. 'I'm in property development and about to retire with several million in the bank. I've just bought a yacht I've christened *King of the Sea*, been married twice before but now looking for love or something that passes for it.'

As he paused, I realised this was my opportunity to speak. 'Well, I'm Lydia,' I began cautiously. 'I'm an antiques dealer and my husband of over fifty years passed away recently—'

'Very sorry to hear that,' he said cutting across me. 'But Lydia we only have two minutes and what I really want to tell you is I think you've got the most fantastic body.'

I blinked in surprise. 'Er, thank you.'

Marcus leaned across the table earnestly as I took a sip of wine. 'I mean it. The moment I saw you, my first thought was, Mummy stop it!'

'What?' I spluttered almost spitting my wine out.

Mistaking my surprise for gratitude, Marcus ploughed on. 'I love an older woman and I have to say, you really do it for me, Lydia. Seriously, I mean, phwoar!'

I set my wine glass down and glared at him. I might be old but I wasn't stupid. 'If you're here to mock me for being older than most of the young things at this event then can I suggest we cut short our two-minute date and settle for thirty seconds instead?'

A flicker of alarm passed across Marcus's face as he leaned back in his chair and raised his hands in horror. 'No, Lydia, you've got me all wrong. I'm not here to mock anyone. I really like you, you've got a certain Mary Berry quality about you.'

I'd heard enough. Who the hell did this man think he was? Not only was he rude and disrespectful, but he seemed to have me down as some sort of cougar. I wouldn't mind but on closer inspection he obviously dyed his hair and wore make-up – badly applied, I might add. It seemed he was a similar age to myself.

'Well?' Marcus asked hopefully, mistaking my silence once more as serious consideration. 'Why don't we just take off? I've a room booked at the Hilton. You could come back with me. If you're hungry, I'm sure I've got something that would tickle your fondant fancy, eh, Mary? What do you say?'

The sight of his hopeful little arrogant face sent me into a white-hot fury. Before I could change my mind, I got to my feet and threw what remained of my prosecco straight into his cretinous face. 'You're a disgrace,' I shouted. 'I'd describe you as a pervert but I think that's doing perverts a disservice.'

With wine dripping from his forehead, Marcus looked at me in astonishment just as the gong rang, signalling him to move on. Never had the phrase saved by the bell been more appropriate. As I watched him slink off to the bathroom all the while shouting blue murder, I sighed, thinking how right Erin had been about this entire evening – disaster barely covered it.

Twenty-One

Erin

My mouth fell open as I watched Lydia get to her feet and throw a glass of wine in the face of her two-minute date. Wide-eyed, I turned to Ginger who I was fully expecting to storm over and make a fuss but to my surprise instead of losing her temper, she quickly rang the bell signalling our dates were over, then accosted a barman to get a refill for Lydia.

As Lydia's date walked away swearing like a sailor, I excused myself from the spotty looking lad opposite me that was blatantly under age and joined Lydia at her table.

Her cheeks were as red as pokers and from the muscle twitching in her left jaw I could tell she was just as fiery inside. 'You all right?' I asked cautiously.

'Fine,' she replied tightly.

'Fancy some fresh air?'

'What a wonderful idea,' she breathed.

Together we took our drinks out to the pub garden and sat at one of the tables near the road. Despite the balmy temperatures of earlier, the evening had now turned chilly and so we huddled under the patio heater clutching our drinks.

'So what was all that about then?' I asked when I saw Lydia's face return to a more normal shade.

'He was very rude,' she growled. 'If I'd have been closer I would have kicked him in his meringues.'

'What are you talking about?' I asked, baffled, but Lydia said nothing.

I leaned back in the wooden chair and looked at Lydia, feeling concerned. On my way home my thoughts had been full of Jack and Lydia. I was delighted to at last have found an address for him and had planned on telling Lydia all about it after our speed dating evening. Only looking at her now, I wondered whether I ought to say something, after all. There was something about her behaviour that worried me. She was continually changing, wanting to take risks that seemed far too sudden. The moment I got home I found that not only had she had her hair cut into a very flattering bob, but she had found a driving instructor and planned on learning to drive within the next few days. It was all just a bit too much. I mean, I was all for improving yourself and your life but it seemed like Lydia was rushing into things. I half wondered about talking to Luke about it – but with him so far away I didn't want to worry him, especially with a baby due in a few months. Now, as I witnessed another swift change in mood I wondered if it wasn't better to keep this latest development to myself, at least for the moment.

The sound of a glass shattering to the floor behind us dragged me from my thoughts and I turned back to my friend. 'So do you feel like going back inside and checking out the rest of the men?'

Lydia made a face. 'No, thank you, Erin. Once bitten, twice shy.'

'That bad, eh?'

'I have never been so insulted in all my life!' Lydia said in a low voice, the amber light from the patio heater giving her eyes a furious glow. 'That man suggested doing unspeakable things with fondant fancies, Erin. I'm sorry, you were right, speed dating isn't for me at all.'

If the look on her face wasn't so incredibly sad, I would have burst out laughing. 'Look,' I began, keeping my tone gentle, 'speed dating is pretty horrible for most people. In a way you got lucky.'

Lydia looked at me as if I had lost my mind. 'How on earth do you work that out?'

I sipped my fizz and wondered how best to phrase it. 'Well, at least you got the nutter out of the way early so you didn't waste your whole evening. Otherwise you'd have sat through a long line of boring, sexist, creepy dates before getting to the mentalist. This way, you can reclaim some of your night back.'

'I'll drink to that.' She grinned, holding her glass to mine.

As I clinked glasses with her, I took another sip and looked up at the sky. There was a full moon and the stars were out in force, illuminating the creamy stone buildings so they looked almost ethereal.

'So didn't you meet anyone nice then?' Lydia asked.

'Nah.' I shook my head as I met her gaze. 'These things aren't for me either. It's always seemed a very unnatural way to meet someone and you know what, Lydia, I don't even want to. I just want to be on my own for a while. Lick my wounds and recover in peace.'

Lydia leaned over and clasped my hand. 'I'm sorry. I shouldn't have organised something like this without talking to you first. I thought it would be a bit of fun, something we could giggle over. Something to mark off the bucket list.'

'Don't be daft,' I said firmly. 'There's nothing to be sorry about. It was a bit of fun. I mean the way you threw that drink in that man's face was definitely something I'd want to tick off my bucket list.'

Lydia shuddered. 'Vile little man. I hope he never gets his meringues into firm peaks.'

'I'm not even going to ask,' I muttered, taking another sip of wine. 'So is that what the driving lessons are about then? Something else to tick off the bucket list?'

'No, this is something I want to do for me,' she said firmly.

'Okay,' I replied slowly. 'So who is this driving instructor?'

'Tracey.' She grinned, the joy in her voice audible. 'She says she would be more than happy to take me on, that she thinks anyone of any age can drive as long as they're patient and committed.'

I nodded, thinking she sounded very sensible. 'When do you start?'

'Next week,' Lydia sighed. 'I wanted to learn in the E-Type but Tracey says that unless that car has dual controls, whatever that is, she'll teach me in her Fiesta.'

'I think that's a good idea,' I replied. 'You'll feel a lot safer that way.'

'Thanks for your support. I was a bit worried you would think it yet another mad scheme. I do know I'm making a lot of changes and I suppose they must all seem a bit odd. The thing is, Erin, since you've been living with me, I feel young again. You're making me realise anything is possible and I don't want to miss out.'

I burst out laughing. 'Don't look at me for inspiration, my life's one big mess.'

'Don't you dare criticise yourself like that,' she said crossly. 'That's my friend you're talking about.'

At the mention of the word friend, I felt something tug at my heart. In these past few weeks we had become a lot more than landlady and lodger – we had moved onto friendship, and it was wonderful, chaotic and, above all else, fun. I gulped another mouthful of prosecco and eyed Lydia thoughtfully. If we were friends, I didn't want to keep secrets from her any more – she deserved better than that.

'Lydia, I've got something to tell you,' I began boldly.

She said nothing as she gazed dreamily into the distance.

'Lydia, did you hear me?' I asked, trying again over the loud chatter of other drinkers.

'Yes of course I heard you,' she said sharply. 'I was waiting for you to get on with it.'

'Oh,' I said, feeling a little wrong-footed. 'Well, there's no easy way to say this, but, well, I think I've found Jack.'

Her head almost did an *Exorcist* style turn as her eyes swivelled to meet mine. 'What?'

'I think I've found Jack,' I said, my voice unsteady. 'I didn't help Rachel today, I lied. I'm sorry. Instead I went to London, Islington to be precise, and met a lady who is still in touch with him. Vera Elwood.'

'It doesn't ring any bells,' Lydia replied sharply. 'Where did you find this woman?'

'Though a community group on Facebook.' I explained. 'She says she was a neighbour of yours and Jack's. He was best friends with her brother Freddie.'

'Not Vera Burnley?' Lydia gasped. 'You met Vera? I thought she was dead.'

'Still very much alive, and now named Vera Elwood' I confirmed. 'Remembers you and Jack as if it were yesterday. But of course, she didn't have an address for you.'

'Nobody did, it seemed.' Lydia replied sadly. 'How was she?'

'Fine,' I murmured, deciding to leave out the part about her having Alzheimer's for now. 'Though Freddie died last year.'

'Poor Freddie,' she said sadly. 'Always such a kind man. He and Jack were thick as thieves.'

'Well, Jack not only came for the funeral but also wrote to Vera last week,' I explained. 'I've got an address for him, I thought you might like to write.'

I handed over the carefully folded piece of paper I had been carrying in my purse all day. Just the simple act of passing it onto the right person felt like a massive burden had been lifted from my shoulders. As Lydia unfolded the note, she read the words on the sheet and then looked at me doubtfully.

'Paris?' she asked. 'Are you sure?'

I nodded. 'Quite sure. Vera says Jack has been living there for a few years now. He apparently started a new life for himself after his wife died.'

'He was married?' Lydia gasped.

'As were you,' I pointed out gently. 'He could only wait so long.'

She clutched the piece of paper to her chest and I was alarmed to see tears stream down her cheeks like rivers. I quickly moved beside her and wrapped an arm around her shoulders, wanting to hold and comfort her as if she were no more than a child.

'Are you all right? I was so worried about telling you, and I can see I shouldn't have. All this is just a bit too much to deal with isn't it? Especially on top of meringue man.'

At that Lydia laughed, and pulled away from my embrace.

'Don't be silly,' she sniffed. I watched her pull out a neatly ironed hankie from her handbag and smiled. Despite all the changes Lydia had been making in her life, it was good to see some things remained the same.

'Is that why you didn't tell me you were going to London today? Because you thought I'd be upset?' she asked eventually.

'I wasn't sure,' I said truthfully. 'I didn't even know if Vera was genuine. The last thing I wanted to do was get your hopes up if it turned out to be someone winding us up.'

Lydia patted my hand. 'Very thoughtful, dear, but I'm not upset, I'm excited. It looks as though after all these years I'm going to be reunited with Jack, and, Erin my darling, it's all down to you.'

Twenty-Two

Lydia

Saturday morning, Erin and I had got up with the lark once more for our second antiques fair, this time in Swindon. After the disastrous speed dating evening a few days earlier, it felt good to get back to normality and forget the whole thing. The incident with the meringue man, as I had started to think of him, had left me shaken. I had never courted anyone in this modern era and frankly I never wanted to again if that's what men were like in the twenty-first century. Where were the manners? The chivalry? The old-fashioned romance? All gone, like the snap in some of these youngsters' knicker elastics.

I could well understand why Erin didn't want to date anyone else in the future. In fact, if I were her, I'd probably resign myself to being single for the rest of my life. But then with a pang I thought of Luke. They weren't all bad, in fact some of them were downright good. I pulled my new phone from the pocket of my mac and checked the calendar – 18th of May. In just four months' time their baby would be here, and

I would be a grandma! Just the thought of a new life coming into the world after so much heartache made me feel joyful, as did the revelation Erin had found an address for Jack.

If I was honest, after so many false starts, I didn't think it would be possible to find him. I'd assumed that he, like Harry, might have died. I should have thought of Vera when we began to trace him. She was always a right old busybody, even when we were kids. Couldn't keep her nose out of anyone else's business. I remember how she had caught me and Jack canoodling, I suppose you'd call it, behind the pub at the end of our street. With her big round face and eyes filled with glee, you would have thought she was ogling a peep show not a pair of teenagers, young and in love. At the memory I felt a shiver. I could remember these strong, masculine arms wrapped around my waist pulling me so close I could feel the beat of his heart thrum against mine.

The sight of a customer smiling brightly at me while she held up a blue and white china vase brought me swiftly back to the present. As I deftly wrapped her antique and encouraged her to call again, I tried to push the memory of the last time I had seen Jack from my mind. It seemed as if it were just yesterday I had waved him off at the train station, doing my best not to shed a single tear.

'I'll write to you every day,' Jack had promised, squeezing my hands tightly.

'And I you,' I had said desperately. 'This won't change anything, Jack, we'll still talk to each other all the time, it will just be by letter that's all.'

'Course it will, my love,' Jack had said, his tone fierce and determined. 'You and me together forever, that's all that matters.'

'That's all that matters,' I'd echoed, unable to keep the tears at bay.

As they fell like rivers down my face I had allowed my gaze to roam across his, desperate to commit every one of his features to memory. The cleft at the end of his nose, the mole on his upper right cheek and the frown line that always appeared in the middle of his eyebrows when he was concentrating. I didn't want him to go, the pain of it too brutal.

Seemingly Jack had understood and as his eyes locked onto mine, he'd gripped my hands even tighter then bent down and whispered in my ear, 'You're the love of my life, Lydia, it has and always will be you.'

With that the whistle for the train had blown and Jack had left without a backwards glance leaving me feeling bereft.

Now, I shook my head to return to the present and shoved my hands in my pockets to keep out the morning chill. What a silly little fool I had been. Of course I wouldn't write every day, and neither would Jack, I thought crossly. We had been young, just as Jack had been when he wrote that letter to me just before I got married all those years ago.

With a start, I wondered if he had ever thought about that letter and if he did, had he dismissed writing it as the action of a silly child? After all that was what we had been really when all was said and done. What if he had never really loved me? What if he was grateful I had never replied? After all, he had married – what if he really did find his soul mate and I was nothing more than a teenage distraction? Then again, what if he had always loved me and never forgave me for marrying someone else and ignoring his letter? We had made promises to each other; what if he hadn't dismissed them? I never had.

'What on earth's the matter with you?' Erin asked, appearing behind me with a cup of tea in each hand.

I took the paper cup gratefully. 'Just thinking.'

'Well, don't make a habit of it,' Erin laughed, perching on the edge of the trestle table. 'The look of horror on your face will frighten all our customers away.'

Sticking my tongue out at Erin, I sipped my tea. 'I'll have you know I've made three sales already while you were queuing for the drinks.'

Erin had the good grace to look impressed. 'You've got the magic touch. Though I did think we'd be busier today.'

'It's early yet.' I shrugged, looking at the few people roaming the field filled with stalls. 'We might be out of bed at this hour, but not everyone else is.'

'I suppose so,' she sighed, looking dejected.

I wanted to laugh. The look on Erin's face resembled Harry Enfield's Kevin the Teenage character I used to enjoy watching on TV in the nineties. 'While we're quiet, why don't we start writing a letter to Jack?'

'Now?'

'Why not? I don't want to waste any more time, Erin,' I said decisively. 'I need to know the truth about that letter.'

'I don't have my iPad or laptop,' she protested.

'Oh my God! However will we manage?' I gasped theatrically. 'Oooh, I know, we could try using this very modern invention called a pen and paper, not sure if you've heard of it, but what you do—'

Erin held her hand up to stop me, 'Yeah, all right, Lydia, I get the message. You know, sarcasm is the lowest form of wit?'

'But the highest form of intelligence,' I fired back, delving under the petty cash box for the notepad and pen I always carried with me. 'Now enough of this chatter, how do you think we should start?'

'How should I know?' Erin replied, clearly still smarting. 'You're the one with all the intelligence, you figure it out.'

This time I couldn't help it and roared with laughter. With her bottom lip stuck out and her head bent moodily over her slender frame she looked even more like Kevin. Yet catching the look of anger that quickly passed across her features, I wiped the smirk off my face.

'Sorry,' I said. 'I was being silly.'

Erin glowered at me as she took the pad and paper from my hands. Setting her cup down, she took the lid from the biro and began to write.

'What are you putting?' I asked, my voice rising an octave in panic. 'Don't just write anything, this needs to be right.'

Erin shot me a look that would sour milk. 'Lydia, would you just relax please? So far all I've put is your address, today's date and the hallowed words, *Dear Jack*.'

'Oh, all right.' I replied mollified. 'What do you think we should put next?'

'Erm, how are you?' Erin replied.

I made a face. 'That sounds like I just saw him last week. You can't start a letter to someone you haven't seen in over fifty years with that. It needs to be more heartfelt.'

We fell into a silence then as we mulled over what to put next. I realised I hadn't actually given much thought to what I'd say to Jack if or when we found him. The simple act of tracking him down seemed monumental enough, never mind what to say. I mean, what was the perfect way to say, hi there, sorry for such a delayed response, your letter arrived late, about fifty years too late and I'm still reeling from the discovery that you, love of my life as I considered you to be are actually still alive and not dead as I thought?

'Maybe you should just be honest,' Erin suggested, breaking the silence.

'How do you mean?'

'Tell him the truth about what happened,' she said. 'Sometimes there's nothing like the truth.'

I took another gulp of tea, the morning chill still biting through to my bones before feeling sudden overwhelmed. 'There's so much to say I don't know where to start,' I wailed. 'This letter will come as a complete shock anyway, I don't want to give him a heart attack.'

'No, good point.' Erin nibbled on the end of the pen. 'How about we leave it for now? We could just brainstorm instead.'

'Oh, you mean scribble down ideas as they come to me?' I asked, already liking the sound of that.

'Exactly.' Erin smiled. 'You can't expect to just dash something of this magnitude off in a heartbeat.'

'True,' I replied, just as my phone buzzed with a tone that I knew indicated a message.

I pulled it out of my pocket and looked at in alarm. It was another Facebook message from Erin's mother. I felt a wave of guilt crash over me. I still hadn't arranged a time to meet Rosie – I'd put the issue on pause. I hated keeping secrets from Erin, especially after we'd had such heated discussions lately over betrayal, but something told me this secret was for the greater good. If I could just hold my nerve, there was every chance I could reunite Erin with her family and all this guilt would be worth it. Still, I didn't want to take the risk of reading the message in front of Erin.

'Do you mind going to get us another cup of tea?' I asked, quickly draining my cup. 'I would go myself, but I'm expecting another trader who's interested in some of those walking sticks to pop by at any moment and I don't want to miss him.'

Erin looked at me suspiciously for a moment before responding. 'All right. Just a tea?

'Perhaps a teacake too if they have it,' I called. 'I'm getting a bit peckish.'

I waited until Erin had walked a few metres away before I risked taking the phone out of my pocket. Clicking onto the message, I was all set to read Rosie's latest message, when I heard the sound of a man clearing his throat.

Glancing up, I saw a tall older man with a pretty short blonde standing next to him.

'Is this the Simon and Garfunkel Antiques Brigade stall?' he asked in plummy tones.

I nodded. 'How can I help you?'

'It's actually Erin we're here to see,' the girl next to him piped up. 'We've been trying to find her and saw from your Facebook post that she would be at the fair here today.'

I glanced from him to her, suddenly recognising them both. With her cheap smile and his sleazy gaze, the penny dropped. This was no ordinary couple; this was that bastard Brad and trumped-up little floozy Cara. For some reason my eyes were drawn to her hands, and it was then I caught sight of the rather vulgar diamond adorning the ring finger of her left hand.

I choked back the fury rising inside of me. Something told me why Cara had been trying to get hold of Erin so desperately, and I knew this would definitely be something she didn't need or want to hear.

Twenty-Three

Erin

The queue for tea and coffee was long, but to be honest I was so desperate for caffeine I'd have crawled on my hands and knees for a flat white that morning. Since I'd told Lydia about Jack, I'd been desperately trying to think of the right way to approach him. I'd thought of getting back in touch with Becki to ask if Jack was on Facebook, but social media seemed too impersonal an approach.

I shuffled further forwards in the queue. I'd hoped that Lydia would know just what to say but she didn't have a clue either, which only made the problem seem bigger somehow.

Giving my order to the guy behind the counter, I pulled out my phone and idly scrolled through the screen as I waited for the drinks. Was a phone call a better way to approach it? Or would it be better for Vera to say something in a letter to Jack? Becki had offered to contact him on Lydia's behalf but I had said I didn't think that it was a very good idea and it would be better coming direct from her. Now, as

I took the cups and handed the guy a fiver for his trouble, I began to wonder if a more personal approach might be better. I mean, this was big news, a letter didn't seem to do the whole thing justice.

Deep in thought, I made my way back to our stall and tried to turn my attention to the day ahead. We had another good haul of stock and while I had been working at Phil's café all week, Lydia had been labelling, cleaning and sorting. She said that she had found more treasures amongst the things Harry had been hoarding and she even found a beautiful bright red vase that was incredibly rare and worth at least £5,000.

I had to admit the stall had far exceeded my expectations. We had been getting a lot of interest on social media, especially since our first event in Bridgwater a fortnight ago. Our Facebook page was inundated with queries from people wanting to know where we would be next and what sort of things we would have on offer. Lydia's passion for Asian art was clearly popular and even though she was beginning to get a bit forgetful there was no denying she was good with the customers and the business.

Watching her now as she chattered away with a couple of customers who had their back to me, I felt a thrill of excitement. Lydia was so animated and full of life – she seemed like a woman half her age. Watching Lydia talk about the antiques she loved was a pleasure in itself and I learned something new every time. It had been a revelation to me for example to discover that for an antique to be classed as an antique it needed to be at least a hundred years old. Lydia had suggested we go to an auction house soon to build up my knowledge which I was looking forward to immensely.

Nearing the stall however, I felt my blood run cold as I realised I recognised the customers Lydia was talking to.

'How many more times have I got to tell the pair of you?' she said furiously. 'Get out of here now before I call the police.'

'The police? For what?' I heard Brad's voice scoff.

As I caught the slight upward lilt of his Cheltenham accent, I felt like I had come home and I could have kicked myself for being so stupid. The guy had shown he was a dick, a lying cheating dick at that, so why couldn't my heart catch onto what my brain had been telling me for weeks?

Fuelled with anger, I watched Lydia lean forwards menacingly and poke Brad in the chest, 'For threatening an old defenceless woman, that's what.'

'You don't look defenceless to me,' Brad scorned. 'Now please, for the final time, where is Erin?'

'Right here,' I replied loudly with a braveness that I didn't feel. 'And I'd be very grateful if you'd leave my friend alone or it'll be me that calls the police for harassment.'

Immediately, Brad and Cara whirled around to face me and I felt my stomach lurch onto the spin cycle once more. They exchanged a brief glance, then turned to me and smiled as if in sync. It was nauseating and as my gaze flickered from one to the other, I saw neither one of them looked battered or torn at the events of the past few weeks. Instead, they appeared happy and content. The perpetual worry lines that adorned Brad's forehead had disappeared and Cara's hair looked even glossier than usual if that were possible. They were like some sort of walking, talking model couple you would find in *Vogue* magazine and I hated them both for it.

'What do you want?' I managed eventually. 'Swindon's not exactly on your doorstep, is it?'

Brad let go of Cara's hand and took a step towards me. 'Erin, it's wonderful to see you.'

As he leaned forwards to kiss my cheek, I moved my head back and regarded him coldly. 'I can't say the same. And for the record, I don't think we're at the air-kissing stage yet, do you?'

Brad had the good grace to look contrite. 'Sorry. But it is good to see you Erin, I, well, we have really missed you.'

Right on cue, Cara gambolled like a lamb to his side and fixed her radiant smile on me. 'Brad's right, Erin,' she said, her voice oozing false concern. 'We've been trying so hard to get in touch with you. I've phoned you loads but you didn't return any of my calls.'

'Which ought to tell you that she's not remotely interested in anything you have to say,' Lydia snapped.

I looked over at her behind the stall. Lydia was quite clearly furious. Her arms were folded and her face was as red as the vase that had pride of place in the middle of our trestle table.

'Lydia's right,' I said, pushing passed the happy couple and making my way around to the other side of the table to stand beside my friend. 'Now if you don't mind, we've got work to do, so leave.'

'You don't understand,' Brad said tightly, his jaw clenched.

I immediately recognised the signs. This was the face he made before he lost his temper, when things weren't going his way. How strange, I suddenly thought, that I knew this man standing before me so well, yet he was also a complete stranger to me now.

'Erin, we won't stay long. But we wanted you to hear it from us,' Cara said firmly. 'I know you won't like it, but the thing is, well—'

'We're getting married,' Brad said abruptly.

My jaw dropped open and I stared at them in disbelief as images of our lives, interwoven throughout the years, flooded my brain. Memories of me and Cara playing on the swings, Brad and I taking our first mini-break together in Nice and him ordering champagne on the flight. How was it possible that I could have experienced such happiness with these two people when they were now standing before me, responsible for the fact I was in so much pain? I had thought that finding them in bed together would be the worst thing in the world, but as I stood there and caught sight of the sparkler on Erin's ring finger, I felt as if I was falling.

I willed myself to say something, anything would do, but I couldn't find the right thing to say. I felt myself mentally scrambling for something appropriate, but nothing would come. In fact, the only thing I thought was that I hoped they'd rot in hell.

'I think you're mistaking me for someone who cares,' I managed, as I remembered I was still holding onto Lydia's tea and handed it to her.

'Erin, don't be like that,' Cara tried again, her eyes flecked with hurt. 'We haven't come here to torture you. We've come here because we respect you.'

'You call sleeping with your best friend's fiancé respect?' Lydia snorted. 'Christ almighty, if I were Erin, I think I'd prefer it if you didn't respect me.'

Brad eyed Lydia coldly before turning back to me, his expression softening. 'Is there somewhere we could all go to chat? In private?'

'I think you've said all that needs to be said,' I snapped. 'Now go.'

'But Erin,' Cara said hesitantly, 'there's something else.'

My head was beginning to spin with the shock of it all. I didn't want them here any more. The pain of seeing them together again was bad enough, never mind having to keep it together while I was at work with my new friend, trying to carve out my new life.

I looked at Cara intently, urging her to recognise the look in my eyes that said the matter was closed. 'There is nothing else I have to say to you,' I said firmly. 'And there is really nothing else you can say to me that I want to hear. Now please, if you say you respect me then you'll leave.'

At that they turned away and I allowed myself the luxury of a sigh of relief at the very welcome view of their retreating backs. Finally, I could pick up the pieces in private.

Only then Brad seemed to change his mind as he said something to Cara and turned back towards the stall.

'What is he doing?' I wailed to Lydia.

'Trying my bloody patience,' she said through gritted teeth.

'What now?' Lydia demanded as her stood before the stall. 'You're putting the customers off with all this to-ing and fro-ing.

'There's just one more thing we came here to tell Erin.' Brad said, his tone insistent.

He's got his business head on I thought, as I narrowed my eyes and stared at him. Whatever it was he wanted, he was going to get it no matter what. Brad had always been ruthless; whatever he wanted, he got. With a start I realised the pair of them were made for each other as Cara never took no for an answer either. I watched them now, his eyes mildly hesitant before Cara gave him a gentle nod of encouragement.

'The thing is Erin, not only are we getting married, Cara is also pregnant,' he said bluntly. 'We're expecting a baby. That's the other thing we wanted you to know, we're going to be a family.'

As the happy couple delivered their final blow, I wasn't sure if I was going to throw up or faint. This time there really were no words. How could this be right? How could my ex-best friend and ex-fiancé cheat on me, then suddenly find all this happiness overnight? This wasn't justice! Surely there ought to be some payback? Surely they didn't get to be *this* happy, that was the last thing they deserved.

Suddenly I felt Lydia's arms around me, and the strength that had left me the moment I saw them returned.

'Did you hear me Erin?' Brad tried again, his voice impatient now, as I didn't give him the nod of approval his voice usually commanded.

I looked at him, staring at me expectantly as if he were waiting for the very words to come out of my mouth that would make this horrible thing okay. I knew the real reason they had come here, and it had nothing to do with respect and everything to do with guilt. Cara had always said that she would want to make sure that everything in her world was perfect before she had a baby. I knew that the way she met Brad and the fact she had lost my friendship over it was about as far from perfect as it could get for Cara. Now she would be in salvage mode.

The fury I had been holding onto since I saw them was now at boiling point. It just wasn't possible to even try to think of the right thing to say so instead I roared with laughter. This whole situation was so beyond ludicrous I felt as if I were in an episode of *Hollyoaks* or something.

'Erin, are you all right?' Cara asked, her eyes narrowed in confusion.

The sight of her looking at me with fake concern brought me swiftly back to reality.

'Oh, Cara,' I said, controlling my laughter. 'I'm absolutely fine. Congratulations to you both.'

Brad and Cara exchanged brief looks of doubt before turning back to face me. 'Are you sure, Erin?' Brad said gently.

'Oh yes,' I smirked, arms folded. 'Because when karma comes knocking at your door she'll be a bigger bitch than I'll ever need to be.'

Twenty-Four

Lydia

'Is that all you've got to say?' I asked Erin, a little surprised.

'My question exactly!' Brad snapped. 'That's not very nice, Erin.'

I looked at him with utter contempt. 'Shut up, you bloody fool.'

'Are you all right?' I whispered to Erin, who seemed fairly calm.

'I'm fine.' She shrugged. 'I just wish these two would sod off so we could get back to doing what we came here to do.'

'You heard her,' I said, turning to Cara and Brad who looked as if they had no intention of leaving. 'I think you've said enough; now bugger off and leave her alone, once and for all!'

Brad ignored me and glared at Erin. 'I can understand why you may not want to congratulate me, but Erin, Cara has been your best friend since childhood.'

'And it's for that reason alone I haven't slapped her, Brad,' Erin said coldly. 'That and the fact I'm busy today and don't have time to wipe slut off my hand.'

'Now that's enough,' Brad snarled, leaning forward menacingly over our stall.

'You're damn right it's enough,' I said. 'What were you expecting from Erin? For her to lay out the bunting and throw you a party? It's a bloody wonder she hasn't flung something at you – if it were me you wouldn't have been so lucky. Now go before I call the police and have you arrested for harassment.'

Cara tugged at Brad's sleeve. 'They're right,' she said, her tone calm, much to my surprise. 'Come on, we've said what needed to be said, let's go now.'

It was clearly not the answer Brad wanted to hear as he opened his mouth to protest. 'But—'

'But nothing,' Cara said firmly as she led him away.

I watched in astonishment as he followed after her like an obedient dog, while Cara turned to Erin and mouthed what appeared to be a genuine sorry.

I had to admit the action surprised me. From everything I knew about Cara and had witnessed so far, I thought she was a selfish little madam with only her own interests at heart. Watching her now, head bent low as she soaked up Brad's anger, I wondered if there was a bit more to her than I had first thought. Glancing back at Erin, I was pleased to see she still seemed calm.

'Wherever did you pick up all those one-liners?' I asked in astonishment. 'I've never heard such sauce come out of your mouth!'

Erin smiled weakly, the courage she had shown just moments earlier having seemingly evaporated. 'Sorry.'

I wrapped an arm around her shoulders and pulled her towards me. 'Nothing to be sorry for, my darling. Frankly they're lucky I didn't join in. To accost you here, at your place of work, with news like that is nothing sort of disgusting.'

'I feel sick,' Erin moaned.

I ignored the curious stares of passers-by and continued to hold her to me. 'Do not let this derail you, dear. You have worked so hard to get over their betrayal, do not let them set you back. You are worth so much more than they ever will be.'

My shoulder was now wet with tears and my heart went out to Erin. She didn't deserve any of this.

'I know, you're right,' Erin said through her sobs. 'This was just the last thing I expected. I feel as though I've been kicked in the stomach.'

'Do you want to go home?' I asked kindly.

She pulled away from me and fixed me with a determined gaze. 'Not a chance. That pair have already destroyed enough of my life, they're not taking this day away from me as well.'

A flash of pride surged through me. Erin was made of tough stuff. 'If you're sure?'

'I'm sure.' She nodded. 'Now how about I go and get a fresh round of tea? I don't know about you but I think mine's cold now.'

I smiled. 'That would be lovely dear, thank you.'

Watching her retreating back, I picked up my phone once more and clicked onto my emails. Scrolling through the endless spam offering me discounts and deals for one day only, I soon found Rosie's message and opened it.

Dear Lydia,

I just wanted to drop you a line to check you had received my last message about meeting up. I don't wish to put pressure on you, but I'm very keen to discuss my daughter and our relationship with you.

I know I don't need to tell you how much I've missed my daughter, Lydia. You're a mother yourself, you know how you think of your children every day, how they fast become your world. Life without Erin has been harder than either Tom or I could have imagined. I would give anything to change the last few years but what's done is done, there's no point crying over the past. We have to move forwards.

There is something that you should know, that I haven't told you before, but Erin's father has recently had a triple heart bypass. It has been an immensely difficult time and because I don't want to upset him further, I haven't told him you and I have been in contact. If we are ever going to reconcile with Erin, this must be done with great caution. That said, I would very much like to meet with you soon if possible.

Yours gratefully,
Rosie

As I finished reading Rosie's message, I felt a flash of sympathy for the woman. Knowing her husband had faced a life-threatening operation would put anything into perspective, and I could well understand her desire to reconnect with her daughter. The question was, what effect would this have on Erin? She had endured enough shocks of late, and I hated to think of the impact this morning's little revelation would have had on her mental health. Hearing her father had been through such extensive surgery and she hadn't been told could possibly widen the gulf between them and that was the last thing I wanted. Quickly, I tapped out a reply. Nobody knew Erin better than her mother and it would be Rosie that would know the best way of reaching her daughter.

Dear Rosie,

Sincere apologies for the delayed response to your message. If I'm honest with you, I had been feeling guilty about getting in touch with you behind Erin's back. She is, after all, a grown woman capable of making her own decisions and the last thing she perhaps needs is a meddling old woman like me getting in her way. However, Erin has endured ever such a lot of late, and now, this news of her father, will I'm sure come as something of a shock. However, I also know how much she longs to make things right with you both. Should we perhaps meet in Bristol next week? I could possibly come over to you one lunchtime on the train? Then we could consider the best way to work things out.

Yours sincerely,
Lydia

Quickly I reread the message and once I was happy with it I pressed send, before I could change my mind. Stuffing my phone back into my pocket, I was alarmed to find Erin standing straight in front of me holding out a cup of tea.

'How long have you been standing there?' I snapped guiltily.

'Just a second or two.' Erin frowned. 'I did try and wave at you from the tea stand to ask if you wanted a Bath bun instead of a teacake, but you didn't seem to see me.'

'Sorry,' I replied, taking the tea from her hands. 'I was just trying to type out a message and you know how hard I have to concentrate on the screen. It's all still a whole new world.'

Erin smiled kindly. 'I know, and you're doing so well. My mum and dad are still in the dark ages, refusing to get a mobile phone.' Her smile slipped then as she caught herself. 'Or at least, they were. I don't know if that's true any more. They may have mobiles, iPads and even smartwatches by now.'

Seeing the look of sadness that passed across her face, I felt even more bolstered by my decision to meet Erin's mother.

'Listen, how about we stay here for a couple of hours, then go and get some lunch? My treat?' I suggested, changing the subject.

Erin visibly brightened. 'Oh, that's a lovely idea. But I think if anyone pays for it, it should be me. Honestly, I feel terrible I spoke like that in front of you, Lydia.'

I waved her offer away. 'Don't be silly. I've already told you once you have nothing to apologise for. It was worth it just to wipe that smug smirk off that snivelling little bastard's face.'

Erin giggled, clearly reliving the moment. 'He was smug, wasn't he?'

'And so was she,' I said tightly. 'I meant what I said earlier by the way. I know it's not easy, but I want you to forget this happened today. Those two are nothing to you any more, it doesn't matter what they're doing with their sorry little lives.'

'But a baby?' Erin moaned, as she stuffed her hands in her pockets. 'Brad and I used to talk about how many babies we were going to have and how Cara would be godmother to all of them.'

I reached out a hand to gently steady her. 'That was in the past. I know that's not easy to hear, but you have to move forwards Erin. And one day, when you find the right man who will be the father of your children, trust me, all this will seem like a distant and dreadful memory. Your happy ending is out there Erin, it just wasn't with Brad.'

'You think so?' Erin asked, the hope evident in her eyes.

'I know so. And do you know how you'll know whether or not he's the right man?'

She shook her head.

'Because he won't cost you your family Erin. That's how you'll know.'

At that, Erin fell silent. It was as if I'd suddenly offered her some piece of wisdom she had never thought of before.

'You're right,' she breathed, her expression softening. 'I'm not going to let those two stop me from living my life. In fact, I'm not letting them stop me do anything.'

'That's my girl.'

'Actually, I had a thought while I was queuing for the drinks.'

I raised an eyebrow. 'Sounds dangerous.'

She laughed. 'It's not, but I thought that perhaps there might be a reason you're struggling to write that letter to Jack.'

'Go on,' I encouraged.

'Well, maybe you're not meant to write to him?' she said.

'Erin, we've been through this,' I began, my tone firm. 'I have to lay this to rest.'

'And I'm not saying you shouldn't,' she said hurriedly. 'I'm just saying a letter isn't perhaps the best way to get in touch. Something like this, well, it's so big, I think you should do it in person. I think you should go to Paris.'

Twenty-Five

Erin

'I'm really not sure about this,' I grumbled, sitting in the back of a silver Ford Fiesta.

'You don't have to be sure,' Lydia snapped from the passenger's seat. 'You just have to sit there and be patient, doesn't she, Tracey?'

As I looked at the instructor's furrowed brow, I felt a pang of sympathy. God knew it couldn't be easy teaching a seventy-eight-year-old to drive and this Tracey must be wondering what on earth she had taken on. With her big blue eyes, open face and easy smile, Tracey appeared to be the dictionary definition of calm, but I couldn't help wondering if she would still look that way after an hour with Lydia.

I looked out of the window at the row of houses beyond me and tried to change my attitude. I hadn't wanted to come on this driving lesson with Lydia, but in the week since Brad and Cara had dropped their bombshell Lydia had insisted I was never left alone for even a minute. If

I wasn't at work she made sure she stayed at home, and when I told her I was going for a walk in the park while she went off to the new book group she had found through Facebook, she rang Rachel to babysit me.

Now, she'd said she wanted me to come with her on her driving lesson, not because she was worried about me, but because she said she would need my help when it came to practising what she was learning. I didn't have the heart to tell her she would need quite a few more lessons before I'd even consider going out in a car with her that didn't have the benefit of dual controls.

'So,' Tracey said brightly as she finished making her final assessments. 'I just need to check your eyesight before we get started. Lydia can you read that number plate on the blue car over by the lamppost please?'

I looked over at the resident Mercedes that lived permanently outside our house as Lydia recited the plate perfectly.

'Wonderful, let's go for a drive.' Tracey beamed as Lydia finished reading.

Lydia clapped her hands together in delight. 'So do I get behind the wheel now?'

Tracey smiled patiently and shook her head. 'Not yet, I thought I'd drive you to a nice quiet road and then we'll talk about the car and go through a cockpit drill.'

Disappointment flashed across Lydia's features. 'But how can I learn to drive if I don't drive? And why are we talking about cockpits? It's not flying lessons I'm after, it's driving lessons!'

Lydia looked at Tracey as though she had lost her marbles, and I felt a surge of frustration. 'Lydia, the driver's area is known as the cockpit and Tracey needs to explain all the controls to you so you know how to operate the car. Did you really think you could just get straight behind the wheel and drive off?'

Lydia flushed with embarrassment. 'Well, Harry always made it look so easy.'

'And it can be easy, with practice,' Tracey said, with a smile.

Over the next twenty minutes or so, as Tracey patiently explained the inner workings of the car, I found myself going over the events of the past few days. There was no way of sugar-coating it. Brad and Cara's announcement still felt like a sucker punch to the gut, something I had mentioned to Rachel when I saw her earlier in the week.

Naturally she had been furious on my behalf when I told her the latest development, though like Lydia she had also appreciated the witty one-liners I had thankfully been able to pull out of somewhere. Yet it did mean that she and Lily had begun Operation Cheer-Up Erin. So as well as coming round for dinner tonight with Phil, they were insisting on taking me out dancing along with lots and lots of drinks later in the week.

Turning my attention back to Lydia, who was still struggling to understand the difference between the clutch pedal and the brake, I wondered if we ought to bring our night out forwards by a couple of days. Something told me I was going to need booze once this lesson was over, and glancing at Tracey's pinking cheeks, I had a feeling I wasn't the only one.'

'No, Lydia, you press the clutch when you want to change gear,' Tracey explained for the umpteenth time.

'So I don't use it instead of the brake?' Lydia asked, still clearly confused.

I leaned forwards and slid my head between the two front seats. 'No, you press the clutch when you want to bring the car to a stop *and* you press the brake then as well.'

Lydia squinted at me in bemusement. 'So why can't I use it instead of the brake?'

'Because that's not how the car works,' I said impatiently.

Tracey turned and shot me a sympathetic smile before turning back to Lydia. 'Why don't we move on and we can come back to that later? There's no hurry and some people take more time to learn things than others.'

'You're not kidding,' I muttered, flinging myself against the backseat.

Ignoring my outburst, Tracey continued to run through the basics of driving with Lydia, who looked more and more confused with every instruction. I hadn't wanted to say I told you so, and honestly, I was proud of the fact that Lydia wanted to try something new, but really, driving lessons at seventy-eight? I was all for living life to the fullest and age being no barrier, but surely Lydia had to realise that this wasn't the best idea. Unlike my idea of going to Paris to find Jack.

I thought we could even make a weekend out of it, yet the moment I had suggested it Lydia had looked at me in such horror, I hadn't pushed it.

Mentally, I resolved to talk to her about it again tonight. Perhaps if there were witnesses around, Lydia might be more amenable. But then again, I didn't want her to feel ambushed either. I watched her now, finally getting the hang of the difference between the clutch and the brake and wondered if bringing the subject up tonight was a good idea after the pressure of her first driving lesson.

Still, I thought with some surprise, Lydia seemed to be doing quite well as under Tracey's watchful eye she began to drive the car down the quiet residential street.

'Oh look, I'm doing it,' she squealed, joyfully.

Despite my reservations I felt a flash of pride. Lydia's face was a picture of concentration as she stared out of the windscreen at the road ahead. And although her shoulders were hunched over the wheel, I couldn't miss the flash of pleasure in her eyes as she realised she was capable of so much more than she had ever been given credit for.

'You are doing it!' I called encouragingly. 'Well done, Lydia.'

'It's as I said, Lydia, age isn't a barrier,' Tracey said. 'Now, could you change gear from first to second just as I showed you a minute ago?'

Obediently, Lydia pressed the clutch to the floor and slid the gear stick into second. I had to admit I was impressed as she almost glided down the road.

'That's wonderful, Lydia,' Tracey said, her voice full of praise.

'I know,' she said proudly as a car suddenly appeared behind us.

'Okay, Lydia, don't worry about the car behind us.' Tracey said soothingly. 'Just let them go past us if they want to, you've every right to be here.'

'I know that,' Lydia said firmly. 'That pillock will just have to work around me, I'm going nowhere. This is my right of way and that road hog will just have to accept it!'

Meeting Tracey's gaze in the rear-view mirror, we both quickly looked away, too afraid of roaring with laughter at Lydia's outburst. Yet as the 'road hog' came into view it took all my self-control not to give into the laughter that threatened to erupt like Vesuvius as a mother of three in a very nice people carrier patiently passed us at a top speed of 25 mph.

Once the car had gone, Tracey patiently issued Lydia with another instruction. 'Now, there's a crossing coming up and a pedestrian clearly waiting to cross, so I want you to stop gently.'

I looked at Lydia expecting her to follow Tracey's instruction, but it was as though she wasn't there.

'Lydia,' Tracey said sharply. 'Can you stop please?'

Suddenly, Lydia came to and appeared to snap out of whatever trance she had been under. Sadly, it wasn't in time to stop for the crossing as Tracey had requested, which meant the instructor had to bring the car to a stop rather suddenly, jolting us all forwards in our seats.

Watching the bewildered pedestrian cross the road in front of us, I glanced across at Lydia. She had gone from confident to frightened rabbit in seconds. It was so strange – almost as if she hadn't seen the crossing.

'Are you all right?' Tracey asked quietly.

'Fine,' Lydia said. 'I'm so sorry. I think I was concentrating so hard on the car I didn't register your instruction to stop.'

Tracey smiled sympathetically. 'I understand that, Lydia, but if I give you an instruction, you must do as I say. Not just for your own safety and the safety of your passengers, but the safety of other road users too. Do you understand?'

'Yes, of course.' Lydia smiled. 'I'm sorry, dear, it won't happen again.'

Tracey nodded. 'All right then. Drive off when you're ready. Clutch to the floor, into first and off you go, just as we practised.'

Seamlessly Lydia carried out Tracey's instruction and for the rest of the lesson did just as Tracey asked. By the time we arrived back at home, Lydia seemed listless and despondent. I couldn't understand it. Aside from the blip at the crossing she had done brilliantly. Turning to Tracey, I watched her pull out a notepad and pen, and begin to tick things off.

'So, Lydia, I think you have the makings of an excellent driver.'

Lydia nodded, her eyes downcast. 'Thanks.'

'Would you like to book another lesson?' Tracey asked gently.

Slowly, Lydia lifted her gaze and shook her head. 'I don't think so, Tracey. Thank you but I think my driving experience ends here.'

'Why?' I gasped, unable to help myself. 'You were great. You can't stop just because you made a mistake, people with years of driving experience make mistakes all the time.'

'It's nothing to do with that darling,' Lydia said quietly. 'It's because it wasn't a case that I didn't hear Tracey's instruction or was a million miles away at the pedestrian crossing. The simple truth is I didn't see the crossing or the pedestrian.'

'But we've all done that,' I said. 'I'm not saying it's ideal but it does happen.'

There was a pause then before Tracey spoke. 'I don't think that's what you meant, is it Lydia?'

'No,' Lydia replied, turning to me, her eyes filled with fear. 'I mean I literally couldn't see the pedestrian until it was too late.'

I felt a flash of understanding as I took in the enormity of what she was saying. 'Oh, Lydia, I'm so sorry. Why didn't you say you were having trouble with your eyesight?'

'Did the optician say it was all right for you to learn how to drive?' Tracey asked gently.

'He didn't say not to.' Lydia sighed. 'He warned me my eyesight was deteriorating though.'

'I thought so,' Tracey said. 'And that number plate I asked you to read earlier, you could only do it because it was from memory, wasn't it?' Tracey gave her shoulder a sympathetic squeeze. 'I'm so sorry, Lydia.'

'Don't be.' Lydia shrugged. 'I was stupid, I thought it didn't matter, that it would be all right. Obviously it wasn't and I feel terrible. I have been so foolish.'

'Lydia,' I began, only for her to put a hand up to silence me.

'No, Erin, I let my heart rule my head. I didn't want it to be too late for me. I've already missed out on so much because of Harry's lies. I didn't want to let something as stupid as eyesight ruin this chance for me as well.'

My heart went out to her – when you were presented with the crushing truth there was nothing you could do but suck it up and face it. I had learned that the hard way and now it looked as though Lydia was about to have to face up to some pretty brutal truths as well.

Twenty-Six

Lydia

I've often wondered why the moment you feel as though you're making progress, life comes along and knocks you back down. '*Loi de gazon*' my darling dad always used to say, or sod's law, as Harry called it.

Whatever it was, I had a feeling I'd had a good dose of it, and the trouble was I couldn't shake the feeling I had brought it on myself. Watching new and old friends tuck into the risotto I had thrown myself into cooking the moment I got home from that disastrous driving lesson, I tried to fight the feeling of stupidity. I had a nagging feeling my eyesight would be a problem, but cynically thought the optician was just trying to get me to spend more on glasses. But when Tracey had told me to stop for that zebra crossing I had known I was in trouble. I couldn't see the crossing anywhere until it was far too late, and then of course, when I realised I could only read a number plate from memory, well, I knew it was game over, as the kids say. I couldn't carry on and risk putting someone's life in jeopardy.

I glanced across at Erin who was deep in conversation with Rachel. I knew she was upset with me for not being more forthcoming about my eyesight and I didn't blame her. Harry always used to go on about the daft old codgers who didn't know when to stop driving. 'They're a bloody nuisance and a danger to others,' he used to shout, and I would agree. Now, here was I doing just the same thing, and all because I had some stupid notion that I had missed out somehow.

I turned my attention back to the table and watched everyone chatter away. Erin had made a pretty floral centrepiece and all our guests seemed to be having a good time. Lily and Erin were deep in discussion about the subject of highlighters versus bronzers, while Phil and Rachel shared memories of when she was a student.

Idly, I pushed the risotto around the plate with my fork. I didn't have much of an appetite and actually felt quite tired.

I pushed my chair back. 'Just popping out for some air.'

Phil's face was full of concern. 'You all right, Lydia?'

'Fine,' I replied, patting his hand. 'It's been a long day, I'll be back in a minute.'

Without waiting for a response, I grabbed my jacket and walked outside, enjoying the feel of the cool evening air against my flushed face. Leaning my head against the stone wall, I tried to gather my thoughts.

'Thought you might like this.' Phil's voice pierced the silence.

Turning round I saw my friend, holding out a rather large glass of Malbec. 'You seemed as if you were struggling a little inside.'

Taking the glass, I smiled gratefully at Phil as I took a sip. 'Yes, today has not been one of my finest.'

'So I heard,' Phil replied. Leaning against the wall next to me he didn't say anything but the warmth from his body gave me comfort.

I turned to face him. 'This might sound silly but I can't help wondering what Harry would make of all this.'

Phil looked at me blankly. 'All what?'

'You know, Erin, Jack, me learning to drive, changing my image.' I pulled at the leather jacket I had been so proud of a few weeks ago. 'He'd say I was losing the plot.'

'Judging by the last few weeks, Harry wasn't exactly the patron saint of sense,' Phil pointed out. 'You're doing what feels right for you now, Lyddie. Don't forget you're still grieving; it makes us all do funny things. It's been what, three months since Harry died?'

I nodded, enjoying the comfort of Phil's advice. If anyone should know how tough death was to cope with it was Phil. He had been devastated when his wife had passed away. 'So do you think me trying to track Jack down is a funny thing? Erin wants us to go to Paris and see him in person, would you believe.'

Phil sipped his wine before he spoke. 'I'm sure she means well. But the young are full of passion for life, they don't understand that as you get older you want to take fewer risks. And given what happened today, I can see why you feel that risk taking is not for you.'

'But surely it's all about taking a calculated risk,' Erin called from behind me.

'What are you doing here?' I asked, whirling around to see her face illuminated by the light from the kitchen window.

'I was worried about you,' she said kindly. 'You've hardly eaten anything.'

'I'm fine. Phil and I have just been talking about the joys of being an old so and so.'

Phil gave me a playful nudge causing me to spill some of my wine down my jacket. 'You speak for yourself.'

'Why are you feeling old Lydia?' Erin asked, the clouds she made with her breath in the cool evening air distorting her face.

'I don't know.' I sighed. 'I suppose today has just been a wake-up call. I'm realising I can't do all the things I want to do any more. It's sad.'

With a start I realised that was just how I felt – sad. It was sad that my mind and my body were beginning to let me down.

'But it doesn't have to be like that for everything,' Erin began urgently. 'You perhaps just have to make your choices a little more carefully. Think about the risks you can take that will actually work.'

'Like flying to Paris you mean,' I said pointedly.

'Yes,' Erin said firmly before turning to Phil. 'Lydia has been having trouble writing a letter to Jack. I said let's not waste time with a letter, let's get out there and see him in person.'

'Lydia has just been telling me,' he said gently to Erin before turning back to me, 'You know, Lydia, it's not a bad idea.'

'It's a terrible idea,' I growled. 'I might give the poor man a heart attack.'

'Or you could have the most wonderful moment of your life,' Erin reasoned.

'Are you really worried about Jack having a heart attack or is this more to do with the fact you no longer like to fly?' Phil asked bluntly.

I felt a flash of anger. My recent fear of flying was something I preferred not to talk about, and something I had forgotten I had told my old friend during an evening sampling some of the Patxaran, he had brought home from his latest trip to Madrid.

'I didn't know you were afraid of flying.' Erin frowned. 'You know it's one of the safest forms of travel, right?'

'True.' Phil pointed out.

I narrowed my eyes at him. 'And you know that's not what I'm worried about.'

Erin pounced. 'So what is it about?'

'I don't want to say,' I said falteringly. 'I would just rather change the subject.'

'And I wouldn't,' Erin said firmly. 'Come on Lydia, we're friends. I'm here for you, please tell me.'

I looked at Erin and despite the situation, couldn't help roaring with laughter. She was giving me her very best puppy dog eyes, and annoyingly, even though I knew she was playing me like a Stradivarius, I was falling for it. Something told me it was time to tell her the truth. 'It's not that I'm afraid of flying Erin. I don't like all the hassle of airport security, the chaos, and I also just don't like being away from home.'

Confusion flashed across Erin's face. 'Why?'

'Because I'm worried I'll get so confused I won't be able to find my way back.'

'But why wouldn't you be able to get back?' she pressed.

I turned to Phil who gave me a silent nod of encouragement. 'Because I'm starting to lose my memory, Erin. It's been happening for a while and I'm frightened.'

'Why?' Erin asked gently, with all the naivety of the young. 'I forget things all the time.'

'Yes, but not like this.' I said haltingly. 'The thing is Erin, my memory is the reason Harry died.'

At that Phil wrapped an arm around my shoulders. 'You've got to stop saying this. It is not your fault Harry passed away.'

I gave in then to the tears I had been desperately trying to keep at bay.

'Why is it your fault Harry died?' Erin asked, her eyes straying from me to Phil as if trying to keep up with the story.

Phil gave me another squeeze before he spoke. 'You know that Lydia and Harry were in my café when he had a heart attack. What you don't know is that when it happened, Lydia reached into Harry's chest pocket for the mobile he had recently bought, then stared at it because for a split second she couldn't remember how a phone worked. I saw what was happening and immediately rang the emergency services myself from the café phone.'

Hearing the story aloud, pain sliced through me like a knife to my heart. How could my memory have failed me at such a crucial time? Erin stepped forward then and took my hand. 'Lydia, this is not your fault, you can't think like that. My God, in the moment, none of us know how we're going to react.'

'Erin is right, Lydia,' Phil added. 'I have told you time and time again, it was a moment's hesitation and the ambulance would not have arrived any earlier had you called them a second before I did.'

'But how could I forget what to do? I keep going over and over it,' I protested. 'There's something wrong with me, I know there is. If I've learnt anything this afternoon it's that.'

There was a pause then as Erin and Phil exchanged concerned glances.

'Have you actually been to the doctor?' Erin asked gently. 'Have you told them you've got memory troubles?'

'After Harry died, when things seemed to be getting worse,' I confessed. 'She said it was nothing to worry about, just the shock of losing my husband.'

'There you are then.' Erin smiled, the relief on her face obvious. 'There's no reason not to go away. I'll be with you the whole time if you feel like you're in trouble, and we could even make it a working holiday, as there's an antiques fair on, the last weekend of June. With a familiar routine, and familiar things around you, then you might find it's not as bad as you think and you could finally lay this piece of your past to rest. Surely it's worth a try?'

As Erin pressed her phone into my hand, I looked at the picture of the antiques fair on the small screen. She was right; the Paris Antiques Fair was a big one, not as large as the one in September, but big enough to attract buyers and customers alike from all over the world.

'This was the fair Harry and I used to go to every year,' I said with a smile. 'It was the highlight of our year, and where we held the annual general meeting of the Simon and Garfunkel Appreciation Society.'

Erin's eyes lit up at the news. 'Well, how perfect is this? Come on, Lydia, you and I can recreate the society once more, what do you say?'

I looked from Erin to Phil. He was smiling and shaking his head all at the same time. He had never understood my love for Simon and Garfunkel, but aside from that there seemed to be encouragement in his eyes.

'All right,' I said nervously. 'Let's go.'

Twenty-Seven

Erin

Life seemed so topsy-turvy I didn't even know what was troubling me most. Was it Lydia's revelation about her memory? Was it the fact she had finally agreed to go to Paris to track down her long-lost love? Or was it Brad and Cara bringing what was surely going to be the spawn of Satan into the world?

As the early morning sunshine peeped through the clouds, I made my way out to the front of the café and wiped down the tables in readiness for the first customers. I always opened up for Phil on Thursday and Friday mornings. Bath always looked at its most beautiful at the end of May when the stone buildings were permanently bathed in a golden glow. Yet even the promise of another day in the most gorgeous city in the world couldn't shift the bad mood I had found myself in since I woke up.

'Stop thinking about that bloody ex! If only for the sake of your wrinkles, woman,' called a voice.

Glancing up, I saw Rachel striding along the pavement towards me. Dressed in a black tailored business suit, as she pushed Matilda down the road in a pram, she looked every inch the powerful, working mother that had it all.

'You look fabulous,' I said, leaning in to give her and Matilda a kiss.

Rachel tugged at the waistband of her trousers and frowned. 'I still haven't lost all the baby weight, and it's my first day back at work – this was the only thing that fitted.'

'Well, you look wonderful,' I declared, and meaning it too. 'Coffee on me to celebrate.'

At that Rachel's face lit up. 'Thanks! But don't let me have one of Ginger's divine pastries for breakfast, that's what got me into this mess in the first place.'

'I thought it was this little bundle of joy?' I asked.

'Possibly,' Rachel grumbled as we walked back inside the café. 'Ignore me, I'm in a foul mood. If I'm honest, coffee isn't the only reason I'm here.'

I raised an eyebrow as I fired up the machine and pulled down a cup and saucer. 'Oh?'

'Yes, Lily has to go up to Elstree Studios tonight and won't be back for the rest of the week. I know I promised you drinks later to take your mind off things, but I don't think I'll find a babysitter at such short notice.'

I set down a cappuccino in front of Rachel and smiled. 'Don't worry about it. To be honest, I'm grumpy myself and an early night might be a blessing.'

'Really?' The look of relief on Rachel's face was obvious.

'Really,' I promised, turning back to the coffee maker to make myself a drink.

'So have things settled down a bit?' Rachel asked taking a gulp of coffee.

'Depends what you mean by settled.' I sighed. 'I've been wondering if it's a good idea to take Lydia to Paris after all.'

'I think it's a great idea,' Rachel said firmly. 'It will do you both good.'

I wrinkled my nose. 'But what if Lydia can't cope or does something stupid?'

Rachel raised a quizzical eyebrow. 'Has she done anything stupid since you've known her?'

'Aside from lying about the fact her eyesight wasn't good enough to drive, shouting at tourists in the street and going on a complete image overhaul you mean?' I said wryly.

'Fair enough,' Rachel chuckled. 'But a lot of that could be grief. I know she says she's getting forgetful, but you also told me that the doctors have said she's fine. Your initial instincts about going to Paris were right, this could be just what Lydia needs to lay these ghosts to rest and face the rest of her future.'

'Perhaps…' I rested my chin on my fist. 'She's just so up and down at the moment. Today she's going to Bristol for a meeting with some antiques dealer and she's been really jittery about it all week. I offered to go with her, but she looked at me as if I'd just offered to chop the head off a donkey and said it was important she went on her own. It's all a bit weird.'

Matilda let out a little cry then and Rachel kissed her daughter's forehead, soothing her immediately. 'Not really. Perhaps she's still upset about what happened with the driving lesson. Maybe she needs to prove to herself and to you that she's still capable.'

I drummed my fingers against the countertop and regarded Rachel thoughtfully. 'Perhaps. I hadn't thought of it like that. And that driving lesson must have really shaken her. It's such a shame as she was actually doing brilliantly once she got going.'

Taking another slug of her coffee, Rachel banged her cup noisily against her saucer. 'It must have been hard for her to realise like that, but honestly, after what happened at the top of Milsom Street the other day, thank God she found the courage to confess.'

'What happened on Milsom Street?'

'Didn't you hear?' Rachel said in hushed tones. 'Some kid stepped out into the middle of the road, and an old duffer who was driving got the brake and the accelerator muddled up.'

'You're kidding!' I gasped. 'Was the child okay?'

Rachel grimaced. 'The child was fine. Some bloke saw what was happening and pushed her out of the way in the nick of time.'

'Oh, thank goodness,' I cried.

'Not for the poor bloke that rescued her,' Rachel sighed. 'He was taken straight to hospital and died from internal injuries.'

My hands flew to my mouth in horror. 'Oh my God! That's horrible. That poor man.'

As Matilda gurgled, Rachel lifted her from her pram and clasped her tightly to her chest. 'It doesn't bear thinking about. But it shows what can happen if people aren't responsible about when to give up driving. The poor old sod was so shaken apparently he needed sedation, and of course he's going to be wracked with guilt over what he's done.'

I could do was hope that once they were reunited all this subterfuge and deceit would be worth it. It didn't help that guilt had been gnawing away at me for days now. To my surprise I had found myself sympathising with Harry. Had he felt as conflicted as I did, I wondered, acting for what I imagined he thought was the greater good? But then I recalled the moment I had discovered Jack's letter and felt that familiar flash of anger. This betrayal was nothing like Harry's.

'Lydia?' came a voice.

My head snapped up and I smiled at the woman standing in front of me. In the flesh she looked even more like her beautiful daughter. 'You must be Rosie.'

'Guilty as charged,' she said, warmly before pulling out the chair opposite and making a face. 'Sorry, solicitor humour. I'm so nervous.'

'Me too,' I said appreciating her honesty.

As she smiled back at me and studied the menu, I took a moment to drink in her appearance. Dressed simply in well-fitted jeans, white embroidered blouse and raincoat, I knew she was in her late fifties but she looked a lot younger than I had imagined her to be. She didn't just have the same build, hair, eyes and nose as Erin, but there was something about her that told me she had her same sense of loyalty and determined spirit too. It was obviously far too early to be making those kinds of assumptions having only just met, but I got a vibe from her, as Luke always said, that reminded me of the way I had felt when I first got to know Erin.

'You have a wonderful daughter,' I blurted, before catching myself. 'Sorry. I'm nervous too, but you're so like Erin.'

Rosie shot me a genuine smile. 'Thank you. And thank you for taking such good care of her at such a difficult time in her life.'

I waved her concerns away and watched in alarm as I saw tears pool at Rosie's eyes. 'Come on, there's no need for all that,' I said gently. 'We're here to sort this out.'

'Yes of course, I'm sorry,' she replied, wiping her tears away on a napkin.

I reached across the table and clasped her hand. 'I think we both need to stop apologising and talk. Why don't you order yourself a drink and we'll start all over again and work out how we're going to resolve things once and for all.'

Rosie nodded shyly and catching the attention of a young barista, ordered herself a latte and me another cappuccino.

'Now that's out of the way,' I said, 'shall we try again?'

'Lovely idea,' Rosie laughed. 'So, Lydia, let me thank you again for all you've done for Erin.'

I raised an eyebrow. 'I rather think we've covered that, and besides she's helped me in a way I never could have imagined I needed when she moved in.'

'Direct,' Rosie chuckled. 'I can imagine Erin likes that, she never did have time for anything fake.'

'She still doesn't,' I said bitterly, thinking of how she had been so recently deceived by her best friend and fiancé.

'How is she?' Rosie asked quietly.

I paused for a moment as the barista set down our drinks before us. The truth was she was doing much better, but I knew she was still devastated at Brad and Cara's latest news.

'She's well,' I said eventually. 'Erin is remarkably strong.'

'Erin has always been strong,' Rosie replied. 'I remember as a child I sent her away on a school trip for a week expecting tears and tantrums as she had never been away from home before. Yet she simply accepted it, waved me goodbye as the bus set off and helped take care of Cara who I believe was crying her eyes out all week long at being apart from her mother.'

At the mention of Cara's name, I grimaced. It still amazed me that one person could take so much from another person and apparently not feel an ounce of remorse.

'From your messages I got the impression you weren't that fond of Cara,' I ventured.

Rosie wrinkled her nose as she sipped her drink. 'I never took to her – selfish and rude, too busy blaming the fact her parents separated for the problems in her life rather than looking to herself. I hoped Erin would see the light one day, but she never did. When they went to separate universities, I hoped that they would drift apart then but of course they didn't. Cara leeched from Erin just as she always did. I think she rather got used to playing one parent off against the other and learned very quickly how to manipulate others to get what she wanted.'

'You never said any of this to Erin?' I asked.

Rosie let out a snort of derision. 'You know as well as I do, Lydia, you can't tell your kids anything, so Tom and I let it be.'

'So what was so different about the relationship with Brad?' I asked bluntly. 'Surely you could have let that relationship fizzle out too?'

'It was a mistake,' Rosie groaned, holding her head in her hands. 'I just couldn't stand the idea of that creep taking advantage of my daughter. When we said to Erin it was us or him, we didn't expect it to ever get that far, Erin was always so level-headed.'

'And you were never tempted to build bridges?'

Rosie looked thoughtful then as she gazed into the distance. 'I was tempted every day to pick up that phone and say let's forget it. The trouble was, with every passing day it got that much harder and I genuinely believed that the best way to force them apart was to withdraw our support. I had seen what had happened to my own sister, the last thing I wanted was for my daughter to go through something similar. And I suppose, rather selfishly, I couldn't stand the idea of history repeating itself either.'

I took a sip of my cappuccino and regarded Rosie thoughtfully. 'I can only imagine how hard it must have been on you both. But it's time to look forward not back.'

'That's what I think too,' she said with a small smile.

'What does Tom think?' I asked.

'Tom doesn't know about any of this,' she said quietly. 'He's still recovering from surgery, he had a few complications and I don't want to give him any unnecessary shocks.'

'But surely if you all made up this would be a comfort,' I said. 'You know, give him strength.'

Rosie sighed. 'It would, but I don't know. He's so closed off about Erin. He was heartbroken when we all fell out. The two of them were so close. Now what I want is for Tom to focus on his recovery, he can't know about any of this.'

I frowned. Although Rosie had mentioned Tom's surgery, she had also mentioned taking tentative steps towards a reconciliation. From what I could tell, more lies weren't the best way of building bridges. 'So what is it you propose?'

She leaned forwards in her chair. 'I thought we could remain in touch, and you could update me on Erin's progress, just as a go-between. I want to reconcile with Erin more than anything in this world but both Tom and I are hurting too over this, and I want to make sure this goes well. With Tom's health the way it is, I'm not sure we're quite ready to reunite with Erin properly just yet. It would be a tragedy if it went wrong, so we must be careful.'

I looked at her, aghast. 'May I be blunt?' I asked, without waiting for an answer. 'In my experience, my dear, lies and betrayal only ever leads to more lies and betrayal, no matter how well intentioned. You say you want to wait until Tom is better, but what happens if Tom never gets better? What would happen if Tom had a heart attack tomorrow and he and Erin never got the chance to reunite? Take it from me, Rosie, I know what it's like to be faced with the unexpected and I know what it's like to have to clear up the unexpected mess that is invariably left behind. Take my advice and sort it out now.'

'But it's not the right time,' Rosie wailed. 'I can't risk everything going wrong again, I can't go through all that pain again. It took Tom and I a long time to live with the anguish of our estrangement from Erin, we even had therapy over it. I won't be rushed over this, I just won't, Lydia, we need to take this gently.'

'There's no such thing as the right time,' I snapped. 'You're worried about the impact this reunion could have on your husband's recovery, but what if it did him the power of good? And what about Erin? She's been through hell and back. She needs her mother now more than ever and, as the mother and the one who instigated this ridiculous estrangement, I suggest you start making amends. You're being selfish, Rosie. You have a chance to put everything right. Take it before it's too late.'

As I drew my speech to a close, Rosie shrank back as if I had visibly struck her. I could tell my words had hit home. Meeting her eyes, I could see they were filled with fear, but I refused to apologise. I meant every word. This whole situation was ridiculous and to try and stagger a reunion with me as go-between was possibly the worst idea I had ever heard.

Glancing down at her cup, Rosie picked it up and drained the last of her coffee. Setting it back down on the saucer, she eyed me beadily before she got up and slid her arms into her coat. 'I'm sorry, Lydia, I can't do more at this moment.'

'Can't or won't?' I fired angrily.

'Can't,' she replied firmly. 'I really am sorry, Lydia, believe me, I want to make up with Erin more than anything in the world, but I won't be rushed into something until I'm sure the time is right. I'll be in touch.'

With that, she got to her feet and stalked out of the door, never once looking back.

Twenty-Nine

Erin

I pressed the bell to Rachel's flat and winced at the noise. It was loud enough to wake the dead so why Rachel was having so much trouble hearing it, I wasn't sure. She'd texted me earlier to tell me to come round at eight, it was now ten past and she still wasn't answering.

Irritated, I set the bottle of chardonnay that was now getting warm in my hand on the floor. Then I reached for my mobile and rang her. I could tell she was feeling bad as she answered straightaway rather than leaving it to go straight to answer machine. Her fear of actually talking to someone was legendary.

'Erin, I'm so sorry,' Rachel babbled. 'I had to stay late at work, you know what it's like, I had to show willing on my first day back. I'm just collecting Matilda so can you give me half an hour?'

Inwardly I sighed. Of course I understood that Rachel had to work, but the last thing I felt like doing was hanging about outside her flat like a waif and stray. Still, what choice did I have other than to go back home? Given Lydia had been in a really weird mood I thought I'd give her a wide berth for the night.

'Yeah all right. I'll go for a drink in the pub on the corner, come and find me when you're done.'

'Will do,' Rachel said, 'and sorry again Erin, I'll be as quick as I can.'

With that the line went dead and I picked up the wine, slinging it in my bag as I made my way to the Hope and Anchor.

Pushing open the door, I tried not to wince at the sight of the garish pub red carpet and clashing, maroon velvet curtains. The place was such an old man's pub it was almost fashionable again – almost, but not quite.

Catching the barman's eye, I smiled and ordered half a lager, then found a seat in the corner near the door – all for an easy getaway. Glancing up at the roaring telly I saw all eyes were glued to the screen. A darts match was in full swing and I suppressed a smile at the identikit men with matching beer bellies and pints as they all stared intently at the TV. David Beckham himself could walk in right now with Victoria naked beside him and these fellas wouldn't even glance in their direction.

I turned my attentions back to my own drink – although this place had always been a proper old man's boozer, it still had a special place in my heart. Believe it or not, this was the place me and Cara always used to visit when we were home from uni, largely because it was even cheaper than the union.

Smiling at the memory of too many wasted nights lying face down on that grotty red carpet, I felt a pang of affection for the memories Cara and I had made. It was a shame it had all gone to waste, but that was life. I had learned that the hard way. Some mountains were just too big to climb and making up with Cara was something bigger than Everest.

Checking my watch, I saw that there was still a good twenty minutes before Rachel was due to arrive so I flicked idly through my phone to pass the time. But scrolling through endless cat pictures on Instagram wasn't holding the same appeal it usually did. I was too restless, my brain too full with thoughts of Paris, Lydia, driving tests, Brad, Cara, weddings, babies and even my parents.

They had been on my mind a lot since Brad and I had ended but no matter how much I wanted to, I just couldn't bring myself to get in touch and tell them the news I knew they would want to hear. Daft as it might have sounded, I was terrified they might reject me again and I wasn't sure I could handle that. So much time had passed now, what if they decided too much water had flowed under the bridge for us to go back?

Taking a sip of my drink, I realised the thing that troubled me most was that I didn't really know my parents any more. Sure, I had happy memories, but now we had been estranged for so long I wasn't sure who they were or even if there was any place for them in my life. Suddenly, I tried hard to bring my dad's face to mind and with a start realised I couldn't recall the shape of his eyes.

I gulped down another mouthful of beer and pushed the unwanted thoughts out of my head. I'd had a good day, I'd booked the flights and hotel to Paris, Lydia and I were finally going to track down Jack – things were moving forwards.

My eyes strayed to the empty table beside me where that week's local paper had been left. I reached for it, grateful for the distraction. Usually I managed to find a spare few minutes at the café to read the week's news, revelling in the mundane planning applications, classifieds and stories about residents up in arms about something or other, but today I had been too busy fetching and carrying for the language group that had been in the cafe most of the day.

Idly I flicked through the pages, until a photo of Brad caught my eye on page three. That familiar pang of longing and regret stabbed at my heart and it took a moment to steady myself and read on. Glancing back down the page, I saw it was a photo his mum, Sue, had taken on his last birthday when they had come down from London and taken the four of us out to dinner. We'd had a lovely time, drinking champagne and planning our future, but now, as I took in the headline, '*Local Hero Killed in Tragic Car Crash Named*', I felt a wave of horror.

The hero who died valiantly saving the life of three-year-old Bethany Carson was named today as local businessman, Brad Masters.

Brad, an architect employing over three hundred at his architectural firm, Brad Masters Associates, saved the life of the toddler after a car failed to stop in Milsom Street on Monday. He was treated at the scene but died hours later at Bath General Hospital, aged 47. Friends and family have been paying tribute to this much-loved hero who was known in the community as one of life's good guys.

'Brad was one in a million,' business partner Andrew Howson said. 'We are all devastated at the news. It seems especially cruel that he died saving the life of a child, when he had just discovered he and his fiancée Cara Hughes were expecting a baby.'

I felt sick. Throwing the paper down to the ground, I raced towards the ladies' and threw up everything I had in the grubby basin. Eventually, when I had nothing left to throw up, I sank to the floor and leaned my head against the cool tiles. Brad was dead! My Brad – dead! Except he wasn't my Brad any more. He hadn't been my Brad for a while now. He was someone else's Brad, and that someone else was carrying his child. Did I even have a right to grieve?

At the sound of the door being pushed open, I tried to scramble to my feet, but it was only Rachel with Matilda sleeping soundly in a papoose. Her face was flushed, and her eyes wide with concern, as she held Matilda close to her body in one hand and knelt down and wrapped the other arm around me.

'I saw your coat and bag next to the article,' she exclaimed. 'I figured you'd be in here. I can't believe it.'

'Me neither,' I replied miserably. 'Brad's dead, Rachel, he's the one that was killed saving a child.'

I leant my head against her shoulder. I wanted to cry, but no tears would come. 'This is all so messed up,' I wailed angrily. 'How can he have died saving a child? How can we live in a world where something like that happens? He might have been a cheating bastard, but this, well, this is just so very wrong, Rach.'

'I know,' my friend soothed. 'I keep thinking about the last time I saw him. I screamed at him that he'd get his comeuppance sooner or later for what he'd done to you.'

A chill ran through me as I lifted my head and looked at Rachel in surprise. 'Did you? You never told me that before. When?'

Rachel looked uncomfortable. 'When I went to get your stuff. He was still there. I told him what a shit he was and that he might be happy now but no bad deed goes unpunished.'

'Do you think he suffered?' I blurted. 'You know, at the end? Do you think he was in pain?'

'Oh no sweetheart, no,' Rachel cried. 'It was all so quick, he wouldn't have known anything about it.'

'Do you really think that?' I begged, somehow unable to bear the idea of Brad suffering.

'I'm sure if it,' she said confidently.

There was a pause then before Rachel spoke again. 'Are you going to see Cara?'

I closed my eyes at the sound of her name. I couldn't imagine how she must be feeling. 'I don't know.' I sighed. 'I have no idea what I'm supposed to say or do. I mean, am I allowed to be upset? Should I be upset?'

'Of course you should,' Rachel whispered into my hair. 'Oh, my love, you were together a long time, you were going to get married.'

'But we broke up,' I said simply, wiping the tears away with the back of my hand. 'He's with Cara now. She's having his baby. I still hate her for what she did, and I still hate him, but at the same time I feel so desperate for them both. I mean that child is going to grow up without a father.'

It was the thought of Brad's child all alone in the world that sent me over the edge and I sobbed my heart out. I sobbed for the Brad I had known and loved, for the tragedy that had ended his life so suddenly and for his lost chance at fatherhood. I even wept for Cara. Despite what had happened between us, I wouldn't wish something like this on my worst enemy. I thought back to the last words I had thrown at them – that karma was a bigger bitch than me. What a terrible thing to have said, I wished I could take the words back.

'Why don't we find out when the funeral is?' Rachel suggested interrupting my thoughts. 'Perhaps pay our respects that way?'

I shuddered at the thought. 'I can't go to his funeral.'

'Why?' Rachel asked.

'Because, because…' I trailed off miserably.

There was no reason why I shouldn't go to Brad's funeral, other than the simple fact that I didn't want to. Deep down it felt healthier to keep hating him for the way he'd cheated on me. By dying he'd effectively taken that right away from me, leaving me with what? Love? Acceptance? Sorrow? If I went to his funeral, I was admitting that he'd died and I couldn't hate him any more.

'Just because you go to his funeral doesn't mean you forgive him,' Rachel said, reading my mind. 'It just means you've got closure and honestly, Erin, I think you'll regret it if you don't.'

As Matilda let out a sleepy gurgle, I looked down at her contented little face. She was so innocent, I wanted her to grow up in a bubble, where she was always happy and nothing ever went wrong. But life wasn't like that. The one thing I could hope for her was that she would find a friend just like her mum, who was the kindest woman I had ever met, with the added benefit of always being right.

Thirty

Lydia

Stepping off the train at Bath Spa, I felt a funny mix of anger and sadness. For the umpteenth time since Rosie Matthews had walked out of the café I'd been consumed with a fury so blind I was ready to lose my temper with anyone who got in my way. Already, I'd snapped at the train conductor and barged a woman with a baby in a very large buggy out of the way as I found a seat.

I knew I was behaving badly, but I didn't care and pushing my way through more crowds of tourists who had stupidly gathered in their droves by the exit, I knew there was only one person who might help me feel a little more like myself: Phil.

With a renewed sense of purpose I quickened my pace and within minutes had reached the sanctuary of Phil's café. I stood outside for a moment, immediately transported back to the time when Harry and I had owned our shop next door. It was a florist now, but the black front door

Harry had hung himself was still there, as was the chip to the window frame he had made hanging it.

I smiled ruefully. They had been happy times, and lately I had to admit I felt happier in the past. It was a place where I felt secure. But as I stared at the shopkeeper saying goodbye to a customer armed with a huge bouquet of roses, I knew I really ought to face the fact that times change. Life marches on, fighting that fact was not only a waste of energy but utterly pointless. What will be, will bloody well be, as Doris Day famously said in that dreadfully chipper way of hers. I pushed open the door and found Phil up to his eyes making coffee.

'Bad time?' I mouthed, catching his eye.

'It's Erin's language class she arranged.'

'Well, where is she?' I asked, shucking off my coat and hanging it on the back of my chair.

'Tea-break,' he said. 'She's full of bright ideas and it's all good for business so I can't complain when my café is thriving.'

'It's not our generation any more,' I sighed. 'I was only thinking that as I stood outside the shop reminiscing about the past.'

Phil said nothing for a moment while he finished frothing the milk for his last cappuccino. As he handed the tray to one of the customers waiting at the other end of the bar I waited for him to sit down.

'So is that why you're here? To reminisce about the past?' he asked.

'I was rather hoping for a coffee and a chat with an old friend actually.'

Phil raised an eyebrow and set two cups under the expensive looking coffee maker. 'Sounds serious.'

'It's not,' I replied quickly before remembering Phil knew me of old. 'Well, it is. I met Rosie today.'

'Erin's mother!' he gasped over the roar of the cappuccino maker. 'You never said.'

'I wanted to keep it quiet,' I admitted, 'I didn't want Erin getting wind of anything.'

Phil reached into the glass chiller for a slice of Congress tart, fresh from the cooking course he had taken in Cornwall last summer. I gave him a smile as he set it in front of me. 'I'm guessing it didn't go well.'

I took a large bite, enjoying the rush of sugar that fizzed through my body. 'She says she wants to make up with Erin but not right now. Her husband's got trouble with his heart and has just recovered from an operation. He's not to have any shocks apparently so it's all better left for a while.'

'In a way she may have a point,' Phil said, setting a coffee down next to my plate.

'How can she have a point?' I argued through a mouthful of tart. 'Life's full of bloody shocks! Not only that, it's her duty as a mother to be there for her daughter. The girl's having a terrible time.'

'But Erin has got you, Rachel and me,' Phil pointed out. 'She's not totally alone. And Lydia, has she even said anything about making up with her family?'

I gave a small shake of my head. 'That's not the point. Of course she wants to make up with her family. Who on earth wants to be estranged? It's nobody's first choice.'

'I'm not saying that, but perhaps this is like a cake when you take it out of the oven before it's ready.'

'What are you talking about?' I said a little hotly.

'I mean that if you take a cake out of the oven before it's ready, it's ruined,' Phil said, in a patient tone. 'Maybe it's the same with Erin and her family, maybe they all need to be in the right place to forge a new relationship. After all, it's not like picking up where they left off Lydia. It will take time, patience, work, effort. If they start something now when none of them have the right mindset to nurture that relationship, then it may end up being permanently destroyed. This is not necessarily a bad thing, at least Rosie wants to make up with her daughter. Time never hurt anyone.'

I finished my mouthful of Congress tart and fixed my gaze on Phil. With startling clarity, I realised I had been so determined to repair the relationship between Erin and her family, I hadn't stopped to consider anything else.

'You're right,' I said slowly. 'You're absolutely right. Perhaps the last thing we should be doing is rushing this.'

'Trust me.' Phil smiled. 'You've at the very least opened the door now for Erin and her parents. That in itself is a step forward.'

I nodded. How could I have been so dense?

'I wonder if I ought to text Rosie now,' I said thoughtfully. 'Let her know that I understand.'

'How bad did you make her feel Lydia?' Phil asked bluntly.

I winced at the memory. I knew I hadn't held back. My face must have told Phil everything he needed to know as he gave me a knowing smile. 'I would suggest a brief note saying you weren't yourself might be in order.'

I made a mental note to compose a nice message through Facebook when I got home.

'In the meantime, I hoped to talk to you about something else,' Phil began.

I glanced at him and saw he looked a little nervous. He had that tell-tale red flush he always got up his neck whenever he had something to say that he really didn't want to talk about, that and his eyes were darting this way and that like a nervous pigeon's.

'What's wrong Phil?' I asked, my voice full of concern.

'It's nothing serious,' he began, his voice taking on a serious tone. 'But I want to talk to you about an idea I have. You see, I am thinking of expanding. Your old shop next door is about to go up for sale. I wondered about taking it over, making more of this place. Since Erin joined us we've been rushed off our feet. She's got a good head for business, that girl.'

My mind was in overdrive as I tried to process everything my old friend was telling me. H and L Antiques as I always thought of it was about to be put on the market again, and Phil, rather than slowing down, was thinking about speeding up.'

'But you're eighty-two next year,' I managed eventually. 'Don't you think you should be thinking about retiring rather than expanding?'

Phil let out a throaty laugh. 'You would think so yes, but I have a lot of life in me yet and to be honest you have inspired me, Lydia.'

'Me?'

'Yes you!' Phil laughed again. 'With all your personal trainers and your new clothes and of course, the fact you are starting your business up again.'

I looked at him doubtfully. 'Can I remind you that I barely lasted one session with the PT and I'm only running the antiques business again because I have to, and I have help, thanks to Erin.'

Phil shrugged as he wiped down the counter. 'It's just an idea, Lydia, but I love what I do so why not think big before, you know... before it's too late?'

As his voice trailed off awkwardly, I clasped his hand tighter. I knew exactly what he meant. He wanted to live his dreams before anything happened to him like dying suddenly as Harry had done.

'I understand,' I said quietly. 'Does anyone know?'

He shook his head, his eyes downcast as he reached for my hand. 'I wanted to talk to you first, my oldest friend – am I making a mistake? Would you be hurt about me taking over your old stomping ground, the place where you and Harry were so happy for so long?'

I thought for a moment. Would I find it strange to see Phil in the shop that Harry and I had once thought of as home? As I turned back to face Phil, I knew that I couldn't think of anyone I would rather take over the old place. 'Phil, I think you should do it.' I beamed. 'Life is too short for regrets, we both know that.'

Phil put down his cloth and reached across the counter to grasp my hands. 'Thank you Lydia.'

'You've nothing to thank me for,' I replied honestly. 'I can't wait to see what you do with the old place.'

'In that case, could I trouble you for another favour?'

I raised an eyebrow. 'Pushing your luck today.'

Phil smiled nervously. 'Perhaps, but if you don't ask you don't get.'

'True,' I conceded. 'So go on, what is it?'

'Will you go to the doctor's again about your memory problems? I know it's been on your mind, especially since that driving lesson. You might find it's not the issue you think it is.'

The words may have come out of Phil's mouth, but it felt as if they had hit me squarely in the stomach. He was right, I had been deeply worried since my disastrous driving lesson. I was terrified my mental health was deteriorating but should I really investigate it when I was already coping with so much?

I opened my mouth to reply, but no words would come out. It was as though Phil had tapped straight into my helplessness and ordered me to face it head on. I looked at him again, his eyes filled with nothing but kindness, and gave him a brief nod of my head. Sometimes life was full of cruelty; that was something else you simply had to accept.

Thirty-One

Erin

I've never liked churches. It's got nothing to do with religion. It's more the fact they're cold – even when it's a scorching hot June day like today – draughty and, in my experience, usually only full whenever there's some extreme emotionally charged event like a wedding – or in this case, a funeral.

There were many things in life I never thought I would do. Abseil down a large building, cuddle a snake or bury an ex fiancé who had been just forty-seven. This morning I had woken up feeling sick to my stomach, still umm-ing and ahh-ing over whether or not I should go. I had sat at Lydia's kitchen table nursing a cup of tea for over two hours, pondering. After all, it wasn't as if I was part of Brad's life any more. But he had been such an enormous part of mine, it somehow felt wrong not to say goodbye.

It was Lydia who had helped me come to that conclusion. That morning she had found me, taken my stone-cold cup of tea and replaced it with a fresh one.

'You know, when I said goodbye to Harry I felt like you do now, I didn't want to go to his funeral,' she said in a tender voice, her warm hands clasping my cool ones.

I lifted my head and met her concern-filled eyes. 'But you had a lifetime together. Of course you were upset, you had every right to be. What right do I have to grieve over Brad? The last time I saw him I wanted to tear him limb from limb.'

Lydia raised an eyebrow. 'As I recall he deserved it.'

I managed a small smile. 'Even so, I'm still not sure I should be at his funeral. It doesn't seem right somehow.'

'You may not think so now, but in time you will recognise Brad was a very important part of your life,' Lydia offered. 'Just because you hated him, just because he treated you appallingly and just because you were no longer together doesn't mean he isn't worth saying goodbye to. You're doing it for yourself, my darling, as much as for him.'

'Whatever do you mean?'

Lydia paused then as if considering her response. 'Look, Erin, my reasons for not wanting to say goodbye to Harry might be very different to yours but at the same time I knew that by doing it I would be able to close a chapter and start afresh. Over the years I've been to some funerals of people I couldn't stand.'

I felt laughter bubble up inside of me. 'Why?'

'Because they played a big part in my life, Erin, and it allowed me to honour them and tie up any loose ends I might have had with them.'

'So it gave you closure?' I ventured.

Lydia wrinkled her nose in disgust. 'Dreadful American term, but yes, it did give me closure and allowed me to grieve for a part of my life that was now over. Trust me, Erin, you will always regret it if you don't go.'

Now taking my place on a pew at the back of the church, I felt grateful for her comforting presence beside me as the familiar notes of Morecambe and Wise's 'Bring Me Sunshine', rang out through the church. I raised a smile. This had been the song Brad said he always wanted played at his funeral. He was adamant there were to be no tears, and that his funeral, whenever it would be, should be a celebration of his life. I wasn't sure Cara would have had the nerve to follow his wishes. She always said the most appropriate funeral song was 'Angels' by Robbie Williams. Watching her now at the front, standing next to Brad's mum and dad as the pall bearers carried the coffin inside, I felt my insides crumble. It dawned on me that Brad had really gone, the coffin right there, just a few metres away confirmation his life had been snuffed out and we none of us would ever see him again.

As the vicar took to the altar, I took a moment to glance around. Brad had always been popular so unsurprisingly the church was packed to the rafters. Everyone from the architectural firm was there, along with all his family and friends. Then there was the family of the little girl whose life Brad had saved. I recognised them from the paper, and my heart went out to them as I saw the woman who I guessed was the little girl's mum dab at her eyes, no doubt thinking how it could so easily have been her own daughter lying in that coffin.

On the other side of the church were Cara's family, all sitting alongside Brad's. At the sight of Jean, Cara's mum, wiping the tears from her eyes as her daughter leaned over to comfort her, I felt my blood boil. She should be there for Cara not the other way around, but then Jean had always been selfish. I remembered how Jean used to come over to my mum's house for dinner occasionally and then talk endlessly about herself, never once asking Mum anything. It wouldn't have mattered, except Jean was so boring – she worked in insurance as an admin manager, but the way she carried on you'd think it was MI5 as she told us every detail, and I do mean every detail, about her day.

I always wondered how Cara had managed to turn out so differently but looking at them together now, Cara leaning on Brad's mum for support, I realised that actually the apple hadn't fallen that far from the tree. As I saw Cara's head turn my way, I slunk further down in my seat ignoring the look of reprisal from Rachel.

'Sit up,' she hissed in my ear. 'You have every right to be here and nothing to be ashamed of. If anyone should be ashamed of their behaviour, it's bloody Cara.'

'I shouldn't have come,' I whispered. 'People are looking at me like I'm a circus freak.'

'Nonsense,' Rachel said firmly.

'Bollocks!' hissed Lydia.

Rachel stifled a giggle. 'What she said.'

I turned to look at Lydia and saw her mouth was set in a mutinous line as she gazed determinedly to the front.

Somehow her vehement outburst made me relax and although it was wildly inappropriate in a church, it was what I needed to hear. With that I lifted my chin, faced front and as I felt the weight of my two closest friends next to me, I realised just how right they were. I did have every right to be here, to pay my respects and say goodbye.

For the rest of the service I focused on saying goodbye to Brad and all he had meant to me. It wasn't as hard as I had been expecting, and as the vicar talked about love, bravery and the impact Brad's soul would have on the little girl he had saved, I felt lighter somehow. Yes, of course it was desperately sad he had been killed, but at least his death hadn't been in vain. He had died in the pursuit of saving someone else, how many of us would be able to say that?

My gaze landed on Cara, and I saw that she wasn't finding the same comfort in the vicar's words as me. Her shoulders were shaking, and great big sobs were convulsing through her body. I was surprised to find I felt sorry for her. Although she was no longer my friend, I knew she had a tough road ahead – alone, bereaved and pregnant.

As the funeral drew to a close, I made my way out into the fresh air, intending to leave without fuss. Brad was having a cremation and I knew that many of the well-wishers would be going to the pub nearby for the wake, but I planned to make my excuses and leave. Putting my hand on the cold metal gate, I felt relief I'd managed to avoid Cara, when a loud squeal made me pause.

'What's wrong?' I asked, whirling around to find Lydia looking frantic.

'I forgot my handbag,' she groaned. 'I left it inside.'

'Do you want me to go back and get it for you?' Rachel asked, knowing I wanted to get away. 'You two can go on ahead then.'

Lydia waved her suggestion away. 'That's kind of you, but I ought to go. The vicar is the same one that performed Harry's funeral and I should pay my respects.'

Rachel made a face. 'He also married me and Lily. I ought to say something too.'

I looked at them aghast. 'You can't leave me here on my own! I'll be a sitting target! Look, they're all pouring out of the church now, I'll never escape all their questions about what went wrong between me and Brad as well as their looks of pity.'

We all turned and looked at the throng gathering outside, some making their way towards the gate.

'Well, why don't you go on ahead of us? We won't be long and will catch you up.' Rachel suggested.

'Are you sure?'

'Of course.' Lydia smiled. 'See you in a few minutes.'

With that they turned to go, and I laid my hand back on the gate, only to hear the voice I had been dreading hearing shout suddenly from behind.

'Erin! Erin, wait!' a voice called.

Dread flooded through me as I turned around and came face to face with Cara.

'You came,' she said with a wan smile.

I gave a brief nod of my head as I took in her appearance. She looked awful. Her face was tear-stained and blotchy, bags hung under her eyes that were so deep, even Lily would have struggled to disguise them with make-up. That, and she'd lost huge amounts of weight, which I knew for a pregnant woman was far from ideal.

'I'm so pleased,' she breathed, placing a hand on her stomach to steady herself. 'Brad would have wanted you here. He still loved you, you know.'

I took a deep breath and said nothing. I wasn't in the mood to be patronised by Cara. 'How are you coping?'

'Fine, okay, you know,' she said, tears starting to pool in her eyes. 'Mum's been with me for support.'

At that we both rolled our eyes in understanding, sure of just how much support Jean would have been.

'And the baby?' I tried again. 'You look like you're not really taking care of yourself.'

Cara stroked her stomach. 'It's been difficult, I haven't really felt like eating since Brad's been gone, there just hasn't seemed much point...'

Her voice trailed off and I felt myself melt just a little. 'You must try Cara, for the baby's sake, if not your own. You have to think about him or her now.'

'I know,' she said quietly. 'But don't you think it's ironic that Brad's life had to be snuffed out in order for his child's to carry on?'

'Don't say that,' I said, walking forwards and suddenly taking hold of her hand. 'This was just a horrible, horrible accident. This child you're carrying is a part of Brad, he will always be with you.'

Cara nodded and the tears she had managed to keep at bay for the past few minutes now streamed like the Niagara Falls down her cheeks. 'I know. I just don't think I can carry on without him Erin.'

With that she fell to her knees and I joined her, pulling her close towards me as if she were no more than a baby herself. 'You will never get over this,' I said, remembering the words Lydia had so wisely said to me just a few months earlier. 'But you will learn to live with it. It will get easier.'

'It won't,' she sobbed, her tears soaking through my coat. 'It won't, Erin, and you know what, I don't want it to. Because this pain that I feel is a way of honouring all that Brad was. I don't want to live if that means living in a world without Brad in it. I need him, Erin, I just can't function without him, I don't know what to do.'

As Cara sobbed her heart out, I said nothing as I held her tightly. I had never seen Cara so upset, so heartbroken before. Sure, she had been upset when Ian had cruelly dumped her but there was something about Cara's behaviour now that was frightening me.

'Cara, you're really going to have to try,' I said gently. 'Brad would hate to see you like this, you must know that.'

'I do,' she replied, her voice trembling. 'That's just what makes all this so hard Erin. I feel like I'm letting him down.'

'You're not letting anyone down,' I soothed.

She pulled away then and looked at me with her big red-rimmed eyes. 'I let you down Erin. I keep wondering if Brad died because of the way I took him from you. Is this my punishment? I'm sorry, Erin. If I could go back and change everything I would. I should never have taken him from you. I would never, ever have taken him from you if it meant he would have lived.'

'Cara, you have nothing to apologise for,' I began earnestly. 'Because you know what I'm beginning to realise? You and Brad were meant for each other in a way we very clearly weren't. You shouldn't say sorry for taking him from me, because he was never mine in the first place.'

PART TWO

Thirty-Two

Lydia

My eyes roamed over the noticeboard in the hospital waiting room. Alongside notices for charity walks, factsheets on how to act FAST in a stroke and the importance of eating your five a day I saw a box marked Fun Quiz, with 'take one to pass the waiting time' written carefully underneath.

I rolled my eyes – as if a quiz could make an interminable wait regarding your future any better. I had been biding my time in this sad little room for over an hour now and did my best to bite back my feelings of annoyance as I waited for my consultant to see me. Flicking through a dog-eared copy of a magazine I tried to be patient. This, after all, should be the easy part. I had spent the last month taking memory tests and assessments, had spoken to numerous specialists and now I was here – in a yellow hospital waiting room, waiting for the results of a test that would shape my future.

'Lydia Harper,' a nurse called loudly from the front of the waiting room.

Standing up, I was relieved to see she gave me a broad smile. As I followed her down the corridor towards the consultant neurologist's office, I told myself that if she had bad news then, surely, she wouldn't have grinned at me. Surely she would have offered me a sympathetic gaze or perhaps squeezed my arm.

'Mr Evry will be with you in just a minute,' she said, showing me to the office at the bottom of the corridor. 'Take a seat.'

Obediently I sat in the chair opposite the desk and tried to remain calm. Whatever the outcome of these tests, at least this was a diagnosis and I could move forwards.

Just then Mr Evry walked into the room clutching a bulging paper file.

'Goodness!' I smiled, getting up to greet him. 'Surely that's not all mine?'

'Afraid so,' Mr Evry replied with a grin, gesturing for me to take a seat. 'Now, Lydia, as you know we've run many tests and today I want to talk to you about the outcome of those tests and what that means.'

'All right,' I said slowly.

'Did you bring any family members here today?' he asked, looking over my shoulder as if I had somehow got the Waltons right behind me.

'It's just me,' I said bluntly. 'Nobody else knows I'm here.'

'Right, okay.' Mr Evry leafed through his notes.

I felt a pang of sympathy then. Mr Evry, or Craig as he had invited me to call him in previous visits, was a young, charming man with a good sense of humour and large family, judging by the photos of his husband and what I guessed were several relatives that lined his desk. We had hit it off from the moment we met, and his no-nonsense, down-to-earth but relaxed manner had set me at ease as he guided me through repeated tests and answered my endless questions.

After Brad's funeral, I had thought long and hard about Phil's suggestion I get my memory checked out. He was right, it had been playing on my mind for some time that something was wrong, and it wasn't just forgetting what I'd walked into a room for or misplacing my handbag. I was worried about my mood swings and of course my failing eyesight. I needed glasses for almost everything now, a far cry from twelve months ago when I was proud of the fact I not only had all my own teeth, but only needed reading glasses.

So the following day, I had found the courage to return to my GP after our chat. I told her I was worried my memory problems weren't just down to grief over losing my husband, but that there was something very wrong. She had been wonderful, patient, kind, interested and agreeable. She said she thought that it was still most likely grief, but felt there would be no harm in referring me for further tests. I had been lucky or unlucky depending on how you looked at it and been given a cancellation early the following week.

Now it was a sunny morning towards the end of June and I found myself wishing I was in the park, in Phil's café, or generally just anywhere but here as I sat waiting for him to tell me the news. 'Whatever it is, Craig, you can tell me now,' I said in what I hoped was a dignified tone. 'I can cope.'

Craig nodded. 'If there's one thing I've learned about you recently, Lydia, it's that you're a lot stronger than I imagine many people give you credit for. So, if you're sure, I'll get right to the point and tell you that I'm afraid tests show you do have Alzheimer's.'

'But my GP said she thought my problems were most likely down to grief,' I managed. 'Are you quite sure?'

As Craig leaned over the desk to clasp his hands over mine, I felt panic grip me. Despite the fact I had prepared for this moment, Alzheimer's sounded so final – so serious. My brain felt scrambled as I tried to take in what this would mean. Would I need to go into a home? What about Luke, Hannah and the baby? My grandchild would never get to know me. To them I would just be some dotty old woman in the loony bin back in England, not a living, breathing woman full of stories, laughter and love. Then there were the practical considerations. Was I dying? Would I die soon? Or would I face a miserable and long drawn-out death?

'Lydia, I know this is a shock,' Craig began gently. 'No matter how well-prepared people think they are, they aren't. It's a big deal and I imagine you have a lot of questions.'

I stared into his kindly blue eyes and shook my head, 'No. I mean, yes, of course I do have a lot of questions, but you're right. This is not what I expected.'

'I understand. How about I talk generally for a bit about what we do now and how we go from here and then you can jump in when you like?'

I sat back in my chair as I tried to concentrate on what Craig was telling me. He explained that my symptoms showed I was in the early stages of Alzheimer's, but there was no need for alarm just yet. He said that although there was no cure for Alzheimer's there were treatments that would slow down the symptoms and that could mean a far better quality of life for around a year and possibly longer. Then he went onto tell me that it wasn't the death sentence it used to be – that there was more and more money being poured into research and new discoveries being made all the time.

I held up my hand then, begging him to stop. I was feeling a bit overwhelmed, and I just couldn't listen any more. 'I'm sorry Craig, this is all a bit much now. Would you have some leaflets or something I could take away?'

Craig nodded and reached into his folder. 'Before I give these to you though, I want you to think about next steps. I don't want to bombard you, Lydia, but will you at least talk all of this through with your friends and family before you come and see me again next month?'

Images of Luke, Phil and Erin flashed into my mind. What would they say? I could imagine Luke's face. He would no doubt worry just like his father, then rush to take charge, all in a bid to protect me of course. The truth was I wasn't sure what I wanted yet, or how I wanted to handle it.

'I think I need some time,' I said eventually, 'I need to work out how I feel about all of this myself.'

'That's understandable,' he replied, 'but don't take too long. Support at this time is crucial. Your loved ones can really help you see that there is still plenty to be optimistic about. If you take care of yourself, Lydia, it's possible to keep the brain working as it should as much as possible.'

I raised an eyebrow. 'Such as?'

'No more alcohol, lots of exercise and fresh air. Crossword puzzles and reading. We want to keep the brain active – it's like a muscle, you have to keep using it,' Craig said, his face as enthusiastic as his tone.

I said nothing. As childish as it sounded, the idea of giving up alcohol and becoming a crossword nut sounded about as appealing as Alzheimer's. I looked up at Craig, about to tell him just that, but the sincere look in his eyes told me this wasn't the time for one of my usual jibes.

'Well, thank you again, Craig,' I said instead, getting to my feet.

'You're welcome, Lydia. Arrange an appointment with me for a month's time and we'll see how you're getting on and whether you want to think about medication.'

I nodded, then walked towards the door. As I placed my hand on the doorknob, I swung around with just one question I wanted answering. 'I'm supposed to go to Paris next week. Will this be a problem?'

Craig smiled. 'Not at all. You can still have a life, Lydia. Alzheimer's doesn't mean sitting around waiting to die.'

'Thank you,' I said, giving him a small tight smile as I turned to leave.

Outside, the fresh air was something of a relief and I decided to take some of Craig's advice and get some exercise, walking at least some of the journey across the city back home. As I concentrated on placing one foot in front of the other, I did my best to make sense of the news, but it was too much for my brain. It was as though I'd been overloaded and my brain just wouldn't put the pieces together. Instead I thought about the upcoming trip to Paris. There was still so much to pack and organise. Although this trip was primarily about finding Jack, Erin and I had agreed to make this a working holiday and enjoy the chance to thrive in Paris. I hadn't been for many years, though it was a fair Harry and I had adored when we ran H and L antiques. Over the years we had got to know many of the vendors and together would often spend many an evening, once the customers had gone home, chatting into the night, a bottle or six of red wine between us as we talked antiques.

Once we had retired, Harry still went back to the fair, spending time chatting with our old friends and revisiting old haunts. I had never fancied it myself, preferring to look forward not back. Harry had insisted he wanted to keep his hand in for the online business. Naturally I had thought nothing of it, only now of course the online business was something else he had lied about, so what had he been doing in Paris Did he have a life then that I knew nothing about?

At the thought of Harry's lies, I felt a flash of anger. How different life could have been if only I hadn't been so gullible, so afraid to stand on my own two feet. In that moment I felt a rush of determination. Craig was right, I wasn't dead yet and I wasn't about to let what was left of my life slip through my fingers without a fight. This trip was the chance to set things right and start afresh, Alzheimer's or no Alzheimer's.

Carrying on down the road with a renewed sense of purpose I felt my smartphone vibrate in my bag. Pulling it out, I screwed up my eyes to examine the screen and saw to my surprise it was a message from Rosie.

Jabbing at the phone the message popped open and I used my thumb and forefinger as Erin had shown me to zoom into the message.

Dear Lydia,

I hope you're well. It was a pleasure to meet you recently and I'm sorry things didn't go perhaps the way either of us had planned. When I returned home our meeting played heavily on my mind – so much so I ended up telling Tom all about it a few days later. He was astonished to hear we had been in touch, and even more astonished I didn't come home with you to meet Erin there and then. In short, Lydia, he doesn't want to wait, he wants to reconcile with Erin now if you think she's agreeable. We wondered if there was somewhere neutral perhaps for us to meet. That way there won't be any pressure or expectation and it will be easier if things don't go as well as we want them to.

Truly, Lydia, I want to say I'm sorry for how I handled things when we met. I don't know what came over me, I can only put it down to the fact I was overwhelmed by a situation I had dreamed of for so long. Both Tom and I have talked now and agree we will happily travel to the ends of the earth to reunite with our daughter – it's the only thing in the world we want.

Yours in sorrow,
Rosie

Immediately I pressed reply, pausing for just a second before I began to type. Rosie wouldn't have to travel to the ends of the earth to meet her daughter again, but she and Tom might want to dust off their passports. Paris might have a bit more on offer than either Erin or I had initially planned.

Thirty-Three

Erin

'This jade ring is highly collectible,' I explained to the woman examining the antique. 'We always find them rather difficult to get hold of.'

'Is it a dragon or a dog?' the woman asked, turning the ring over in her hands.

'It's most likely a Foo Dog,' I replied, 'cut into foliage and it probably belonged to an archer.'

'An archer? My word,' the woman exclaimed, pulling out a pocket loupe from her handbag to examine the ring in more detail.

Turning to Lydia, I saw the corners of her mouth were upturned in a knowing smirk, forcing me to look away before she had me in fits of hysterics. I had done a few fairs with Lydia now and had long since discovered that those customers who were the most clueless were the ones that tended to bring their own magnifying glasses for a closer examination – all the gear and no idea, as Rachel would say.

As the woman put her loupe away, she gave me a warm smile. 'I'll take it, thank you. Is there any movement on the price?'

I shook my head. 'I'm so sorry. I'm afraid not. As you will know already I'm sure, these jade rings are incredibly hard to come by and we have priced it as competitively as we can in order to encourage genuine art lovers to pick up an affordable piece that will serve them for years to come in the future.'

The woman paused for a moment, and looked lovingly at the ring, 'Okay then, I'll take it.'

'Lovely,' I grinned. 'That will be four hundred pounds please. I'll just write out your receipt.'

As Lydia handled the cash I wrote out the receipt in our book, and handed it over. Bidding her goodbye, I sank onto the little stool and took a sip of the lukewarm coffee I had dashed across the field to buy an hour ago.

We had been rushed off our feet all morning and I was delighted at the chance to take a breather. Today we had got up earlier than the crack of dawn to go to an antiques fair just outside Birmingham. It was one of the largest fairs in the UK and with Paris on the horizon next week, we thought it would be a good idea to try something a little larger to get us warmed up. Consequently, we had stuffed the van – sorry, delicately packed the hire vehicle – with some of our best pieces, keen to test our selling skills. I had to say that so far things were going really well. Not only had we turned over two thousand pounds in just under two hours but Lydia and I had got into a steady rhythm. It was thanks to Lydia I had developed a certain knowledge about the more general pieces but for anything more specialised she was on hand to help answer customers' and fellow dealers' queries.

'You handled that customer very well.' Lydia said admiringly. 'Very nice touch there, inferring she was an expert on those rings.'

'You taught me well.' I smiled, raising my paper cup to clink hers. 'I even managed not to roar with laughter when she pulled out that loupe.'

Lydia wrinkled her nose in disgust. 'These amateurs.'

'These amateurs keep us in tea and biscuits,' I said warningly.

'True,' Lydia said, her tone relenting. 'Though speaking of which, did you notice how little stock we have left now.'

I nodded. We had gone into the attic last night to sort through the items we wanted to take this morning and our stock had seriously dwindled. With all the fairs and the online selling I had introduced through a new website last month, we had seen a huge surge in turnover. In a way, of course, it was a good thing; Lydia needed to sell everything in order to pay for the losses Harry had left her with. But I would miss working with Lydia. She had not only taught me how to handle antiques customers, she had also become more than a landlady and business partner – she had become my best friend. Looking at her now, jabbing at her phone, I smiled delightedly as I watched her bring our website up for another dealer who had stopped by to say hello.

'I must say, that's a lovely looking website,' the man I knew to be called David said.

'It's all Erin,' Lydia said, a hint of pride in her voice. 'She's revolutionised our business, takings have been through the roof.'

David scratched his chin thoughtfully. 'Really? How much do you reckon you sell through it then, in a week?'

Lydia and David looked at me expectantly. 'Since we went live we've sold over £10,000, but I haven't listed everything, just the things I knew would sell to a more specialist collector, or to the overseas market.'

'The overseas market...' David raised an eyebrow. 'You reckon it's been worth it then?'

'Without a doubt,' Lydia said triumphantly, as an alarm sounded on her phone. 'Look, we've just got an order now – for that chest, Erin.'

The oak tall boy was something we were never going to shift at a fair, it was so large and bulky. However, I'd read an article about Americans liking bigger pieces and wondered if it was the sort of piece New York housewives would like. Apparently, they had taken to collecting them as the perfect accompaniment to their Upper East Side homes.

'Is it an American?' I asked.

'Yes, just as you said,' Lydia said excitedly.

'My word, how did you work all that out?' David asked.

I shrugged, and got up from my stool as a customer approached to look at one of the silk scrolls I had laid out. 'Research. Lydia helped me get a feel for it all.'

'You two make quite a double act,' David said. 'She's better looking than your Harry ever was, that's for sure.'

At that, Lydia roared with laughter and David walked away. Shaking my head, I turned back to our customer and answered her questions about the scroll. Twenty minutes later and she had walked away a satisfied customer.

'Do you realise that with the sale of that scroll, we've taken more at this fair than we ever have before?' I pointed out, flicking through the receipt spreadsheet I had created on my laptop.

'Don't forget all the online sales this week as well,' Lydia pointed out. 'Harry and I could have done with you years ago!'

I laughed. 'Years ago, I wouldn't have had the first idea about a business. Working at Brad's taught me a lot.'

'You have a natural eye. It's the architect in you,' Lydia said kindly. 'Do you never think about picking that up again?'

'To be honest, no. You spend a lot of time in an office as an architect. Working with you, I've realised how much I love being in the great outdoors and talking to people.'

Lydia beamed. 'It's been a pleasure for me as well, to see how you've picked up the antiques trade.'

'I like it,' I admitted, 'which is a surprise. I always thought I'd end up in architecture – possibly as Brad's partner or something. At least that was a plan we talked about.'

'You've hardly mentioned him since the funeral.' Lydia said quietly. 'I haven't liked to pry, but how are you feeling now?'

'All right,' I replied honestly. 'I sort of feel Brad and the life I had with him is firmly in my past. It's not my place to grieve for Brad any longer. I did that when he left me for Cara. Now, it's Cara that should be grieving for all she's lost.'

'Have you heard from her?'

I shook my head. I had told Lydia and Rachel about the conversation Cara and I had in the graveyard. Initially each of them had been outraged Cara could have hijacked me in such a way but it hadn't felt like that to me. To me it felt as though it was the perfect time to let go of the hold Cara and Brad had over me. The funeral hadn't just allowed me to say goodbye, but it had allowed something inside me to shift. I could look forward in a way that I hadn't before, and as a result I had thrown all my energy into the Simon and Garfunkel Antiques Brigade. I had been designing logos, building customer order forms, adding blog articles and forging links with other dealers around the world. It had been good for me, I felt more like my old self, and judging by the money we were now taking in, my new-found confidence was paying dividends too. If nothing else, it proved I did have what it took to make my own way in the world.

'Has Phil spoken to you?' I asked Lydia, suddenly changing the subject.

Looking up from the antique clock she was now pushing to the front of the stall, she gave me a knowing glance. 'I take it from your tone he's told you about his expansion plans into the florist's?'

'Yes, I think it will be good for him.'

'I wondered about offering to manage it for him.' I gulped. 'Or do you think that's a silly idea?'

As Lydia stood there looking at me, opening and closing her mouth like a guppy struggling for the right words to say, I took that to mean that she thought it was an atrocious plan. 'Is that something you would want to do?' she asked eventually.

I ran a hand through my hair as I considered my answer. I had thought about the prospect of managing Phil's café for him ever since he told me he wanted to take over the florist's lease. I mean, I knew that taking a bigger part in

Phil's business, assuming that was what he would even want, wasn't using my degree, but I liked working with Phil and it would be a job I could throw myself into, even though I knew it wasn't exactly what I had always wanted to do.

'I think so,' I said slowly. 'Recently, I've felt more capable and I've loved getting involved in the coffee shop – finding new customers, bringing the takings up... And the way things are going, after Paris our little antiques empire will have finished too, we'll have sold everything. I'm going to need to make sure I'm gainfully employed and like I said, I like being around people.'

Lydia nodded. 'You're a natural when it comes to business, Erin. But, darling, you're young and full of ideas. Okay, things are a bit up in the air for you work-wise but they won't stay that way. You need to channel all this creativity and energy you've got into what you really want to do. You're in the prime of life – you need to grasp whatever's out there with both hands, just think about how to really use your talents.'

As a customer approached the stall to look at the clock, I let Lydia handle him, and sat back onto my stool. As I watched her make another sale, I passed her the book. She looked delighted with herself, and I was delighted for her. Whatever came next, I knew it would be hard to beat the job I had working with Lydia. Just how often do you get to find a job where you spend the day with your best friend?

Thirty-Four

Lydia

Zipping my suitcase shut, I took a deep breath and looked at my reflection in the mirror. Dressed simply in navy trousers, cream V-neck jumper and the leather jacket I still loved slung over one arm, I took a deep breath to steady myself. My appearance was wan and there were bags under my eyes from all the sleepless nights I'd been enduring over the past couple of weeks, but a little Touche Éclat had done the trick.

Come on, old girl, you can do this.

'Lydia are you ready?' Erin called up the stairs, breaking my train of thought. 'The taxi's outside.'

'I'm just coming,' I replied, giving my jumper an anxious tug.

Pulling the door open, I carried my little case down the stairs and saw Erin waiting for me at the door.

'You all right?' she asked gently.

I gave her a brief nod of my head. 'Of course.'

'I understand,' she said encouragingly. 'Soon we'll be at the airport and you can relax. If nothing else, you can get a well-deserved G&T into you.'

I said nothing and simply smiled as I followed her out into the early morning sunshine where the taxi driver picked up my bag and placed it in the boot. This was the day I had been dreading and looking forward to in equal measure. Today was the day I was going to get on a plane and find my first love. Today was the day I was going to find Jack Harrison and tell him the truth about what happened all those years ago – to say I was a little terrified is an understatement. I had always been dreading the trip, anxious about what would happen if I strayed out of my comfort zone, but not only that, I was scared stiff about seeing Jack again. For the umpteenth time since waking that morning, I wondered what on earth had possessed me to agree to this? I mean, who on earth went chasing long lost loves around the continent? Certainly not ones that were old enough to know better. And what if Jack didn't want to see me? What if he looked at me in disgust? He might want nothing to do with me? Or worse, what if we did meet and we no longer liked one another? Wouldn't it be better to leave the past where it belonged? After all, at the moment I had very fond memories of Jack. What if he had turned into some dreadfully bitter old man since I last saw him?

I paused for a moment to take a deep breath and calm down. Since my diagnosis, that panic had risen to epic levels. This morning all I had really wanted to do was crawl under the blankets and stay there, but to do that would be letting Erin down. She had invested so much of herself, not just into finding Jack, but organising the trip and of course, our involvement with the antiques fair. I just couldn't do that to her.

Just then my phone buzzed with a text message. Taking it from my pocket, I smiled as I saw it was from Luke.

Just wanted to say good luck, Mum! Lx

Typical – always a man of few words. Surprisingly, Luke had been rather good when I explained what I was up to. I had fretted for ages about telling him that his father had kept secrets from me, and I wondered if he would think I was betraying Harry in some way with my quest. Yet Luke had simply shrugged during our video chat and said his dad might have been wonderful but he had his faults too, and he could understand why I needed to find Jack.

Putting the phone back in my bag, I clambered inside the cab that would take us to Bristol Airport. Erin shot me an encouraging smile and I felt more than a pang of guilt ebb away at me. I was as bad as Harry at keeping secrets from her, but I simply knew that at this time it was for the best. Although I had stuck to my decision to keep my Alzheimer's diagnosis to myself, I still felt guilty for not confiding in Erin, Phil or even Luke. I knew Craig had encouraged me to talk to my family and loved ones but the moment I had been given the diagnosis I felt as though this was something I wanted to keep private, at least for now, I didn't want their sadness, their disappointment – I wasn't ready for all that.

But of course, that wasn't the only reason I felt guilty. Since inviting Rosie and Tom to Paris to reconcile with their daughter, I had been ready to open my mouth and blurt out the words to Erin. Yet I had lost my nerve at the eleventh hour, each time resorting instead to asking Erin to top up my wine glass or pass me the salt. With the numerous requests I had made at the dinner table lately, Erin could be forgiven for thinking I had an eating disorder.

Now as I glanced across at Erin checking through the travel documents, I couldn't help feel a flash of pride. She was a changed woman since Brad's funeral, becoming more relaxed and clearly feeling more at ease and confident in life. It had been a wonderful thing to see, especially as I knew just how important it was that she attended the funeral. I knew Erin had wondered about her place there and had dreaded having to face that awful Cara girl, but if anything, I think that had been the thing that had changed her view of Brad. It was as if that day she had finally exorcised all those wretched demons and was ready to face the future. The big question now, was I?

'So when we get to Paris, do you want to go straight to the hotel or would you rather get some lunch first?' Erin asked.

'Well, it will be quite early for lunch won't it?' I said, glancing at my watch and seeing it had just gone six in the morning. 'Why don't we get our bearings? Besides, surely we'll get a meal on the plane?'

Erin smirked. 'Not likely. It's budget travel. We might be able to buy something on board though.'

I raised an eyebrow. 'Tell me you're joking. Next you'll tell me you don't even get a complimentary Bloody Mary on board and with my nerves this morning I'm going to need at least one.'

Erin smiled encouragingly. 'You'll be fine. I thought you were feeling much better about going to Paris now. You've got your phone; we'll write the name and address of the hotel on a note in your bag in case we get separated.'

'You're making me feel like a child,' I grumbled

'You know I don't think that,' Erin said softly, 'You've been my rock over the past few weeks. When Brad died, well, you know I would never have got through it without you or Rachel. I just want to repay the favour that's all. I know you're a bit worried about the trip and meeting Jack after all this time. It's natural, I just want to look after you.'

'And I appreciate that, Erin.'

'You don't need to appreciate it,' Erin said, her green eyes filled with affection. 'Just accept it. I'm so grateful to you for your friendship, I just want you to know that.'

I shifted uncomfortably in my seat. 'Well, you can show me how grateful you are by getting me a drink on board.'

'Oh, Lydia,' Erin chuckled. 'You're in for a surprise.'

Just twenty minutes into the flight I could see what Erin meant. Everything on board cost extra! Leafing through the menu I was astounded to see that they didn't even give you any complimentary nuts with whatever aperitif you ordered.

'Three pounds for crisps!' I shrieked.

'Okay, calm down Lydia,' Erin said soothingly.

'But it's a bloody liberty.' I jabbed my finger at the menu. 'And look at this, five pounds for a gin and two pounds for a tonic! It's downright criminal.'

'Ssssh,' Erin said warningly. 'People can hear you.'

I glanced over the top of my menu and saw that Erin was right, other passengers were looking at me. 'So what?' I shrugged in a Gallic fashion. 'I'm probably just saying what they're all thinking.'

Turning my gaze back to the menu I saw the man in the aisle opposite chuckling. Tall and about my age with flecks of grey in his largely brown hair, he seemed to be travelling alone.

'Quite right,' he said catching my eye. 'I'm wondering what on earth happened to the golden age of air travel.'

'Judging by this menu, that's long gone.' I sniffed. 'And what on earth is the matter with these seats? I feel like a sardine.'

The man snorted. 'Yes, they do try and squeeze as many in as possible. It's all bums on seats these days.'

'Literally,' I muttered. 'I mean why on earth don't people complain? In my day you stood up for yourself, you said what was what. It was the British way for heaven's sakes. 'Couldn't agree more.' The man smiled, holding out his hand, 'I'm Jerry.'

'Lydia,' I said, 'and this is my good friend, Erin,'

'Pleased to meet you,' Erin muttered before burying her head back in her guidebook. Perhaps she didn't want to chat and make a new friend, but I did.

'Let me be honest with you, Lydia. In my opinion, too many of these youngsters these days worry about whether or not we've offended someone. I'm all for speaking my mind,' Jerry said conspiratorially.

'Me too,' I exclaimed. 'There's too much of this pussy-footing around, if we were a bit more upfront about our feelings, well, I can tell you this Brexit and the mess that's followed would never have happened.'

'Oh God,' I heard Erin groan.

Out of the corner of my eye I saw her slump down a little lower in her seat and I stifled a giggle. The young today were too easily embarrassed.

'Quite right,' Jerry grinned. 'So will you allow me to buy you an overpriced gin and tonic when the trolley dolly comes round.'

I roared with laughter at the un-PC comment. 'I'd like that very much.'

It didn't take long for Jerry to catch the air steward's attention and within seconds I had a wonderfully cold gin and tonic, complete with a bag of nuts pressed into my hands.

I raised my plastic glass and clinked it against Jerry's in gratitude, then took a sip of my drink, enjoying the feel of the ice-cold liquid trickling down my throat. I closed my eyes and sank back into my chair, the numbing effect of the alcohol quickly taking hold. I didn't know if it was the gin, the flight, or even Jerry, but I was no longer the bag of nerves I had been when I woke this morning. Instead I felt calm, confident and even excited. I was about to face my past and embrace my future; something told me that not only would I survive this trip, but I would bloody well enjoy it as well.

Thirty-Five

Erin

The last time I went to Paris had been with Cara. We were eighteen and decided to go inter-railing together the summer before we started university. Despite the very best of intentions to see, Italy, Greece, Spain and Croatia we actually only got as far as Paris. The two of us fell in love with the city so quickly that we took summer jobs. I got a job as a cleaner in the Louvre, Cara found work in a bakery and we became fluent in French!

Because we both worked early morning shifts, we often had most of the day together to bum around enjoying lunches of bread (from Cara's bakery), cheese and wine on the banks of the Seine. Then in the evening we would cruise up to a little bar in the fourteenth arrondissement, around the corner from where we had rented a tiny studio flat near the university.

It was an amazing summer. It was a place where Cara and I fell in love – with each other, with the city and also two very cute French brothers who ran the bar we spent most of our evenings in. Cara lost her heart to Patrice, the older of the two brothers who cooked most of the food, while I fell for Theo, a broad-shouldered, tall and frankly smouldering French wine wizard who spoke fluent English but rarely chose to use it. Instead he would communicate with passionate kisses and big glasses of Côtes du Rhône. It was no surprise neither Cara or I wanted to go anywhere else.

Now, as Lydia and I clambered out of the cab at the top of the Champs-Élysées, I felt a thrill of excitement and inhaled the sights and the smells. The gorgeous tree-lined street was buzzing with cars, pedestrians and fancy ladies gabbling in fast French into their mobile phones while the air itself seemed to smell of flowers, coffee and meat – after the devastating fire at Notre Dame it was wonderful to see the city pulsing with life and feeling, well, completely and utterly unmistakably Parisian! From the corner of my eye I could just make out the large Louis Vuitton gold initials that famously adorned the store and I turned to Lydia, delighted to see a smile as big as my own on her face.

'I had forgotten how marvellous it all is here,' she breathed, her head whirling around like a nervous pigeon as she tried to take it all in. 'This city takes your breath away.'

I nodded as I reached for her case. 'Let's get inside then we can explore.'

It didn't take long to check into our hotel near the Champs-Élysées. Lydia had decided that as we had made more money than either one of us could have anticipated from the antiques fairs, we should stay somewhere lovely, so she had chosen this old world, gorgeous hotel right in the heart of Paris.

Listening to the receptionist give us details about breakfast on the third floor and the champagne bar at the top I found myself daydreaming about what it would be like to live in this wonderful city. It had been so perfect the last time, what if I just upped sticks and came back? After all, aside from Rachel and Lydia there wasn't really a lot to tempt me to stay in Bath. I had no family, no job, no boyfriend – perhaps this was the time for a new start?

But of course I said none of that to Lydia as we found our rooms and oohed and ahhed over the complimentary toiletries and the view of the Parc Monceau. Instead, I focused on Lydia and Jack. They were the reason we were here, I reminded myself as I ordered us two black coffees from the pavement café we found ourselves in near the hotel.

'So what do you want to do first?' I asked.

'Do first?' she raised an eyebrow. 'Well, I thought I'd start by auditioning as a dancer for the Folies Bergere! What the bloody hell do you think I want to do Erin? I want to find Jack!'

I held my hands up in defence. 'Okay, okay. I was only asking. I just didn't know if you might like to settle in a bit first, sort out any final arrangements for the antiques fair...'

My voice trailed off as I took in the serious glint in Lydia's eye. It was true we had discussed the fair to the nth degree at home and I personally had overseen every bit of stock we were transporting through a specialist company. I had also dealt with our booking for our stall at the expo centre along with the accreditation and with Lydia's help answered numerous enquiries through the website. I could see the last thing she wanted to do was talk any more about antiques and I had a feeling that the sooner we got on with our mission to find Jack, the better.

'I take it you have his address?' Lydia asked, getting straight to the point.

'Yes, he doesn't live far actually. In the twentieth arrondissement,' I replied.

Lydia smiled. 'Where the Pere Lachaise Cemetery is. Typical of Jack, he did always love to be around the great and the good.'

'So you really want to go now?' I asked doubtfully.

'No, next week,' Lydia snapped, before her expression softened. 'Ignore me, I think I'm a bit nervous.'

I hid a smirk, privately thinking that the amount of gin she had knocked back on the plane with the strange new friend she had made might have had something to do with her tetchiness. However, I knew better than to suggest she had a hangover. According to my good friend she had never had a hangover, merely the odd headache or poor night's sleep that occasionally coincided with an extra glass or two of wine.

'Well, if you're sure, let's go after we've had these coffees,' I said, slipping a handful of euros on the table to cover the bill.

Lydia needed no encouragement and downed her espresso in one. As she stood up, she slammed her cup on the saucer and looked me squarely in the eye. 'Let's go.'

I wasted no time hailing a taxi and an hour later we had arrived at the address Vera had given us. Clambering out of a car for the third time that morning, I paid the driver and stood back to marvel at the house in the warm summer sunshine.

There was no getting away from it – the house was impressive. A large white building set over two storeys with big picture windows and balconies. Set well back from the road, in the grounds of a large garden that appeared to be beautifully tended, the place looked as gorgeous as a hotel – a fact that wasn't lost on Lydia.

'Are you sure this is the right address?' she said, peering at the house, hands shielding her eyes from the sun.

I looked down at the address and checked it with the map on my phone. 'We're definitely in the right place. Look, there's a big board over there too with Maison Retrait on the front.'

'Retreat House,' Lydia murmured. 'I just didn't picture Jack somewhere so modern. And are these flats?'

I looked across at the large wooden double doors and saw a woman with a pushchair coming through one side, while a man with a Zimmer frame used the other.

'It appears so,' I frowned. 'Funny, Vera didn't say that he lived in a flat.'

Lydia shrugged her shoulders as she tugged at the hem of her dress. I saw she had left the leather jacket at the hotel and instead changed into a soft summery floral dress that showed off her petite frame.

'I suppose she wouldn't have necessarily known. I mean, Retreat House could as easily be a block of flats as it could a country manor,' she replied, her tone giving nothing away.

'Shall we go in then?' I asked brightly, walking towards the door.

Glancing behind me, I saw Lydia was still rooted to the spot, her eyes roaming across the building. I felt a flash of concern. I should have known that this huge step wasn't something to rush into. I should have instead insisted that we spend the day settling in and getting ready for the antiques fair in the morning. Quickly I returned to Lydia's side and gave her shoulder a gentle squeeze.

'Are you all right?' I asked softly.

Lydia came to then, and swung her face around to smile at me. 'I'm fine. I think it just hit me that the moment really has arrived. No more putting it off, no more excuses. I'm now going to see Jack Harrison in the flesh and let him know I've only just discovered he's still alive.'

I nodded proudly. 'Do you know what you're going to say?'

Lydia shook her head then, and I couldn't miss the flash of anxiety in her eyes. 'I thought I'd know exactly what to say when I saw him, but now, well...' Her face fell. 'Now I wonder if I shouldn't have prepared something after all.'

A gentle breeze caused her hair to flutter and the look of vulnerability in Lydia's eyes wasn't lost on me. But in that moment I caught something else too: optimism. And I knew that the very worst thing we could do would be to walk away and leave this for another day.

'I think you should trust your instincts,' I said earnestly. 'You wanted to speak from the heart so that's what you should do. The right words will come to you when you need them.'

'Do you really think so?' Lydia asked, wide-eyed with fear.

'I know so,' I promised. 'You've come all this way; you're bound to be nervous. But you can't let those nerves get in the way of this. You'll never forgive yourself. What's happened to that determined spirit that wouldn't even let me finish my coffee an hour ago?'

Lydia chuckled. 'Sorry about that.'

'No harm done.' I smiled. 'Why don't you make it up to me by going in there, knocking on Jack's door and asking if he wouldn't mind putting the kettle on?'

'We're in France, dear,' Lydia said drily. 'I rather think it will be the cafetière.'

I rolled my eyes. If Lydia was being a smart arse, she was clearly feeling better. 'Come on.'

With that, she took a deep breath and then without waiting for me, marched across the road and straight up the path. Quickening my pace, I hurried to keep up with her and only just managed it as she pushed open the heavy wooden door.

Walking inside the huge light-filled lobby, I felt a surge of optimism myself. This place was gorgeous with big bright vases of flowers lining the windows, and the sounds of calming classical music filling the room.

Spotting a large white desk in the corner, we walked up to the very elegant French woman who was tapping away at a computer screen and wearing a name tag that said she was called Cecile. I gave her my best smile as she looked up. 'Excuse me, we're hoping to see Mr Harrison. Can we go on up?' I said in my very best French.

'One second if you don't mind,' the woman replied in perfect English. 'Is he expecting you?'

Lydia shook her head. 'No, but we wanted to surprise him. I haven't seen him in over fifty years you see.'

Cecile's face lit up. 'Alors! You are an old love, yes?'

'Yes,' I grinned, knowing how the French were a passionate race. 'We've waited a long time to see him.'

'Oh, Monsieur Jack is a wonderful man. So polite, so generous. Let me just check where he is,' she said, tapping away again at her screen.

'Do you keep tabs on all the residents?' I asked politely.

'Not all,' Cecile said shaking her head. 'Only the ones who are here with us for care.'

'For care?' Lydia quizzed.

Cecile nodded as she gestured around her. 'We are a multi-generational assisted living facility. We house the old and the young in these apartments. The young people help the older people who are frailer stay, how would you put it, young at heart when their health isn't so good any more. In return we are able to offer them cheaper rent while the young also benefit greatly from our older residents' wisdom.'

There was a silence between us as suddenly the penny dropped that this wasn't Jack's home, instead he was in a home. I glanced at Lydia and was shocked to see how pale she had suddenly become.

'Ah! I have found him,' Cecile smiled, interrupting our thoughts. 'He is upstairs in his apartment – number twenty-two. Take the lift at the end of the corridor to the second floor and turn right.'

'Thank you.' I smiled, before turning to Lydia. 'Are you ready?'

Thirty-Six

Lydia

As I followed Erin down the carpeted corridor towards Jack's apartment, I felt so nervous I thought I might faint. My stomach felt as if it was on full spin cycle and as for my heart, I was worried that was about to give out at any second.

The ludicrousness of this idea was really beginning to sink in now. What on earth was I doing travelling to France to meet a man I hadn't seen since I was scarcely more than a child? The confidence I had felt on the plane was now beginning to wear off along with all those lovely gin and tonics Jerry had bought me. The past was the past, surely it was better to leave it there?

As I saw the gold number plate against the green door, I leaned against the wall for a moment to try and gather myself. I couldn't stop now, not after everything Erin and I had been through. I had to carry on, didn't I?

Spotting I wasn't by her side, Erin swung around to look at me. 'Are you all right?'

I nodded weakly. 'I'm fine. It's just, well, the moment is finally here.'

'It is. But if you don't want to do this Lydia, you really don't have to. Maybe it's enough to have just seen where he lives?'

The idea shook me. To have come all this way and not see it through was unthinkable now. I had to know what lay beyond that door. I had to know for my sake, Jack's sake and to some extent Harry's too. I owed it to the girl I had been before and although I was nervous, it was better to find out now. 'No,' I said, standing up and taking another deep breath. 'No, I'm not leaving now, come on.'

With renewed determination I walked straight to the door and rapped on it so hard, I made Erin jump. Immediately the door swung open and in that moment the years fell away as I took in the sight of the man before me. Tall, with those same sparkling blue eyes and thick black hair, he oozed the same easy charm I had always remembered as he stood there smiling in welcome at me and Erin.

'Jack,' I breathed, 'after all this time, is that really you?'

The man frowned. 'No, sorry. I'm Jacob – Jack's my grandfather. Do I know you?'

I couldn't seem to find the words to speak then, but Erin came to my rescue. 'Pleased to meet you.' She smiled, stretching out her hand towards Jacob. 'I'm Erin and this is Lydia. Lydia's an old friend of your grandfather's, she's come from Bath to meet him.'

'Bath?' Jacob frowned once again. 'Does Jack know you're coming?'

Suddenly I seemed to find the right words. 'No,' I said emphatically. 'But I think he'll want to see me.'

Just then a loud voice as familiar to me today as it was yesterday boomed down the corridor. 'Jacob, who is it? Not bloody salesmen, is it? Tell 'em to bugger off.'

Jacob gave a brief smile of apology. 'No, Granddad. Old friends of yours apparently. From Bath?'

'Bath?' Jack's voice came again. 'But I don't have any friends in Bath.'

'Yes you do, Jack,' I suddenly found myself saying. 'It's Lydia.'

There was what felt like the longest pause in the world then before Jack spoke again, his voice incredulous as it carried up the hallway. 'Lydia? Lydia Day? Is that really you? It can't be.'

'It is,' I breathed, almost crying with relief now that he knew who I was.

Just then the sound of footsteps almost running down the corridor echoed out into the hallway and then there he was – Jack. My Jack, as lovely and full of life as he had always been. He still had a full head of hair, though now it was white, and of course he had a few wrinkles around his mouth and brows, but to me all I saw was the light in his eyes as he stood there, mouth wide open gaping in astonishment. In that moment, all I saw was the same Jack I had fallen in love with all those years ago.

'Lydia?' he gasped. 'Lydia, I can't believe it's really you.'

'It's me,' I said, tears rolling down my face. 'It's taken over fifty years, but I found you.'

The look of love in his eyes that I recognised just as if I was a shy teenager all over again sent my heart soaring, and before I could stop myself I pushed past Jacob and ran the few steps left along the corridor towards Jack. Even as

I neared him, I recognised that same citrusy musk he had always smelled of and I let out a little gasp as the memories of our time together came rushing back. As he held out his arms, I fell into them and together we buried ourselves in each other, both weeping for all those lost years and the sheer pleasure of just being together again.

A little while later and Jack and I had managed to calm down enough to sit next to one another and drink a cup of tea, beautifully made by Jacob, I might add. It still felt so shocking to see Jack again after all these years and I kept sneaking a sidelong glance at him just to check this was really happening.

'So I still don't understand how you found the letter after all this time.' Jack frowned. 'I know you said you never got it at the time, but what I can't grasp is how you found it now.'

I sighed. Erin and I had already explained the story of Harry's death and how we had come to find Jack's letter but as I said the words aloud I could see how this story could be seen as the stuff of fantasy.

'Erin found it in a box of antiques when we were clearing out the attic,' I explained. 'When he died Harry had left me in such a terrible pickle financially that the only way of making any money was to sell the antiques we had stored.'

Jack shook his head in disbelief. 'And my letter was just there? Amongst it all?'

'All purely by chance,' Jacob interrupted from his chair on the other side of the room.

'It really was,' Erin confirmed from her chair next to his. 'Up until then, Lydia thought Jack had died.'

At the mention of the word death Jack's face clouded over. 'I'm just so sorry, Lydia. The idea of you thinking I was dead is just terrible.'

I leaned over and squeezed his arm. I had, of course, had many months to get used to the idea that Jack was alive and not dead, but for Jack and to some degree Jacob, I appreciated this must all be very hard to comprehend.

'But worse for your poor mum,' I countered softly, 'I feel so dreadful knowing she went to her grave thinking you had died.'

'It's something I've had to learn to live with,' Jack sighed. 'It should never have happened. When I found out about the mix-up, I was furious. Of course, my CO apologised personally, but it wasn't enough. This mistake had cost me my family, it had cost me you,' he said as he leaned over to squeeze my hand for added emphasis. 'I could never stay in the Army after that even though they offered me a wonderful position with the Signals. I just had to get away, I couldn't forgive them for all they had done so I returned to London and tried to start again. I met Lizzie and we moved away, eventually having two wonderful sons – Michael, who is Jacob's father, and Simon.'

'Where are they now?' Erin asked politely.

'London.' Jack smiled. 'It seems to me everyone goes to London, though of course Michael is talking about retiring out to the Cotswolds.'

'He's been saying that for a long time, Granddad,' Jacob chuckled. 'Mum will never let him leave, she's terrified that she'll have to start sheep shearing if they move out to the country.'

I laughed; Jacob was as easy to be around as his grandfather. Since Erin and I had arrived he had done his best to be as welcoming and accommodating as possible, but also taking care not to step on his grandfather's toes and allowing him to talk when he needed to. He obviously had a lot of affection for his grandmother, but was kind enough to realise what a shock and unexpected delight this was for both Jack and me. I was touched at the empathy he showed.

'Do you live in London then?' Erin asked before I had a chance.

Jacob nodded. 'Yes, I work in advertising.'

'He doesn't just work in advertising, he's just turned thirty and runs the company,' Jack added proudly.

Jacob's cheeks flamed with colour as he batted his grandfather's pride away. 'I don't run the company, I'm a partner – there are five of us.'

'Even so, that's amazing,' Erin exclaimed.

'Not really,' Jacob made a face. 'What is amazing though is I get to spend a lot of time in Paris with Granddad.'

'That is amazing,' Jack agreed, 'best thing about your job.'

'How often are you over here?' I asked, helping myself to one of the chocolate biscuits Jacob had thoughtfully laid out.

'Between one and two weeks a month. We have a lot of clients out here and so I'm the one that meets with them and takes care of them, all while dossing down in Granddad's spare room,' Jacob explained.

'I must say you have a beautiful apartment,' I said admiringly. 'The grounds are gorgeous.'

'It is beautiful, and perfect for me,' Jack replied

'So what is this place?' Erin asked, her face twitching with bemusement. 'It seems as though it's half flats and half care home.'

'It is a bit like that,' Jack admitted. 'The French authorities had this marvellous idea a few years ago that the young could help keep the old young at heart while the old could help teach the young 'uns a thing or two.'

I laughed, feeling at ease in Jack's company now. 'What a wonderful idea. Though I will say it seems to me that it's the youngsters teaching us a thing or two. Before Erin, I didn't have a clue what a website was, never mind a smartphone. She's very technological.'

'What is it you do?' Jacob asked as he turned to Erin.

Erin made a face. 'Not much. I'm a waitress.'

'You are not just a waitress,' I protested hotly before addressing Jack and Jacob. 'This young lady is not only a fully trained architect but she has also helped me get the antiques business back on its feet. She has a wonderful eye for jewellery, has set up a website for us, handles all the trade and customer enquiries, deals with the tax man and generally takes on all the day to day running, which on top of a day job helping run a café is no mean feat.'

I was pleased to see Jacob and Jack had the good grace to look impressed. It was impressive, I just wished Erin would believe in herself a bit more.

'You're putting us to shame.' Jack nodded approvingly.

'She certainly is,' I added. 'Not only that, but once she found out where you lived, she was the one that organised our stall at the antiques fair tomorrow as well.'

Jacob looked surprised. 'You're here for the market? That's a coincidence, that's what brought me to Paris this week.'

'Oh, are you into antiques too?' I asked in surprise.

'Not me,' he grinned ruefully. 'Don't know the first thing about them, but my client is, and she's at the fair tomorrow too.' He checked his watch and got to his feet. 'Actually Granddad, I ought to get going. Sandrine is waiting for me at the hall.'

'Of course, son.' Jack said, getting to his feet to see his grandson out. 'I'll see you tomorrow,'

'Nice to meet you, Jacob,' Erin said. 'Perhaps we'll see each other tomorrow at the fair.'

'Absolutely.' Jacob smiled. 'Unless you'd like to come with me now. I mean I could help you set up and that way we can leave these two to talk about old times without boring us to death.'

'You cheeky sod,' Jack said gruffly, though I could tell he was teasing.

A look of relief followed by doubt passed across her face. 'I would love to get on actually as I'm a bit behind, but Lydia, is that okay with you?'

'Of course,' I said in what I hoped was a reassuring tone. 'I'll get a taxi to take me to the hotel and see you later.'

'If you're sure?' Erin still looked worried.

'I'm sure.' I sighed. 'If I have any problems I'll give you a ring.'

'And I can promise I'm not an axe murderer,' Jack teased. 'Criminal in the kitchen yes, but that's about it.'

As everyone laughed, Erin followed Jacob out to the corridor. 'I don't want to put you to any trouble.'

'It's no trouble,' he replied. 'Besides, maybe you can teach me something about antiques so I can impress Sandrine a bit later on.'

'Deal,' she replied before turning to me. 'Right, see you later. Jack, a pleasure to meet you, I hope I see you again soon.'

'I'm sure you will, my dear,' he said, bending down to give her a goodbye kiss on the cheek.

Waving farewell to Jacob he shut the door, then turned to me and smiled. 'So, it's just us then.'

Thirty-Seven

Erin

'Is this everything?' Jacob asked scratching his head thoughtfully as he surveyed our stock.

I nodded, feeling a surge of alarm. 'Yes, why?' I babbled.

Jacob paused for a moment before he spoke, his lovely blue eyes temporarily filled with concern. 'No, it's fine, really, I just thought you would have more than this. There's not really enough here to fill a trestle table.'

Drinking in the scene before me with fresh eyes I saw he was right – we didn't really have enough stuff. Although I had done plenty of research into this fair, ensuring we kept our most bespoke pieces back for Paris that would appeal to collectors and dealers I hadn't quite appreciated just how big this fair was going to be. The courier had taken everything we had left, and I reasoned it was about the amount we had for one of our usual Saturday fairs. Only here, in this vast space alongside other dealers it looked as though we had brought just a handful of items. I wanted to wail in despair. How could I have got it so wrong?

'Look, I'm sure it's not that bad.' Jacob said reassuringly. Walking towards the stall he looked at the pile with his arms folded as if assessing the situation. 'What about if you spread the items out a bit? Really go for a high-end presentation?'

'I guess that could work,' I said gloomily. 'Perhaps if I make it more of a bespoke area people will be more interested.'

'Exactly.' Jacob smiled, his eyes dancing with delight. 'And think about it – you can just act as though you sold a lot of your items really early on because all your stuff is so good. You know Parisians, it's all about image.

I roared with laughter and was delighted to see he joined in. 'I can see why you're in advertising, you know just how to turn a terrible situation into a good one.'

A flash of embarrassment passed across Jacob's features. 'I might know the odd thing about spinning a line, but it's true Erin, look at this stuff.' He picked up one of Lydia's blue and white vases with a rare red swirl in the centre. 'This is gorgeous. It truly does look as though you've only got really good quality pieces, unlike a lot of the sellers here who will be trying to farm out any of the old crap they've been hanging onto for the tourists.'

'You can't say that,' I giggled.

Jacob winked. 'You know as well I do it's true, Erin.'

I said nothing, privately agreeing with him. I had been around enough antiques dealers in recent months to know that was exactly what many of them did. I had lost track of the number of Care Bears and My Little Pony Dream Houses that some had been trying to sell for ludicrous amounts of money, marketing them as vintage English toys, rather than cheap eighties fads, no doubt made in China.

'Are you sure you don't mind helping me?' I asked, changing the subject as I began rooting through the first box to set up.

Jacob smiled. 'Of course not. Besides I'm in no rush to get back to Granddad's, it seems as though he and Lydia have a lot of catching up to do. I still can't get over it. Did her husband really keep my granddad's letter from her for all those years?'

'Yes,' I sighed, pulling out a display case I had earlier filled with rings. 'Honestly, it was as though Lydia had seen a ghost when she read it. She had truly believed Jack had died during his National Service.'

'That's terrible,' Jacob said, as he started helping me sift through. 'It's amazing to think what might have happened if she had actually got the letter when she was supposed to. She might never have married Harry; she might have married my granddad instead. History could have been changed.'

'But the fact is, Harry did keep the letter from her, they did get married and your grandfather and grandmother were very happy together,' I said firmly. I had played the 'what if' game far too many times when Bad and I had split up and knew it was far from healthy.

'True, they were made for each other. Everyone always said so,' Jacob agreed, running a hand through his thick black hair. 'So where do you fit into all of this then?'

'I'm Lydia's housemate and she's my best friend too.'

Jacob blinked in surprise before his mouth broke out into a wide smile. 'Really? How did you two meet?'

Pausing for a moment, I wondered how best to sell the circumstances behind my move into Lydia's home. I couldn't put my finger on why, but I didn't really want to tell Jacob all about Brad cheating on me with Cara behind my back which then made me jobless and homeless in turn. I wanted to look forward not back, and I didn't want to do or say anything that might make Jacob think less of me, or worse, feel sorry for me.

'We were introduced through a mutual friend, and I moved in after I split up from my fiancé,' I said truthfully.

Jacob nodded as if reading between the lines that there was more to the story but he wasn't going to push it.

'And was it through Lydia you got into antiques?' he asked.

I picked up one of the jade rings we had brought with us to sell and gazed down at it to give myself a bit of time to think. I had become quite a ring enthusiast thanks to Lydia, enjoying sorting through our stock to catalogue and price each item. 'Yes, I knew nothing about it before, but thanks to her I've really fallen in love with it. I'll be sorry to let it all go after tomorrow.'

'Why don't you just carry on with it if it's doing so well?' Jacob frowned.

I put the ring back in the case. 'It was only ever supposed to be temporary. Harry left Lydia in a lot of financial trouble and so her son Luke said that if she wanted to make ends meet she would need to take in a lodger—'

'Which is where you come in?' Jacob interrupted.

'Correct.' I grinned. 'And we would need to sell all the antiques that had been accumulating in Lydia's attic too. Effectively this meant she had to come out of retirement for a little bit.'

'Like Barbra Streisand,' Jacob teased, his blue eyes sparkling with joy.

'Just like Barbra Streisand,' I laughed. 'Anyway, enough about me, what about you? What's the story?'

Jacob looked confused 'What story?'

'Well, you know, doesn't your wife or girlfriend mind you coming to France so regularly?' I asked bluntly.

Mentally I kicked myself. How could I have got straight onto whether or not Jacob had a wife or girlfriend? Couldn't I have started by asking about his work? I looked at him from under my eyelashes trying to work out if he was amused by my question as he ripped through another box, but if he seemed surprised, he didn't let on.

'I don't have a wife or girlfriend,' he said eventually. 'I'm single, I split up with someone recently.'

A flash of guilt passed through me – me and my big mouth. 'I'm sorry.'

Jacob made a face. 'Don't be. We'd run our course. Natasha and I were together six years.'

'What happened?' I asked softly.

'She left me for someone else,' he said, a look of anger and hurt passing across his eyes. 'I came home one day to find she'd moved out. She left me a forwarding address for her mail and I soon discovered that the forwarding address belonged to her new boyfriend.'

As the words hung in the air, I felt a pang of sorrow for Jacob. I knew better than anyone the pain he must have felt.

'If it helps, my ex left me for my best friend,' I admitted quietly. 'And if that wasn't enough, I was stupid enough to fall out with my parents over it – we haven't spoken in years.'

'You're joking,' Jacob gasped, his eyebrows raised.

'Sadly not.'

He scratched his head thoughtfully. 'Wow, Erin, what a bloody fool he must have been.'

'Sorry?' I blanched in surprise.

Jacob's cheeks flushed with colour. 'Erm, I just meant you know, you're lovely, you're talented and you're kind. How many people have you met that become best friends with their elderly housemate and then helped them track down their first love in Europe? You're amazing.'

I put the box down then and gazed at him properly. I knew Lydia would think he was the spitting image of his grandfather but I could see more to him than that. Jacob was strong, kind, funny and charming, and although we had only just met there was something about him that made me feel as if I had known him all my life.

'Thanks,' I said eventually. 'I know I should probably say something more appropriate than that, but truly, thank you. It's a long time since anyone called me that.'

Jacob took a step towards me and reached a hand up to my face. As he pulled a piece of Sellotape from my hair I winced slightly as he held it out in front of me.

'Maybe we could see each other again over the weekend,' he said as I took the tape from him. 'Perhaps we could find out more amazing things about each other.'

'I'd like that,' I replied, feeling my insides start to melt.

Just then the sound of footsteps behind caused us to spring apart like two teenagers caught in the act. Turning around I saw a short woman with petite, angular features, bobbed black hair and bright red lipstick stop behind us.

'Jacob,' she called. 'You're here. I need your opinion on the marketing plan we've got for the fair. Are you free now?'

Jacob paused for a moment before his eyes left mine. 'Yes, of course. Sandrine, allow me to introduce you to a friend of mine who is also exhibiting at the fair tomorrow. This is Erin.'

'Erin Matthews,' I replied, holding out my hand for her to shake. 'It's a pleasure to meet you.'

'Likewise,' Sandrine replied with a genuine smile. 'If there is anything we can do to help you while you are here please let us know. We are in the far left-hand corner.'

I glanced over to the stall she gestured towards and hid a smile. Sandrine's stall was huge and on a completely different level to ours.

'That's very kind,' I said politely. 'What's your speciality?'

'Modern art,' Sandrine explained. 'Oh, and our founder loves pottery.'

'So does my partner. Asian vases are her favourite.'

Sandrine raised an immaculately groomed eyebrow. 'We could be sisters! My partner also has a weakness for Asian vases.'

'Well, perhaps with so much in common we could all get together for dinner later?' Jacob suggested with a smile. 'Erin doesn't know many people here and I think her business partner is otherwise engaged tonight.'

'Of course,' Sandrine exclaimed, her lipsticked mouth breaking into a wide smile. 'We will go to a little place around the corner I know, Erin, and you can tell me all about English antiques.'

'I look forward to it,' I beamed.

'Me too,' Jacob said as he turned to walk away. 'It's a date.'

Thirty-Eight

Lydia

Was it possible to get jaw strain from talking so much? It had been over two hours since Jacob and Erin had left Jack and I to reacquaint ourselves and we had chatted non-stop. We had covered all of the usual things at first: jobs, home life and holidays. I learned that Jack and Liz had been together for forty-one years but when she died ten years ago Jack had chosen to live in Paris and make a fresh start. The two boys were old enough to look after themselves, he reasoned, and he felt that a new city where he knew nobody would be the perfect place to deal with his grief. It was something I understood and I had occasionally wondered myself in the long months since Harry's death if I wouldn't have liked to have done something similar. If it hadn't been for the fact my darling husband had left me high and dry, who knew where I might have ended up – drinking cocktails in Aruba perhaps, waited on by scantily clad waiters! Well, everyone can fantasise.

'Where have you gone?' Jack's voice interrupted my daydreams.

I smiled as I took the glass of wine he had offered me. 'I'm sorry, I was miles away.'

'Reminiscing about the past?' Jack asked kindly as he took a seat next to me.

'Something like that.' I grinned, taking a sip of a delicious Burgundy. 'So, what's your life like here?' I asked, setting the glass down. 'I've heard about the past but what about the future?'

Jack guffawed. 'What future? I'm eighty next year.'

'Stop it immediately,' I scolded. 'Plenty of life in you yet, I mean look at you, you're living in this wonderful apartment in one of the most beautiful cities in the world. I should think you've got plenty of future ahead of you.'

'You're still doing that then, I see?' He smiled softly, his blue eyes dancing with merriment.

'What?'

'Still giving everyone a good dollop of your common sense – whether they ask for it or not!' He chuckled, topping up my wine from the bottle on the table.

I held out my glass appreciatively. 'You've either got it or you haven't, Jack Harrison.'

'And you've always had it,' Jack said tenderly.

'Too true,' I said, clinking my glass against his. It felt so good to just be in his company again, I had forgotten just how wonderful it felt when Jack shone his light on you. He always had this knack of making you feel as if you were the most interesting person he had ever spoken to and as his blue eyes bored into mine, I felt as if liquid sunshine were being poured into my soul.

'So how have you adjusted to life as a widower, Jack?'

'It was very difficult at first,' he admitted. 'Lizzie and I had enjoyed a wonderful marriage together, it was half the reason I felt I needed a fresh start. I knew things were never going to get any better for me than they had been; I needed something different.'

I nodded in understanding. 'So Lizzie never visited Paris?'

Jack shook his head. 'Funnily enough no, she always loved Italy, but never came to France. I had not been here before even though it's so close to London – it just seemed like a natural place to come for a fresh start, besides I see plenty of the family.'

'Do you get back to the UK often?

'Oh yes, every couple of months and the boys visit often enough. Then of course, Jacob is over here all the time.'

'He seems a lovely boy.' I said admiringly.

Jack flushed with pride. 'He is, he's my favourite grandson.'

'I thought you said he was your only grandson,' I laughed.

'I'd say it even if that wasn't true,' Jack replied good-naturedly. 'He can't do enough for me and the two of us are more like friends. He's very calm, always good in a crisis and is someone I just enjoy spending time with. You know the best thing about him, Lydia?'

I listened, agog.

'He doesn't treat me like a bloody old person. To him I'm not an inconvenience, I'm just Jack and I can't tell you how good that makes me feel.'

'Erin is the same.' I smiled. 'Oh, she tells me off every now and again but she's my best friend.'

'You never used to really have female friends,' Jack exclaimed. 'Always too busy with work, your family or studies. Has all that changed now?'

I shook my head. 'No, but it's different with Erin. I never expected to find someone like her but I've discovered something wonderful since Harry's death Jack – the sheer joy of having a best friend. It doesn't matter that she's young enough to be my granddaughter, the years between us have no bearing whatsoever.'

'She's a lovely girl,' Jack said softly. 'You were lucky to have found her when you did.'

'Don't I know it,' I said resolutely, taking another sip of my wine. 'If it hadn't been for Luke of course, I would never have so I suppose I ought to be grateful for his bullying.'

Jack rolled his eyes. 'I suppose we all should be grateful for our children's bullying on occasion.'

'But when they treat us like inconvenient burdens you feel like slapping them,' I chuckled.

'Couldn't have put it better myself.' Jack laughed, clinking his glass against mine. 'Lydia, I have missed you.'

'Me too,' I said, startled by the confession. 'I'm so very glad I found you again.'

'I always hoped you would,' Jack said softly. 'I prayed in my heart every day that one day you would find me again.'

'I just feel so terrible that you thought I had abandoned you,' I said sadly. 'You must have hated me for thinking I had ignored you.'

Jack looked at me stricken. 'I never hated you Lyddie. Oh, my darling, I could never hate you, I understood entirely. When Harry came to see me and explained you were getting married and you were happy, of course I was furious, but I understood.'

My heart began to beat wildly at this sudden revelation. What meeting? When on earth had Harry and Jack met? 'What do you mean when Harry came to see you?'

Jack looked at me in wide-eyed horror, as if realising his mistake. 'Oh my God, I'm sorry Lydia. I shouldn't have said that.'

'You still haven't answered my question,' I said, trying to keep my voice from shaking. 'You said you and Harry met. When was that?'

There was a pause before Jack set his glass down and took hold of my hands. 'When I wrote you that letter, Harry got in touch. He wrote to me at the address in London and suggested he and I meet.'

'Why?' I asked, my heart beating so loudly I could hardly hear Jack's voice.

'He told me that he suspected you still held a torch for me and that you believed I was dead. He felt it would be better for your future happiness if you still believed that. He said you had gone through so much to get past what you believed had happened to me and if I were to suddenly reappear, it would throw your life into turmoil. Harry told me you were settled, you no longer suffered from nightmares, you had a future to look forward to and I had no wish to upset any of that.'

I looked at him, those blue eyes that had just moments earlier seemed as familiar to me as my own now belonged to a stranger. I felt sick. I couldn't believe that these two men, the men I had adored most in the world had conspired to keep the truth from me.

'Didn't you think, as a grown woman, I deserved the right to know so I could decide for myself?' I said eventually. 'I'm sorry, Jack, but for years I felt nothing but guilt at moving on. I thought it was terrible that I got to have a future while yours had been so cruelly snuffed out.'

Jack hung his head; he was clearly sorry but it cut no ice. 'I thought I was doing the right thing. Harry was so persuasive. He seemed to love you so much, we both did, I just didn't want to cause any more hurt. I was still grieving over the loss of my own mother; I couldn't stand the idea of anyone else being in pain. I wanted you to have the world, Lydia, I thought this was the best way of doing that. I got it wrong, and I always regretted it.'

'Did you?' I couldn't help asking.

'Of course,' Jack growled, lifting his head those stranger's eyes meeting mine once again. 'I have thought of you every day for the past fifty odd years. I had often wondered what had happened to you and I wanted to go back and change what had happened. I adored Lizzie, but I always felt I didn't handle things the right way with you. I was so broken when I came back from the Army and discovered my mother had died and you had gone. I couldn't face the idea of hurting you or me any more, so when Harry said you were happy and suggested we left things as the status quo it seemed like the best idea. When I grew stronger and as more time passed, I realised that had been the wrong thing to do. I'm truly, truly sorry Lydia, please forgive me.'

I closed my eyes, I felt as if I were spinning, it was all so much to take in. I got to my feet, the walls closing in on me, I was desperate for some fresh air and to think clearly.

'I have to go,' I blurted.

'Lydia, no.' Jack got to his feet and reached for my hand, but I shrugged it off.

'Look, Jack, I'm not unsympathetic to what you've said,' I said softly. 'But you must understand that this has come as rather a shock and I need time to digest what you've said.'

'But will I see you again? Please Lydia, I've dreamed of this day for so long, I can't bear for it to end like this.'

To my horror I saw tears pool in Jack's eyes. Confusion ebbed away at me, I was so angry with him, with Harry, but on the other hand I felt overwhelmed with affection for both of them. Both of these men in my life had misunderstood me, underestimated me, but they both seemed to have done so for the very best of reasons – love. I didn't know what I felt, but I did know I just needed some time for me. 'Oh Jack, of course we'll see each other again,' I said eventually. 'I think that all this has just shocked me a bit, I need some time.'

'I understand,' Jack said. 'But please let's not leave it like this. Can we have dinner together on Sunday. The four of us?'

I nodded.

'I'm so sorry, Lyddie. I should never have done it,' Jack said with a watery smile.

'You shouldn't,' I said sadly. 'But what's done is done. It's in the past, but right now, it's my present and I just need some time to think it all through.'

With that, I reached for my coat and walked past Jack. Pausing at the door, I turned to look at him then, doing his best to put on a front that he was fine. The sight of it shocked me; it was the same look he wore when I said goodbye to him at the train station as he went off to do his National Service – a lost, scared little boy dressed like a man.

'I'll see you on Sunday,' I said, before opening the door.

Shutting it firmly behind me, I didn't look back as I hurried down the hallway towards the lift.

Getting downstairs I asked the nice lady at reception if she would call me a taxi to take me to my hotel and then went outside. The cool night air was like a balm for my poor aching head and I rested it against the stone pillar, trying to make sense of the day.

Just then I felt my mobile beep. Pulling it from my pocket I saw it was a message from Rosie.

Hi Lydia,

Just a quick note to let you know Tom and I have made the Eurostar and are now in Paris. We'll see you at the fair tomorrow and are so excited to see Erin again – and you, of course.

Love, Rosie

I shoved the phone back into my pocket and let out a shaky sigh of relief. At least that was one thing that was going to plan. All I could do now was hope that the second reunion of the weekend would go a lot better than the first.

Thirty-Nine

Erin

The fair was nothing like how I imagined it to be. Don't get me wrong, we had been busy enough, having already sold most of Lydia's vases and a good half of the jade rings I had come to adore, but there was something missing.

I wasn't sure if it was the lack of bacon sandwiches filling the air or the fact the customers were more well-heeled than we were used to, something just felt different. I sneaked a glance across at Lydia who had been staring into space for the past five minutes and wondered if she was feeling it too.

'Has it always been like this?' I asked.

'Sorry what?' Lydia said, coming to from her daze.

I narrowed my eyes. She had been behaving strangely all morning. For a start she had hardly said a word over breakfast and when I asked her how things had gone with Jack she had clammed up and said everything was fine. I hadn't liked to pry but I could tell that something wasn't right.

'So you said we were meeting up with Jack and Jacob tomorrow night before we go home on Monday?'

'Yes, that's right.' Lydia replied, her face expressionless.

'What happened last night?' I tried again. 'You and Jack were getting on so well when I left, I thought you would be on cloud nine this morning.'

'I'm fine,' Lydia replied evenly. 'I don't want to talk about it, if you don't mind. I'm tired, and really I would rather just focus on the fair.'

'All right.' I shrugged, knowing there was no point trying to persuade Lydia to talk if she didn't want to. 'Anyway, you didn't answer my question.'

'I didn't hear you ask me a question.'

I felt a stab of frustration. I was tired and at that moment didn't have the patience for yet another of Lydia's mood swings. She might not want to talk about her personal life, but the least she could do was keep her mind on the job.

'I asked you if the fair was always like this?' I hissed.

Lydia blinked at me in surprise. 'There's no need to take that tone with me young lady, you want to respect your elders.'

'Respect cuts both ways, regardless of age,' I snapped. 'And if you had the slightest amount of respect for me, for the work I've done in tracking Jack down, helping you get your antiques business back on track and putting up with your tireless backhanded insults about my age, you might even go out of your way to answer one simple question.'

I didn't wait for a response. I turned my back on her and focused on the customers that were beginning to flock to our stall. I had come to adore Lydia but she was driving me up the wall this morning and for once I didn't feeling like hiding my frustration.

Instead, as I talked to our customers through the history of our pieces just as Lydia had taught me, I felt myself relax, and was delighted to see our stock disappear thick and fast. Then of course there was the fact Jacob was working at Sandrine's stall right across from me. Much to my surprise, I had found myself gazing at him whenever his back was turned, and for the life of me I didn't know why. I mean, yes, he was gorgeous but it wasn't like anything could happen between us. His life was here and London, mine was... well, actually I wasn't sure where it would be once all this was over. However, I didn't want a boyfriend, I wanted to focus on myself when I got home. I was sick of men getting in the way of my plans. That still didn't stop the little thrill of excitement I felt in the pit of my stomach whenever I caught Jacob's eye and he smiled at me.

All in all, a morning of flirting and working was exhausting, and come noon, when we found ourselves enjoying a quiet moment for once, I was more than ready for a breather in the posh restaurant above the fair.

I was just about to turn to Lydia and ask about her lunch plans when I felt a tap on my shoulder. Turning round, I saw Lydia looking contrite.

'Sorry,' she said gently. 'You were right, I've never really thanked you properly for everything you've done, have I?'

All the anger I had felt towards her disappeared in an instant. 'It was my fault as much as yours. I shouldn't have snapped. We've both done a lot for each other, I think I'm just tired.'

Lydia squeezed my arm. 'Then let's say no more about it.'

I nodded, keen to put the argument behind us.

'Mind if I nip off for a sandwich?' I asked over the rumble of my stomach.

'Now?' Lydia asked in alarm.

'Err yes,' I said. 'I won't be long.'

'I know that,' she babbled, 'but we're about to get a rush on.'

I cast my gaze around the hall which was practically empty. 'All the best customers have been and gone,' I pointed out, 'and look, apart from one vase we've got no stock left anyway.'

'Just hang on a bit longer,' Lydia begged.

I sighed, perhaps Lydia wasn't feeling very confident at handling things alone but didn't like to say. I felt a flash of guilt. Was that the problem rather than something to do with Jack? Was she having a hard time with her memory? After all she had been so good since we arrived, I had almost forgotten there was ever a problem.

'Course I'll stay,' I said softly.

The relief on Lydia's face was palpable. 'Thanks, we'll need to clear up soon anyway, then perhaps we could have lunch together.'

I ignored the deafening rumbles in my stomach and plastered on a smile. 'Sounds great.'

At the sound of footsteps nearing our almost empty stall, I swung around ready to greet our latest customer, but nothing could have prepared me for what I saw. There in front of me were two people I hadn't seen in almost four years and wasn't sure I ever would again – my mum and dad.

As I took in the image of my parents – so much older, but still just the same – I tried hard to form a sentence. Was this a coincidence? Did they know I would be here? Why were they here? The last time I saw them it had ended so badly, they had thrown Brad and I out of their home.

'What are you doing here?' I managed.

'We heard this was where you would be,' Mum said hesitantly. 'I hope it's okay that we've come.'

'We wanted to apologise, Erin,' Dad added, taking a step towards me, a faint trace of his American accent still there.

I looked from Mum to Dad, a mixture of shock and disbelief pulsing through me. A million and one questions raced through my mind. Why now? Why here? Why after all this time did they want to apologise? Had they heard about Brad's death? Was that something that had triggered all this? I didn't know what to think, I wasn't prepared, but as I took in Mum's slightly greyer hair and the lines that were now etched across Dad's forehead, I realised it didn't matter why they had come, all that mattered was the fact they were here. Too much time had passed already and I didn't want to lose any more. I looked from one to the other, feeling as if I were a five-year-old girl who had got lost in the supermarket. All I wanted was to cuddle my mum and dad and never let them go. Unable to stop myself I ran round the front of the table and wrapped my arms around them. For a moment I said nothing, happy to drown in the all too familiar scent of washing powder and coffee that was uniquely my parents. God, how I'd missed them.

'I have dreamed of this moment for so long,' I said, my voice cracking with emotion.

'So have we,' Dad whispered. 'We made some mistakes, Erin, some very stupid ones. You are our world, you always have been, we should never have let you go because of Brad.'

My heart banged against my chest as I looked at him. Were those tears in his eyes?

'I keep going over and over it,' Mum added falteringly. 'I wished we had done things differently. We always encouraged you to be yourself, to find your own path in life and when you did just as we had raised you to do we turned our back because we didn't approve, because I was so worried you were going to end up alone and penniless like Sandra.'

'It was a shock to us that we had behaved that way,' Dad admitted unable to look me in the eye. 'We were embarrassed by what we had done and dug our heels in.'

'So stupid, so, so stupid,' Mum echoed.

I stared from one to the other – this was all so unreal. I glanced beyond them and saw Jacob staring quizzically at me. I smiled, surprised that I found myself wanting to explain everything to him before turning back to my parents.

'It's not just you who should apologise,' I said earnestly. 'We both made mistakes. I broke up with Brad and should have come to you then, but pride got in the way and I was terrified you would reject me.'

I caught a flicker of guilt pass across Mum's face. 'Erin, you have always been full of grace, but truly the mistake is ours not yours.'

'We know about Brad, Erin, Lydia has told us, well your mother all about it. To be honest, we hated seeing you with him,' Dad said. 'You are worth a thousand of him.'

'As for that so-called best friend of yours,' Mum said, her face darkening. 'She's always been out for what she could get.'

'We wanted you to have the world, Erin,' Dad put in. 'That's why we behaved as we did. We never wanted you to settle for second best and that's exactly what we always felt Brad was.'

'Quite right,' Lydia agreed hotly.

I turned to look at her in surprise, only for Mum to start talking again. 'Your dad and I have been foolish, Erin, and it's thanks to your wonderful friend here that we have realised just how very wrong we have been.'

I swung back to look at Lydia and saw that she wasn't as shocked as I was to see my parents. In fact, she was sort of glowing. A smile lit up her face and the way she was hugging her arms to her chest told me that she knew something.

'You were in on this,' I gasped. 'You planned it, didn't you?'

Lydia nodded, her eyes full of contrition. 'I'm sorry if I interfered, Erin. After Harry died, and knowing how I had gone through life not knowing the truth about Jack, I realised just how short life could be. To see you so upset over some dreadful man and woman who betrayed you, well, I thought you needed your mum and dad. And I thought this was the perfect time for you to be reunited.'

I gaped at her in surprise. I thought Lydia had been lost in her own world of finding Jack and getting over Harry. I had no idea she had gone to all this trouble. I mean, she had been there for me of course, but to think that all this time this was what she had been plotting was staggering. I walked back around to the table and hugged her. 'You have nothing to apologise for,' I sobbed into her neck. 'I can't believe you would do all of this for me.'

I pulled away then and smiled as Lydia reached up and ran a hand down my cheek. 'Oh, my darling, you are worth it. I just hope you realise quite how much.'

Gently she kissed my cheek, before turning back to my parents. 'Why don't you all get some lunch and talk?'

'I would like that very much,' Mum said shakily.

'As would I,' Dad added.

'Then let's go.' I smiled, before turning to Lydia in alarm. 'Unless you don't want to be left alone. I mean, can you manage?'

Lydia threw her head back and roared with laughter. 'Contrary to what several people think, I have managed to get through life largely unscathed for the past seventy-eight years. I think I'll manage the rest of the afternoon myself – especially as there's hardly any stock left.'

I shook my head in disbelief. Lydia Harper was one tough cookie, make no mistake. I looked at her. This woman in front of me had given me the world – a home, a new life, and become the best friend I never knew I needed. Without taking my eyes off her, I reached into my pocket and pulled out the tiny box I had been carrying since we left Bath.

'What's this?' She frowned as I passed her the box.

'Open it,' I said.

As she did, I saw a flash of surprise pass across her face. 'This is your engagement ring,' she gasped. 'Why are you giving it to me?'

I laughed. 'I'm not giving it to you, I'm asking you to sell it. Do you remember when I moved in, you very wisely told me to keep the ring. You were right, but now I think the time has come to sell it.'

'Are you sure?' Lydia asked gently.

I nodded. 'I've been thinking about it for a while, it's why I brought the ring with me. I wondered if I could try and sell it at the fair. Mum and Dad turning up like this is proof that this is the right time to say goodbye to the past and, Lydia, you're the person I trust most of all to sell this for me.'

There was a pause then as Lydia gave the ring a final glance then shut the box with a smile. 'Best decision you'll ever make. I'll get you a good price, don't you worry.'

I hugged her again. 'I know you will Lydia, you've always had my back.'

Forty

Lydia

I can honestly say that watching Erin and her parents walk away, cocooned in one another's love, was one of the most satisfying things I had ever seen. It was how a family should be. Knowing I was partially responsible for reuniting them felt wonderful.

The afternoon had been as quiet as I had expected and had given me the chance to chat with a few of the other traders I had known over the years. It had also given me the opportunity to sell Erin's ring to a jewellery enthusiast I knew. I could have sold it to a punter, who would no doubt have loved the one-carat radiant diamond that was a lot more valuable than Erin had suspected. Yet like me, the trader had known immediately what it was and offered me a very good price. However, I'd had the devil about me and haggled, securing Erin with more money than either she or I had a right to expect.

Now, as I sat in the hotel bar with an illegal gin and tonic I knew was against doctor's orders, I found myself imagining just what it would be like to be a part of Erin's family reunion. But then, I thought, savouring a delicious sip of bitingly cool gin, it was a rather private affair, just as my reunion with Jack had been.

At the thought of Jack, I felt a shiver of delight and a pang of disgust. I had hoped that after a good night's sleep I would feel a lot calmer about everything but I was still as upset as I had been when I left him. The same question had been burning in my mind all day – why on earth did the men in my life feel as if I couldn't cope? I had been raised by a father who was rather ahead of his time and believed women weren't frightened little mice that needed to be protected. Instead, he raised me to believe that women were just as strong as men, so when did that change? What had Harry seen in me that made him think I needed protecting from every little thing that could go wrong, and when had I allowed that to happen?

I managed a smile. Perhaps the fault was just as much mine as it was Harry and Jack's. *I* had allowed this to happen. *I* had allowed them both to believe I couldn't cope – they hadn't just suddenly decided.

I took another sip of my drink and stared out of the window at the passers-by strolling along the Champs-Élysées basking in the late afternoon sun, without a care in the world – or at least that was how it seemed to me.

Finishing my drink, I signalled to the waiter to fetch me another and tried to relax and enjoy the city as I always used to. This hotel had been a favourite of Harry's and we had always enjoyed such happy times when we stayed here. After the fair, we would often return to the champagne bar and celebrate a fabulous day's takings or commiserate at how much we had lost over some poorly judged purchases. We would be joined by friends and would drink well into the night, laughing and chatting about all our latest news and calling order on all the Simon and Garfunkel Appreciation Society antics. I shook my head in sadness at the memory – that was it now, all my best days were behind me, what did I have to look forward to?

Just then, the waiter returned with my drink. 'For you madam, and also, reception have telephoned me to let you know you have two visitors. Are you happy for me to send them up?'

I frowned. 'I'm not expecting anyone. Did they say who they were?'

The waiter shook his head. 'I can send them away if you'd like?'

I was about to nod and say I'd rather be left alone, when I remembered that earlier that morning I had got chatting to an old friend, Pierre, who ran a stall in Lyons with his wife Yvette. We hadn't seen one another for years and I had suggested they drop by the hotel for drinks and indulge in a little Society reunion.

Giving the waiter my best smile, I cleared my throat. 'Send them up and could you bring us a bottle of your finest Sancerre please and three glasses.'

I was used to company during these fairs and it would be nice to share a glass with someone else. I took another sip and savoured the taste before my guests arrived, the illicitness of the act only making the drink taste all the more delicious. I had promised myself that my drinking days would be over after this trip, but for now, I simply wanted to enjoy the moment.

Just a few moments later the waiter set down the bottle and glasses. I looked up to thank him, only to drop my jaw in shock. My visitors were not Pierre and Yvette, but Jack and Jacob. As they threaded their way through the tables, I felt alarmed to see Jack had a rather determined look in his eye.

'What are you doing here Jack?' I hissed as he arrived at the table, Jacob standing sheepishly behind him. 'I told you I needed time.'

Ignoring me, Jack sat down and glanced at me defiantly before gesturing for Jacob to do the same. I lifted my chin and met his gaze.

'And *I* wanted to talk to you,' he said firmly. 'This is silly, Lydia.'

I turned to Jacob who I noticed with some satisfaction looked a little more hesitant at being here than Jack. 'What do you think?'

'Me?' Jacob looked at me in horror. 'This has nothing to do with me at all, Lydia. I said to Granddad that this was a bad idea, but he was insistent.'

'I can well imagine,' I said drily before turning back to Jack. 'So now you're here what is it you want?'

'There's no need to be like this, Lydia, really,' Jack tried again. 'Surely it's all water under the bridge now, it was so long ago.'

'Maybe to you,' I snapped, 'but all of this is very new to me, so you must forgive me if I can't suddenly let it all go overnight and laugh it off as you and Harry did.'

'Harry never did that,' Jack said, leaning forward in his chair. 'Believe me, he was in agony over all this. I could tell he felt conflicted, but he was terrified of losing you.'

'But that didn't stop you going along with what he suggested. You could have talked sense into him, Jack. Made him see that I could make up my own mind.'

Jack looked uncomfortable and I saw him glance longingly at the bottle of wine and empty glasses the waiter had set on the table. 'Well, I thought it was for the best once Harry came to see me and explained everything. You had been through enough – I didn't want to cause you any more pain.'

'And as I said to you last night, it was up to me to decide,' I said, breaking off with a sigh. 'Look, I don't want to go over all this again.'

'And that's not why I'm here,' Jack began again. 'It really has been such a pleasure to see you, Lydia. Despite our row I haven't felt so happy in such a long time. None of us are getting any younger, don't you think we can just let this pass now? Move on, eh?'

Reaching for the wine, I said nothing as I poured out three glasses. As I pushed one towards him, I found myself seeing Jack with fresh eyes. I remembered how Jack hadn't just hated being told what to do but he had also detested rows and confrontation too, preferring the easier life. As for me, arguments weren't something I enjoyed but they weren't something I had ever shied away from either. I preferred to clear the air in a way that allowed us to grow. It was something Harry and I had in common from the outset. It wasn't that we made a point of arguing, but we had always insisted on talking through an issue, usually while listening to a Simon and Garfunkel song. We would stay up until the wee hours sometimes, but we had always sorted out our problems and had never once gone to bed without settling our differences first.

Now, after so long, the truth was beginning to dawn on me – despite my doubts when I found that letter, Jack was never my first real love or my soulmate. It had been Harry all along. He and I had built a life together, growing with each other, learning from one another, leaning on one another through bad times and good. I couldn't honestly say whether or not I would have chosen Jack over Harry had I received his letter all that time ago as he intended, but looking at Jack now, I realised I had been looking at the past through rose-tinted glasses. Jack had been good for me as a teenager but who was to say if he would have been good for me as an adult? It was Harry who had held me after I gave birth to our son, Harry who had kissed away my tears when my beloved father died and Harry I had spent nights laughing uncontrollably with over something that had happened in the shop. He made me happy, he made me feel safe and he had always put me first, just as he had by seeking Jack out when his letter came through the door and asking him to leave me alone. He would have known he was taking a huge risk going behind my back, but he did it anyway because he loved me. It was the same reason he had hidden the truth from me about our finances, and now I felt all the anger I had been carrying over Harry's betrayal melt away. I realised he hadn't acted out of malice or spite; it had been pure and simple love.

It was time to forgive, forget and look to the future. Erin had done that very thing this afternoon by embracing her parents and saying goodbye to her past – I needed to do the same.

'I think you're right, Jack.' I lifted my glass. 'We are too old to let this drag on. How about we toast to friendship and the joy of finding one another again after all these years?'

Jack's face lit up. 'I'll drink to that.'

'So will I.' Jacob laughed in relief as he clinked his glass against ours.

Taking a sip of wine, I felt contentment slide through me. It had been good for me to come here and lay old ghosts to rest. And yes, there had been some surprises in store, shocks I hadn't expected, but there had also been some joy. Watching Erin and her parents walk through the doors of the champagne bar, I got to my feet and smiled.

'Over here,' I called.

As the trio threaded their way through the tables, I signalled to the waiter to bring us three extra chairs and another bottle of wine with extra glasses.

'You all look rather happy,' I said, taking in their beaming faces.

'I think we are,' Erin said shyly, as she took a seat next to Jacob. I couldn't miss the gentle yet knowing smile that passed between them. These two could be a good match, I thought, but that was something for them to find out – my meddling days were over.

'I think we're on cloud nine,' Tom chuckled, sitting next to his daughter and filling her glass.

'Wonderful!' I grinned, raising my own drink towards them as I introduced them to Jack and Jacob.

'So will you be staying in the city long?' Jack enquired politely.

Rosie shook her head. 'Alas, we have to get back tonight. I've so much paperwork to catch up on before I'm in court later this week.'

'That's a shame.' Jacob smiled politely. 'Perhaps we'll see you again.'

I couldn't help myself and burst out laughing. 'From the way you and Erin have been gawping at each other since you met, I should say it's highly likely you'll meet again.'

Erin's cheeks flushed. 'Lydia,' she hissed. 'Be quiet.'

'Darling, love issh a wonderful thing,' I slurred, the wine clearly having taken a slight hold.

'I have to say I agree,' Jack said, winking at me. 'I think you two would make rather a lovely couple. Don't they remind you of us when we were younger, Lyddie?'

'Oh yessh.' I nodded emphatically. 'Only I think they're probably even more smitten than we were.'

'Stop it, both of you.' Jacob glowered. 'Erin and I are just friends.'

'Exactly,' Erin put in. 'I've told you all I'm not ready for a relationship and I meant it.'

At that Rosie, Tom, Jack and I fell about laughing while poor Jacob and Erin looked at one another aghast. They looked so upset I almost felt sorry for them. Yet as their gaze fell upon each other once more, any sympathy I had vanished, and I exchanged a knowing look with Jack. Unlike us, these two had their entire future ahead of them.

Forty-One

Erin

'Are you sure I look all right?' I asked, as I twirled this way and that in the hotel room. I had put on the new floral maxi dress I'd bought especially for the trip but as I stared at my reflection in the mirror I couldn't help wondering if it seemed a bit much.

'I think you look gorgeous.' Lydia smiled, from her position by the window. 'Jacob's a very lucky young man, and to be quite honest Erin, from what little I've seen of you together, you seem very well suited.'

Surprised at the compliment, I turned to look at Lydia and saw that she was busy trying to balance the books after our final morning at the fair. It had been an incredible event. We had not only sold the last of our stock, but thanks to the sale of my ring, made more money than ever before. Lydia had tried to give me the cash she had raised for the ring, but I had refused and said that after all she had done for me, I wanted to put it back into the business.

I'd expected a bit more of a fight but after I made the suggestion, she went along with it quite happily. Now, as I watched her type something in what I could clearly see was the wrong column on the spreadsheet, I tried not to let out a groan of despair. Lydia's online book-keeping was so dreadful I knew I was going to have to go over it myself later. Yet in that moment, I felt so happy and so grateful for having Lydia in my life I couldn't bring myself to mind.

'Do you think Jacob will like it?' I asked shyly.

Lydia let out a snort of disbelief as she peered over the top of the laptop. 'Who cares? You should dress for yourself not for a man. That said, I think he would be a fool not to like you in that get-up. Where is he taking you?'

'A little café-bar he said he knows,' I replied. 'I won't be long, and I'll be back in plenty of time for our dinner.'

Lydia waved my concerns away. 'Don't be silly. And honestly, Erin, it's a lunch date not a marriage proposal. Stop worrying about it and enjoy a date with a handsome man sat opposite you. Trust me, when you get to my age, these invitations will be few and far between.'

I sank onto the bed, suddenly feeling rather exhausted by the events of the past few days. 'How are you feeling now? About Jack, I mean?' I asked, aware that Lydia had kept rather quiet about their reunion. 'You and he were very civil with each other over drinks last night, but I got the feeling you were keeping something back. Did something happen after Jacob and I went for dinner with Sandrine?'

Lydia snapped the lid of the laptop shut and gave me a half-smile. 'No, I haven't been very forthcoming, have I? The thing is, Erin, I had pictured this wonderfully romantic reunion in my head. Don't get me wrong, I didn't expect to fall in love all over again, but I thought seeing Jack again would be more magical.'

'And finding Jack hasn't been magical?' I asked.

'No, it has, it's been wonderful,' Lydia said firmly. 'But wonderful in a different way than I expected. You see, I was worried all this time that Jack had been thinking I left him in the lurch, but the truth is that Jack knew all along that Harry never gave me the letter.'

'What?' I gasped, sitting bolt upright at the revelation.

I found my jaw dropping open as Lydia then told me the events of the past couple of days. 'I can't believe it,' I said, feeling incredulous as Lydia finished her tale. 'Why didn't you tell me any of this before?'

'Because I knew your parents were coming and I didn't want to put you off your reunion with them,' Lydia explained.

'And what about after?' I demanded. 'You should have told me.'

Lydia flushed with embarrassment. 'I'm sorry. It's just you were so happy when you got back from your meal last night, I didn't want to ruin that for you.'

I walked over to the leather chair Lydia was sitting in and crouched down beside her. 'I'm your friend,' I whispered. 'I'm always here for you, Lydia.'

To my surprise I saw Lydia's eyes fill with tears. 'The one thing I've realised during this whole trip, Erin, is that I was looking in the wrong place to find the love I thought I needed.'

My eyes flickered with concern. 'I don't understand.'

'I mean, that all this time I've been looking to the past,' Lydia said, her blue eyes shining with tears and happiness.

'I've been looking at my defining relationships with Jack and Harry thinking they were the ones that were important. But really, what was actually important was the present.'

I nodded. I was beginning to see what she was getting at. 'So you feel all right with what happened with Jack now?'

Lydia tilted her chin in defiance. 'It's all water under the bridge now, Erin. Jack did what he thought was right at the time. And Harry, well my Harry always acted in my best interests, or what he thought were my best interests – for Harry it was another act of love and I've decided to see it as such.'

'That's a good idea,' I agreed. 'If there's one thing I've realised these past few months it's that anger eats you up – you taught me that.'

'And you taught me the true value of friendship,' Lydia whispered. 'This trip should have been a celebration of me and you, an opportunity for the Simon and Garfunkel Antiques Brigade to go out on a high.'

With that, she fixed her eyes on me and I felt a surge of love for the woman sat before me. She had been there for me when I had nowhere else to go, supported me, encouraged me, provided a shoulder to cry on and helped me move my life forwards in a way I could never have predicted.

'I'll never ever forget what you did for me with my family,' I said fiercely. 'Nobody has ever done so much for me, and I doubt they ever will. Lydia, I want you to know you truly are the best friend I could ever wish for. It might sound funny now, but you know what, I'm glad Brad and Cara went behind my back because if they hadn't, you and I would never have become friends.'

At that Lydia giggled. 'I think I know what you mean.'

'I'm not very good at emotion,' I said.

'Neither am I,' Lydia smiled. 'But, Erin, you and I have had such wonderful times together. I don't think I've ever laughed so hard.'

I smiled at all the memories we had created, the incredible moments we had shared together flickering through my brain like a Pinterest board. 'The time you tore shreds off that poor tourist.'

'And the time you threw insults at Brad and Cara,' Lydia countered.

'Or the time you threw your drink all over that dreadful speed date,' I giggled.

At that, Lydia looked at me blankly. 'The what?'

'The speed date,' I laughed. 'You remember? At the event Ginger organised. You said you had never been so insulted in your life.'

'Oh yes!' Lydia clamped a hand over her mouth. 'How could I forget?'

I looked at her, feeling unsettled. She had seemed so well on this trip, that I had forgotten her memory was ever a problem.

'I want you to know, that living with you over the past few months has given me more joy than I could ever expect.' Lydia smiled, clasping her hand over my own. 'Taking you in as my housemate has given me such a lease of life.'

'We've got plenty more of those moments to come yet. We've only just started, Lydia, just think what's around the corner for us.'

With that, Lydia squeezed my hand even more tightly. 'Thank you,' she whispered.

'I mean it. Look how well the Simon and Garfunkel Antiques Brigade has done. I've been thinking about this. There's no need to end it all now just because we've sold all our stock. Why don't we keep going? You've got brilliant contacts, we've got oodles of profit, even after you've paid back everything you owe. I know how to organise – together we make a brilliant team! What do you say?'

As I left my question hanging in the air, I looked at Lydia expectantly, only to see that she looked anything but excited about the idea.

'It's not that I don't want to, Erin,' she said eventually. 'But there's a lot to think about.'

'What is there to think about?' I demanded. 'We've done so well – we're the dream team.'

'I know that,' Lydia laughed, 'but running a business is hard work. Let's talk about it when we get back all right?'

I gave a brief nod of my head. I had learned that there was no point trying to push Lydia into something before she was ready.

'Well, I'd better be off,' I said eventually. 'Will you be all right while I'm gone?'

Lydia rolled her eyes. 'I'll be fine. Stop worrying about me. I have got my own life you know.'

'All right, all right.' I held my hands up in mock defence. 'I'll see you tonight.'

'For our last supper,' Lydia murmured as I walked through the door.

Shaking my head I hurried out into the fresh air. I saw Jacob straightaway, leaning against a tree dressed in jeans, T-shirt and blazer. Walking across the road towards him,

I saw he was tapping one hand against his thigh; he was clearly as nervous as I was.

'Hello,' I said.

Slowly he reached for my hand and as our fingers entwined I felt my heart bang against my chest and cursed myself. What was wrong with me? I was behaving like a teenager.

'Nervous?' Jacob asked, reading my mind.

'A bit,' I said, surprised at how easy it was to be open with Jacob.

'Me too,' he admitted. 'I didn't expect to be, but then all this has taken me a bit by surprise. I never expected to find you.'

'Nor I you,' I said haltingly. 'I don't know what this is Jacob, but I just know I like being with you.'

We carried on walking then through the streets of Paris, not saying much, just enjoying the thrill of being with one another. With Jacob by my side I felt as if the city had been switched to Technicolor as I took in the sights and smells around me. Dazzling hydrangeas, roses and delphiniums stood in immaculate lawns that lined the Parc Monceau, perfectly manicured gardens adorned the area around Notre Dame, while the scent of cherry blossom filled the air. The city looked so beautiful, it was as though I was seeing it with new eyes. As we continued to stroll along, content with just each other, I soon caught sight of the Bateaux-Mouches up ahead and herds of tourists basking in the sunshine.

'Have you noticed where we are?' I laughed

'The banks of the Seine,' he said wryly.

'All we need now is a bottle of wine, a baguette and some cheese,'

We stopped then and looked at each other for just a moment, seeing each other with what felt like fresh eyes.

'Instead, all I've got to offer you is this,' he said softly, bending down to kiss me.

At the feel of his lips against mine, I realised how strange this felt. This was the first kiss I had exchanged with anyone other than Brad for a long time. His touch felt so different, softer, less abrupt, but as we began to get to know each other's lips, bringing them together to fit like two pieces in a jigsaw, I felt fireworks fizz and dance inside of me. I never wanted it to end.

Forty-Two

Lydia

'This the last of it then?' I asked, pushing what I hoped was the final document back towards the solicitor, or notary as they were better known in France.

He offered me a smile as efficient as his paperwork. 'The very last one, Madame Harper. Your affairs are now in order.'

'Thank you,' I said, getting up to show him out of the hotel room. 'And thank you for coming at such short notice.'

The notary shrugged in classic Gallic fashion. 'Anything for a friend of Mr Harrison's.'

Once he had gone, I sank back into the chair and allowed myself to relax. Now everything was in order I felt as if I could breathe. I had known that I couldn't leave my head in the sand for much longer. It wasn't fair on Erin or Luke and it certainly wasn't fair on me. I knew my health was only going to keep deteriorating and the last thing I wanted was to be a burden to those I loved.

The conversation with Erin earlier had shocked me, and made me realise the decision I had made about my future since we arrived in Paris was the right one. I truly had no idea what she was talking about when she mentioned the speed dating incident. I'd remembered the tourist – anyone that vain and stupid would stick in the mind of even the most far gone of dementia sufferers – but the speed dating evening had thrown me. I wanted to scream at her that she'd got it all wrong, but I knew that wasn't the case. The problem was with my brain not hers. And so I pretended I knew what she was talking about – something I was getting surprisingly good at but finding increasingly tiring.

Getting to my feet, I gave the hotel room a final once-over. It was a nice room, sunshine-filled and pleasant. I would miss it when I left. The notary had helped me get my belongings together. Surprisingly, he had told me that he was often asked to help with just this type of situation and he hadn't batted an eyelid as he straightened and tidied. Letters for Luke, Phil and Erin were left squarely in the centre of the table and my bill was already settled with the front desk.

Reaching for my coat, I slipped it on, checked my appearance in the mirror and patted a stray lock of hair in place. My mind may have been deteriorating but that was no reason for standards to slip. I walked through the door and didn't look back – whatever came next, I was ready.

Forty-Three

Erin

'Come on, you look fine as you are,' Jacob wheedled as he pulled me in for a kiss.

'Fine!' I shrieked playfully. 'Fine!'

Horror flooded Jacob's face. 'No, not fine, beautiful, more than beautiful, exquisite, gorgeous… aaah!'

I burst into laughter at the look of fear on his face. 'I'm teasing, you idiot! But seriously even if you think I look beautiful, exquisite, fine or whatever else you said, I do need to check on Lydia.'

'Okay,' Jacob sighed, and I was glad he brooked no argument.

Although I hadn't told him all of Lydia's private business, I did tell him that she was having memory problems. Jacob had been very understanding, explaining that many of the residents at Maison Retrait suffered with memory problems including dementia. He said that living with the young gave them a fresh perspective and helped them maintain their focus. Having spent time at Jack's apartment I didn't doubt it. The place had felt so positive and was a million miles away from the care home my gran had ended up in when she couldn't look after herself any longer.

As we turned the corner, Jacob pulled me towards him and then I felt his lips on mine. The only thing I could think about was the gorgeousness of his kiss. We had done a lot of kissing that afternoon. We had also done a lot of talking, strolling, cuddling and I personally had done a lot of lusting. With every moment I spent with Jacob I felt as though my heart was going to leap into flames. He wasn't just undeniably gorgeous but he was smart, funny and exciting too.

I had already secretly texted Rachel an update about our date. Naturally she had demanded information at every turn, wailing that now she was an old married woman she was living vicariously through me.

But I knew I had to return to reality and check Lydia was all right before I could enjoy seeing Jacob and Jack at the restaurant.

'Come on, I'll see you in an hour.' I grinned, extricating myself from his arms.

'But it's too long,' he wailed, making me laugh even harder.

'Go!' I laughed, shooing him away.

Back inside the hotel I didn't bother with the lift back up to my hotel room. I was so high on life I felt as if I could climb the Eiffel Tower three times over. Like an excited child I couldn't wait to tell Lydia everything.

Gingerly I knocked on the door of her hotel room. At Lydia's insistence we had booked adjoining rooms but I didn't want to invade her privacy and so I had never used it.

Still no answer, so I tried again but nothing. I checked my watch. There were now less than forty minutes before we had to meet Jack and Jacob for dinner. Our flight back to the UK was first thing in the morning and tonight was a celebration – our last chance to enjoy all that Paris, along with friends old and new had to offer.

Suddenly I felt a buzz in my pocket. Pulling out my phone I saw Mum's name flash across the screen. I felt a flush of excitement as I saw it, the novelty of being able to talk and text my mum was still fresh and new.

Hi Erin, just wanted to say hello. Hope you and Lydia are enjoying yourselves in Paris. Safe journey home, love Mum and Dad xxx

I felt a sudden glow and resolved to send Mum a message the minute I found Lydia. It was all down to her I was even receiving texts in the first place and although I knew there was no way to repay her for the kindness she had shown, I wouldn't rest until I'd tried.

As I tapped away again at the door, anxiety began to gnaw away at me. What if she had fallen or was hurt? I felt a flash of exasperation as I realised I was going to have to use the adjoining door after all.

Stepping inside, I snapped on the light and gasped in surprise – the room was spotless. The bed was freshly made, all of Lydia's belongings, like the water bottle, laptop and glasses case she had left on the bedside table had gone. And the coat she had slung casually over the back of the chair since we arrived was nowhere to be seen.

A knot of worry began to form in my stomach. I raced over to the wardrobe and flung the doors open – it was bare, as though Lydia had never been here.

I sank back onto the bed and tried to think. Just because she had taken all her stuff this didn't necessarily mean anything. It was possible she had taken her things to Jack's for some reason, or even gone home because there was a problem back in Bath. I thought back to the last time I saw her. She had seemed happy and upbeat, there was no cause for alarm. Anxiously I checked my phone for any message from her, but there was nothing.

Quickly I dialled her number, but it rang and rang, and I cursed myself for not taking the time to show her how to set up her answering service so people could leave a message.

I got to my feet and pinched the bridge of my nose. *Think, Erin, think.* But I had no idea. There was only one person who might know, I realised: Jack. I scrolled down to find Jacob's number and felt a surge of relief as he picked straight up.

'Missing me already?' he teased, his warm tones making my insides turn to mush.

'Jacob, have you or Jack seen Lydia?' I asked, getting straight to the point.

I heard an exchange of voices before Jacob returned to the line. 'No, why?'

'All her stuff's missing,' I said, finally giving into the fear that had been building inside. 'She's not answering her phone and I don't know where the hell she is.'

'What?' Jacob sounded as shocked as I felt. 'Hang on.' Once again I heard another exchange of voices but above the noise of the street I couldn't work out what they were saying.

'Erin, we're not far from the restaurant. Can you meet us there now and we'll work out what to do? Granddad says the last he heard from her was this afternoon. She rang him asking if he knew of a solicitor he could recommend.'

'A solicitor? Why?' The knot of worry now becoming a massive great ball.

'No idea,' Jacob said. 'But look, get down to the restaurant as soon as you can and we'll find her. Don't worry Erin, we'll find her.'

As Jacob hung up, I took a deep breath and buttoned my coat back up. Just then my eyes strayed to the table under the window, and I saw a series of envelopes. Cautiously I stalked over to them, fearful of what they might contain as if they were an unexploded bomb. To my surprise, I saw two were addressed to Phil and Luke, and a fat one had been left for me.

Anxiously, I ripped it open, and at the sight of Lydia's careful handwriting a sob caught in my throat.

Dear Erin,

Firstly, I'm sorry for the cloak and dagger way I've done this. I've taken the coward's way out, I know that, but I couldn't stand to see your face as you tried to talk me out of it. The truth is, my lovely friend, I haven't been entirely honest with you. You see this trip wasn't just about finding Jack, selling our antiques or even celebrating our friendship as I said to you earlier. It was in fact about me – about celebrating the end of my life as I know it. As you know Erin, I've been having problems with my memory and a few weeks ago I finally had the diagnosis I had fretted over confirmed. I have Alzheimer's.

In a way, having a diagnosis has been something of a relief. Now I know exactly what my future holds and precisely what it doesn't. I've decided to take control and I have you to thank for that. What I've realised on this trip is that I have spent too long letting others control things for me. This is my life and I want the final say over what happens now. Erin, I won't be coming back with you tomorrow. I know this isn't the best way of breaking it to you but I've made my mind up and I don't want you or anyone else to talk me out of what I'm going to do next.

You, my darling girl, have a wonderful future ahead of you and that's why I have made provision. Phil and I are so very fond of you, Erin, and we have talked about you long into the night. We have both come to realise that neither one of us likes getting old and after many a heart to heart, Phil has decided not to expand the café after all. After much reflection, he thinks it will be too much. When you return to Bath, I want you to go straight to my solicitor – Edward Delacroix in George Street. He is expecting you and will have a bundle of papers for you, but amongst them will be the deeds to the florist's next to Phil's café which I have bought for you with the profits from the business and the sale of the E-Type which has been handled by Phil while we have been away. Thanks to you, Erin, we have done better than I could ever have dreamed, I have paid off the debts and there's far more than I ever anticipated– it's only right you are rewarded accordingly. As well as the shop, you will find all the profits from our business, along with all my books, treasures and anything remotely connected to the Simon and Garfunkel Antiques Brigade. These are for you to set up your own antiques business, or in fact anything else you might choose. You have a real flair for antiques and you have such a good business head on your shoulders I know you can set the world on fire. I have put the house on the market, but the proviso is that you are free to stay there until you have found suitable accommodation. Mr Delacroix has strict instructions to ensure you have enough money for a deposit from the sale to buy a place of your own – the rest will go to Luke and I hope will help him, Hannah and their new addition forge their way in life.

I'm going to sign off now. I know this might sound ridiculous but I don't want you to worry. I want you to remember me as your old friend Lydia, rather than some old woman who had trouble remembering her own name. I don't want anyone to think of me that way.

Erin, getting to know you has been the greatest love affair of my life and that will always be a memory I shall treasure.

Yours affectionately as always,
Lydia

As I finished reading the letter, tears gushed from my eyes like Niagara Falls. I felt as if my heart was breaking as I read and reread the letter. My poor lovely friend – her worst fears realised. I knew that no matter how tough

Lydia was, discovering she had Alzheimer's after all she had endured would have left her bereft. But the worst thing about it all was that she felt she had to deal with this alone. How could she just leave? And how could she make all these plans without talking to me? How could Phil? Why did nobody say anything to me? Rereading the letter again, I felt a sickening sense of dread – surely she wasn't going to do something stupid? Like a newborn lamb I got up and stumbled over my feet, racing out of the room. This situation suddenly felt very urgent. I had to find my best friend, and I had to find her now.

Forty-Four

Lydia

Believe me when I say I thought long and hard about my future. I went through all the ifs, buts and maybes but eventually I came to the right decision for me and now I've done it, well it's as though a rather lovely weight has been lifted from my shoulders. I hate clichés but the moment I made my mind up about what to do next, it was as though I could see the way ahead clearly and accept what was in store. It feels as though it has been years, not months, that I've been working to try and stay the same, no matter what challenges I've faced and I am now utterly exhausted. I know many of me as a tough old broad – and that's how I've always thought of myself, but I can't stand the idea of becoming something so different before the eyes of those who love me.

Perhaps it's a pride thing, or a generational problem, but I have no desire to be a burden or the victim of what I call hushed whispers. That dreadful thing where people look at you with pity in their eyes and talk about you behind your back with concern – that's not something I ever want. For me, the kindest thing in the world for my friends, family and for me, would be to slip away quietly, into the night and that is exactly what I intend to do.

I know that for many people this cruel disease doesn't stop them living their life, indeed some are optimistic about the future and the research being done. I have always admired these people and wish I could be as strong as them. I know my plan is very weak and perhaps even foolish, but I also know it's the right decision for me. Naturally I don't want to hurt anyone along the way, but I can't deny that having come to a decision I feel much more at peace.

All that's left to do now is continue making my way through the winding streets of Paris and head for the Metro. There is one last piece of my jigsaw, one final thing I must do, then all my affairs will be in order. The only thing left will be one final adieu.

Forty-Five

Erin

Sweat trickled down my forehead and by the time I reached the restaurant I was panting so hard the waiter brought me a glass of water without me even having to ask.

'Jesus, Erin!' Jacob gasped as I threw the glass of water down my neck in one as if I had trekked across the Sahara Desert. 'Did you run all the way here?'

I nodded, setting the glass down. 'It was quicker than waiting for the Metro.'

'Have you got the letters?' Jack asked impatiently.

I had called them en route to tell them I was on my way and explain about the notes Lydia had left. I had also called Phil who was on the way to the shop, but he was as surprised as me to discover Lydia was saying her goodbyes. He had spoken to her yesterday after she had taken over the lease on the florist's, and had arranged for the E-Type to be collected by its new owner. They had promised to catch up the moment she was back from Paris and said nothing about the fact she wouldn't be returning. Now, as

I handed Jack his letter and mine, I saw the fear in his eyes that echoed my own as he ripped the envelope clean open. His eyes scanned the page and I couldn't help willing him to hurry up and reveal the contents.

'Well?' I demanded as he put the letter down and rubbed his hand wearily across his face.

'See for yourself,' he replied, handing me the letter.

As I took it from him, I saw it was only a few lines long.

Dear Jack,

I can't tell you good it has been to see you again. Being with you these last few days has taken me right back to when I was a girl in London and we would spend every spare moment of every day together. We made such a good couple back then, but I have realised that is precisely where you and I belong – in the past.

Don't get me wrong, it's got nothing to do with the mess you and Harry cooked up. I've forgiven you both for that, I know you were both only acting with my best interests at heart and for that, I thank you. It's dawned on me these past few days that rather than feel angry I should feel fortunate. I've had the love of two good men throughout my life and it's this knowledge that has spurred me on to take this next step towards my future. You see, the one person I have to love now is myself. It's time for me to put my best interests first, just as you and Harry thought you were doing all those years ago.

I have Alzheimer's, Jack, and the doctors have warned me that I need to change my lifestyle. You know as a girl I was never very good at being told what to do and I'm certainly no better now. I've always tried to live life

347

on my own terms. Now, I've got a choice, and I intend to make that choice for me, by me, with nobody else's involvement.

I am so grateful for the past few days we have had together Jack, and for your kindness at recommending me a solicitor without asking why. Not many people get a chance to put their past in order before they face their future – together you and I have done that and for that, I thank you.

Your Lydia

As I finished reading, I looked at Jack in despair. 'What did she say to you when you spoke? What does she mean about her facing her future?'

'Just what she says in her letter, Erin,' Jack replied desperately. 'I had no idea she had Alzheimer's though – did you?'

I shook my head bitterly, feeling a pang of anger and regret. I had suspected something was wrong but had shied away from finding out more.

'I don't understand what she's doing,' I wailed in frustration.

Jacob took my letter and his grandfather's and read them through himself. 'Well, it sounds like she's saying goodbye,' he said doubtfully.

'I know that,' I snapped. 'But why? What sort of goodbye does she mean? Is she going somewhere? Is she, oh God, is she going to kill herself?'

Up until now I had shut that thought from my mind, unable to believe Lydia would do such a thing. But on reading her letter to Jack, I couldn't see what else she intended.

'Wait a minute,' Jacob said, jabbing at my letter as the cool wind whipped around his head forcing his fringe to blow into his eyes. 'I'm not sure what her intentions are, but it seems clear to me that she's seen this trip as an opportunity to get everything in order. It seems she's going out of her way to say goodbye to everyone that matters – is there anyone else she needs to say goodbye to before she goes onto do whatever she wants to do?'

'What about that old friend of hers from the café – Phil?' Jack said hopefully.

'She's left a letter for him, and for Luke too.'

'Do you think we should give Luke a ring?' Jacob suggested hesitantly. 'He might have some idea where his mum's got too.'

I bit my lip anxiously. 'I don't really want to until I have to. His baby's due any day and I don't want to have to give him or his wife something to worry about when they're so far away and we might still be able to manage this by ourselves.'

'Okay,' Jacob said. 'You said earlier that she used to come to Paris a lot when she and Harry ran the antiques business.'

I nodded, keen to encourage whatever train of thought he was following. 'Yes, at least twice a year – they held the annual unofficial Simon and Garfunkel Antiques Society AGM here after every fair, and even saw a Simon and Garfunkel concert at the Olympia here. It was special because that's when she told Harry she was pregnant with Luke.'

'Here? In Paris?' Jack quizzed.

'Yes, they came over specially,' I explained. 'Lydia told Harry he was about to become a dad right after the concert.

It was the perfect way to celebrate a new start as a family she said.'

Jack let out a gasp of astonishment. 'I've got it. I know where she is.'

My heart banged against my chest in excitement. 'Where?'

'I may not have seen Lydia in a long time but she hated loose ends. These letters,' he exclaimed, waving the envelopes in his hand as if to demonstrate the point, 'are proof of that.'

Jacob reached a hand out to steady Jack's arm. 'Granddad, calm down. What do you mean?'

'I mean that Lydia always does things the right way,' he said in exasperation. 'You must have seen that, Erin.'

'Yes of course, but I don't understand how that helps us now.'

'It means she's got one last person to say goodbye to before she does whatever she's going to do next – she needs to talk to Harry,' Jack said in exasperation.

'But Harry's dead,' I pointed out.

Jack shook his head. 'No! She's saying her goodbyes at the Olympia. If that's where she told Jack about Luke, then that's where she will have gone to say goodbye.'

'The circle of life,' Jacob said thoughtfully.

I exhaled shakily with relief. 'I think you're right, Jack!'

'I'd put money on it.'

Jacob lifted his hand to signal for a taxi. 'Well, don't throw that cash away on the bookies just yet Granddad,' he said as the car slowed. 'Save it for the fare instead.'

As we clambered into the back of the taxi, I listened to Jack say something in fast French, and we were off, the taxi zipping at breakneck speed through the streets. I closed my eyes and found myself praying to any God that would listen. *Please let us find our friend before it's too late.*

Forty-Six

Lydia

I leaned against the tree and stared up at the Olympia. Smiling, I closed my eyes and was instantly transported to that day over forty years ago when I told Harry he was going to become a father. I did it here, right at this very spot. We had fallen out of this concert hall high on life and full of hopes and dreams for our future. The business was going well, after many years and false starts, the house renovation was on track and, as Simon and Garfunkel's final song 'Old Friends' played out to rapturous applause, I grabbed hold of Harry's hand and pulled him out of the concert hall.

He'd laughed at me, thinking I was about to suggest some late-night bar, but I had other ideas. I'd dragged him to this spot, then stood before him and had taken his hand placing it on my belly.

Always in tune with one another, he had looked at me, eyes wide with joy, before jumping up and down, shouting, 'I'm going to be a dad.' It had been the most magical night of our lives, and after an impromptu celebration with the members of the Simon and Garfunkel Appreciation Society that were in the city, we had talked long into the night about our hopes and dreams for our child.

Tonight, as I stood in the chilly night air looking up at the bright red lettering ablaze on the front of the Olympia, I still felt that same pulse of happiness. Just being here made me feel as if Harry were by my side and I couldn't help holding my right hand out to reach for his left, just as I had always done.

'When I found out what you had kept from me, Harry,' I whispered, 'I thought I'd lost you. I thought you weren't the man I had fallen in love with. I started to think everything we had shared was a lie.'

I paused then to gather my thoughts. This goodbye was important, I wanted to take the time to get it right. As my eyes strayed down from the front of the Olympia to the street sprawled out in front of me, I couldn't help but marvel at all the human life laid out before me. Lovers entwined arm in arm, strolled along the street, a new mum desperate for some sleep pushed past me with her pram, while smart men in business suits working late into the night, spoke into mobile phones as they hurried to the Metro.

Life really was a whirlwind and it passed in an instant. I thought back over my own life, wishing I had savoured more of the sleepless nights when Luke was teething or the grief I had felt when my father died. As ridiculous as it sounded to want to treasure those things, they were all moments that made me who I was today and life, whether good, bad or ugly, deserved to be savoured – along with those you were fortunate enough to love and cherish along the way. My dad always told me that everything, bad and good, passes and he was right. I had carried around these feelings of anger towards Harry ever since he died. But now, as I stared back up at the music hall where we celebrated the most magical of beginnings, I only felt love towards my husband. He may have behaved like a fool, but he was afraid and doing what he thought was right.

'I forgive you,' I whispered. 'I've realised I could forgive you anything. But you should have let me prove to you how much I loved you. I would always have chosen you, my love, I'm just sorry you went to your grave never knowing that.'

'Oh, I think he would have known, Lydia,' Jack said softly. 'It would be impossible not to spend a lifetime with you without knowing how much you were adored.'

I whirled around in astonishment and to my surprise found Jack, Erin and Jacob standing in front of me looking for all the world as if they were about to cry with relief.

'Where have you been?' Erin cried, flinging her arms around me before I even have a chance to reply to Jack or answer her question. 'I've been so worried about you.'

I wrenched myself from her embrace. 'Didn't you get my letter?'

'We all got your letters Lydia,' Jack said exasperatedly. 'But what we don't know is what you mean? What's all this about saying goodbye and a new future.'

Jacob took a step towards me then and smiled softly. 'I think what Granddad and Erin are trying to say is that your letters weren't as clear as you might perhaps have hoped they were.'

'Lydia, are you here to kill yourself?' Erin blurted, cutting across Jacob.

I stared at them all in disbelief. 'Kill myself?' I ventured, aghast. 'Why on earth do you think I'm ready to kill myself?'

'Because your letters were full of how you wanted to say goodbye,' Jack explained. 'You said you didn't want to be a burden to anyone now you knew you had Alzheimer's.'

'And because you've left instructions with your solicitor in Bath,' Erin put in. 'You said you're selling the house, you've sold Harry's car and have bought the shop next to Phil's café for me. Why would you do that for me unless you were going to do away with yourself?'

My hands flew to my mouth in horror as I realised how those letters could have appeared. 'That's not what I meant,' I gasped. 'I just wanted to say goodbye to you all properly.'

'And we know that now,' Jack yelled. 'But what we don't know is where the bloody hell you're going!'

I lifted my chin and glared. 'Where I'm bloody going is none of your business, Jack Harrison, and if you don't mind you're rather ruining my last goodbye of the day with Harry.'

'Lydia please,' Jacob tried again, his tone even. 'Can you just tell us what this is all about? Granddad didn't mean to upset you. Surely you can see how worried we have all been?'

I took a deep breath. This hadn't been part of the plan at all. The plan had been to make a dignified exit, not scream and shout with those I cared for in the middle of the street. 'If you must know I've arranged a place at the sister home of the one you reside in, Jack.'

'What sister home?' Jack narrowed his eyes in confusion.

'It's a home in the twentieth arrondissement,' I explained. 'It's a bit like the home you live in, filled with young and old, but this one has a bit more care, shall we say, for those who are suffering from Alzheimer's like myself.'

'Oh, Lydia,' Erin exclaimed. 'Why didn't you just tell us that? You didn't have to be so cloak and dagger about it all.'

'I'm sorry, my dear,' I said softly, seeing the relief on her face. 'I didn't mean to make you worry so much. Truly I didn't consider you would think I was about to end things from my letter. I was just trying to clear everything up while I was still in full possession of all my faculties.'

'But you were going to leave without telling us where you were going,' Erin pointed out.

I felt a flush of shame creep up my cheeks. 'I was,' I admitted. 'I thought it would be cleaner this way.'

'Why?' Erin demanded. 'We're your friends, how could you ever think it was all right to just leave without saying anything?'

Rightly or wrongly, I felt a flush of anger surge through my chest. This was my moment, my goodbye that was being hijacked.

'Because I don't want you to go through what I did,' I said fiercely. 'My father died of Alzheimer's. I nursed him through his illness, I listened when he asked me where my mother was and I held his hand when he cried out in agony. It was the most painful thing I have ever witnessed and I will not do that to you, Erin, I won't do it to anyone.'

With the truth finally out there, I gave into the tears I had been holding in for so long. I had adored my father, he had been my world, but towards the end it had been heartbreaking. Dad had been such a wonderful man, and to see him become something that he wasn't had devastated me. I knew in his more lucid moments that it devastated him too. I didn't want that for me or my family. Instead I wanted to see out my days being cared for by strangers so I didn't have to inflict the anguish of my suffering onto anyone else. I would live on in the minds of those that I loved simply as Lydia – fierce old bag.

As my gaze met Erin's I was shocked to see a mixture of pity and shock in her green eyes. Slowly she stepped forwards and put an arm around me. 'But Lydia,' she began slowly. 'Even though you said it was a painful time for you to look after your dad, do you wish you hadn't done it?'

'Not at all.' I said defiantly. 'I would have walked to the ends of the earth for my father. It was just a part of the journey we had together.'

'And what about if he'd simply left you without explanation at the beginning of his diagnosis,' Jack ventured. 'How would that have made you feel?'

'Terrible,' I admitted, understanding what they were getting at. 'I just didn't want to be a burden to you – to any of you.' .

With that, Erin clung to me, as though she was terrified to let me go. 'You will never be a burden to me, Lydia Harper.'

'I'm sorry.'

'Don't be sorry,' Erin whispered. 'Just don't shut us out.'

'Lydia, your father's path doesn't have to be yours,' Jack said gently. 'Why would you want to cut yourself off from those that adore you? Especially when you're about to face the challenge of your life?'

'Because I'm frightened,' I admitted, through tears.

'Then let us help you,' Erin offered. 'I know I could stand here and lecture you about how Alzheimer's has changed, that there are drugs that slow the disease down, that you can still have a life, you can still have hope, but that's not what you need to hear right now. What I do think you need to hear, though, is that we're your friends – please let us help you shoulder this burden.'

'We're all here to take some of the load,' Jack ventured with a smile. 'All you have to do is ask.'

In that moment, I saw the hope in Jack, Erin and Jacob's faces and realised how wrong I had got it all. I may have had the best of intentions by leaving without a word but although I would be leaving with all my loose ends tidied up, I would be leaving a gaping hole in their hearts as well as my own. The journey I was on wasn't going to be fixed by abandoning those I loved. Like climbing Everest or running a marathon it was a lone effort but there were always others on hand who made that effort possible. I had come to Paris consumed with a desire to uncover the truth about my marriage and to track down an old flame. What I had actually achieved exceeded my wildest expectations. Because what, I had actually discovered was the value and raw power of beautiful friendships.

Epilogue

Seven months later – Erin

As the taxi whirs through the streets, I can't help smiling as I lean out of the window and admire the sights. The last time I was in a cab driving through Paris it was because I was terrified my best friend was about to kill herself. Now it's because I'm coming to see her to celebrate a milestone – her seventy-seventh birthday.

Usually Jacob picks me up from the airport, or the station if I've taken the Eurostar. But because today is such a special day we've all taken a cab from the airport. When I say we, I mean me – obviously – and Jacob, Phil, Hannah, Luke and little baby Joe, who at six months old is the cutest thing I have ever seen.

'Are you guys holding up all right?' I ask, directing my question to Hannah and Luke who have flown in on the red eye from New York.

Hannah and Luke exchange knowing looks. 'We're fine. In fact, I think we both managed more sleep on the flight than we have done since Joe was born.'

I laugh. I have to say they do look surprisingly well. Since Lydia decided to stay in Paris, the four of us have all got to know each other pretty well. Firstly, I made Lydia fly to New York with me, not only to tell Luke her plans in person and reveal her diagnosis, but to meet baby Joe too. I told her she would regret it if she didn't, in what I had hoped was a tone that brooked no argument. It worked. She had a fantastic time, as did I. Getting to know Luke better was brilliant too and we spent a good few nights talking into the small hours about Lydia and what her future looked like.

Hannah joined us on a few occasions and the following month, when Lydia moved into La Belle Maison permanently, Luke, Hannah, Joe, Jack, Jacob and I all helped her settle in. It was an emotional moment for all of us as we tried to help Lydia adjust to the new order of things. Luke was endlessly upbeat with his mum, telling her that there was a lot of hope for Alzheimer's sufferers now. In the end Hannah told him to button it before I did. I mean, I'm all for positivity but it just felt like he was trying too hard.

'So how's the business going, Erin?' Luke asks dragging me back to the present.

I shoot him a smile. 'Brilliantly. You'll be glad to know your mum and dad's old shop is in the care of a very responsible owner.'

'I don't doubt it.' Luke smiles. 'Mum would never have bought it for you, if she didn't believe in you, but you know, I never saw you in antiques.'

I shrug. 'I never saw myself in antiques either until recently, but I always saw myself working with people'

'And business,' Phil chimes. 'All that social media you do, posting photographs of the latest stock, where you've been, I would never think to do anything like that.'

'It's just the way business is done now,' I say, my cheeks flushing with embarrassment.

'But you're so good at it though,' Luke enthuses. 'You've really got a flair for antiques, and driving the business into the twenty-first century.'

'Yes, the shop is always so busy,' Phil adds.

I beam at my old friend. After a lot of conversations with Lydia, Phil has taken a bit of a back seat with Ginger taking over as manager of the café. That doesn't mean I see any less of Phil though. Instead, he spends most of his days popping in to see me and I have to admit I quite like having him in the Box of Delights. That's not a euphemism by the way, that's actually the name of the shop. It was Lydia's idea. She said it was her favourite book as a child and funnily enough when I was a child it had been a novel I had adored too – just another example of how we were basically the same person, just a few years apart.

'What about the store in London?' Luke asks. 'When will that be ready to open?'

'Next month, I hope,' I say, crossing my fingers.

Jacob squeezes my knee affectionately. 'You don't need to hope, I know it's going to do well.'

I never planned to have two stores, but the Bath shop has been doing so well and so many of our customers were coming down from London that Jacob suggested I use some of the profit to set up a small outlet just off the Finchley Road. Given he has a flat a ten-minute walk from there, I thought it was a brilliant idea. Of course, I didn't do it without seeking advice first, but Lydia beamed when I told her and just shouted, "Atta girl."

'My friend Courtney was on your website the other day and she is desperate to buy that gorgeous Japanese necklace you've got online,' Hannah says over the roar of the traffic. 'I said I'd talk to you about it this weekend.'

'Tick it off your to do list,' I reply triumphantly. 'The necklace is Courtney's.'

Hannah's eyes light up with pleasure. 'Oh, she'll be delighted.'

'Let's hope the rest of the weekend is as easy,' Luke puts in as the cab draws up outside Lydia's home.

As we step out, I'm delighted to see Jack waiting outside, his arms piled high with gifts.

'You robbed a Galleries Lafayette, Granddad?' Jacob teases, clapping Jacob on the back in affection.

'Not yet, though never say never.' Jack smiles, bending down to kiss me on the cheek.

I kiss him back, delighting in the affection. Jacob and I travel to Paris most weekends to see Jack and Lydia, and it's always the highlight of our week as, not only do we get to see our loved ones, but we get to spend time together in the most romantic city in the world. Of course, Jacob doesn't stay with his granddad any more. Instead we usually stay in a hotel not far from the Opera. It's going so incredibly well with Jacob, and my mum and dad adore him.

It's also been going well with them too, as we've talked over what happened and learned to reconnect. I feel like it's been good for us in a funny way. Although I would never wish estrangement on anyone, it's given us the chance to discover who we are independently. The one thing we have all realised is how fragile relationships can be, and how important it is not to take the other for granted.

Together, we follow Jack inside the home, and I'm delighted to see the crisp winter sun is shining. Like Jack's apartment, Lydia's is filled with light and set in beautiful grounds where the kids who live here can play and the older ones can watch.

It doesn't take long to find Lydia. She's where she always is, holding court in the communal living room. Today she's playing 'Mrs Robinson' on the piano while many of the residents, young and old sing along.

As soon as she sees us, she gives us a bright smile, but doesn't stop until she's reached the end.

'Et voila!' She smiles, getting to her feet. 'I must go now – my public await.'

With that she gives a little bow and trots off to greet us.

'Nothing changes' I wrap my arms around her, pulling her in for a cuddle.

'I should bloody well hope not,' she chuckles, pulling away from me to kiss everyone else and take baby Joe for a cuddle.

I take a moment to look at her as I always do when I visit. I want to assess her health and see how she is. Like a lot of Alzheimer's sufferers she has good days and bad days, but what's changed since she moved into this wonderful home is her attitude. After we found her outside the Olympia all those months ago, she was so sure her life was over. Now she says it's as though her third act has just begun and she seems so much happier and settled. Lydia keeps in regular contact with Mr Evry her neurologist. I've met him a few times and he's a lovely man. Together we all had a long chat and Lydia decided to take the drugs in the end to try and halt the symptoms for a while, but she's also become the most fantastic advocate for those with Alzheimer's. She's been fundraising, getting involved with charities and will proudly tell anyone she meets now that she has the disease, insisting that there's nothing to be ashamed of.

The change in her is fantastic to see, and as I watch Helene, a six-year-old who lives here with her mum Simone, dance around Lydia's legs, I see how she lights up in her company.

'So, Helene, shall we see if any of this lot have brought us any nice presents?' Lydia smiles down at the little girl. 'What is it we always say?'

'It's your presents not your presence that counts,' the little girl says innocently, taking care to stress the 't' in presents as I know Lydia will have taught her.

'Too right it is,' Lydia agrees, 'and anyone that says otherwise is lying.'

I can't help roaring with laughter. 'Nice to see you're corrupting young minds.'

Lydia winks as she hands Joe back to his mum. 'I'm only telling the truth. Plain speaking we called it in my day.'

I sink into the nearest chair and throw my head back onto the cushions dramatically. 'Please not any more of your "in my day" crap, we've only just got here.'

'Ha! It's my birthday – I get to do just as I like. So if you don't like it I suggest you help yourself to that champagne in the bucket over there.'

My eyes light up. I walk immediately over to the table, and start to pour everyone a glass. As I offer one to Lydia, she shakes her head and turns to Luke instead. It's a small gesture but her refusal is a stark reminder of how different things are now. I sit back down and watch her as I take a sip of champagne. Change doesn't always have to be a bad thing, I realise. Lydia is more alive than I've ever known her. I watch her eagerly collect her parcels.

'It's nice to see you, Mum,' Luke grins as he kisses Lydia on the cheek and hands her a large bag.

'And it's nice to see you as well, son, but it'll be even nicer to see what's in that lovely gift bag,' she quips.

I smirk as Lydia rips open the paper to reveal a stunning bracelet.

'Oh, Luke, it's just gorgeous,' she breathes, running her fingers over the precious metal.

'Always said you were like a magpie,' Jack teases good-naturedly.

Lydia wags a finger at him. 'You watch out or I'll tell Madame Parker you don't know how to talk to a lady.'

Jacob and I exchange knowing looks. Jack has started seeing one of Lydia's neighbours and it's fair to say Lydia thinks it's hilarious that he's found love again at his time of life.

'You know you won't put her off me,' he says loftily. 'In fact, I was thinking about asking her to move in.'

At the baldness of the statement everyone's jaws drop open in astonishment.

'Granddad, are you sure?' Jacob asks at last.

'Yes, that's a big step,' I offer.

Jack shrugs. 'When you know you know.'

Lydia claps her hands together, and little Helene joins in without really knowing why. 'Bloody marvellous,' she says, and then it's as though a penny drops. 'You know, if Madame Parker lives with you Jack, that means there'll be a spare flat going here. What about you two?' she asks turning to us.

'What about us?' Jacob asks cautiously.

'Oh, don't give me all that what about us claptrap,' Lydia says. 'You two should clearly be living together, don't you think, Luke? Hannah?'

'Don't drag us into this,' Hannah laughs.

'Yes, Mum, don't think just cos you've got Old Timers you can get away with saying whatever you like,' Luke giggles.

The rest of us join in with his laughter – since Lydia's diagnosis we've often found that the best way through the harder days and even the easier days is with a good dollop of humour.

'I'm only saying what you're thinking,' Lydia protests, a twinkle in her eye. 'So what about it? Don't tell me you haven't missed living with your old friend, Erin?'

I can't help laughing. Lydia knows how much I've missed her at home. Living with her was the best part of my life, even if our unusual arrangement was forced upon us. Perhaps living in an old and young community, like this Parisian venture, would be the start of more unusual but happy memories for me, Lydia and Jack and Jacob too.

Jacob turns to me and smiles. 'I'm game if you are.'

'But what about the shop? I need to be there in the week.' I ponder, thinking I ought to sound like a proper businesswoman now.

'We'll commute like we always do,' he says. 'We'll just do it in reverse. Now the house in Bath has gone through, you're about to become homeless. You don't open on

Mondays and you were going to divide your time between London and Bath anyway and take on a manager to help with the day to day.'

He's got a point. I am about to be homeless but now Rachel and Lily have moved into a bigger place, they have said I can always rent a room from them when I need. Shyly, I find myself nodding as I look at Lydia's face and then Jacob's. Jacob sweeps me up in his arms and twirls me around while all our friends clap and cheer, and I feel blessed. Suddenly Lydia starts banging a spoon against her water glass.

'I think it's time for a toast,' she cries over the chatter.

'About time,' Jack says, a twinkle in his eye. 'How about to new beginnings.'

'To new beginnings,' Lydia says holding her glass aloft before she turns to fix her eyes on mine. 'With the very best of friends.'

Acknowledgements

Writing a book is hard work! And like any tough endeavour it takes an entire team. That's why big thanks must go to my fantastic agent Kate Burke of Blake Friedmann – I am grateful for your support on a daily basis. Likewise, I have been lucky enough to have the most gifted editor in Hannah Smith. Hannah, I cannot tell you how much I appreciate your ability to make a good book a brilliant one – thank you a million times over for your fantastic suggestions, oh, and the pack that I am lost without these days that we all know is yours really! To Vicky Joss who makes social media look like a walk in the park rather than the art form it really is – thank you so much for your patience with my stupid social media questions and for all your brilliant hard work to make this book a success. Thanks must also go to the lovely Laura Palmer who believed in this story from day one and has been kind, helpful and unbelievably generous with her time.

To everyone at the Alzheimer's Society, huge thanks to you for your help and patience with my research, it's very much appreciated. Any errors contained within these pages are entirely of my own making.

To all the Aria authors: thank you for being so darned supportive! Truly, you are a fantastic, welcoming bunch and I'm very proud to be a part of the Aria family.

And of course a very special thanks must go to my family and friends who forever put up with me scribbling an idea down during a lunch date, or running plot ideas past them. I know it's dull, but I love you all for never saying so.

Lastly, and perhaps most importantly, a huge thank you to you, dear reader, for picking up this book and taking a chance. There are a gazillion, zazillion (real number, I'm an author, I checked) books out there for you to read and the fact that you chose to spend time in the company of Lydia and Erin is something I'm thrilled about so thank you.

Like every author I love to connect with readers and although I have written this book under the name Abby Williams, if you would like to say hello, then you should know my real name is Fiona Ford and you can find me at facebook.com/fionafordauthor.

About the Author

Abby Williams is the pseudonym for Fiona Ford, writer of romantic up-lit and historical fiction. Fiona started out as a freelance journalist for titles such as *Grazia*, *Sunday Mirror* and *Stylist* before realising her passion lay in novels. Now she spends her days immersed in made-up worlds and reckons she has the very best job in the world. When she's not writing, Fiona is a gym nut, but only so it means she can eat lots of cake and drink lots of wine - not necessarily in that order. She lives in Berkshire with her husband and two cats who she sometimes thinks she might love just a little bit more than all the humans she knows. *The Time of Our Lives* is her first romantic novel and she is now busy scribbling away her second.

Hello from Aria

We hope you enjoyed this book! Let us know, we'd love to hear from you.

We are Aria, a dynamic digital-first fiction imprint from award-winning independent publishers Head of Zeus. At heart, we're avid readers committed to publishing exactly the kind of books we love to read – from romance and sagas to crime, thrillers and historical adventures. Visit us online and discover a community of like-minded fiction fans!

We're also on the look out for tomorrow's superstar authors. So, if you're a budding writer looking for a publisher, we'd love to hear from you. You can submit your book online at ariafiction.com/we-want-read-your-book

You can find us at:
Email: aria@headofzeus.com
Website: www.ariafiction.com
Submissions: www.ariafiction.com/
we-want-read-your-book
Facebook: @ariafiction
Twitter: @Aria_Fiction
Instagram: @ariafiction

Printed in Great Britain
by Amazon

53418635R00214